Bound by Blo

Bound by Blood

Rick Nelson

Thomas Dunne Books
St. Martin's Minotaur New York

This is a work of fiction. All of the characters, organizations, and events portrayed in this novel are either products of the author's imagination or are used fictitiously.

THOMAS DUNNE BOOKS.
An imprint of St. Martin's Press.

www.thomasdunnebooks.com
www.minotaurbooks.com

Library of Congress Cataloging-in-Publication Data

Nelson, Rick.
Bound by blood / Rick Nelson.—1st ed.
p. cm.
ISBN-13: 978-0-312-37264-4
ISBN-10: 0-312-37264-7
1. Detectives—Louisiana—New Orleans—Fiction. 2. New Orleans (La.)—Fiction. 3. Death row inmates—Fiction. 4. Domestic fiction. I. Title.
PS3614.E4494B68 2008
813'.6—dc22 2007039947

First Edition: February 2008

10 9 8 7 6 5 4 3 2 1

For my father, Keith Nelson,
and my mother of blessed memory,
Florence Nelson

Acknowledgments

Writing for publication is a team sport, and I have a great team. I first wish to thank Toni Plummer, my editor, who gave me this opportunity. Her insight and guidance made this book a better novel and a very enjoyable project. Thanks also to the entire staff at Thomas Dunne Books and St. Martin's Press who contributed greatly to the final product.

Thanks to fellow writers Marty Braniff, Marcia Gerhardt, John Oehler, and Jack Thomas for their keen criticism and unwavering encouragement; to Eleanor Lane for championing my writing; and to the rest of the gang for their support. Special thanks to Chris Rogers, who was there for me at the right time, proving that when the student is ready, the teacher will come.

Thanks to my children, Tami Nelson Kent and Lisa Nelson de Mendez, for making me proud of them. My greatest gratitude goes to my wife, Ginny. Her love, patience, and friendship help me through everything.

Bound by Blood

1

Everyone in New Orleans knows that when you crack open a crab shell and a pungent ammonia odor smacks you in the face, the crab was dead before it hit the boiling pot. But the acrid air blasting my nostrils as I entered the Second District squad room Monday morning wasn't foul shellfish. It was the cleaning crew's liberal application of caustic wash to the linoleum floor. As I reached my desk, the phone rang and I lifted the receiver, not knowing I was about to rip open something that, unlike a putrid crab, I couldn't toss away.

"Detective Brenner."

"Jack, this is Neil Gross." The nasal voice belonged to a public defender whose father generously supplemented his son's income rather than let him join his law firm.

I settled into my chair. "A little early in the day for you."

"I have an arraignment before a judge with a ten o'clock tee time. I'm on my cell phone sitting in traffic."

It was July and a hundred percent humidity, but Neil no doubt had his Porsche's top down. "So whose case are you pleading out today?"

"I'm the poor schmuck who got stuck defending that redneck scumbag Emmett Floyd Graves."

"All your clients are scum, Neil. Isn't he the guy who stabbed a corrections officer to death trying to get off the bus to Angola?"

"I pled him on drug dealing. Now it's capital murder."

"Then my advice is to lose the case."

"Listen. I called you because Graves was in Bon Terre when your cousin David was killed."

Hearing my cousin's name caused my face to flush with the heat of July 1972. Static crackled in my ear.

"Jack? We don't have such a good connection.

I clenched the receiver. "What's your client got to do with David?"

"Oh, good. You . . . there. I . . . recharged the damn . . . Graves . . . he can—"

A dull hiss replaced the sputtering on the line. I returned the receiver to the hook.

"Smells like cat pee in here." My partner, Ferrell Arceneaux, walked up wiggling his nostrils with his thumb and forefinger. A few months earlier, he was shot, almost fatally. He had lost weight from the surgery, but his belt was still a good six inches below the bottom of his tie. I was now working with a temporary partner until he was released for full duty.

Arceneaux sat at the desk across from me twitching his nose. I looked past him into another decade, my mind rapidly scanning through dark childhood images.

"What's eating you?" he said.

My eyes refocused on Arceneaux. "You know a guy named Emmett Graves?"

"Yeah. He sliced up a guard trying to escape during transport to the Farm. Why?"

"Neil Gross is defending him. Says Graves was in Bon Terre when my cousin David was killed doing civil rights work there."

Arceneaux pulled his lower lip. "David's the one they named the chapel for at your temple, ain't he?"

"The library."

"What the fuck could Graves have to do with your cousin?"

"Don't know." I watched the fans spinning from the high ceiling. "Maybe he knows something about his murder."

"Did he tell Gross that?"

I turned up my palms. "Neil's cell phone went dead before he could finish."

Arceneaux drummed his knuckles on the blotter. "Whatever it is, don't get involved with Graves. I'll tell you a story I heard about him when I was a uniformed in Lafayette."

I leaned back in my chair.

"Emmett Graves came down here in the sixties from the red clay country up around Monroe," Arceneaux said. "He got a job digging trenches for a natural gas line near the Atchafalaya in the middle of summer. The basin was boiling like a schoolhouse furnace, and Graves was slapping at mosquitoes in a ditch filling up with water almost as fast as the crew could sling out the mud. The working conditions didn't bother him, but the black boy alongside him did."

Arceneaux looked around, then leaned across the desk and hushed his voice. "He complained to the foreman about having to work with a nigger. The foreman told him nigger work was all Graves was fit for, so Graves cursed the man and walked off the job.

"The black kid didn't show for work the next day neither. Someone cut off half his hand the night before." Arceneaux drew a finger across his palm.

"That afternoon, the parish sheriff found Graves sitting without a shirt on the bank of a bayou holding a cane pole with a line in the water. There was a whiskey bottle and a brown paper sack next to him. One deputy lifted him up by the armpits and another grabbed the rod from Graves's hands and pulled the line up. The hook looked like a burnt piece of pork sausage with a dull, hard covering at one end. When the deputy reached down and picked up the sack, he saw four black fingers in it and he spewed his lunch into the bayou. Then Graves says, 'Can't catch nothing with this bait. Don't even a gar eat nigger meat.'"

Arceneaux sat upright and resumed a normal tone. "An all-white jury convicted Graves of simple assault. Nine months later, he was out, doing odd jobs and driving stolen cars to Texas."

"This one of your Cajun yarns?" I asked.

"No siree. This is for true. I'm telling you. Don't mess with Emmett Graves."

The phone rang and I quickly grabbed it. "Brenner."

"Sorry we lost contact." Neil Gross's voice was as astringent as the ammonia searing my nostrils.

"What's this about Emmett Graves and my cousin?" I asked.

I heard him rev the Porsche's engine. "He says if you visit him at Angola, he'll help you find who killed David."

The skin tightened across my forehead. "What's he told you?"

"Not a damn thing."

"How do I know this isn't some sort of con shuck?" I asked.

"I'm a lawyer, not a mind reader. Let me know if you want to talk to him."

I heard the Porsche downshift and the tires squeal around a corner.

"What'd Gross say?" Arceneaux asked as I hung up.

"Graves wants to talk to me about David's death."

"Cons always say they have information. He's jerking your chain. Or Gross is trying to use you to muddy the waters at trial."

"Neil isn't that smart," I said. "And he doesn't care about his clients."

"Well," Arceneaux said. "No disrespect to the dead, but this is 2003. Whaddaya think you're gonna do about it now?"

"What he's gonna do is get that fine-looking butt of his out to the car." My temporary partner, Keisha Lundy, stood over us like a five-foot-ten sculpture of polished obsidian. "We gotta meet with the DA before we get on the stand and put Frank Marino away."

Arceneaux looked up at her with fretful eyes. "Sorry. Didn't mean nothing by sitting at your desk here."

"It's your desk, Ferrell," she said.

"Don't look like it." Arceneaux scanned the gleaming white blotter, always hidden by files, loose sheets of paper, and Styrofoam cups when he'd worked there.

"You'll get your desk and partner back soon enough," Keisha said. "But I'm not returning the fingernail clippings you left in the bottom drawer."

Arceneaux stood, catching his heel on one of the chair wheels. A thin red line formed around the edge of his collar. "Gotta get back to work. Guidry's got me so's I can use the computer now."

"The desk work's been tough on him," I said to Keisha as Arceneaux shuffled up the aisle.

"Better than the alternative," she said.

"Yeah." I followed her toward the door. "Thanks for coming to get me. I got distracted."

"Tell me on the way if you want." Keisha pinched her nose, then snorted. "Did someone in here piss in his pants?"

I finished telling Keisha about my conversation with Neil Gross as she pulled into the courthouse garage. When I stepped out of the car, an electric arc shot up my left calf. I reached down to massage it.

"Therapy not helping?" Keisha asked as she shut her door.

"No. But I go anyway. I like sitting in the hot tub." I'd torn a tendon in my calf chasing the man who shot Arceneaux.

Keisha walked slowly with me into the building.

"Think Graves really might have something about your cousin's murder?" she asked.

"Who knows?" I pushed the elevator button. "Maybe I should leave it alone."

Keisha dropped her eyes. "Some things don't get finished." Then she turned and looked directly at me. "But if there's a chance, why not take it?"

"Like I can handle more than I already have. Utley has us working double shifts a couple of times a week and—"

Keisha held up her hands. "Hate to tell you, but the lieutenant caught me on my way to get you."

"Oh no. Not tonight."

"Yeah."

I jabbed the elevator button several times more with my thumb. "I'm supposed to take Alexis to Emeril's. She's going to be pissed."

"Not your fault," Keisha said.

"With her, it's always my fault."

"Don't mind the OT myself," Keisha said as the door finally opened and we entered the elevator. "No one at home for me to disappoint."

"I was hoping to have some quality time with Alexis while Sarah and Carrie were away at summer camp." And maybe improve our faltering relationship. "Going to Angola to talk to Graves will mean even more time away from home."

"David was family," Keisha said. "She'll understand."

"You'd think." I rolled my eyes and pulled out my cell phone. "Wait for me outside the courtroom."

The doors opened and I found a quiet alcove to call Alexis. I got her voice mail. "Guess you're busy. The lieutenant stuck us with a double shift tonight so it'll be another late one. Sorry about missing dinner. I'll cancel the reservations." I started to shut off the phone, then drew it back. "Love you."

Catching up with Keisha in the hallway, I saw her talking to someone in a wheelchair. My jaw grew taut and my hands felt numb, the way I felt when last winter's first cold front forced its way across Lake Ponchartrain into the city. The last time I saw Mary Evans.

"Hi, Jack." Mary looked up at me with familiar, molten sapphire eyes. "Nice to see you. It's been a while."

I turned to Keisha. "When did they put a second prosecutor on the Marino case?"

Mary tugged at my coat sleeve. "We won't be working together on this one. I just happened to run into Keisha. She tells me the job's spoiled your evening plans."

I stuffed my hands into my pockets and shrugged. "Didn't know you two knew each other."

"We're both in LEPIK," Mary said.

I threw my partner a puzzled look.

"Law Enforcement Professionals Investing in Kids," Keisha said. "A child protection organization."

Mary grabbed the controls of her electric wheelchair. "Gotta go, guys. Knock 'em dead."

"It's not a capital case," I said.

"Lighten up, Jack. It's just an expression." Mary smiled as she turned her chair. "Good to see you again."

"Same." I watched her vanish among a group of empanelled jurors a bailiff was herding into a courtroom.

Keisha moved next to me. "I feel like I just turned the TV on in the middle of a movie."

"What do you mean?"

"Honey, there was something going on there besides idle courthouse chitchat."

"We worked together on a case. That's all."

"That's not all. She looked at you with a woman's eyes, not a lawyer's."

"I didn't notice." I started down the hallway.

"Brenner." Keisha's voice stabbed me from behind. "The sorry thing is, you probably didn't."

I was twelve when I finally beat my cousin David at fifty yards, but he was a distance runner. He'd set a Tulane record in the three-mile run a month earlier and barely missed qualifying for the NCAA nationals. His senior year was still ahead of him.

We jogged from his house to the high school track. Our bare chests glistened as we loped along the asphalt steaming from the showers that rush across New Orleans every summer afternoon. The musty smell of wet oyster shells rose from the shoulders of the road.

The crushed-brick running surface had a sun-baked firmness and the earthy musk I always associated with David. I dug small holes in the red clay for footholds. He took a standing start and dug just one.

David let me call the starter's signals and I thrust my arm and leg forward, keeping low, as he'd trained me. The yellow post at fifty yards grew closer. Our feet made rapid crunching sounds as they tore into the track. He'd taught me to look straight ahead, that I couldn't keep a stronger competitor from overtaking me, that my only purpose was to direct my own potential to the finish, to hope it was enough, and be satisfied if it was not.

I heard him breathing hard beside me as I began to lean. The line I'd drawn across the crushed brick flew beneath me and I turned my head to see him crossing just behind me.

"I did it! I did it!" I skipped twice, then stumbled forward, bending over to relieve my burning lungs.

"It was just a matter of time." David trotted past, his breathing returned to normal. "I'll give you ten minutes rest and we'll race a quarter."

"No way!"

"Okay. But next time we do a hundred." He smiled and ruffled my hair.

We jogged back home. Sitting on his front porch, we watched kids play in the street as dry lightning flickered in the darkening sky like lavender fireflies. We drank from half-gallon jars filled with sun tea and hunks of ice and we mopped our faces with the cool condensation.

I loved him like a brother.

"Hello-o-o, Jack," Keisha said as we drove back to the station. Water from a late-afternoon shower trickled into the gutters along the curb.

"Sorry. Just thinking about what you said earlier. Some things don't get finished. But all I have are recollections from when I was twelve. It'd be nice to have some real information if I decide to talk to Emmett Graves."

"How about your friend at the television station?"

"Odell Harris? What could he do?"

"Maybe dig up some old stories. He's been around a long time and he's helped you before."

I chuckled softly. "In exchange for exclusive information. I've nothing to offer this time."

She lifted her right hand from the steering wheel and held up her palm. "New-millennium cop solves thirty-one-year-old crime. Sounds like high ratings to me."

"That's what I'm afraid of. He'll push me into something I don't want to do."

Keisha slapped me on the arm. "And when was the last time that happened?"

The sun burst from behind the thunderheads moving over the lake. My eyes tracked the transient wisps of steam rising from the concrete. "Maybe I can catch Harris after the five o'clock news."

"Detective Brenner!" Odell's eyes gleamed when he saw me standing at his door. His salt-and-pepper hair was mostly salt. He gestured for me to enter. "Have a seat."

He removed his navy blue suit coat and carefully placed it on a wooden valet. He glanced at three flickering monitors on the opposite wall, then sat behind his desk. "What brings you by? Not another high-profile murder, I hope."

I took a visitor's chair. "Not a recent one. Do you remember the young civil rights workers who were killed in Bon Terre in 1972?"

"Yes. One white boy, one black boy. I was with the newspaper then and covered the story."

"The white boy was my cousin."

"My gosh." Odell's sharp brown eyes briefly softened. "David Brenner. I never made the connection. You must have been about—"

"Twelve." I swallowed and thought about the day I'd learned David was missing. "I want to see if you can dig up anything about the murders."

"I can pull articles from the archives. Should be able to find my notes as well."

"You have notes from a thirty-one-year-old story?"

"It's a compulsion of mine. You never know when an old story might shed light on a new one. I have one bedroom and half an attic full of files." He lifted his chin slightly. "What's caused your interest in your cousin's murder now?"

I told him about my conversation with Neil Gross.

Odell's eyes focused briefly on the monitors behind me, then met mine. "This could be some story."

"Only if Graves gives me information and I decide to act on it. I don't want any publicity until that happens."

"Nothing will come from me without your say-so."

I'd come to know Odell Harris as a straight shooter, but I had the same uneasiness about doing business with a reporter that most people have about being around cops.

"I must warn you," Odell said. "You don't know who else Neil Gross or Emmett Graves will talk to. They may have already talked to the press. You can't control that. The sooner you meet with Graves, the better your chances of influencing who else he does or doesn't talk to."

"And the sooner you get a story."

Odell smiled. "I'm only offering advice. I've seen what happens when sources start broadcasting their stories to anyone who'll listen."

I rose. "Call me when you've found your notes."

Later that evening, Keisha and I sat at our desks catching up on paperwork. We were the only detectives in the cavernous squad room. The faint scent of ammonia still rose from the tiles.

"Quiet night," I said near the end of our shift.

"It's not over." Keisha stared over my shoulder.

"Black male DOA." The night sergeant recited the phrase I heard almost weekly.

I spun around in my chair to face him. "Where?"

"Napoleon and Miro outside a convenience store."

"Robbery?" I asked.

"Drive-by. He was at a pay phone."

"Drugs." Keisha and I spoke in unison.

As the sergeant walked off, Keisha locked her desk drawer and stood. "This'll take till O-dark-thirty, Jack. Better call home."

I stared at the phone. I wouldn't be getting voice mail this time.

2

We arrived at the convenience store five minutes after leaving the station. A uniformed officer held up a hand as we attempted to turn into the parking lot. Keisha rolled down the car window and flashed her shield at the patrolman. The muggy night air invaded the interior.

"Glad to see such good security on the scene," she said. "We don't always get it."

"With Al Roque, you do." The gangly cop directed a thumb toward a tall, muscular officer standing outside the yellow tape that marked the inner perimeter of the crime scene. Then he waved us past, staring at Keisha the way most did at the rare sight of a female homicide detective.

Roque walked up as we opened the car doors, tipping his visor and nodding to Keisha. "Haven't seen you at the gym lately, Brenner," he said.

"The police basketball league's gonna have to do without me for a while," I said.

Roque slapped the back of his hand against my stomach. "And you're gonna have to do without second helpings."

"What've we got, Roque?"

"Young black male. Took a slug by the phone booth over there. The receiver's still dangling. You can see a pager hooked to his belt. The store manager heard three shots and tires squealing."

"How about the patrons in the Blue Pelican?" Keisha asked, pointing to a bar known as a hangout for drug dealers that faced the side street just beyond the store.

"Nobody admitted to hearing anything."

"Figures. Let's have a look at the body," she said.

Drops of moisture teemed in the halogen lamps set up around the scene. As we neared the body, I stopped short.

"What is it?" Keisha looked up at me as she knelt by the victim, facedown on the asphalt.

"His windbreaker. That's the Ben Franklin falcon below the entry wound." I knelt beside her and studied the lettering on the forest green nylon shell. "Franklin track. I used to have a jacket like that."

"Isn't Franklin that school for smart kids up near the lake?" Keisha asked.

"For about the last ten years. When I went there, it was on Carrollton near St. Charles."

"This boy must have studied chemistry." Keisha's face was as hard as the line she took on drugs. "I get tired of seeing kids pull this shit."

I looked up at her. "Let's not jump to conclusions."

"When did this start looking complicated to you?"

My calf started to cramp, so I pushed myself up with the other leg. "The manager see anything, Roque?"

"Heard the shots, but didn't see nothing but the boy lying on the pavement."

Keisha pointed toward the intersection. "If the manager didn't see the car, the shooter must have turned off of Napoleon and sped down Miro past the Blue Pelican."

Two members of the crime scene unit drove up. Keisha walked over to greet them.

Roque's eyes followed her. "We caught this at end of shift, Brenner. You guys got the scene?"

"Yeah, go on. Leave the statements you took and we'll canvass tomorrow."

He backhanded my belly again as he left.

Keisha returned with the ME. Before we could request it, he bent down and lifted a wallet from the boy's back pocket and handed it to Keisha.

"Got a name?" I asked.

Keisha flipped open the wallet. "Driver's license says Steven Bowen." She lifted heavy brown eyes. "He's seventeen."

As I focused on Steven's forest green windbreaker, the thought of our next task chilled me. *Parents.*

I awoke the next morning in a gloom that began hours earlier when I'd watched a man under the pallid aura of a lonely porch light hold up his wife, who'd collapsed after hearing their oldest son was dead. Our new lieutenant, Forrest Utley, liked to see his detectives in the mornings, and being on a scene in the middle of the night before was no excuse. I slipped into the squad room around nine.

"Glad you could make it, Brenner." Forrest Utley stood over the desk of a seated, more punctual Keisha Lundy. The crisp white cuffs of Utley's shirt separated his lush navy blue suit from his deep mocha skin. "What did you get from the victim's parents last night?"

I threw my jacket on the coat rack. "Not much. They were real shaken up."

"Never a good time to interview parents of a dead child," Utley said. "You'll talk with them further today."

I sat at my desk. "We told them tomorrow. They have arrangements to make."

"And we gotta canvass the neighborhood." Keisha said.

Utley scowled. "All right. Drugs involved?"

I glanced at Keisha. "No evidence yet."

"Ballistics?" Utley looked at me intently.

Keisha came to the rescue. "The ME dug a thirty-eight slug outta the boy."

"Did you tell me a moment ago there were three shots fired?" Utley asked.

"But no other slugs found," Keisha said. "And no shell casings in the area where the shot came from, which means the shooter either used a revolver or the casings ejected inside the vehicle."

"Or you weren't thorough," Utley said.

Just then, Arceneaux walked toward us holding a coffee mug. He stopped suddenly when he noticed Utley, but it was too late.

Utley turned his head. "Detective Arceneaux. I need to talk to you. There's a problem with that file you gave me yesterday. Follow me."

"Sure, boss," he stuttered. A film of coffee slid down the side of his mug and onto his hand.

Keisha leaned forward when Utley was gone. "I bet Arceneaux's thinking that lieutenant's one uppity nigger."

"Come on, Keisha. Arceneaux's not really like that."

"Child, that's what I'm thinking, too."

I laughed. "I'm thinking Utley's interfering with my sleep and personal relationships."

" 'Least you got a relationship to be interfered with," she said.

"You're too picky, Lundy."

"Nothing to pick from." She grabbed the store manager's statement and threw it across her desk to me.

Women detectives intimidated most men.

We spent the next few hours finishing our reports. Around noon, I stopped to call Emeril's for reservations. Thanks to a cancellation, I got a table for two at eight o'clock, then left a message for Alexis saying I'd pick her up at seven-thirty. I'd just reported my good luck to Keisha when the phone rang.

"Brenner."

"This is Odell Harris. I haven't found my old notes yet, but I remembered I did a TV segment a few years ago on local civil rights heroes. Doing the research, I found that one of the students who worked with your cousin is a woman named Faith Tilden. She owns a restaurant in Bon Terre called Meal Time."

The name Faith tugged at a dim memory.

"And the FBI agent who investigated the murders was from the New Orleans field office. Ennio Cribari," Odell said. "We have a phone number for him."

I wrote it down. "What about the local law? Any of them still around?"

"The sheriff's name was Vernon Hammond, but he was shot to death six months later by a motorist he'd pulled over. A deputy named Rhino Perrot took over his job. He's still sheriff."

"Thanks for your help."

"A small investment of my time," he said.

Hoping Cribari's number was still good, I dialed it, then swung my chair around, facing away from Keisha.

"Hello?" A soft, high-pitched man's voice answered.

"Ennio Cribari, please."

"Who's calling?"

"Jack Brenner. New Orleans police."

"Is there some trouble?"

"No. But I need to talk to Mr. Cribari."

A deep exhalation followed. "Hold on."

I listened to the faint sounds of classical music in the background until a sonorous voice came on the line, one with a native New Orleans accent outsiders mistake as Brooklyn.

"This is Ennio Cribari. What can I do for you?"

"I need to talk to you about a case you worked on. Two boys killed in Bon Terre in 1972."

There was a pause before he spoke. "That was a long time ago."

"You don't forget murder cases," I said. "Especially the ones you never solve. A man named Emmett Floyd Graves says he knows something. Maybe you can give me some background before I talk to him."

"Emmett Graves." Cribari recited the words as though they were an evil incantation. "Come by at six-thirty," he finally said. Then he dictated his address.

I softly slapped the receiver against my palm, feeling both accomplishment and apprehension. When I swiveled around to hang up, Forrest Utley glared at me.

My skin felt like hardened paste. "Uh, I was checking the store manager's work schedule. We want to interview him again before we canvass the neighborhood."

"Report to me at six today," Utley said.

Shit. That would mean not meeting Cribari. "People won't be home from work until then."

Utley nodded. "Okay. Then in the morning. Eight sharp."

There was no way to complete the canvass, see Cribari, and still make it to Emeril's. I watched Utley until he moved out of hearing range.

"We won't finish in time for me to meet Alexis," I said to Keisha. "I can't stand her up two nights in a row."

"Hang with me till seven and I'll finish up. Lord knows I got no dinner date. But you owe me."

"What if I hang till six?

Her eyes narrowed. "O-o-kay. For lunch at Clancy's."

"Deal."

After leaving Keisha on Miro Street to finish questioning the neighbors, I drove to the north part of the French Quarter and found a space to park on Esplanade. Water from an afternoon rain puddled in low spots on the broken sidewalk. Breathing in smells of damp concrete and auto exhaust, I walked three blocks to the address Cribari gave me. The residence hid behind a white-painted brick wall abutting the sidewalk. I pressed a buzzer on the frame of a red arched wooden door.

The intercom speaker embedded in the wall crackled. "Who is it?"

"Jack Brenner. I called earlier."

I heard an electric hum and opened the door and found myself in a courtyard brimming with begonias and impatiens. Bushes thick with red, white, and fuchsia roses lined a high brick wall.

A slight man with a full head of gray hair, holding an unlit pipe, tottered through French doors. A younger man watched from the doorway. He had sandy hair and wore pressed jeans with a tan button-down shirt. The man with the pipe was dressed in gray slacks and a burgundy knit mock turtleneck.

"Ennio Cribari," he said as he shook my hand. Then he motioned me toward a patio table and chairs in the corner of the L-shaped courtyard.

"Your roses are gorgeous." I pulled out a chair and eased into it.

He sat and crossed his legs. "Tending them is more relaxing than chasing bombers and gun dealers."

Talking to a law officer about an unsolved murder is like asking a basketball player about missing a last-second shot and losing a championship game. I wasn't sure how to start.

Fortunately, Cribari spoke first. "You wanted to talk to me about Emmett Graves. I read where he killed a guard. You say he knows something about a case I worked on in Bon Terre?"

"His lawyer says he does. One of the boys who was murdered was my cousin."

Cribari's breath slipped slowly from his lips as if he were expelling thoughts he couldn't articulate. "David Brenner. I missed the connection."

"Any chance Graves could know something?" I asked.

Cribari shrugged. "Why's he bringing this up now?"

"He wants to stay off death row."

He smirked. "Guys on death row develop good memories about unsolved crimes. They'd rather sit in a witness chair than lie on a gurney."

"What if he's telling the truth?"

"It'd be a first," Cribari said.

"Tell me what you know about him."

His milky blue eyes rolled up in recollection. "His love of violence goes back to childhood. I questioned some people in his hometown as part of the investigation. They told me he tortured animals. He used a magnifying glass to concentrate the sun on little birds and burn them in their nests. But what he liked best was luring cats so he could grab them by their tails and scrape their assholes with a dried corncob dipped in turpentine."

"I'm sure his neighbors at Angola have similar profiles," I said.

"And like them, he graduated from animals. He was in third or fourth grade when a little girl who'd moved to town the summer before took a liking to him. After noon recess, she folds up a love note and drops it on his desk. He looks up and says, 'What's this?' The other kids are standing around snickering. The girl doesn't know Graves can't read. Some form of dyslexia. Letters look like bird droppings to him.

"So the girl says again, 'I wrote it for you, Emmett. Open it.' The kids laugh louder and Graves's face gets redder. Then the girl says innocently, 'Open it and read it, dummy.' "

Cribari leaned back in his chair. The metal creaked like a bone twisted from the joint. "Graves grabs a pencil and rams it clean through her cheek and into her tongue."

"Jesus." I looked across the paving stone at the rose petals that had fallen from the rain.

"It was the last time a kid, or adult, for that matter, brought up the subject of his disability."

"Obviously hasn't handicapped his criminal pursuits," I said.

"Graves is the smartest illiterate you'll ever meet. Interviewing him was like playing twenty questions with a starving cottonmouth." He tapped the bowl of his pipe into his palm "I know how you feel about your cousin, but let the system finish Graves off."

I drew in the scent of roses and wet masonry and sat forward, gripping the edge of my chair with both hands. "Begging your pardon, sir, but you don't know how I feel about my cousin."

An awkward silence was broken by the brass click of the handles on the French doors.

"Ennio." The sandy-haired man stepped out onto the paving stone.

I gave Cribari my card. "I need your help."

He rose from his chair. His eyes, now gray, sank into the white skin pasted hard across his cheekbones.

I stood with my arms crossed as he walked slowly toward the house while the younger man focused worried eyes on me. Cribari stopped in the entryway, reached into his pocket, and pulled out a book of matches. He struck one and held the flame near the bowl of his pipe and drew in. I hoped this meant he was thinking as hard as I was about Emmett Floyd Graves and the murders of two young men over thirty years ago.

3

I rushed into the squad room the next morning with seconds to spare. I'd been late picking up Alexis, and we almost lost the reservation. This led to our perennial quarrel about how I'd be working regular hours if I'd take an administrative post at the department.

"How was dinner?" Keisha asked.

"The meal was flawless. Thanks for finishing up. Anything else turn up last night?"

She patted her notebook. "Nothing but more names and numbers. No one saw or heard anything helpful. But briefing Utley isn't what I'm dreading."

"Me either." The image of a ghostly porch light shone in my brain.

After an unexpected meeting with the superintendent of police limited Utley to fifteen minutes of grilling and second-guessing us, we drove to the Bowen home. This wasn't the first time I'd questioned parents after the death of a child, but experience doesn't make it easier. The one thing I've learned is to never say you understand.

The neighborhood was a quarter mile from where Steven Bowen was shot to death and a two-mile jog to Audubon Park. The gloom no doubt pervading the Bowen home wasn't visible from the street. Perennials and variegated shrubbery lined the white, green-trimmed house. Because of the cars parked out front, we pulled in two houses up and walked back. I rang the bell. The sun shone directly on the porch, and the morning humidity joined the weight of our task to send rivulets of sweat down my neck.

A short, thin man in a dark gray suit opened the door. "You must be the police. I'm Edgar Bowen, Steven's grandfather."

His bony fingers motioned us inside. Two dozen people were spread around the combination living-dining room. Voices drifted from the kitchen along with the aroma of shrimp and sausage. Someone was preparing jambalaya or gumbo. The elder Bowen led us to an enclosed back porch. Two water oaks shaded the room and the entire yard. A floor fan at one end sucked in conditioned air from the main house. Mr. and Mrs. Bowen were settled on an old couch.

"Need anything, son?" the elder Bowen asked.

Steven's father shook his head. Keisha and I sat across from the Bowens on a pair of rattan chairs.

Keisha spoke softly. "Once again, we're sorry for your loss. Mr. Bowen, you told us the other night that you'd been at work until shortly before we arrived. And Mrs. Bowen, you were home all evening. Is that right?"

They both nodded.

"Mrs. Bowen," Keisha said, "you said Steven had left the house not long before he was killed. Did he say where he was going?"

"Meeting up with some of his friends at the arcade," Mrs. Bowen said. "We let him go out nights during summer recess."

"Which arcade?" I asked.

"Up on Broad."

The convenience store would be on the way. "Do you know why Steven might stop to use the phone?"

"No." Mrs. Bowen's whisper had the heaviness of a thousand whys.

A call received twenty minutes before Steven was shot was stored in his pager. It had beeped again as the ME loaded the body for transport to the morgue. The pager was old technology, meaning there was no way to trace the call to a specific residential phone or cell phone. It accepted only numeric messages input by the caller. The second page had the same callback number as the first. Arceneaux was going to use a reverse directory to identify the caller.

"Did your son always carry a pager?" Keisha asked.

"I know what y'all are thinking." Mr. Bowen's eyes seared us. "Steven didn't have nothing to do with drugs. We gave him that pager so we could keep up with him."

"I didn't mean to imply that, Mr. Bowen," Keisha said. "Maybe one of his friends paged him to tell him about a change of plans. Who'd he hang with?"

Mrs. Bowen's jaw quivered. "He had a lotta friends."

"Can you tell us who?" I asked.

Mrs. Bowen rolled her eyes upward and began retrieving names and uttering them with a slow rasp.

I scribbled down the names, all boys.

"No girlfriends?" Keisha asked.

Mrs. Bowen shook her head. "Between his studies and his running, he didn't have time. He'll be into that soon enough—"

Her eyes flooded as though she'd suddenly become aware it would never happen.

Mr. Bowen put his arm around his wife. "Is that all?"

Keisha and I traded glances, then nodded.

Mr. Bowen called into the front room, "Andy. Come sit with your mama."

A boy appeared, six inches of wrist showing below the cuffs of his suit coat, eyes fearful of new responsibility. He looked to be the same age I was when David died.

Mr. Bowen squeezed the shoulder of the young man who was now his oldest son, then motioned us onward. "I'll show you out."

We reached the front porch. Swells of wet heat rose from the concrete.

"It was real hot Monday night," I said to Mr. Bowen. "Your son wore his track jacket."

A faint glow appeared in his eyes. "Always took it with him. He was real proud of it."

Muffled laughter seeped from inside the house. The kind that comes from family, even in painful gatherings. Maybe this buzz of undying linkage caused me to tell Mr. Bowen about my own connection to his son. "I understand your son's pride. I ran track at Franklin High, too."

"Steven set a school record in the mile this May." His eyes gleamed as though daring death to rob him of his pride for his son. "I miss some meets 'cause I work shifts, but I saw him do it."

David's record. Suddenly, the sultry air seemed frosty as I drew in a breath. "My cousin held that record. Wish he could have seen Steven break it."

Keisha and I returned to the car.

"Did you hear what Mr. Bowen said about Steven breaking David's school record?" I asked.

The springs creaked as Keisha shifted in the seat. "Spooky."

I sat silently remembering the last time I'd seen David run. Then I looked at Keisha. "There's something I didn't tell you yesterday."

She stared ahead, her expression a mixture of curiosity and hurt. "Yeah?"

I told her about meeting Cribari. "I can't let this go. But I'm sorry I kept you in the dark."

Keisha moved her gaze from the windshield and leaned toward me. "Look. I know you're anxious to have Arceneaux back."

"Keisha—"

"It's okay. You two've been partners for a long time. You've built up trust. I'm just glad I got the chance to work with you. You've been helpful to me ever since I got my shield. No other guy would give me the time of day. That's why I asked to fill in when Arceneaux was shot."

"I didn't know," I said.

"What I'm saying is, I know you gotta take care of business with this Graves creep. Like I said, maybe you can finish it. Sometimes people don't get that chance. You need my help, you need me to cover for you like I did last evening, I'll do it."

"Thanks. Over the years I've had nightmares about David's death. Guess I'm in for another round of them."

I looked back into the rearview mirror. The cheery exterior of the Bowen home belied the grief inside. Putting the car in gear, I noticed Keisha had turned her head to the side window. The glass reflected troubled brown eyes.

"What is it?" I asked.

"You're not the only one with bad dreams," she said. "I have them every time I see a dead kid like Steven."

She reached over and turned down the air conditioner, reducing the rumbling fan to a dismal hiss. "My brother was seventeen when he was shot. He got in the way of a drug dealer. The bastard broke our door down and shot him in the face. I think Steven got in the way, too. You called it right from the start, Jack."

"Did they ever catch the guy who shot your brother?"

"No. Still out there."

Still out there. Was David's killer still living among us, too? I wondered why I'd never considered it before. Perhaps it was a young boy's psychological defense against deep loss. Now it enraged me. Keisha might never know who shot her brother, but I might have a chance in David's case. The Bowens would damn sure have a chance.

As Keisha and I walked into the station, Arceneaux waddled up from the back of the squad room.

"I got an address for that number on the kid's pager," he said, waving a yellow slip of paper.

"Residence?" I asked.

"These young dealers deliver like they was peddling pizzas," Arceneaux said.

"The vic wasn't into drugs," Keisha said.

Arceneaux sniffed. "Right."

Keisha jerked the note from his fingers. "Let's go, Jack. We're burning daylight."

"Sorry to be so short with Arceneaux," Keisha said as we drove toward the lakefront.

"Believe it or not, he'd understand. He's got some bad memories of his own."

Her face and neck muscles softened as she settled into the seat. A few minutes later she asked, "Do you ever get personally involved in a case?"

"Can't help it sometimes."

"Some vics matter more than others?"

I thought about it as the molten blue sky rippled with heat above us.

"No," I said, recalling something I learned from my cousin, who helped prepare me for my bar mitzvah. "David taught me an ancient rabbinic saying. 'Because we all come from Adam, to take a single life is to destroy the entire world.' That emphasizes the absolute evil of murder. But the second part is this: 'To save a single life is to save the entire world.' Every victim matters because stopping a killer prevents him from taking another life. It saves the whole world."

"So what if David wasn't killed and it was just the other kid?" she challenged. "Would you have gone to Ennio Cribari? Would you even be thinking about driving to Angola to see Emmett Graves?"

I felt no more articulate than the wheezing air conditioner. "Maybe not. The saying tells us all victims are equally important to God. Guess I'm human."

She looked straight ahead and nodded, hopefully as indication my honesty was sufficient.

The address Arceneaux gave us led to a stretch of newly constructed townhouses on the shore of Lake Pontchartrain west of the causeway. We parked in the visitors area and followed a walkway that took us to the lakefront. Each home faced the water and looked down on a shoreline park from entrances well above ground level. We walked up the steps to the front door of the residence whose owner of record was a Jason Meade.

Keisha rapped a solid brass knocker. A minute later, she rapped again. Finally, deadbolts clicked behind the heavy mahogany. A young man with sandy blond hair opened the door halfway, holding on to it with one hand and propping his other arm against the frame.

"Jason Meade?" Keisha asked.

"Yeah?" mumbled the short, skinny kid dressed only in baggy shorts.

Insipid pop music drifted from the back of the house. I held out my badge.

He peeked back over his shoulder. "I took care of those parking tickets, man."

"May we come in?"

He sneered. "Not a good time."

I pressed my palm against the door. "We won't be long."

"If you'll give me your card . . ."

"After we leave." I shoved the door forward six inches.

"Uh, look." He gripped the polished mahogany and glanced back into the home's interior. "She's married, man. Guy's president of the Rotary Club."

I released my hand, then pointed to a table surrounded by deck chairs on the tiled porch.

His eyes moved slowly to the furniture. "Hang on. I'll be right out."

Keisha and I took a seat. The lake was calm and the air clear enough to see the causeway to Mandeville all the way to the horizon. Jason was back in a minute. Still no shirt.

He pulled out a chair. "Whadda you guys want?"

"We want to know why you paged Steven Bowen the night he was shot," I said with no certainty that Jason was the one who dialed his pager, but hoping his reaction would tell me.

"The kid from Franklin who got shot the other night?"

"The young man you paged."

"What makes you think I paged Steven Bowen?"

"Your callback number was stored in the pager."

He glanced away, his eyes moving as if tracking the flight of a seagull. Then he smiled and reeled off ten digits. "That the number?"

I nodded.

"It's my sister Jenna's number. We all got cells on my father's family plan."

"Your father named Jason Meade, too?" I asked.

"I'm the second. Not junior."

"And this place is in his name."

"Until I'm thirty-five. That's when the trust comes through. I get a meager allowance in the meantime."

Arceneaux had found Jason Meade's name from the reverse phone directory, then got this address from the parish property tax roles. Either the elder Meade's home was in someone else's name, or Arceneaux hadn't looked far enough.

Jason smirked. "Don't be embarrassed. Mix-ups like this happen all the time."

"Bet there's no confusion about which one of you has a steady job," I said.

The dark pinpoints in his eyes hardened around his pupils in a cold glare.

"You guessed your sister left her phone number on Steven Bowen's pager," Keisha said. "She a friend of his?"

"She's on the track team," Jason said. "Steven was a big star."

"I presume Jenna lives with the senior Jason Meade. You think you could you save us some time and give us the address?"

"Always ready to help out New Orleans's finest." Jason recited the address.

Keisha turned to me with a can't-think-of-anything-else look.

"You can get back to whoever's wife you've been banging," I said.

"No sweat, man."

Keisha and I descended the steps. The lake lay in front of the property like a blue-green lawn, dotted with sailboats.

"Little pissant," Keisha said. "You catch that whiff of weed coming from inside his place?"

"Maybe Jason makes his spending money providing chemical and physical pleasure to older women."

Keisha motioned to a park bench under a tree at the far end of the row of townhouses. "Let's wait a while and see who leaves his place."

It wasn't long before my theory was confirmed.

A woman in black leotards with a lavender and white print wrap skirt descended the steps of the townhouse. She looked to be in her early forties, firm and flat-chested, her salon-blond hair pulled up except for the dozens of wisps clinging to the moisture on her neck. She walked past us briskly, her lips taut, her eyes straight ahead like someone who'd found a twenty-dollar bill on the floor of a store and had decided not to announce it.

The address Jason had given us was in the Garden District. As we pulled up to a white-columned home with a large second-story deck on the side, a dark green Lexus backed rapidly out of the driveway and into the street. The tires squealed as it stopped and lurched forward. A young blond woman wearing sunglasses wrestled the steering wheel to the left and accelerated past us. We parked and made our way up a walkway lined with Asian jasmine.

A woman wearing a French blue shirt and khakis answered the door. When I held up my badge, she stepped hurriedly onto the porch and looked off in the direction of the speeding Lexus.

Keisha followed her gaze. "Your daughter, Jenna?"

"Yes. Is something wrong?"

"She was sure in a hurry," Keisha said.

Mrs. Meade surveyed the shrubbery under the windows that forestalled the encroachment of her manicured lawn. "A boy at her school died. The funeral is today."

"That's why we're here," I said.

Despite the morning sultriness, Mrs. Meade's skin remained smooth and dry, her carriage as crisp as her cotton shirt. "What does Jenna have to do with it?"

I wasn't going to let her know Jenna's cell number was stored in Steven's pager. "We're talking to all Steven Bowen's friends."

"They weren't friends," Mrs. Meade said.

"The whole team going to the funeral?" Keisha asked.

"I suppose so. Jenna broke a dental appointment."

"And your daughter sped off in a huff after you tried to convince her to keep it," Keisha said.

Mrs. Meade's eyes returned to the shrubbery. "They're hard to get."

"Where was your daughter Monday night?" I asked.

The noon heat seemed to evaporate the blue from her eyes. "My husband and I were out. She was here when we returned around eleven. But I think she'd been out with friends earlier. It's awful what happened to the boy, but do you really need to speak with my daughter?"

"Like I said. We're talking to kids who knew him. We'll come back another time."

We descended the tiled steps.

"Mrs. Meade referred to Steven as 'the boy,'" I said as I started the car. "Maybe for Jenna it was boy *friend*."

"Could've had a secret romance going. She pages Steven. He goes to the phone at the convenience store to return her call."

I put the car in gear. "It's the closest pay phone to his house. Probably used it to call her a lot."

"Which means Jenna knows her page got him killed," Keisha said.

Taking the time to follow a lead on David's murder would no doubt upset Alexis and piss off Lieutenant Utley. And Keisha had forced me to admit that no matter how much I'd taken David's teaching to heart in my work as a detective, I probably wouldn't risk the turmoil if the black kid were the only victim of a 1972 homicide. But David was blood. I was going to see Emmett Floyd Graves.

Back at the station, I dialed Neil Gross's cell phone.

"Yeah." Neil spoke above blaring horns and a grinding noise. "Shit. It's starting to rain and the goddamned top won't come up."

"Just have the leather shampooed?" I asked.

"Ah. There it goes. Who's this?"

"Jack Brenner. Set me up with Graves tomorrow morning."

"Kind of short notice."

"Can you do it?"

"Okay. Nine o'clock. It's a two-hour drive to Angola unless you have a radar detector."

That meant Neil's Porsche did it in ninety minutes.

"Fine. Meet you there?"

"Hell no. I have clients who might benefit from my services. Graves's life expectancy isn't any longer than my dick. Let me know how it goes."

I heard tire rubber screech.

Keisha promised to cover for me the next morning. I took the interstate to Baton Rouge, then headed north to Angola State Prison. The sun shone on vermilion cane fields dripping from an overnight thunderstorm as I kept my eyes peeled for changes in the posted limits to avoid the speed traps set up all over rural Louisiana.

The highway eventually turned to blacktop and a few miles later, I pulled up to the prison gate. Inside the unit that housed Emmett Graves, I checked my service revolver with a guard at the first of a series of electronically controlled glass doors. While the guard's face sported a lazy eye and the scars of an acne-ravaged youth, he had the easy demeanor of one certain about his purpose on earth.

"Graves'll be on death row soon," the guard said as he directed me through an X-ray. "Ever been there?"

"Put a couple there," I said, not wishing to mention the one execution I'd witnessed.

"Most of 'ems Christian by the time they get here. It's almost peaceful."

The guard took me down a corridor that smelled of wet concrete and old perspiration, then led me to a ten-by-ten room. "Go on in. They'll bring him through that door yonder."

The door clunked behind me and I heard the tumblers fall into place. I sat in a metal chair at a three-foot-wide table that stretched six feet toward another chair. I tried to push my chair back to stretch my legs, but it was bolted to the floor.

I turned toward a sound like the opening of a vacuum thermos. A man in prison whites, about five feet eight inches tall, stood in the doorway just ahead of the guard. His coal black eyes fixed on me instantly, hard and metallic as the ankle and wrist chains that clinked as he shuffled toward his chair. His gray hair, streaked with black, was pulled into a ponytail.

The prisoner slid into his chair, and the guard attached his shackles to a D ring welded to the surface of the table.

The guard pointed above my shoulder. "Press that button on the wall when you're through."

Again, tumblers clicked into place as he left me face-to-face with Emmett Floyd Graves.

"I've been waiting," he said.

I tried to penetrate his gaze, but his pupils were like black holes from which no light escaped. "What made you think I'd come?"

"You people take care of your own. David Brenner was your kin." His skin was like sun-split leather, but his facial muscles were relaxed.

"How'd you connect him with me?" I asked.

"Saw you on that nigger newsman's show," he said, referring to Odell Harris, who'd interviewed me at the conclusion of a high-profile murder case on his Saturday afternoon program. "Recognized the last name and wondered if you were related. You've got acquaintances here at the Farm. They made some calls."

"Assuming you have anything worth listening to, why didn't you tell it to your lawyer?"

He leaned back in his chair. "I wanted this personal."

"It's a long drive. I don't plan on making it again."

Graves cocked his chin. "Know what commitment is, Brenner?" He paused, watching me. "David Brenner had it. That Jew-boy worked long hours for no pay. Spent long days in the middle of summer slapping at mosquitoes in that nigger church with one old ceiling fan. All to help them poor black folk. That's commitment."

Graves locked his eyes on mine. "You looked up to him, I bet."

"What kind of shuck are you playing, Graves?"

"More like an older brother, huh?"

I wasn't prepared for this aggressive personal intrusion and felt he'd somehow gained an advantage. I pressed my palms on the table and stood. "I've got some yard work to do."

"You'll do what it takes to find who killed him." His eyes rose with me.

"It's ancient history," I said.

Graves smiled shrewdly. "Ain't no such thing with you people."

The skin tightened across my face. "You said *find*. That means you don't know who killed my cousin. Or you know and you don't have proof."

"I have information."

"If it comes from being involved with killing either David or the other kid, it won't buy you a pack of cigarettes. I guarantee that."

"You wanna hear it or not?" He scraped his manacles forward on the table and extended his palms toward my chair.

I sat down slowly, drawn as much by his cold, magnetic eyes as by my aching curiosity. "You don't strike me as the repentant type. What do you want?"

"I want the death penalty off the table."

"Killing a guard in an attempted escape?" I shook my head. "The DA's going to make sure you go down hard."

"Figure a way to convince the DA otherwise."

"What makes you think I can do that?"

"You'll find a way."

"The DA isn't going to let you off the gurney because you have information on a thirty-one-year-old case, which you've given me no reason to think you have anyway."

"I'll give you enough so you'll believe I know what I'm talking about. Then get the DA to settle for life and I'll sing the whole song."

I exhaled. "I'm listening."

"When you go to Bon Terre, say hello to Avery Hammond for me."

He was taking me for a ride. This wasn't the first time a con had tried it, but the stakes had never been personal. "Who says I'm going to Bon Terre?"

"You won't have trouble finding him." Graves was doing to me with words what he'd done to those cats with a corncob and turpentine. "Come back this weekend and tell me what you think."

"You haven't given me a damn thing. If you think I'm going to run all over the state—"

Graves clanged his wrist chains against the steel table. "Guard!"

The guard came in and quickly released the shackles from the iron ring. The room, moisture oozing from the concrete, felt as hollow as my lungs.

Emmett Graves rose. "Commitment, Brenner. When you come back, show me you got it."

4

Commitment. The word echoed off the damp masonry as I trudged back up the long corridor. I retrieved my weapon and returned to the prison block entry, where I pulled out my cell phone and dialed Keisha.

"Get anything from Graves?" she asked.

"Jailhouse shuck and jive and a name. I need to drive down to Bon Terre."

"I was hoping we'd talk to Jenna Meade today."

"I'll be back by late afternoon. There's a meet every Thursday evening at the Franklin track. I bet she'll be there. I'd rather talk to her away from her mother."

"What makes you think she'll be at the meet?"

"She's a runner like Steven was. If she had feelings for him, she might use the competition to manage her hurt. Get any grief from Utley this morning?"

"He asked where you were."

"What did you say?"

"I told him you had the runs and went home to change your slacks. He went 'humph' and marched back to his office."

I chuckled. "You're a pal. See you later."

Closing the phone, I noticed a woman with straw blond hair enter the building. Dressed in a navy blazer with an eggshell blouse, her legs were long for her height. As she removed her sunglasses and slipped them into a large shoulder bag, I recognized her. Even in the flat, institutional fluorescence, her eyes glinted like amber crystals. Sensing my cognizance, or my stare, she looked over to me.

"Willow," I said, recalling hot summer nights on the levee.

She wrinkled an eyebrow, then launched a smile. "Jack?" She walked up and lightly touched my elbow. "It's been since—"

"Since my wife pulled me away from you on the dance floor at our ten-year high school reunion," I said. "But I've seen you recently. I was in Atlanta last fall on a case and caught you on the ten o'clock news. Your voice. Your face. But I didn't recognize the name."

Willow grinned. "Left it behind with the weather-girl job in Chattanooga. Willow Ashe is more audience-friendly than Willow Ashkenazi."

"Meaning more WASP."

She laughed and brushed a blond strand back into place with her little finger.

"What brings you to the Farm?" I asked.

"A story. What else? Hopefully a good one. I've been an investigative reporter in Atlanta for five years and if I don't get the attention of the networks soon, the station will push me aside for someone who doesn't need chemistry to cover her wrinkles. It's an up-or-out business, unless you're willing to settle for winters in Fargo."

"I hope this is the big one for you."

"Me, too." Then she gave me a look that brought back memories of perfume and sweat. "I once thought the big one was you and me." The fluorescent bulbs hummed above us as Willow moved closer and looked up at me. "Then you left me waiting for you at Molly's that winter. I was going to ask you about it when your wife dragged you off the dance floor."

A hard swallow aborted my attempted chortle.

Willow stepped back, but her subtle, earthy scent lingered. "Maybe we can finish that conversation. There's a good chance I'll be in south Louisiana awhile."

"Call me at the Second District," I said, fumbling in my coat pocket for a business card.

She took the card and dropped it into her purse, her eyes riveted to mine.

I drove down to Baton Rouge, then took I-10 toward New Orleans, fearing Emmett Graves was leading me on a futile venture. Ennio Cribari had warned me about Graves's intelligence and I was angry I'd underestimated it. Even angrier that a racist killer might be the lynchpin to resolving my cousin's death. But what vexed me most was my inability to focus on my next move without distracting thoughts of Willow Ashe.

As the interstate crossed the swampland south of Lake Pontchartrain, my mind returned to a summer night on the Mississippi levee, car stereo playing, while remnant lightning from a passing storm and river scents floating through the open windows mingled with the piquant odor of native grasses and feral emotions.

Willow lay on top of me in the backseat, I in khaki Bermudas, she in blue jean shorts, our legs interlocked. My silk camp shirt was unbuttoned and her sweat-soaked tank top was pulled well above her breasts. Suddenly her breath caught. I felt a violent tremble and she began to whimper.

Confused and alarmed, I lifted her face from my neck. "You all right?"

Her eyes opened languidly. Serpentine strands of straw blond hair clung to the perspiration on her cheeks. Her smile was other worldly.

"Absolutely wonderful," she murmured.

"Sure?" I asked in a cracked whisper.

She licked my earlobe. Her breath was hot. "You've got a lot to learn, Jack."

Willow forced her tongue past callow lips, then she slid her hand down my chest and inside my shorts. She clamped her thighs around one of mine, harder and more purposeful than before, rocking with a quickening cadence. Soon she trembled and whimpered again. I quaked with her, as the last resonance of thunder rumbled over the Gulf.

Though actual intercourse took place several nights later, and included protection, we always considered that night on the levee as our first time to make love.

The reverie of my first time with Willow faded just in time for me to catch the 310 turnoff from the interstate. I cut over two lanes and headed south toward Bon Terre.

The endless rice and soybean fields I drove past for the next half hour looked like a waterlogged Kansas prairie. I approached a phalanx of cypress trees shortly past a sign saying three miles to Bon Terre. Soon, an unmarked bridge took me over a narrow bayou and the highway curved into the woods. The sudden shadow blinded me for a second. Then, as my eyes adjusted, the highway burst out of the trees into the hot midday light. But the flicker in my rearview mirror was not from the sun. I looked down at my speedometer. The dial slid below seventy as I tapped the brake. In my side mirror, red and blue sparks burst from the roof of a patrol car. I pulled over and stopped on the shoulder piled with freshly mown johnsongrass.

A voice boomed from the speaker of the patrol car: "Please step out of your car, sir."

I reached back across the seat for my coat so I could display my gold shield.

"Please step out immediately," the crackling voice demanded.

I looked back through the heat shimmering from the asphalt. A lone officer stood behind the open door of the patrol car. I stepped out, hoping my holstered gun would let the officer know I was a cop.

"Remove your weapon with your left hand and lay it on the ground," the voice behind the sunglasses demanded.

"I'm a cop," I called back.

"I don't know that, sir."

I didn't suggest reaching back into the car for my badge. No experienced officer would let my hands get out of sight.

"Walk toward me," the officer said when I'd complied.

The officer ordered me to stop once I'd covered half the ten yards that separated us, then spoke into the mouthpiece of an onboard radio. After nodding and replacing the radio mike, the officer started toward me. Suddenly I realized the officer was a woman.

I grinned as she approached. "Guess the dispatcher who ran my plates told you I'm on the job."

"I'm on the job," she said. "You've violated the law."

"No professional courtesies?" I asked, noticing the nameplate above her left uniform pocket: J. THOMAS. A silver shield was pinned above the other.

"Courtesy would be obeying the speed limit, sir."

"Must have been distracted."

"That just cost you two hundred dollars. Can I see your license?"

"Two hundred dollars?"

"Sixty-five in a thirty-five." She flipped open her ticket book, past several pink receipts.

"I didn't see a thirty-five-mile-an-hour sign," I complained.

"It's right after you take the bend," she said.

I looked stupidly back up the road. Temporary blindness, I thought. No doubt the shadows had hidden her patrol car.

She crisply ripped off a ticket and handed it to me. "Return to your car and follow me, Mr. Brenner."

I was too shocked to question the "Mister." "You're kidding."

"You pay before you leave in Bon Terre. Leave your weapon on the ground. I'll return it to you at the station."

"It's against department regulations to relinquish my firearm," I said.

She pulled off her sunglasses. Her eyes were a shocking blue against deeply tanned skin. "You working a case in cooperation with authorities in this parish?"

Not yet. "No."

"Then return to your vehicle." She was slightly shorter than Keisha, but almost as muscular. Her expression ruled out further protest. "We're two miles out. Follow me and stay in view." She replaced her sunglasses, then retrieved my gun after I closed my car door.

I stayed close behind Officer Thomas's cruiser. As we crept past a turnoff labeled ESCONDIDO ROAD, I noticed a neatly lettered sign: MEAL THYME RESTAURANT. Faith Tilden's place, I thought, chuckling at the spice pun. Then we rounded a gentle bend where a WELCOME TO BON TERRE sign and several billboards lined the road. The largest three stood out. HAMMOND MOTORS. HAMMOND APPLIANCES. HAMMOND INSURANCE.

Avery Hammond? The name Emmett Graves threw out to me like a used soup bone to a starving dog? I was about to pay two hundred dollars to find out.

The highway became Main Street, lined with chains of connected storefronts. Officer Thomas pulled into a reserved space on the left. I parked a couple of slots away, then grabbed my badge from my coat. Taking the ticket from the top of the dash, I got out and stepped onto the sidewalk. She held open the door marked BON TERRE SHERIFF.

Chilled air and the odor of stale tobacco filled the office. A man wearing a short-sleeved uniform sat behind a desk and looked me over. His massive square face was lined, but his wiry dark hair was fuller than mine. The nameplate on his desk read: RHINO PERROT, SHERIFF. The name Odell Harris had given me.

"Whatcha got, Jarla?" asked Rhino.

"Sixty-five in a thirty-five."

"Maybe we can square this." I held out my gold shield. "Second District, New Orleans."

The chair creaked as he leaned back. "You tell this to Officer Thomas?"

"Yes."

"Sheriff," Jarla said, "I asked Detective Brenner to remove his weapon. I checked his plates and badge number. He's for real."

Rhino grinned. "Let him have it, Officer Thomas, and get

back on out there. That bend's got a few more hours in deep shadow."

I wondered what they did for revenue on cloudy days.

Jarla tipped her visor and handed me my revolver. As she opened the door on her way out, the cold air rushed from the office as rapidly as my patience.

"Okay." I laid my ticket on his desk next to an ashtray with three cigar butts.

Rhino looked at the ticket like it was an overdraft notice from a bank. "The sheriff don't collect fines." He grinned up at me. "Gotta see the JP for that." He pointed to a JUSTICE OF THE PEACE placard fixed to a high, wood-paneled counter in the back of the room.

I stared at the unattended venue of rural jurisprudence. It was almost one. Only a few hours before I needed to get back to Keisha.

"He'll be just a minute," Rhino said. He gripped the armrests of his chair, which groaned as he struggled up. Then he moved toward the back of the room and took the step that led behind the counter. "Court's in session," he called out.

The ticket dangled at my side like a broken leaf. "You're the sheriff *and* the justice of the peace?"

"One person, two jobs. The refinery my boy works at in Lake Charles calls it multicraft."

Multi*graft,* I thought. "I don't have two hundred dollars on me," I said, walking to the counter. "Your Honor."

"Well now, that's a problem, son." He leaned into the counter using his ample stomach as a cushion. "The justice of the peace only takes cash. But you can use a credit card to post bond at the bail bond office next door."

I exited the office. After a few paces along the sidewalk, I came to a glass door with purple and white hand-painted lettering: SEVEN ANGELS BAIL BONDS. I could use them all, I thought as I entered the empty room. It was half the size of the sheriff's office and the walls were painted mauve. Photographs of south Louisiana flora and fauna hung on the walls. And it didn't reek of tobacco.

"Can I hep you?" Rhino Perrot appeared at the rear of the office.

"Aren't you taking this multicraft too far?" I asked.

"The missus owns the bail bond business. I keep an eye on things when she's out." Rhino carefully sat at the desk in a wicker chair made for someone much lighter.

I laid my ticket in front of him.

"Let's see," he said. "We can pay that for you on your behalf if you'll just sign this." He pulled a two-part form from the top drawer.

"What's it going to cost me?" I asked.

"The fine amount plus twenty percent, 'cept the minimum fee's a hunnert."

"That's ridiculous."

His eyes danced under his furry eyebrows. "Your time ain't worth a hunnert dollars, son?"

I shook my head, then signed the form and gave him a credit card that he ran through a scanner connected to the phone line.

"Usually takes a few minutes," he said. "What brings a New Orleans cop to Bon Terre anyway?"

"A friend recommended Meal Thyme for lunch."

Rhino looked at me as though listening to a pitch from a timeshare salesman. "Have to do better than that, son."

It was a small town. He'd eventually find out about my mission. "Okay. I'm looking into the background of a former resident. Emmett Floyd Graves."

Rhino reacted as though I'd spoken an obscenity. "Property values went up around here when he got put away for dealing drugs. When he killed that guard they went up some more, 'cause he for sure ain't coming back."

"Graves have any connection to a man named Avery Hammond?"

Rhino squinted into the sun streaming through the glass door. "Mr. Hammond has lots of connections. I don't keep up with them." The credit verification machine clattered and he wrote the approval code on the form. Rhino tore off the pink copy of a three-part form, handed me a copy, and threw the two remaining copies into a tray.

Rhino Perrot obviously knew Emmett Graves and Avery Hammond, but he'd shut off discussion for now. My first interest was Faith Tilden anyway, and I could talk to Rhino later. As I closed the Seven Angels door behind me, I looked up and noticed a red Camaro parked next to my car. I could see bodywork had been done on the front left side, but it wasn't painted. A man stood on the sidewalk between me and the door to the sheriff's office.

"Got caught in the trap?" the man asked, chewing on the earpiece of his wraparound Armani sunglasses. He wore a black knit polo shirt with sleeves tight around his biceps. A black belt with a silver tip and buckle held up tropical-weight tan slacks.

"I contributed to the town coffers," I said. "And Seven Angels."

He focused on my holstered gun. "Not often law gets caught by law."

I looked into his gray eyes. "The law applies to everyone."

The man smiled, but his eyes were as flat as paint on a parish roadworks vehicle. He replaced his sunglasses and returned to the Camaro.

I heard the door to Seven Angels open and close.

"Figured you'd be gone by now." Rhino stepped onto the sidewalk and pulled a cigar from his shirt pocket.

"Just schmoozing with the local populace," I said.

"You'll have to talk English round here, son."

"Who's that guy in the red Camaro?"

"Creed Beaumont."

"I'm guessing he's not a Bon Terre native. But you are. You were a deputy when Vernon Hammond was murdered. He related to Avery Hammond?"

"Brothers." He lit the cigar. "Enjoy your lunch. You'll see a sign for Faith Tilden's place off the main highway on your way back to where you came from. I'd suggest you keep going in that direction afterwards."

On the force when David was killed, I thought. Talking to Rhino again was now critical.

"See ya around, Detective," Rhino said.

"What makes you think I'll be back?" I asked.

"You're after something you ain't telling me about, son. Don't let me find out what it is from someone else."

Back up the highway, I spotted Escondido Road and turned onto a narrow asphalt lane shaded by an oak canopy. After crossing a bayou on a one-lane bridge, I came to a rambling, whitewashed building. A sign with two-foot-high pink and lavender lettering—MEAL THYME—hung from the front beam of the gallery. Planters crammed with pansies and snapdragons lined the railing. Another whitewashed building, with a steeply pitched roof and large double doors, stood just beyond. I parked in the oyster-shell lot and went inside.

A woman, probably in her late twenties, approached holding a menu.

"I'm here to see Faith Ann Tilden," I said.

Her dark brown eyes brightened. "You must be the writer from *South Louisiana Gourmet.*"

"No," I said. "It's other business."

The young woman relaxed her smile and gestured toward an archway. "You can go out through the back. She's in the garden picking herbs."

Entering the kitchen, I recognized the aroma of seafood gumbo—a strong dark roux, with garlic, onion, and fresh shrimp and crab. A forty-gallon garbage can captured the discarded shells. Hints of tarragon and basil told me some of the preparations were more complex than traditional bayou-country fare. A short black woman looked up at me from a chopping board.

Blasts of mint and honeysuckle overwhelmed the kitchen odors as I opened the screen door and stepped onto a covered back porch lined with shrubs and flowers. Below the gallery, the sun wrapped a verdant luster around rows of herbs and peppers. The grounds beyond sloped gently toward the bayou.

A woman wearing a broad straw hat knelt beside a garden near a whitewashed building lined with wisteria.

I took the steps from the porch and walked toward her. "Faith Tilden? I'm Detective Brenner, with the New Orleans police."

She looked up from a wicker basket filled with green onions and basil. Rising slowly, she studied my face as if peering into a mirror in a dimly lit room. Her splotched bronze shoulders contrasted with her chambray jumper. Generous streaks of gray offset the waves of auburn hair cascading from her hat.

Faith smiled curiously, the crinkles around her eyes showing middle age. "Hello, Jack."

"News travels fast in a small town," I said.

She laughed. "We met at Tulane. You were with your father watching your cousin at the conference championships."

The image of David leaning across the finish line in his final race swept past me. "You knew David?"

"I was at Tulane with David. Of course, you wouldn't remember. You were maybe ten?"

"Twelve," I said.

Faith pulled off her garden gloves and dropped them into the grass next to her basket. "David introduced me after his race, but your eyes were on him."

"He set a school record that day."

"And you had it right there on your father's stopwatch."

"I never reset it." I remembered how empty I felt when I looked at the frozen dials after learning David's body had been found.

I jumped back as a bee darted out from the wisteria and hummed around her hat.

Her green eyes shimmered. "Don't mind them, they won't mind you."

I wondered how sharp the sting would be for refusing to leave the past alone.

"Whatever in the world brings you to Bon Terre?" Faith asked.

"Not the *South Louisiana Gourmet.* Your hostess seemed disappointed when I told her."

Faith looked toward the restaurant. "That was my daughter, Grace. She's been on pins and needles since that fellow called to say he wanted to do an article on us."

I swallowed and watched several bees hovering along the wisteria. "I'm here about David's murder. I understand you worked with him."

She reached down, grabbed her gloves, and looped the basket handle over her arm. The smell of newly cut herbs infused the air.

"There's a guy named Emmett Floyd Graves who claims to have information," I said. "I want to see if there's anything to it."

Her jaw tightened. "Emmett Graves is an evil man."

"Most information I get to solve crimes comes from evil people."

Faith rearranged the herbs and onions in the basket. I wondered if she was reshuffling memories as she ordered the greenery.

She lifted her chin and smiled. "Have you had lunch?"

"I'd like you to tell me about David and what happened the summer he died," I said.

"You're stubborn, like David." She took my arm and led me toward the back porch. "We'll talk after lunch. The herbal tea is guaranteed to improve your day."

Faith faltered as we reached the steps. Her grip tightened.

"Are you okay?" I asked.

A fine mist formed in her eyes. "I was thinking about the one other time I saw you. It was when they buried David."

5

The wooden planks groaned as we climbed the porch steps. When Faith set down the basket of herbs, I noticed a sod-encrusted garden shovel resting on the edge of a planter crowded with mint. It reminded me of the one we used, following Jewish custom, to scatter dirt over David's casket. Faith motioned me inside with a distant smile.

I wanted her to talk about David and I was running low on time. But since she'd insisted on having lunch first, I ordered the crab Louie.

"This is outstanding," I said between bites as I sat across from Faith at a window table. "What spices do you use?"

"Not telling." She grinned. "Maybe I'll let the *South Louisiana Gourmet* print the recipe if they give us a good review. Another helping?"

I glanced at my watch, then looked at her with raised eyebrows.

"Okay," she said. "I promised. I was a year behind David at Tulane, but we were in the same French class. I placed out of the first level, and tutored him. He helped me get through math."

"You the reason he was in Bon Terre that summer?"

She glanced away and took a sip of her herbed tea. "Sort of. David was interested in civil rights, so I asked him if he wanted to lend a hand to Deer Jackson and me. We were helping to register black voters. Deer's real name was Elton, but everyone called him Deer. A runner, like David. He's the other boy who was killed. He attended Grambling after returning from Vietnam. Like me, he was home for the summer. Helping his parents out on their farm."

I thought about what Keisha had said. Other people cared about the murders, too. And now the other victim had a name and family. "His parents still live here?" I asked.

"They moved away shortly after. While I was in California."

"California?"

Faith shrugged. "Finding myself. Getting pregnant. But not in that order."

"I remember David being away a lot that summer," I said. "Did he stay here in Bon Terre?"

"With Deer and his family. The two of them ran together every evening."

"I used to run with David," I said.

Faith sighed. "So you were a runner, too."

"Intermediate hurdles in high school. Ran a few marathons in my thirties before my body rebelled."

"Athletic ability must run in your family," Faith said.

"On my father's side." I didn't mention what ran on my mother's side. "So you asked David to join you. You make it sound like a field trip."

She gripped her tea tumbler. "Bon Terre wasn't exactly a boiling pot."

"Then how did two guys get killed?"

Faith's gaze turned hazy. Footsteps from behind caused me to swivel around.

Grace approached our table. "Mom, the man from the magazine just called and apologized for not letting us know earlier, but he won't be here until tomorrow."

"Too bad. I wanted him to try the snapper."

"Well, everyone else did," Grace said. "We're out already."

I looked up at Grace. "Fortunately you didn't run out of crabs. The Louie was wonderful."

"Glad you enjoyed it," she said. "Can't eat it myself. I'm allergic to shellfish."

I grinned. "In Louisiana, that's as bad as having an allergy to beer or Jack Daniel's."

"Our menu's varied enough that I don't starve," Grace said.

"My daughter Sarah's allergic to shellfish, too," I said. "We discovered it when she was four at a friend's crawfish boil. It was a little scary."

"She puffed up and couldn't breathe?" Grace clasped her hands around her own throat.

"Like she'd swallowed a frog."

Grace smiled. "Anything else we have in common?"

"As a matter of fact, you both have olive skin," I said. "And you're both pretty."

Grace's beam broadened as she turned to Faith. "I'd better get going. Grandma needs a break."

Faith made a shooing motion with her hand. "Truman will be by soon with the vegetables. He'll bring me home."

"Good luck with the magazine," I said.

"Thanks." She waved at her mother and turned away.

"Do you have other children?" I asked Faith as the front door clicked shut.

"No. If you don't count my father." Faith smiled at my quizzical expression. "He had a stroke a long time ago, which may have saved his life because it stopped his drinking. But he needs constant attention and it's too much for my mother. So they live with me."

"That's gotta be tough," I said. "I have two girls to worry about." I checked my watch. "When I first mentioned Emmett Graves, you said he was evil. You know anything that could connect him to the murders?"

"He and some of his Klan buddies egged on some white kids into acting up," she said. "But nothing more than verbal taunts and stupid jokes. We never felt threatened."

"This what you told the investigators back then?"

"Yes." Faith leaned forward and covered my hand with her palm. It felt cold. "It's been thirty-one years, Jack."

Then I asked her the same question I'd asked Rhino Perrot. "What connection does Emmett Graves have to Avery Hammond?"

Faith withdrew her hand. "Mr. Hammond employs a lot of people."

I thought about the man leaning against the red Camaro. "Like Creed Beaumont?"

Her lips tightened. "He runs Hammond's casino."

"Hammond's Native American?"

"No. So technically, he doesn't own the casino. But he runs the operations. He sends the tribe a check every month."

"Where is this casino?" I asked.

"About twenty miles south. It's not like the glitzy ones in Lake Charles. Mostly locals go there."

"Did Graves work for Hammond before he got arrested?" I asked.

"I hear Graves made sure people made good on their markers at the casino," Faith said. "And who knows what else?"

I wondered what else, too. Then I heard the crunch of tires in the oyster shell lot.

Faith turned toward the window. "There's Truman. He supplies our organic vegetables."

"Can we talk again?"

"Absolutely," she said, rising. "Bring your family."

I followed her to the front of the restaurant, thinking she knew more. But our time alone was over, and I had to get back to New Orleans.

Faith opened the door. A heavyset man with shoulder-length gray hair and an unkempt beard lumbered up the steps. His round face sported a scar running from the large bulb of his sunburned nose down to his jaw.

The man focused on me, then asked, "You the fellow from the magazine?"

"The reporter couldn't make it today, Truman." Faith gestured toward me. "This is Jack Brenner."

The man studied my face with cloudy blue eyes.

"David Brenner's cousin," Faith said.

The odor of whiskey preceded his "How do you do?" as we shook hands.

"Truman LaRoche is an old friend of mine." Faith put her hand on his shoulder.

"You knew David?" I asked as Faith hurried toward the kitchen.

"I was here the summer he died."

"Can we talk about it sometime?" I asked.

He exhaled another cloud of distilled spirits. A small muscle spasmed below one eye. "If you don't mind listening to the stories of an old ex-priest."

I wondered if the twinge came from recalling David's death. Or had it just been too long since his last drink?

Soon after turning onto the main highway, tiny drops began to click on my windshield. I saw Jarla Thomas cruising toward town followed by a motorist in a black Lincoln, no doubt a soon-to-be Seven Angels customer. The splatters on the glass quickened as I drove toward the city. I imagined a narrow road snaking through fields of tall cane dripping from an early evening shower, with David and Deer moving through clouds of steam hovering above the road, striding with the easy rhythm of champion runners.

The cloudburst had ended by the time I reached New Orleans. Sunlight glistened off the oil-filmed parking lot at the Franklin High stadium, where Keisha leaned against her car.

"Find anything in Bon Terre?" she asked.

"A multicraft justice system," I said.

"Say what?"

"Tell you later. Bring me up to speed while we find Coach Goldberg."

"We're having a communication problem here, Jack. Who's Coach Goldberg?"

"He's been the track coach at Franklin for almost forty years and he runs these summer meets. Since we didn't get a good look at Jenna, he can point her out to us if she's here tonight. Either way, he might know if something was going on between Steven and her."

Keisha moved beside me as we started toward the stadium. "I got the crime scene unit back this morning and we broadened the perimeter."

I glanced at her. "'We' includes me, right?"

"As far as Utley knows, you came right back after changing your soiled britches." Keisha cackled.

I held out my palm.

She slapped it. "But we still didn't find any casings matching the bullet. And we haven't found the other two slugs."

"Only takes one to match a weapon," I said.

Keisha nodded. "The ME and the firearms examiner agree the shooter was fifteen to twenty feet from the victim and fired from the street.

"Consistent with our moving automobile theory."

We passed the stairs leading to the bleachers and stood on the track at the head of the straightaway. I closed my eyes and inhaled. Scents from the infield grass and rubberized running surface, still cool and damp from the rain, drew me back in time. Thirty pounds lighter. Eyes focused on a hurdle ahead. The sound of spiked shoes slapping the track. Willow Ashkenazi waiting in the stands.

"What now?" Keisha loosened my hold on the memory.

I pointed up the straightaway. "There's Coach."

Herman Goldberg was dressed exactly as he'd been the first time David brought me to a track meet. He wore a forest green cap and polyester coach's shorts with a white-collared T-shirt. Three stopwatches hung from his neck. Two middle-aged men in shorts and running shoes conversed with him, most likely former Franklin track men clinging to their youth. A concept I understood. Coach looked up as Keisha and I approached and the men jogged off.

He pointed to my midsection. "You'll never clear a hurdle carrying that."

I grasped his hand, unusually large for a man only five-foot-six. "All I'm hoping to clear these days are my cases."

He studied my spongy physique through Coke-bottle lenses. "Well, good to see you even if you are in shameful condition."

"Sorry it's been so long," I said.

My expression, or the tone in my voice, must have telegraphed that my visit was business. His broad smile suddenly vanished.

"We're working Steven Bowen's murder," I said. "This is my partner, Keisha Lundy."

She nodded. "Coach Goldberg."

Coach dropped his eyes to the ground and shook his head. "Fine kid. I feel bad for his mom and dad. Did you know he broke your cousin David's school record in the mile?"

"Steven's father told me," I said. "He was real proud of his son."

"How can I help?" Coach asked.

"We thought maybe some of Steven's friends would be here," I said.

"Most of the team was at the funeral yesterday. I told them they could skip tonight if they wanted. But I'm sure some of them will show up anyway."

"Including Jenna Meade?" I asked.

"Maybe. But she wasn't at the funeral. I thought it was strange—"

"You sure?" Keisha asked. "When we talked to her mother yesterday, she told us Jenna'd just left for the funeral."

Coach folded his arms. "I'm sure. The team was together. Is there some reason you're specifically interested in Jenna?"

"She paged Steven a short time before he was killed," I said.

Keisha studied Coach's face, then asked, "Does it surprise you Jenna had Steven's pager number, Coach Goldberg?"

"They trained together fairly often. Mostly long, easy runs. Steven did his strength runs by himself or with the other guys."

"Where did they run?"

"On school days, along Lakeshore or over to City Park. But they liked to run in the morning at Audubon Park on weekends and during the summer."

I scanned the track as more runners arrived to warm up. "Was her interest in him more than athletic?"

"I was the first male coach in town to train girls. But I still haven't gotten used to hormonal equity." Coach shook his head.

"So they were an item," I said.

Coach Goldberg nodded. "They were close. That's why I started to say earlier it was strange she didn't come to the funeral. The other kids wondered about it, too."

"Guess we'll wait in the bleachers awhile, Coach. Could you give us a signal if Jenna shows up?" I asked.

"You bet." Then as we walked off the infield Coach called out, "If you're the competitor you were in high school, Jack, I know you'll get the bastard that shot Steven."

While Keisha and I waited in the stands, I told her about my trip to Angola, my speeding ticket, and my lunch with Faith. Forty-five minutes later, Coach looked up and shook his head. No Jenna Meade.

"What now?" Keisha asked.

"We didn't get a good look at Jenna yesterday, but I know some people with kids at Franklin. She'll be in the team picture in the school annual."

"So?"

"So we can identify her when she runs in Audubon Park in the morning," I said. "Let's you and me go for a jog tomorrow."

"I hate jogging. And you have a bum leg."

"Then we'll walk. Meet you at the station at six-thirty. Wear your workout gear."

Keisha rose from her bleacher seat and mumbled something through clenched teeth.

The next morning, Keisha and I left the car on a side street and waited for a St. Charles trolley to clack past before crossing the tracks. A road closed to motor traffic circled a lake that reflected the shadows of old oak trees. Ducks skimmed along the water's surface near the shore. Runners, walkers, and a few rollerbladers traveled in both directions. A group of seniors, mostly Asian, practiced tai chi on the lawn near the edge of the lake, moving their limbs in deliberate motions through the heavy air.

"Hope Jenna shows," Keisha said. "Don't wanna be losing my beauty sleep for nothing."

"Come on," I said. "The exercise will do us good."

Keisha looked down at my belly. "Do *us* good?"

I told her to look out for a lithe blue-eyed blonde. We walked briskly along the road, taking note of every woman runner who passed us, but just as sweat began to seep through my shirt, I felt a twinge in my calf.

"Ah, shit." I pulled up.

We walked toward a bench near the lake, keeping our eyes peeled for teenaged female runners. I grabbed the top of the bench and stretched my left leg out behind me.

Keisha wiped her forehead. "Serves you right for dragging me out in this humidity. We could have watched the road from the lawn where them old folks are doing kung fu."

I lifted my calf to the bench seat and massaged it. "Tai chi."

"Whatever."

As I tested my leg with a few measured strides, a young blonde wearing red shorts and a gray tank top whisked by on the road holding something colorful in her hand.

"That's her." I instinctively broke into a trot.

"Call out her name," Keisha hollered from behind.

"I don't want to spook her," I called back.

Keisha caught up to me, panting. "I told you I hate running."

The girl was putting distance between us, but as I picked up the pace, my calf knotted like a prizefighter's fist. I limped to a standstill, then leaned forward with my hands on my knees, head up.

Keisha came puffing up beside me. "You don't do anything the easy way."

I stood upright and stepped forward gingerly. Shaking my head, I trudged on, angered at the injury preventing me from catching Jenna.

"Look," Keisha said suddenly. "She's slowing down."

"Maybe there's a water fountain ahead." I lengthened my strides.

Keisha grabbed my arm. "Whoa there, jackrabbit. We're placing our bets on the tortoise today."

The girl trotted off the road, then worked her way toward a row of untrimmed magnolias until she disappeared from sight.

Keisha and I soon reached a path leading behind the broad leaves and moved quietly along. On the other side of the magnolias, a grass-covered finger of land protruded into the lake. Lily pads quivered on the water's surface. Sweetgrass framed the shore on either side.

The girl knelt on the moist green carpet, a bunch of flowers in her hand. She laid them on the ground next to a faded bouquet, then picked up the shriveled blossoms and raised them above her head as if she were going to fling them into the lake. But she stopped. The withered flowers slipped from her hand as she covered her face.

Keisha and I glanced at each other, then took a few steps toward the girl.

Keisha spoke softly. "Jenna Meade?"

The girl gasped and twisted toward us. "Yes."

"Don't be afraid." Keisha pulled out her shield and crouched next to her.

I dropped to a knee. "Coach Goldberg told us you and Steven Bowen ran in the park sometimes. We were hoping to find you here."

Jenna clutched the ragged nosegay. "What for?"

"We want to find out who killed Steven," I said.

Her lower lip trembled as she looked down and plucked at the browning greenery in her hands.

"We're real sorry about Steven," Keisha said.

"It's beautiful here," I said. "Did you and Steven come here to cool down?"

"And talk," she said.

"Your mother told us you'd gone to Steven's funeral on Wednesday, but Coach says you weren't there."

"I couldn't. I was afraid I'd fall apart."

"I understand," Keisha said. "But we saw you drive off. Where did you go?"

She let the faded flowers fall to the grass. "I was going to leave these at the cemetery."

"Your parents didn't know about you and Steven, did they?" I asked.

Jenna shifted her eyes to Keisha, then looked at me anxiously. "They wouldn't let me date anyone until my junior year."

"When would that be?" I asked

"This fall," she said.

"We want to make sure we know what Steven was doing the night he was killed," I said. "We know you paged him."

"I came home after going to the movies with some girlfriends. I wanted to see if he wanted to hang out for a while."

"Why'd you call his pager rather than his home phone?" I asked.

She looked away. "That's what I always do."

Ensuring Steven's parents never knew the two of them talked.

"But he didn't call right way, so you called again?" Keisha asked.

Jenna looked confused. "I only called once."

I glanced at Keisha. "Are you sure?"

"Yes." Her tone was firm.

"Your number showed up twice on Steven's pager," Keisha said. "What time did you call him?"

"After I got home. About ten-thirty."

The second call. "Any reason someone would page him and punch in your callback number?" I asked.

"A lot of kids have my cell number, and lots of them know Steven's pager number. Maybe someone was playing a joke on Steven." Jenna crossed her arms as though suddenly chilled. "He got killed trying to call me, didn't he?"

"I'm sorry, honey," Keisha said.

We left her with the solitude she'd come for.

"If Jenna had made both calls, that'd be the end of it," I said to Keisha as we followed the asphalt back to the park entrance.

"That's right. Girlfriend calls boyfriend. No relationship to the shooting."

"We still have a loose end."

When Keisha and I returned to the squad room, sweat clothes still damp, Lieutenant Utley burst from his office, brushed by Arceneaux, and marched toward us.

"Brenner. My office," Utley commanded, then turned away sharply.

I rose and followed the lieutenant. Though he strode briskly, his navy suit hung on him in perfect alignment. He entered his office and went directly to his desk.

"Shut the door," he said.

"What's going on, Lieu—"

"What the hell are you trying to pull?"

"I can explain the way we're dressed, sir."

"Your sloppy attire is the least of my concerns. I've just spent the last twenty minutes on the phone with the department's public relations officer. She tells me—let me emphasize, she tells *me* that one of *my* detectives has reopened a cold case without my knowledge. She further tells me that one of *my* detectives has made a deal with a drug pusher and killer."

"Lieutenant, I never—"

"And since *my* detective apparently wasn't going to inform me, I can hear all about it on the *goddamned evening news.*"

Utley's glare scalded my face. I'd stepped in it big-time. But who had given me away? I thought about the promise Odell Harris had made. "What channel?" I asked.

"I don't know. But it's a national story. Some woman reporter from Atlanta."

Before my heart could recover enough to thud inside my chest, I realized what had happened. *Willow Ashe.*

6

Utley watched my jaw tighten. "I have the pleasure of meeting with the superintendent of police and the district attorney this afternoon to decide how we're going to handle this. The press will hit us hard after the broadcast tonight. At least that reporter had the courtesy to give us a heads-up."

Some courtesy Willow had shown me.

"Which is more than I can say for you," he continued. "In the meantime, don't go anywhere near Angola. In fact, don't leave town. Now get the hell out!"

I trudged back to my desk, hurt more by Willow's betrayal than the precarious state of my job. I flopped into my chair.

Keisha surveyed me. "You couldn't get any whiter."

"Couldn't feel any dumber."

"What happened?"

I told her. "Willow Ashkenazi, Ashe, whatever. I can't believe it. She knew she was going to do this when we talked at Angola. Did I tell you we were high school sweethearts?"

"You left that part out."

I filled her in.

"That's cold, Jack. What now?"

I felt helpless. Not only because Willow hadn't disclosed her mission to me, but also because my chance of investigating David's murder was spiraling down the toilet.

"Let's go home and change clothes," I said.

After returning to the station, I hunkered over my desk and studied the Bowen autopsy and ballistics reports, finding nothing that augmented the summary Keisha had given me in the stadium parking lot. We still couldn't explain the two missing slugs. Could the store manager be mistaken about hearing three shots?

Meanwhile, Keisha called Jenna Meade to get a list of friends who might know both her cell number and Steven's pager number. She got most of the track team and a couple dozen others. We spent the rest of the afternoon tracking down as many as we could. No one claimed to have paged Steven the night he was killed.

A little before five, I headed over to Channel Six and caught Odell Harris walking rapidly out of his office.

He stopped in front of me and grinned. "Heard you've been to Angola, Jack. Cat's out of the bag now."

My eyes narrowed. "How do you know that?"

"I don't reveal sources," he said, still grinning.

Probably the PD public relations officer. "Hopefully this source didn't hear about the conversation you and I had on Monday."

"I told you. I don't reveal sources."

Being a source didn't have a good feel to it, but Odell had always given me information in return.

"Wait in my office," he said. "We'll catch the national news after the local show."

Odell rushed off to the studio. In his office, four mute monitors tuned to different channels flickered from one wall. I pushed the volume control on the one playing Channel Six, then sat on the edge of Odell's desk and watched the local news. Odell did a ninety-second piece on the trial of a local cable company executive near the end of the program.

Eventually trumpets announced *The Evening News with Don*

Samuelson as Odell returned to his office and hung his suit coat on the valet.

"This the right channel?" I asked.

He sat down and leaned back in his chair. "The station Willow Ashe works for is our network."

Since I hadn't mentioned her name earlier, I figured he'd learned it from his source. If Odell had wanted to break this story, he'd be the one in front of the camera.

Samuelson began to announce the evening's top stories.

When he'd finished, I turned to Odell. "He didn't mention anything about a report from Louisiana."

"It's not a hard story yet. They'll play it as human interest."

It came after the first commercial.

Samuelson glanced up from his copy. "Our next story is a reminder that, all too often, justice is neither swift nor sure. Here is Willow Ashe, investigative reporter with our affiliate in Atlanta."

Willow's liquid brown eyes filled the screen. My thudding heart nearly drowned her words.

"I'm standing outside Louisiana State Prison in Angola, the notorious Farm, as it is known in this sweltering delta country, where this year alone, over a dozen lethal injections have been administered. But my story today is about a different kind of execution—the murder of two young civil rights workers. In the summer of 1972, David Brenner and Elton Jackson were shot to death in Bon Terre, a small town south of New Orleans."

A picture of David breaking the tape on a running track flashed on the screen, followed by a photograph of a young black man in military uniform.

"Their bodies were recovered from the surrounding swamplands." Willow spoke over an aerial shot of the wetlands.

Willow returned to the screen. "Inside these walls, an inmate facing a possible capital murder charge claims to have information that could lead to clearing these unsolved murders. Just yesterday, Emmett Floyd Graves met with New Orleans homicide detective Jack Brenner—ironically, the cousin of one of the victims."

Samuelson appeared on one side of a split screen. "Willow, what evidence does Emmett Graves have?"

"He claims to know the location of the shotgun used to kill the victims, whose bodies were discovered in the trunk of David Brenner's car, which was immersed in a secluded pond. However, when I contacted the New Orleans Police Department, they declined to comment."

Shotgun? I flew from the edge of Odell's desk and crowded the monitor as though Willow were standing live in front of me.

"Were any arrests ever made in this case?" Samuelson asked.

"No, Don. Justice has gone unserved. But perhaps this new lead will allow law enforcement authorities to apprehend those responsible for taking the lives of two brave young men."

Back on-screen, Samuelson nodded soberly. "Thank you, Willow. Please keep us updated on the progress of this case."

The sound died and I heard the remote rattle on the desktop. "She sure as hell scooped me," Odell said. "You think Graves really knows where the murder weapon is?"

I turned and faced him. "He didn't say anything to me about it."

Odell lifted his eyes to the ceiling as though beseeching God to spare another fool. "I warned you Graves might talk to people without your knowing. You got played and now you're in trouble. This all happened because you wanted to go it on your own."

My nails cut into my palms. "She told me she was working on some kind of story."

Odell furrowed his brow. "You talked to Willow Ashe?"

I told him about our encounter at the prison, describing her as someone I knew in high school.

"Damn it!" I said. "She never tried to contact me before the broadcast."

"She's too smart. By contacting the department, she can say she checked out her story through proper channels. Since you hadn't informed anyone what you were doing, the department had no choice but to 'no comment.' Willow Ashe made a public relations coup."

"And screwed me royal," I said.

"You dealt your own hand," Odell said. "Willow Ashe did nothing outside the limits of professional ethics. I know it sounds like I'm defending one of my own, but she was just following a story."

I didn't want to explain our past. "You're right."

He leaned back in his chair and thought a moment. "At least your cousin's murder will be investigated. With this kind of publicity the department has no alternative. They either follow up or turn it over to the FBI."

"And after the department suspends me for initiating an investigation without authorization, I can learn all about it watching television at home," I said.

"Now that the story's out, I'll be following it. I might be able to help the department understand how bad the PR would be if they discipline you." He pulled on the cuff of his blue cotton pinpoint shirt. "But I'll need an edge. Tell me about your interview with Emmett Graves."

I smirked. "You mean give you something Willow Ashe doesn't have in exchange for your help."

Odell winked. "You understand our relationship, Detective."

I reconstructed my encounter with Emmett Graves. "He claimed he had information he'd give up if I got the DA to back away from the death penalty. That's all."

"So he told Willow about the shotgun, but didn't tell you. Hmm." He rose and lifted his coat from the valet and slipped into it. "I'm sure she specifically asked Graves if he'd told you about it. When he said no, she had no obligation to contact you and confirm it."

"She didn't confirm shit with me. And she probably got Graves to tell her everything about our conversation."

"Don't assume that. It may be Graves pulling the strings."

I thought for a moment. "Well, he still has his bargaining chip. Willow's report didn't mention the location of this alleged shotgun."

"Graves gave Willow just enough for a story," Odell said, straightening his tie. "She probably pitched it to the network as 'let's see whether officials in Louisiana are so hellbent to execute folks they'll ignore a lead on the murders of a couple of civil rights workers.'"

"There'll be a lot of angry people if they do."

"That's how Graves is betting. He figures public pressure will force the DA to give in." Odell started toward the door. "Smart."

Ennio Cribari had warned me that despite his learning disability, Graves *was* smart. Unlike his lawyer, I thought, suddenly remembering Neil Gross. Did he have something to do with Willow being at Angola? I returned to the car and flipped on my cell phone. Neil picked up on the first ring.

I heard a cacophonous drone. "Sounds like your Porsche needs a tune-up."

"It's the treadmill. I'm at the gym."

"Have time to catch the evening news before putting on your Nikes?"

"Saw it in the locker room," he said. "Some story."

"I'm betting you had something to do with it, Neil."

He puffed into his mouthpiece. "What do you mean?"

"I didn't want any of this coming out yet."

"Hey." He gulped for air. "All I did was respond to my client's request and set up a meeting with you."

"You talked to Willow Ashe," I said.

"No way. I figured you had. Say. I remember from high school. Didn't you and Willow—"

"Yeah. We went out."

"Willow Ashkenazi." He drew out the name. "She's still a hottie. At least on the tube."

"I ran into her at Angola, but had no idea she was there to talk to Graves."

"Me either. And I'm only the guy who's trying to save his life."

Perry Mason in a Porsche. "He may have done that on his own."

"How so?" Neil asked as the treadmill whined as though changing incline.

"Must be banking on public opinion forcing the DA to drop the capital charge in exchange for information about this alleged shotgun."

"Smart."

At least Neil could recognize it in others. "Did Graves tell you he knew anything about the murder weapon in David's case?" I asked.

"If he had, it would be privileged."

That meant no. Odell was right. Graves was orchestrating this. Neil hadn't been a player in setting off the media brushfire. But he'd have to be involved in cutting a deal for Graves with the DA.

"Who's prosecuting Graves's murder case?" I asked.

"Hasn't been assigned yet. The PD know about you going to Angola?"

"They had no idea until the public relations officer got a call from Willow."

Neil laughed breathlessly. The treadmill whirred. "Guess you caught your dick in your zipper."

I drove home and found Alexis standing at the kitchen counter cutting up a roasted chicken. Her dark hair, with streaks of auburn, was pulled back loosely, drawing attention to the silky olive skin of her neck and cheeks.

She spoke without looking up. "Please don't say you were going to tell me about this."

"About what?"

"Your cousin's murder." Her voice was as sharp as the chef's knife.

"You must have seen the six o'clock news," I said.

"No. I was fixing you a nice Sabbath meal. But three of my friends called me after they did."

I'd forgotten it was Friday. We only went to services when someone we knew was having a bar or bat mitzvah, but I usually made it home for traditional Sabbath Eve meals.

Alexis used the blade to separate the chicken, now in bite-sized pieces, from the bones and carcass. "How much time have you spent with Willow Ashkenazi, or whatever she calls herself these days?"

I opened the refrigerator and grabbed a beer. The twist-off cap was as tight as my gut and took three tries to loosen. "About fifteen minutes."

Alexis skewered me with her dark brown eyes. The knife rattled on the counter.

I told her about running into Willow at Angola. "She totally blindsided me. The convict I talked to, Emmett Graves, must have fed her the story. I didn't know she was going to do it on national television."

Alexis scraped the chicken meat into a plastic bowl. "Your aunt Joyce called, too. She was crying and wanting to know what was going on. What could I say?"

I sucked air through my teeth. Aunt Joyce was David's mother. "I'll go see her tomorrow and let her know what's happening."

"How about letting me know while you're at it." She snapped a lid on the container. "Television news doesn't count as communication with your wife."

The phone rang. I grabbed the receiver at the end of the counter, thankful for the interruption. "Hello?"

"Brenner. This is Lieutenant Utley. Be in my office at eight tomorrow morning."

"Okay."

The receiver clung to my ear long after the click as a cold void invaded my chest.

"Who was that?" Alexis asked.

I finally replaced the receiver. "Lieutenant Utley."

"You're not on call tonight."

"He wants to see me in the morning."

"What about?"

"The news broadcast, I suppose. I've been doing this without his knowledge," I said. "Keisha covered for me."

Alexis raked the bones from the cutting board into the trash. "That's so like you, going off and doing what you want without thinking of other people."

Like Odell Harris said, I'd done it my way and I was paying the price. "I wanted to see if there was anything to Emmett Graves's claim before I got others involved."

"Well, you *did* get others involved. And how nice. Willow has a big story. What else did you give her?"

"Goddamn it! I spoke to the woman for fifteen minutes. She betrayed me."

"You feel betrayed? How do you think I feel?"

I stood motionless, the beer bottle warm in my hand.

Alexis wiped her hands roughly with a dish towel, then stalked from the kitchen without looking at me. "There's another chicken in the oven," she called out. "Help yourself."

The stairs rumbled like a swollen thunderhead.

7

When I entered Lieutenant Utley's office Saturday morning, he was at his desk, fingers interlocked. "I want an explanation, Brenner."

I told him about Neil Gross's call and my visit to Graves, including my encounter with Willow but omitting my connection to her. Then I told him about David.

"I wanted to see if Graves had anything substantial before I brought it forward," I said.

"And how were you going to do that?"

I quickly lowered my eyes from his gaze.

Utley slapped the desk. "I know you've already done investigative work. A Sheriff Perrot called downtown and they transferred him to me. You were going to keep at it until this newswoman blew your cover."

I reconnected with his trenchant eyes.

Utley stood and pressed his palms on the desk. "I sympathize with your motives. But your freelancing is inexcusable. The reason we have procedure on this job is to hold our emotions in check. When we don't, people get hurt."

I nodded.

He shook his head as though he'd seen something as incredible as the Saints winning the Super Bowl. "Fortunately for you, the public relations officer convinced the DA and the superintendent of the public relations value of letting you be the lead detective in reopening the Elton Jackson - David Brenner murder case."

Hearing both victims' names reminded me that any chance of success required mustering my usual professional detachment and objectivity. It wouldn't be easy.

"What made the DA decide this?" I asked, curious to know if Odell Harris had acted on my behalf.

"Mostly that Atlanta reporter's doing."

I'd thank Odell anyway.

"I don't know who was using who," Utley said "but Willow Ashe's news stories have forced the DA to cut a deal with Emmett Graves. We can't let the public think we'd sweep an old civil rights crime under the rug. Even if it means letting a peace officer's killer escape lethal injection."

"I understand that, but why me?"

"Graves told the DA through his lawyer he wouldn't deal unless you led the investigation. He'll give information only to you."

Commitment. Graves had told me not to come back without it. Now I also had authorization. "And the DA went for it?"

"Reluctantly," Utley said. "The public relations officer convinced him that letting you run the show would cast the best possible light on the DA's office and the PD. She said we'd definitely get bad press if we disciplined you."

"Guess I caught a break."

"I'd suspend judgment on that if I were you. You're working this case completely on your own. The FBI will give you anything but manpower. Neither Lundy nor any other detective in the department is to spend a minute of their time on this."

"Aren't there some jurisdictional issues?" I asked. "Bon Terre isn't exactly in the Second District."

"That didn't stop you before, Brenner." He delivered the sarcasm with an enigmatic twinkle in his eye.

Good-humored? Maybe not. "Look, Lieutenant, I'm sorry I—"

"Save it. We've resolved the jurisdiction issue. The Bon Terre sheriff has deputized you. He asked me to tell you to drive carefully. Said you'd understand." Utley leaned forward. "When the superintendent and DA agreed on this course of action, I insisted on three things. One. The day you spent at Angola and in Bon Terre goes unpaid. I won't allow my detectives to conduct personal business on department time."

"Fair enough."

"Two. You continue working the Bowen case as well. Arceneaux belongs to you and Lundy full-time. But remember, they only work the Bowen case. And three. That you work this cold case until it's solved, or I decide it's a dead end."

Meaning I'd better come up with something quickly.

"The three of you are authorized for all the overtime you need," he said.

I nodded, thinking how the extra hours would further complicate any attempt to reconcile with Alexis.

Utley rose. His gaze was intense, but his trademark malevolent glower was absent. "I hope you crack this. And not because one victim's your cousin or the other victim's black."

I stood and for the first time met his eyes truly straight-on. "It's because you're a good cop, Lieutenant. Nothing's less acceptable than unresolved murder."

Utley straightened his shoulders, but not in the stiff military manner I was used to. "Get your ass out on the street."

"It'll be great working with Arceneaux again."

"Well, don't get too used to it."

My eyes narrowed. "What do you mean?"

"For her experience level, Lundy's the best female detective I've seen. I'm thinking of making your pairing permanent."

Something cold spun in my gut. "But Arceneaux and I've been together for five years."

"I know. And Lundy's come a long way working with you."

"No one else can work with Arceneaux."

He held up a hand. "My detectives work with whom they're assigned."

I bit my tongue and headed toward the door.

"Brenner," Utley called after me.

"Yes, sir?"

"I negotiated three conditions with the DA and the superintendent, but there's a fourth. No talking to the press."

I smirked. "Don't throw me into that briar patch, Lieutenant."

"I'm very serious, Brenner. Keep away from this Willow Ashe. Our PIO says she's a piece of work. Know anything about her?"

I held up my hands. "Reporters. They're all alike."

I had my assignments and hours of work ahead of me, but the previous night's broadcast had presented me with a family issue to take care of. I drove to my aunt Joyce's house, wondering if reopening David's murder case after all these years would bring her hope for justice. Or would it force her to replay a nightmare?

I walked up the steps to the same porch where we'd been gathered when the FBI agents told us they'd found David's body. Though I'd visited often enough, particularly since my uncle died, I realized how little had changed in thirty-one years. The small house had the same gray-painted shakes with white trim, same neatly trimmed shrubbery surrounding the foundation. The ancient oak still shaded the whole front yard. Only the cat lounging on the whitewashed planks, soaking up the coolness from the ground beneath the porch, was different. But even she was the progeny of David's cat, Sabra.

I rapped on the door. The deadbolt clicked and the door opened inward. My aunt Joyce stared out at me. She'd been free of cancer for three years, but she continued to sport the stylish auburn wig chemotherapy had forced her to wear.

"Jack!" Aunt Joyce unhooked the screen door and pushed it out. "Come in."

"Thanks." I entered and shut the door shut behind me.

"I thought you were Mimi Schwartz," she said. "Services don't start until eleven, but she's always early. You know I just hate depending on other people for rides. Coffee?"

"Sure."

I followed her to the small kitchen. David's older brother, Sam, had tried to convince her to move into a senior facility, but she'd shut off all discussion of it. He and his wife looked in on her frequently and Aunt Joyce had a housekeeper who'd come every Wednesday for years. Sam paid the housekeeper generously to drop by on other weekdays. Eventually his mother quit protesting the intrusions.

Aunt Joyce always used china. The cup jiggled in the saucer as she shuffled toward me. I didn't offer to help because I knew she'd refuse. A thin brown film slid over the edge of the cup as she set the coffee down.

She sat next to me. "I know why you came, Jack. How could you do this without speaking to me?"

Sweet peas climbed a lattice outside the window. We'd sat here before, at a different table, waiting for news about David. "It wasn't really my doing, Aunt Joyce. Some convict that lived in Bon Terre when David was killed is looking for an angle to save himself from lethal injection by claiming to have information."

What I'd said was true. Graves didn't need me to play his hand and Willow could have broken her story anyway. But still, I felt responsible. Comes with growing up with a depressive mother.

"Are they going to investigate?"

"The district attorney agreed not to ask for the death penalty if the convict gives us something useful."

Her dark brown eyes turned moist. "Can you make them stop?"

"I have no say. The DA and superintendent felt compelled by the publicity. But I'll be honest with you, Aunt Joyce. You know how much I looked up to David. I went out on my own because I couldn't pass on a chance to find his killer. I'm going to handle the case. He was my cousin."

"He was *my* child." She stared out at the sweet peas, her lips moving silently as if repeating her last words—*my child.* "I've been comforted by memories of all the kind things he did. What mother could be so blessed? But when I saw the television last night, all I could think of—" Her eyes closed and her mouth quivered. "I don't want to relive it."

Three sharp beeps sounded outside.

"That's Mimi. I've got to go." Aunt Joyce quickly wiped her eyes, as if the blaring horn had paused the tape running inside her head. She rose and patted the wig as if it were her own hair.

I stood on the porch as she locked the door behind her and stepped carefully down the walk to her friend's car. The cat, no doubt disturbed by the noise, had relocated to more tranquil surroundings. I had no hope of similar refuge.

Another person who might be wondering about the consequences of Willow Ashe's broadcast was Keisha. I chanced dropping by her apartment. After knocking and waiting, I walked back down the steps to the visitors lot. I'd nearly reached my car when Keisha drove up.

She lowered her window. "Something up with the Bowen case?"

I shook my head. "Just hoping to catch you home."

"I've been to the grocery store." She studied my face. "This have something to do with last night's broadcast?"

I glanced up at her apartment. "If we talk out here, your milk's gonna spoil."

"I don't drink milk. Hop in."

We drove to her assigned space. She popped the trunk and we got out of the car.

"Need some help?" I asked.

"Looking at a girl's groceries is like looking in her dresser. I can manage."

She looped a half dozen plastic sacks over one hand and grabbed three more with the other. She looked up to her apartment, then back into her trunk. "All right. You can carry the beer."

I grabbed the two six-packs, then closed the trunk and followed her up the stairs.

"What's so interesting in your dresser?" I asked as Keisha set the bags on her countertop.

"You'll never know. Take a beer and go in there while I put these away."

I left the kitchen and stood swallowing my beer while I scanned her living/dining room. It was neat and sparsely decorated, like her desk at the station. A large poster hung above the dining room table—a child holding a teddy bear surrounded by a cop, a woman in a suit, and a robed judge. I guessed it was a promotional photo for the child protection organization she and Mary Evans belonged to. Then I noticed two photographs on an adjacent wall, one of an elderly woman, the other of a teenage boy. No doubt her mother and the brother who'd died. Where was her father?

Keisha entered the room several minutes later holding two beers. She set one on the coffee table in front of an easy chair. "Figure you'll be ready for another soon."

She motioned me to the chair and sat on the couch.

I settled back in the chair and wiped my face with the condensation from the bottle. "Utley was pissed at me for going after Graves on my own."

Keisha's beer clanked onto the glass coffee table before making it to her lips.

"Fortunately," I continued, "the public relations officer convinced the DA and superintendent that I should work the case."

I explained the terms and about Arceneaux joining us. I didn't mention Utley's plan to partner Keisha and me permanently.

"I feel bad you almost got into a beef, Jack. I encouraged you to go for it."

I took a swallow. "I didn't tell Utley you knew what I was doing, but he may question you."

"Screw him. He almost took my partner away."

"You and Arceneaux are going to be spending quality time together."

Keisha took two long swallows. "We're gonna make Mutt and Jeff look like twins."

I chuckled. "So you saw the news last night?"

She nodded.

"What did you think about my old girlfriend?"

"She's a looker. Those are the ones that get you in trouble."

"Right now, I'm in trouble with all kinds of women."

Keisha furrowed her brow.

"I'll tell you about it over the next beer," I said. "At least my daughters like me."

She gripped her bottle. "Your girls are lucky to have such a great dad."

Keisha's eyes locked on something inside her, and I wondered again about the missing picture of her father.

8

"Utley gave Arceneaux the good news about joining the team," Keisha said when I sat down at my desk Monday morning. "He still hasn't been cleared to go on the street, but he's off doing some research on the Meade family now. I know you'll be glad to have him back in action."

Though possibly not as my partner. But my fledgling respect for Utley told me he was sounding me out, and he'd talk to me again before he acted.

As Keisha began catching me up on the Bowen case, my phone rang.

"Jack. Mary Evans here."

I swiveled in my chair, away from Keisha. "Mary. This is a surprise."

"Heard about your new assignment," she said.

I chuckled. "The grapevine works fast at the DA's office."

"I'm a little closer to it than that. I've been assigned to handle Emmett Graves's guilty plea in return for information about the death of your cousin and Elton Jackson."

My ears warmed.

"Looks like we're working together again," she said.

"Maybe it won't be so dangerous this time," I said.

Less than a year ago, quick action on both our parts had saved our lives by disarming a killer. Sudden good judgment, or fear, kept us from having an affair.

She hesitated as if she understood the double meaning. "Amen to that. Listen. I set up a meeting with Graves at nine tomorrow morning. You have to be there."

"Neil Gross, too, I suppose."

"Graves doesn't want him around."

"That'll suit Neil," I said. "He hates getting his Porsche splattered with bugs. I just hope Graves isn't pulling our chains."

"I have to tell you, the DA hopes he is. Then this will all blow over."

I kneaded the phone receiver in my hand. "What about you?"

"I want to see justice done," Mary said. "And I know what this means to you, Jack."

"We'll need an early start. Pick you up at six?"

"Remember where I live?"

I managed a dry swallow. "Sure."

"Who was that?" Keisha asked when I hung up.

"Mary Evans. She's been assigned to work out the deal with Graves. Your friend and I are driving to Angola in the morning."

Keisha cocked an eyebrow. "*My* friend?"

This could be a real briar patch, I thought, pondering my past with Mary. Thinking back over the women in my life is not a simple trip down memory lane. Beginning with my mother, it's a tour de force over a four-lane highway of disappointment and inadequacy. I was about to head for home when I got a call on my cell that steered me farther down my emotional interstate—destination unknown.

"Brenner."

"Jack."

Willow Ashe. A hairpin turn on a slick road.

"I hear you're working your cousin's case," she said.

"What did you have to do with me being assigned to the investigation?" I asked, knowing I was violating Utley's directive by talking to her.

"You looking to thank me?"

“I’m looking to find out who’s pulling the strings. You or Emmett Graves.”

“What if I told you Emmett Graves doesn’t want to face lethal injection and he figures your personal interest is his best security?” she asked.

“I’d say it makes sense, but I’m not sure I believe it. So tell me. Did you inspire Graves’s manipulation of the media?”

“You mean you think I created this news story?”

My jaw flexed. “I mean what do you know about Emmett Graves?”

“Join me for lunch, Jack.”

“I’m on a diet.”

Spider to fly: “Then have coffee with me. Maybe I can answer some of your questions.”

Fly rationalizing: “Okay. Where?”

“Molly’s.”

The place where I left her waiting for me during winter break of our first year of college.

Molly’s was not far from my father’s hardware store on Magazine and was a favorite hangout for Willow and me during high school. We’d decided to date other people in college and had made plans to meet there during winter break our freshman year. Unfortunately, one of her friends let slip she’d had a torrid affair with a Costa Rican graduate student during her freshman orientation at Vanderbilt. I guess I regretted the consequences of our agreement.

I parked a block away and walked up the sidewalk, summer heat rippling off the broad leaves of the magnolias lining the curb. Willow sat at a table next to a large plate-glass window. Perhaps sensing my approach, she turned toward the street. The light streaming through the glass made her face shimmer like a priceless and untouchable museum piece.

I entered what was now called a bistro and sat across from her.

She pointed to the long, plastic-covered page in front of me. “Not the same menu.”

"Times have changed," I said.

She nodded slowly. "So they have."

"But it looks like Molly's still uses college kids." A thin young woman with kinky red hair wound tightly under a white crochet snood walked up behind Willow. Other than the designer name on her baggy T-shirt, she looked much like the Sophie Newcomb girls who served us burgers and fries in high school.

"Can I take your orders?" the girl asked.

Willow looked up at the waitress. "I'll have the chef's special with iced tea."

"Just coffee for me," I said, then waited for the girl to leave. "Willow, breaking that story without warning me was a shitty thing to do."

"All's well that ends well." She flipped back her shoulder-length hair. Though shorter than in high school, it was still straw blond. "You get to investigate your cousin's murder."

"Tell me what you know about Emmett Graves," I said, crossing well beyond the line Utley had drawn for me.

"He did his homework, Jack. Don't ask me how, but he knew all about you. I'm sure he has a huge network of unsavory connections. The idea to use the press as leverage was all his. He never specifically told me that was his goal, but he knew he had a good story."

"*You* knew he had a good story," I said as the waitress set down my coffee and Willow's tea.

"Someone would have broken it."

"Aren't you worried he's taking the DA and the rest of us for a ride, you included?" I asked.

"If he's not, it's the biggest story of my life. If he is . . . I've had my face on national television a couple of times. The Orleans Parish DA is the one who's making this deal. Not me."

"Right place, right time," I said.

Willow tilted her head and smiled. "So tell me what's been going on in your life since our ten-year reunion."

"Until now, a successful career. Two wonderful daughters growing up way too fast."

"Job. Children. What about Alexis?"

I hesitated too long to cover up. I took a sip from my coffee. "Problems come up when you've been married sixteen years."

"I never made it more than four years," Willow said. "Either time. I blamed the first one on being too young. But when my second husband quit telling people he was married to me, I began to realize my business and marriage don't mix."

"So no long-term relationships?"

"I've been with an architect in Atlanta for three years. Trent's sort of gotten used to me standing him up when a story breaks, but he'll get tired of it." Willow sounded no more wistful than an old couple acknowledging they couldn't retire in a beautiful village in Tuscany they'd driven through on their last trip to Europe.

The waitress brought Willow's meal—catfish covered with a crawfish-laden sauce piquant. I declined her offer of a bite, fearing the intimacy that accepting might imply. Our conversation was easy. We recalled funny incidents in high school and people we knew. I spoke about my girls and she told me about every town she'd spent time in working her way up to a large city station and how she and Trent had managed to travel to some fun places, but she couldn't understand how he could be happy sitting at a computer all day and half the night. She didn't try to get me talking about the case. And she never asked me why I'd left her sitting at Molly's years ago.

When she'd finished eating, I walked her to her rental car parked under a magnolia. The shade couldn't keep moisture from infusing my collar.

"I'm glad you accepted my invitation, Jack, but I wasn't sure you would. Why did you?"

"Something besides logic," I said.

She smiled. "Logic's your surface personality. It's why you thought you should be a lawyer."

"Flunking out of law school ended that. My mother and Alexis have never forgiven me."

"Your wife objects to you being a cop?"

"Mostly the part about getting shot at. She's never come to terms with that. Alexis is angry now because she knows I could get an administrative job with the same pay and regular hours any time I wanted."

The eyes that studied me were far different from a reporter's staring at a teleprompter. "You need to be out on the street with the wildness and excitement. Like I do. Maybe that's what's missing from your marriage."

Sorry, Willow. Not biting. "That big network contract you told me about at Angola is for wildness and excitement?"

"Sure, the major networks pay big bucks. But it's not about the money, any more than your being a cop is. It's about being on the edge—the big story, the race to air it, not having to compliment some young weather girl on her new dress."

There—I had it. And it's what I'd known. Her affair with the Costa Rican grad student was Willow pushing the envelope. Grasping the wildness.

"I'd like to see you again, Jack," she said.

I felt like a suspect I'd just offered to help get his story straight for the DA. Maybe there was something in it for me. Maybe a price too high.

"Let me know when you're back in town," I said.

She pulled a business card and a pen from her purse, then wrote on the back of the card and handed it to me. "Here's where I'm staying the next day or two."

I stared at what she'd written. "This is the hotel where we had our ten-year reunion."

A smile spread on her face, the way the long grass on the levee rustles more loudly as the wind rises. "Maybe there'll be another."

9

I brewed a pot of coffee and filled two large travel mugs before driving to Assistant DA Mary Evans's house the following morning. When I saw her waiting under the front porch light, I realized the caffeine would be no antidote for my uneasiness. As I got out of my car, the hum of her wheelchair joined the sounds of predawn bird twitters and distant power lines buzzing in the heavy air. When she reached the end of the walk, I helped her into the passenger seat, then folded her chair and placed it in the trunk.

"Smells wonderful in here," she said, as I slid behind the wheel.

"This one's yours." I tapped on the lid of a stainless-steel mug in the cup holder.

I started the engine, telling myself I'd be happy to sip my coffee in silence the entire two-hour trip to Angola. We drove up Carrollton and soon turned up a ramp onto I-10 traveling west. The concrete whirred beneath the wheels as we crossed the swampland south of Lake Pontchartrain in the dark.

"I know you're uncomfortable working with me again," Mary said halfway to Baton Rouge.

"Uncomfortable?"

"You're a worrier, Jack. With what happened between us—and please don't say nothing happened because we didn't have sex—I'd expect you to be uncomfortable."

"We won't have any problem doing our jobs," I said.

"I'm not concerned about that. We're both professionals. But I want to be friends." The murmuring air conditioner almost masked Mary's sigh.

Professionals. I thought about that, but mostly I thought about being friends. I had no women friends. Not something Alexis would permit, anyway. The sky had grown pink and orange above the tips of the tall pines bordering the interstate.

"Tell me about the agreement we're going to ask Emmett Graves to sign," I said.

Mary summarized the deal, her voice cool and professional.

"Graves's lawyer has to review the document before we can act on it," she said.

"I thought Graves was leaving Neil Gross out of this."

"Legally, he can do that. But the DA doesn't want any technicality to stand in the way of future prosecution. He's even instructed me to get Graves to sign a waiver that he's voluntarily talking to us without counsel today."

"Has Neil seen the agreement?" I asked.

"I didn't have the final draft approved until nine last night. I faxed it to his office and sent him an e-mail with the file attached."

I gripped the wheel and glanced at Mary. "So he hasn't looked at the agreement."

The cool turned to freezing. "I checked my office voice and e-mail from home before we left this morning."

"Shit. Try calling him now. I'm not sure how long my string is and I sure as hell don't need bureaucratic delays."

"Sure." Mary stared at me as she pulled out her cell phone. She called Neil Gross's office and mobile numbers. No answer. Then she tried her voice mail again. Finally she asked an assistant to check her e-mail.

"Nothing." She shoved the phone back into her purse.

"Sorry-ass lawyer." Suddenly noticing I was well above the speed limit, I backed off the accelerator. "Why the hell are we making this trip if Graves can't tell me anything?"

"He can tell you anything he wants," Mary said. "You just can't act until Neil Gross says it's okay. We're making this trip because I have to get Graves to sign the agreement and he insisted you be there when he does."

"I don't know which is worse. Neil Gross's incompetence or Emmett Graves jacking me around."

"You don't mind playing puppeteer, but you don't like having your own strings pulled, do you, Jack?"

A deep incision from someone who'd offered friendship. Or maybe she was being straight with me the way friends are supposed to be. "I'm sorry. I'm letting this case get too personal."

"Understandable, but this is a team sport. Though I'll settle for being teammates, I'd prefer we were friends."

I smiled and tapped her arm with the back of my hand. "Friends."

Mary smiled and flipped back her dappled blond hair, strands of gold reflecting the sun.

As we entered the waiting area at Angola prison, my eyes involuntarily scanned the room for Willow. Like my last trip to the Farm, the guards searched us, secured my weapon, and led us through the dank, sweat-infused corridors. Soon we entered the interview room with the bolted-down chairs and six-foot-long gray metal table. As I sat, Mary started to position herself in the middle of the table. Not wanting her close to Emmett Graves, I stopped her. She maneuvered her wheelchair next to me, briefcase in her lap.

Graves entered the room. His shackles jangled as the guard locked them to the iron ring fixed to the table. His black eyes burned into mine like a soldering iron. His ponytail was pulled tighter than before. Thick black streaks wormed through his silver hair.

"Glad to see you back, Brenner," Graves said as the guard left. "Shows commitment."

My skin prickled. "Graves, if this is a shuck—"

Mary placed her hand over my arm. "We have business to conduct."

Graves still focused on me as if Mary were only a voice in the room.

"Mr. Graves," she said. "I must advise you that you have the right to have counsel present for this discussion. If you wish to forgo that right, the Orleans Parish district attorney requests you to sign an acknowledgment before proceeding."

Graves's gaze didn't waver. "Let me have it."

Mary pulled the release from her briefcase and handed it to me. I pushed the document, along with a pen, toward Graves. He made two rapid motions with the pen on the paper, then shoved them back at me and continued staring.

Graves finally turned to Mary. His leathery skin crinkled around his eyes.

She met his glare with ice blue composure. "The special agreement we've drafted is very simple, Mr. Graves. You provide evidence leading to the identification of the person or persons responsible for the death of David Brenner or Elton Jackson. In return, the state agrees not to seek the death penalty against you for the murder of the guard during your attempted escape. The agreement is null and void if it's determined that you conspired to kill either David Brenner or Elton Jackson, had any foreknowledge of anyone's intent to kill either, or if you performed any act which directly or indirectly caused the death of either. The agreement is also null and void if you provide us with any information that is materially false. Do you understand?"

Graves smirked. "Yeah. If I helped kill 'em or change my story, I fry."

Mary lifted the special agreement from her briefcase. "If you choose to sign this agreement, your counsel must review it with you before it can take effect."

"Gross ain't seen it?" Graves asked.

"We completed this late last night," she said. "He hasn't yet had the opportunity."

I refrained from rolling my eyes.

Mary's were locked on Graves. "You requested this meeting and we didn't wish to postpone it."

"How mannerly," Graves said.

I took the special agreement from Mary and pushed it, along

with the pen, toward Graves. He immediately flipped to the last page, signed it, and slid it back.

I flexed my pointer finger at him. "Pen, too, Graves."

"No telling what hole this might've got stuck in." He rolled the pen across the table, plastic rattling against metal.

"Mr. Graves. I think I've been complete in summarizing the special agreement, but don't you want to read it first?" Mary asked.

I recalled what Ennio Cribari had said about Graves's dyslexia, but said nothing.

"That's what my lawyer's for," Graves said.

"Very well." Mary dropped the agreement and pen into her briefcase.

I leaned toward Graves. "Now tell me what you've got."

He refixed his smoky glower on me. "Not until my lawyer tells me it's okay."

I slammed down my palm. The metal table banged like a rim shot off a snare drum. "Goddamn you, Graves. You didn't want him here."

"The little lady here says this ain't no deal till my pissant lawyer reads it."

I stood and shook off Mary's hand from my elbow. "He's going to okay it whether he reads the goddamned thing or not. You're wasting time."

"Commitment, Brenner. Remember? You need to prove you have it."

"This some sort of perverted test?"

Graves raised his fists as high as the manacles would allow, then sent them crashing into the metal. "Guard," he hollered.

Instantly, the tumblers clicked. The guard appeared and unfastened the connection to the iron ring. Graves rose, the guard's hand on his arm. He backed into the doorway, raven eyes still locked on mine.

"Come back soon," he said. "I'll give you what you need. And more."

10

I sulked over being played by Emmett Graves the whole way back to New Orleans, but my mood improved when the kitchen phone rang later that evening.

"Hi, Daddy!" It was the blended voices of Sarah and Carrie.

"Hey, guys. We weren't expecting you to call tonight. Your mom's not here right now."

"Sarah bet Jenny Adams she could beat her by two full seconds in the fifty fly," Carrie said. "Jenny put up ten minutes on her calling card."

Sarah chortled. "I kicked her butt, Dad."

"What did you put up?" I asked.

"To finish her stupid nature project, but it's not like I was taking chances."

"Of course not," I said. "You guys still having a good time?"

"Yeah," Carrie said. "We went to Carowinds yesterday. I rode the Cyclone four times."

"After all that outdoorsy stuff, you needed a day of thrill rides and video games," I said. "How about you, Sarah?"

"It's all right. Most of the stuff is for kids Carrie's age."

"You had fun at Carowinds," Carrie protested. "You rode the Hurler with Ben Garfinkle."

"Who's Ben Garfinkle?" I asked.

Carrie giggled. "He's from Atlanta and he's in love with Sarah."

"Shut up," Sarah snapped. "Dad, he's the only boy that can outswim me."

"He must be a fine young man."

"Are you and Mommy having a good time without us?" Carrie asked.

I knew she was jesting, but the question hit hard. "Some. I've been having to work a lot."

"So what's new?" Sarah said. "Take advantage. You're getting us back in three weeks."

"Can't wait."

"We'll call back on our regular night," Sarah said. "Unless Jenny wants to try me in the backstroke."

"I love you, Daddy," Carrie said. "Tell Mommy I love her."

"Most definitely."

"Bye," Sarah said.

"Bye, guys. I love you."

I hung up thinking how much I missed the girls, but also how, without the convenient distraction of the children we both loved so much, Alexis and I were being forced to confront our ailing relationship.

My new friend Mary called me at the station late the next morning. Keisha sat at her desk pretending not to listen.

"I tracked down Neil Gross," Mary said. "He read the special agreement with Graves while walking on the treadmill at his health club. He has no problems with it."

"Didn't figure he would," I said. "If Graves could read, he'd be better off acting as his own counsel."

"Graves can't read?"

"The FBI agent in charge of the investigation in Bon Terre thirty-one years ago told me Graves has some form of dyslexia."

"I wondered when he signed the agreement so fast," Mary said. "I certainly thought it foolish to trust the lawyer he has."

"Is having Neil for a lawyer grounds for appeal?" I asked.

"Shhhh!"

I chuckled.

"Neil's set up another meeting for you with Graves at four today," Mary said.

"Graves better not jerk me around this time."

"If he does, tell him the state has a large supply of potassium chloride. Let me know how it goes."

"Thanks."

She clicked off.

"Catch all that, partner?" I asked without glancing up.

"Only your end," Keisha said.

I dialed home and left a message for Alexis that I'd be late that night.

The first tropical storm of the season had churned through the Gulf. Though never reaching hurricane status, it had caused severe flooding along the coast from Houston to Beaumont. The dying depression moving northeast pelted rain on my windshield as I drove west to Angola.

I left the volatile winds and rain behind and entered the immutable prison atmosphere—dank clouds of sweat, testosterone, and desperation beneath a bleak fluorescent glare. Graves was waiting for me when I entered the interview room. His flat, black eyes followed me like those of a water moccasin watching an approaching rodent. I sat across from him and waited. The light fixture hummed above us.

Finally his wrist chains clinked as he clasped his hands and leaned on his elbows. "Bet it really galls you that you need help from a racist, gentile criminal to find your cousin's killer."

"You're helping yourself. And I'm glad you said gentile. You're sure as hell not a Christian."

"You're gonna see this through even though doing business with the likes of me makes your insides churn," Graves said. "That's commitment."

"Dealing with your kind is my job," I said. "Getting sick to my stomach is an occupational hazard. Now give me what you got, or I walk and you die."

His lips curled. "Did you give my regards to Avery Hammond like I asked?"

"Didn't get the chance," I said.

"You know he just about owns the whole town."

"I gathered that, but talk about Avery Hammond isn't getting us anywhere."

"It's going somewhere you might notta thought it'd go." His eyes held me as though my own were manacled to them. His grin dissolved. "There's a big oak tree behind Hammond's house. Dig about twelve feet from the trunk, between the tree and the bayou that runs along the back of the property. You'll find the shotgun that killed your cousin and the nigger."

"How do you know it's buried there?" I asked.

"Put it there myself."

"Remember, your deal's no good if you were the one who shot them," I said.

"I wasn't there when that happened." Graves sat up in his chair, his upper body erect as a rising viper's. "I just cleaned up."

Bam, bam, bam. The storm battered the trailer door. With all the thunder and lightning outside, Emmett Graves could barely hear the moaning woman in his bed, her loins quivering tight against his hips. He hated bitches that took so long to come, but he had a reputation of making it happen.

"Oh, baby," she finally shuddered.

Bam, bam, bam. It wasn't the thunder.

"Goddamn!" Graves rolled off the woman and grabbed his jeans from the floor. The rain clanged like shrapnel against the aluminum walls.

"Be right there!" he hollered toward the door.

"Don't, Emmett." The woman's voice was husky. "What if it's—?"

"If it was your husband, honey, he'd a-blowed off the locks by now, and whatever slugs he had left over would be in my butt and your brains."

The woman hopped out of bed, snatched her clothes from a chair, and disappeared through the bathroom door.

Bam, bam, bam.

Graves pulled a pistol from the nightstand. "Hang on, goddamn it. I'm coming."

He approached the door, stood aside, and eased it open.

"I need you to do a job for me," the visitor announced. Water sluiced from the brim of his tycoon straw hat. Graves laid his gun on the floor and stepped out into the rain, his eyes flicking toward a mud-splattered vehicle. "Can we talk in your car? Got someone inside."

The man glanced at the trailer, his hat shading his face from the flickering lightning, then slapped Graves's shoulder and motioned him toward the car. The two men sloshed through the water rushing over the muddle of soil and gravel.

"Hate to interrupt your Friday-night recreation," the man said to Graves inside the car. "But I have a problem I need you to remedy right away. I'll tell you this one time: what you don't understand, don't ask about."

Graves didn't care that he was sopping and shoeless and shirtless. He felt a payday coming.

The man laid his arm across the backrest. "There's two bodies and a car outside the Negro church on Escondido Road. Make them disappear and make sure no one sees you."

Graves knew a place to dump a car and two bodies. But how could he drive the car there and get back to his own car at the church without help? He thought about that a moment.

The man watched Graves intently. "You'll be rewarded for your difficulties."

The jon boat, Graves thought. He knew the bayous around Bon Terre. "Okay. That all?"

"Something else. It's in the trunk."

They got out. The rain glimmered like strands of spun silver in the flashing lightning. Small branches and leaves clung to the car, only to be blown away and replaced by more debris.

The visitor slowly lifted the lid. "Make sure no one ever finds this."

Graves looked into the well. The trunk light revealed a long object wrapped in a plastic sheet, lying on a blanket.

"Roll up that shotgun in the blanket and get rid of it," the man said, grabbing Graves's hand and slapping a roll of bills into it. "There's ten fifties for the job, ten others for the extra trouble. You get another thousand cash in a year if the gun's not found."

Graves shoved the soggy bills into his jeans pocket. He leaned into the trunk, wrapped the shotgun in the blanket, and pulled it out.

The man faced Graves. Though his eyes were in deep shadow, Graves knew they were set firmly on him.

"You haven't asked me who's dead or how they died," the man said.

"You told me not to," Graves said.

A twisted smile flickered beneath the brim of the tycoon straw hat.

The cranking of the car engine was muffled by the thunder and hammering rain and thrashing tree limbs. Graves carried the rolled-up rug like firewood, slogging and slipping his way to a shed behind his trailer. The shotgun was safe there for now. What a night, he thought. The hurricane had ripped through the coastal marshes and bayous as furiously as the woman had torn off his shirt and pressed her lips hard to his, the taste of bourbon on her tongue.

Graves shuddered like a wet dog as he stepped inside the trailer. He saw the outline of the woman sitting on a footstool in front of his easy chair, the tip of a cigarette burning in the dark. Lightning flickered on the side of her face and Graves noticed the parted curtain above the bed.

The woman pulled the cigarette from her lips and blew the smoke upward from the corner of her mouth. "What in the world would Avery Hammond be doing out in this godawful storm?"

Another problem to fix.

. . .

I spread my fingers on the table. The backs of my hands were as sallow as old parchment in the fluorescent light. "You got rid of the woman?"

"Playing on your mind, ain't it?"

"Only the guard's murder is covered by your agreement, Graves. If—"

"Don't get your innards in an uproar, Brenner." The chains jangled as Graves spread his palms. "The woman's alive and well in Baton Rouge, I hear."

I sat back and took two methodical breaths. "If you didn't kill her, how'd you fix your problem, her seeing Avery Hammond?"

"She never told anyone. Never will."

"The woman could corroborate your story," I said, though whether Graves was lying about her or not, I needed physical evidence.

"Once I convince someone of the virtue of silence, they stay convinced. Unless you're prepared to do something worse than she knows I'd do, she ain't talking."

"You can't hurt her now," I said.

"Don't bet on it," Graves said. "You wanna hear the rest of this story or not?"

I balled my fists, knowing he could hardly wait to tell me about dumping David's body.

Emmett Graves took the knife he used to gut deer and held it against the woman's cheek, the tip pressed into the skin just beneath her eye.

He tightened his grip on her hair. "Seen anyone come by here tonight?"

Her lips formed a voiceless no.

"You understand there's nowhere I can't find you?"

She nodded slowly as Graves drew back the knife.

The woman put her clothes on. Moments later, Graves

watched her car fishtail in the mud as she sped away. Disposing of the car and bodies would be easy. The logistics would be tricky. Graves pulled his small jon boat from the muck behind his trailer and loaded it into the bed of his pickup, then retrieved a small outboard he kept in his shed. Fifteen minutes later, he was in a labyrinth of dirt and gravel roads winding in byzantine patterns among swamps and cane fields. Avoiding the dirt roads for fear of being mired in the mud, Graves soon found a spot close to the bayou that would be his escape route. He unloaded the jon boat and motor, then drove off.

The rain and winds had not relented, but the sizzle was gone from the lightning. Erratic flickers exposed dense and twisting vegetation along a road that never strayed more than fifty yards from the bayou. Rocks pinged the truck's underside until the gravel surface eventually turned to asphalt. Several minutes later, guessing he was a quarter mile from the nigger church, Graves turned onto a hardpan path. Would it hold? He killed the lights, but left the engine running and got out to check. Satisfied the ground was solid, he returned and drove the truck slowly toward the bayou to a spot local niggers used to launch their fishing boats then sit around afterward drinking whiskey while they cleaned their catch and played dominoes. He could navigate his way back in his jon boat, even in the storm, by keeping close to the bank.

Even niggers wouldn't be out on a night like this. Money had propelled Graves's own venture into the turbulent night. And a duty that brought him the prospect of more. He left the truck and hiked up the blacktop to the church, which was set near the bayou. As Graves approached Beulah Baptist Church, raindrops beating on the brim of his fishing cap, a fleeting flash outlined the modest structure. He saw nothing else in the jet black night. Then another ephemeral glimmer lit the oyster-shell parking area on the side of the church. He saw a hulking shadow, like a boulder in powdered snow. The car? Graves looked back over his shoulder. No way anyone driving by could see the parking lot in this lashing rain and darkness.

Marching toward where he thought he'd seen the form, he

placed a hand inside one of the deep pockets in his slicker. The pistol grip felt hard. Then he reached into the other pocket, pulled out a flashlight, and turned it on. Graves saw a body just ahead on the slick, wet shells. He moved forward and knelt beside it. The light framed the face of a nigger. Graves had seen him before—college boy stirring up the local coons. The boy's eyes were open and white as bone. Graves moved the flashlight beam down the body. The boy's stomach spilled out organs, as if someone dressing a buck had been called away before completing it. Next to the body, raindrops dimpled a large, red pool. The nigger had taken the shotgun blast at close range.

He let the light travel away from the body. The car. Graves rose and followed the ring of light. Loose gravel crunched beneath his feet. No need to worry about footprints with these interminable torrents. Approaching the vehicle, he noticed the driver's door was open. He looked down and saw two shoes, then two crumpled legs, one dyed crimson, kneeling in a pool of blood and rainwater. The torso was facedown on the seat, as if the person had been trying to escape when he was shot.

Though he couldn't see the face, Graves knew from the green *Tulane* jacket whose body it was. The white college boy who'd been getting niggers registered to vote. What had caused Avery Hammond, a man who solved problems with money and influence, to use such extreme measures? But Graves quickly discarded the thought when he saw his job had been made a little easier—keys dangling from the ignition. No need to hot-wire the car. Open the trunk, stash the bodies, and off we go.

Graves leaned back in his chair, the jingle of his chains echoing off the gray cinder block.

I'd seen videotapes of serial killers recounting their deeds in clinical fashion, as a glassblower or jewelry maker might describe his craft. And death camp officers recalling their ability to improve the efficiency of the trains and ovens as though their talent should be admired.

"I dumped the car in a sinkhole near where I left my boat," he said. "It was deep and had a pretty good drop-off, so the car went under quick. When I got done, I set my boat into the bayou and glided back to my truck. The whole thing was pretty easy, 'specially not having to hot-wire the white boy's Ford."

"David's Ford," I said.

"Yeah. From the way his leg was blowed off and his body being halfway onto the driver's seat, I guessed he drug himself to the car, then bled out before he could get it started. Two bad it couldn't a been the nigger that suffered."

Too bad I can't make you suffer, Graves. "Why didn't you dispose of the shotgun like you promised?" I asked.

"Avery Hammond paid me well for odd jobs over the years, but I figured if I ever got in a jam, I'd have me some insurance. I unwrapped the blanket and plastic the next day. Saw smudges I figured was fingerprints."

"Why didn't you go for a big score and blackmail him at some point?" I asked.

"No need. I was fine with things the way they was."

"Until you were arrested for drug trafficking and you killed a guard," I said.

Graves grinned. "You might got an ace, but you can only play it once."

I nodded. "So when did you bury the shotgun on his property?"

"A couple nights later, while the ground was soft from the rains and it was easy to put the sod back in place. And in case you're worried about the condition of your evidence, I wrapped a half dozen plastic garbage bags around the blanket and wound duct tape around it all."

"Ever question Hammond about the gun or the boys being killed?" I asked.

"When you do a job for Hammond, you don't ask details. That's what got me busted."

My eyes narrowed. "What do you mean?"

Graves's smile evaporated. "Not your case, Brenner."

"All right." I wondered what connection Hammond might have

to Graves's botched drug deal. "Why would Avery Hammond kill these boys?"

"Didn't say he did."

"Or cover for someone else."

"You got what I agreed to give you. Go figure out the rest." Graves clanked his manacles on the aluminum table, then stood. "Guard!"

11

The storm that had followed me from New Orleans had strewn splinters of cane across the highway between Angola and Baton Rouge. The rain had stopped, and hints of blue dappled the western sky, but my thoughts were fully overcast. Was Emmett Graves's story an elaborate hoax to forestall a death sentence, or was he playing a game for his own wicked entertainment? I discarded the second notion. No doubt Graves lusted after the physical and mental torment of others, but I believed each violation had personal gain as its purpose. Though he'd taken pleasure in it, terrorizing the woman in the trailer before sending her away into the thunderstorm was part of his contract with Hammond. So I had to believe his story—faithful, embellished, or fabricated—had motive beyond self-amusement. Escaping death row was as good as any.

And I had no option but to accept Graves's account as truth. Which, I suddenly realized, meant digging up the property of the most influential man in Bon Terre. I doubted Rhino Perrot would gladly execute a warrant. I could do it without him, but I wanted him on my side. And what if I did find a shotgun? Could I prove it was the weapon that killed David?

Even the weather was confused. I drove the interstate into New Orleans under cobalt skies, the usual late-afternoon thundershowers preempted by the cloudless wake of the rushing tropical storm, by now well up the Natchez Trace in Mississippi. I'd made good time. Maybe Alexis would like to go out to dinner. I flipped on my cell phone and called home.

I was curious about Graves's statement that Avery Hammond was somehow connected with his drug conviction, so I stopped by the station the next morning and asked Arceneaux to talk to his former colleagues in Narcotics and gather some details about Graves's arrest.

"No problem," he said. "But while you're here, let me tell you what I found about the Meades. Daddy's an oil company exec. He's high enough up so his salary and bonuses are public information."

"Meaning he can provide for his children," I said.

"For true. He's set up major-league trust funds. The kids get allowances from them at twenty-one. Jason became of age two years ago. That's when Daddy bought him the home on the lake. They get the whole enchilada when they turn thirty-five."

"He told us about that. Characterized his allowance as meager."

"It sure as hell ain't meager for a cop." Arceneaux smirked. "But maybe it is for him. Jason's got two bank accounts, each with triple-digit balances. Some months the trust allowance don't cover his mortgage and credit-card charges. And he's been hitting the casinos all over Louisiana and Mississippi since he became legal."

"Wonder if the companionship and marijuana he's providing older women cover his losses?" I asked.

Arceneaux shrugged. "Who knows? But he don't pay taxes on it."

A silver mirage on the horizon above the hot asphalt led my way to Bon Terre. Shitty weather for me, but the rice and soybean fields on each side of the road loved it. I parked in front of the sheriff's department and went inside. The office was empty, though the odor of cigar smoke told me I'd just missed him. I decided to try Seven Angels Bail Bonds next door. As I stepped back outside, Creed Beaumont shut the door of his Camaro, new red paint gleaming on the low-slung body like tanning oil on a swimsuit model.

He hopped up onto the sidewalk. "Officer Thomas catch you again?"

"Fool me once, shame on you," I said.

"Quick learner. Maybe what I have to tell you will stick." He pulled off his sunglasses and twirled them casually. "I don't know what Emmett Graves has told you, but he's a liar." His voice was as flat as his stern gray eyes, revealing neither regional nor ethnic ties. Nor emotion.

"Guess I'll find out soon enough."

"This is a peaceful town, just like it was when your cousin was killed. Everyone's sorry it happened, but there's nothing anyone can do about it now. We'd all be better off if you'd leave it alone, so things can stay peaceful."

"You say *we* like you were born and bred here. You're not from the South. What brought you to Bon Terre?"

"Mr. Hammond offered me work after my discharge from the military."

"For your special skills?"

"One. Loyalty. In a place like this, powerful people like Mr. Hammond are vulnerable to those with conflicting allegiances. I answer only to him."

"Did Emmett Graves answer to Hammond?"

"To me," Beaumont said. "He was useful keeping cheaters and riffraff out of Mr. Hammond's casino, but Graves has no loyalties. He'd have never made a soldier. Take my advice. Honor your cousin's memory by going back to New Orleans and bringing current-day killers to justice before any more reporters come snooping around."

Willow's piece was on national news. I didn't recall any local footage or press interviews. "You've had reporters in Bon Terre?"

"A TV newswoman came by Mr. Hammond's today. I ran her

off, though I wouldn't mind seeing her again. She'll get your pecker harder than space-age metal."

My face burned as if standing too close to an opened oven. It had to be Willow.

"That's why I took my sweet time shooing her away," he said. "She was pumping out pheromones faster than a little kid dousing ketchup on french fries." Beaumont replaced his sunglasses and stepped off the covered walkway. "If she got those long legs of hers wrapped around you, I guarantee she'd squeeze you off more than once."

Creed Beaumont watched me as he eased his car onto Main Street, his Armani wraparounds showing no more animation than his eyes. As I started toward Seven Angels Bail Bonds, the pastel-lettered door opened, and a woman emerged followed by Rhino Perrot, an unlit but well-chewed cigar in his hand.

"Morning, Sheriff," I said.

The woman had a familiar look. She appeared to be my aunt Joyce's age, hair short and silver, her eyes gray-green.

She turned to Rhino. "This the New Orleans policeman who's stirred up all this trouble?"

"Some people would say that, ma'am," I answered for him.

Though slightly more than five feet tall, she glared at me like a schoolteacher admonishing a misbehaving child. "You got the media digging up this old mess all over again. Isn't there enough real live suffering and mayhem for them to cover?" She pushed past me and walked briskly from the walk to her car.

"Who was that?" I asked Rhino.

"Constance Tilden."

"Faith Ann's—"

"Mother. She came over to demand I put a stop to this circus. Some reporter's over at Meal Thyme right now. If I weren't minding Seven Angels for my wife, I'd go on over and check her out myself. Maybe that's something you could do. *Deputy.*" He winked at me and reached into his pocket for a lighter and relit his cigar. "Mrs. Tilden says she's as blond as a Biloxi whore."

"I need to tell you something before I go, Sheriff," I said, hoping to tell him about the shotgun before he heard about it from another source.

"Talk to me later, son." Rhino started past me. "This month's utility bill just got paid."

A silver Mercedes 380SL pulled into a parking space, Jarla's cruiser on its tail.

I arrived at the restaurant well before the lunch crowd. Only a green van sat on the oyster shells in front of Meal Thyme. I hopped onto the veranda and went inside.

Faith Tilden's daughter, Grace, called out as the door harp pinged. "We're not open yet, but I'll bring you some raspberry tea if you'd like to wait." Grace looked up from the table where she was setting silverware. "Oh. Hi, Detective Brenner."

"Hello, Grace. Your mother in the kitchen?"

She lowered her voice. "She's out with some news lady. When she showed up, Grandma left in a big huff and went to complain to the sheriff." Grace shook her head. "Those two boys were friends of my mother's. You'd think Grandma would want to find out who killed them."

"Sometimes it's easier to let things be forgotten."

"My mother and Grandma are good at that." Grace grabbed more silverware from a plastic tub, snapping each utensil into place as though punctuating internal thoughts.

I strode through the dining room and then the kitchen, nodding to the smiling cook. Faith and Willow turned toward the creaking screen door as I stepped outside. They were a picture of town and country—Faith in her loose denim jumper, Willow with tailored gray slacks and an ecru silk blouse. Both held glasses of iced tea laced with sprigs of mint.

Willow took aim at me with luminous amber eyes.

Before either could speak, I said, "Faith, I declined Grace's offering of raspberry tea a minute ago, but I believe I've changed my mind."

"I'll get you some right away," she said. "And I guess I don't need to introduce you two."

"That's correct." I wondered exactly what Willow had told her.

Willow looked curiously at me, possibly searching for a good-to-see-you-again look on my face that wasn't there.

"I'll be back," Faith said. The screen door creaked.

I walked past Willow to the far end of the porch and looked out toward the bayou.

"Following me, Detective?" Willow asked.

I turned to face her. "I found out you were here from Faith's mother. She isn't pleased either of us is in Bon Terre."

"When are people ever pleased to see a cop or a reporter?"

"Avery Hammond wasn't glad to see you, either. What did you want with him?" I wondered if she'd spoken with Graves after I had.

She grinned. "I knew you were following me."

I hadn't expected an answer. "Creed Beaumont told me he turned you away this morning. Don't try him again. A guy like that quickly loses his charm if you try to get past him."

"I've been bullied before."

"We're talking disappearance and dismemberment here," I said, working from feeling rather than fact. "Beaumont's no different than Emmett Graves."

"Just doing my job." She sipped her tea, her gaze never losing mine.

"The problem is, it's interfering with mine."

She stepped close to me. "Then let's work together."

"Not into one-night stands, Willow," I said. "Particularly if I end up paying for it."

She raised a soft, stenciled eyebrow. "Pretty cynical, Detective. I could be a fantastic partner if you'd let me. Or have you forgotten?"

The sharp scent of mint chafed my nostrils. "I haven't forgotten the freshman orientation you got from that Costa Rican graduate student at Vanderbilt."

The cosmetic blush faded from her cheeks.

"Your friend Karen Stern told me about it during winter break," I said.

"So you left me waiting at Molly's because of a bruised ego," she said, her eyes hardening. "Karen also told me about you and Alexis. So maybe you thought that when we agreed to see other people it only applied to you. Or do you always reconstruct history in a way that makes you the good guy?"

She had me there, and I could have ended the discussion by calling a truce. But perhaps a fragile ego still governed my actions.

"Willow, I didn't screw the first woman I met at college before even taking a class."

Her lips parted without words.

"I'm sure your Latin American interlude met that need for wildness and excitement you talked about the other day. Like hot and sweaty nights on the levee with the lightning crackling, and me the naive high school boy who just happened to be there while you got all hot and bothered. Now it's the big story you're getting off on."

Willow's eyes fogged over as if searching for the locus of a forgotten pain.

The acid in my stomach had just worked its way to my throat when the screen door creaked.

"Jack. Here's your tea," Faith said.

I looked over Willow's shoulder. Faith held a cut-glass tumbler with both hands.

Willow moved closer, the back of her hand touching mine, her breath hot against my neck as she whispered hoarsely, "You're terribly wrong, Jack. It wasn't the lightning. It was you."

She patted a strand of moisture on her cheek before turning around and approaching Faith. "I have to go now, Ms. Tilden. Deadlines, you know. We'll talk some more another time."

"Now remember you said—"

"Don't worry." Willow patted Faith on the arm. "Everything you gave me was merely background material."

"You two looked like you were talking about something important," Faith said once Willow had left.

"Just background material."

She watched me guzzle the tea she'd given me. "I need to get back inside. Stay for lunch?"

"I'll come back when you're not busy," I said.

"Stop by my house after two."

"I'm not sure your mother will let me in."

"It's my house," Faith said.

I left with the address, a smoked turkey sandwich with herb dressing, Gouda cheese, and avocado, and a piece of pecan pie. Pulling out of the lot, I remembered Emmett Graves had said the church was on Escondido Road, near the bayou. I hadn't seen a church driving from the main highway to Meal Thyme, so I turned right rather than left and headed along the asphalt under a canopy of water oaks and cypress trees.

I stuffed a napkin Faith had given me into my shirt collar to keep the dressing from dribbling on my tie, a Father's Day present from Sarah and Carrie. As I munched on the sandwich and scanned the land along the road for a church, I thought about the moisture in Willow's eyes and was convinced it was real. Had I been unfair or too hard on her? Was her passion in the backseat of my father's car really ignited by a shared spark—the unique flare of energy that tells two people they're soul mates? Did such a thing even exist?

After driving five miles without seeing a church, I concluded it no longer existed. Something to ask the sheriff when I told him what I needed to do. As I started to turn around, I noticed a fork in the road ahead. After considering the risk of getting lost, I decided to stick with my plan to do a one-eighty and return to the main highway. Until I saw the sign: HAMMOND LANE. I veered left past rows of sun-illumined emerald cane.

Five minutes later, my car crept along a narrow wooden bridge above a creek marked HAMMOND'S BAYOU. I knew the diminutive stream wasn't the bayou that ran behind Meal Thyme. After another mile, I reached the head of a long oak-lined drive. I couldn't see any buildings, but the interlocking brick pavers suggested wealth beyond the trees.

I turned in and soon came to a clearing where the drive looped in front of a massive white two-story home, a plantation big house that surely belonged to Avery Hammond. Though raised four feet from the ground, it was built in Victorian Renaissance style rather than the Greek Revival of most great Southern houses, with modest columns and modest amounts of gingerbread work around the first-floor windows and second-story dormers. Ferns, white ginger, and pink and yellow hibiscus surrounded the foundation.

Knowing Rhino Perrot would have a fit if my first encounter with Hammond was unescorted, I considered continuing through the circle and returning to Bon Terre. On the other hand, I'd get a better feel for the man if I talked to him before he had reason to be defensive. I parked, then walked toward the steps, catching the sound and scent of horses before the ginger overwhelmed my nostrils.

Moments after knocking, the brass lock clicked and a dark-haired woman pulled the ten-foot-high door wide open. She was barefoot and richly tanned. Two buttons barely restrained her large breasts within a sleeveless denim blouse. Beltless white shorts clung to her hips well below her navel. She was not the butler I expected.

"The B-and-B's a mile that way." She gestured with her eyes, mosaics of emerald and golden brown, while cradling a tall glass filled with chipped ice and a cranberry-colored liquid.

"I'm here to see Avery Hammond." I fought to keep my eyes on neutral territory, but she didn't leave many options. "What makes you think I'm a tourist?"

"Figured you're a reporter like that newswoman who came by this morning. She's staying at Trahan's Bed and Breakfast. Lord, that woman wanted to be a blonde real bad."

The herb dressing turned sour in my mouth. Willow had set up camp close to the story.

"Uncle Avery," the woman hollered, offering a side view. Definitely not the butler.

She turned back to me and grinned, giving me a visual undressing as though mocking the behavior I tried to avoid.

"Christ, Annie," a voice echoed. "Please let someone with manners answer the door. That's what I pay Cho for."

Annie glanced over her shoulder. "You don't have to pay him anything. We've been playing gin rummy in the kitchen and I've taken ten years wages from him."

A man dressed in a white short-sleeve safari shirt appeared behind her. "Then why didn't he answer the goddamn door?"

"He's taking a leak. These cosmopolitans make him piss every fifteen minutes." She smiled at me like a four-year-old using a bathroom word in front of her mother's friends.

The man took Annie's shoulder and gently shoved her out of the way. "I apologize for the behavior of my family. What can I do for you, sir?"

"Avery Hammond?" I asked.

"Unless you're the IRS I am." Unlike the starched, buttoned epaulets of his shirt and crisply pressed khakis, the corners of his eyes crinkled beneath gold-rimmed glasses. His hair was pure white, precisely trimmed around the edges, with several dozen strands combed straight back. His brows, bushy and dark, were streaked with gray.

"I may be worse than the IRS," I said.

"Not if you were the devil himself. Or a reporter."

"I understand you've already had one of those thrown off your property today," I said.

Hammond grinned, his eyes scanning over my shoulder. "My associate had the good luck of greeting her, but I got a look from the window. She's got the best ass I've ever seen on a white woman. Please come in, Detective Brenner. I've been expecting you."

I wasn't surprised. "No doubt thanks to Creed Beaumont. Would he have turned me away if he'd answered the door?"

"Well now, Annie didn't do much of a job of it, did she?"

I stepped into a long hallway, typical of old Southern homes.

Annie had disappeared. Hammond led me to a brightly lit study overlooking a garden, and beyond, a motor court with a six-car garage.

"She called you uncle," I said, taking the chair he offered. It was soft, the leather a deeper shade of tan than his designer loafers.

"Yes." Hammond sat and crossed his legs in a matching chair on the other side of a cherry occasional table. "Her mama named her Angélique, but I started calling her Annie after her mother took off because Angélique sounds like a couch dancer's name. Though that's pretty much what she's become, except she doesn't charge for it."

"Creed Beaumont told you I was in town today," I said. "But I presume you learned all about me from Sheriff Perrot."

"You've come to avenge a kin's murder." Neither his tone nor his expression suggested admiration or Godspeed.

"Vengeance and justice are two different things," I said.

"Only when justice puts things back the way they were. Which is almost never. Whatever you think you're going to find around here isn't going to bring anyone back. Neither your cousin, who I'm sure was a fine young man, nor Elton Jackson, who I know was."

"Your brother Vernon died shortly after my cousin was killed, so I guess you know about moving on."

Hammond gripped the leather armrests, then relaxed his hands and smiled. "It's been my duty, but an honor, to raise his son and daughter."

"Never brought his killer to justice?"

"Whatever happened was the Lord's will. Maybe something for you to consider."

"God's the only force you wouldn't go up against, judging from all the signs around here with your name on it."

He chuckled. "Don't forget Infernal Revenue, my friend. I personally funded the Iraq war."

"How about the press? You allowed a cop into your home but you ran off a reporter."

"Cooperating with authorities, even if inconvenient, is my duty,

Detective. Besides, you can get warrants and subpoenas and all that crap. But I cherish my privacy, and no goddamn reporter is going to drag my family or my business into millions of living rooms with people eating off TV trays. That said, I have nothing to hide."

Unless a murder weapon's buried out back. "Whether you do or not, you've done a pretty good job of securing yourself. You have quite an impressive spread."

"My great-granddaddy built it, everything from the bayou north of here. And I'm not talking about the dipshit creek we named Hammond's Bayou, either. I'm talking a five-mile-wide swath from Bayou L'enfant all the way to the main highway. And other bits and pieces scattered about."

"Not to mention the power and influence," I said.

"Hell. My great-granddaddy collected the land, but you don't buy power and influence. That comes with respect. I've provided livelihoods for many a man and woman. Bon Terre is a great place to raise a family. It's safe here. It's a little piece of Eden that I hope to goddamn hell doesn't get spoiled by reporters and television crews kicking up mud."

"A place where the wolf lies down with the lamb," I said.

Hammond's bushy eyebrows became one. "Thought it was lions and lambs."

"Common mistake. But it's the same concept."

"You know how many murders we've had in these parts since Elton Jackson and your cousin were killed?" He held up his hand, thumb tucked into his palm. "Four. That's one every seven years. Three of them were domestic squabbles and the other was the drifter who killed my brother. I'd say the lions around here are pretty goddamn tame, wouldn't you?"

"I have a theory that the lambs are safe only as long as the carnivores get fed so well and often it's not worth the trouble dining on lamb."

Hammond pushed up from his leather chair. "This Bible talk gives me a goddamn headache. Let's go out back and have some lemonade. Don't worry. It never gets to ninety under the big oak tree."

Hammond led me toward the rear of the house, calling into the kitchen as we passed by, "Cho, tell Annie to play solitaire for a while. Bring us some lemonade out on the patio."

Hammond grabbed a white tycoon hat from a table next to the French doors leading outside to a covered veranda. Stables and an oval track lay a hundred yards to the left. Fifty yards directly behind the house flowed a wide bayou, not the "dipshit creek" I'd crossed getting here. A bass boat and a jet boat were moored at a pier. Cypress trees lined the shore, but the land between the house and the bayou had been cleared, leaving a monstrous live oak, its gnarled, moss-laden limbs spreading out like an aerie of griffins. Then a realization stung me the way a wasp's bite burns the back of your neck long after its retreat. Circling the spreading oak, a tiled patio encased the ground where Graves said he'd buried the shotgun.

We walked down the steps from the gallery and crossed the lawn. The temperature dropped from blistering to mild entering the shade of the oak. Our heels clicked on the hard surface as Hammond led me to a wrought-iron table with padded chairs.

"This spot's been in perpetual shade for over three hundred years," he said, lifting his eyes to the serpentine branches. "The breeze off the water and the stone surface keep it cool even in the summer."

I focused on a spot twelve feet from the base of the oak in the direction of the bayou.

He waited until he caught my eyes. "You seem to be admiring my patio. The slate's from the Green Mountains in Vermont."

An Asian man approached with a tray, two glasses, and a pitcher of lemonade with orange and lime slices floating on top. A silver flask stood next to the pitcher.

"Thank you, Cho," Hammond said as the small, middle-aged man laid the tray on the table. "When you go back in, tell Annie to put on some clothes. She won't be able to cheat you blind at cards if you can keep your eyes out of her cleavage."

"No can tell Miss Annie what to do, Mr. Avery." Cho nodded ceremoniously, then plodded toward the house, right leg dragging.

"Cho used to groom my quarter horses till one of them kicked him in the knee. Won't go near the stables now." Hammond poured the lemonade, then spilled some of the flask's contents into one glass. He raised his brows at me. "Grey Goose?"

I grabbed the undoctored drink and took a sip. It was cold and tart, quenching my thirst, but somehow leaving me wanting.

Hammond took a long draw from his glass. "So, Detective. What do you expect to dig up?"

12

My cheeks and neck burned as though I'd lifted the lid on a pot of boiling crabs. I gulped my lemonade, sloshing part of it down my windpipe, then covered my mouth and hacked.

Hammond smiled at my distress. "Sure I can't get you a shot of vodka?"

Dig up. I shook my head and hacked some more, cursing myself for reacting to what I hoped was a coincidental selection of words.

"I know I can't stop you from carrying on with your wild goose chase," Hammond said. "I respect what you're trying to do, but please go about things quietly so the media doesn't circle around like buzzards over dead nutria."

"I don't control the media." I coughed into my fist.

"Suppose not." Hammond grabbed the silver flask and spiked his lemonade again. "Though I wouldn't mind giving that blond news lady an exclusive interview."

The sound of the French doors slamming suddenly drew our attention. A man wearing a blue blazer over a white button-down shirt hurried down the steps and marched toward us. His hair was cropped short and his dark eyes fumed like funnel clouds.

"What are you doing home?" Hammond called to the man.

"I cut off Buddy Lejeune's line of credit," he said.

"Why the hell did you cut off Buddy Lejeune?" Hammond asked.

"He owes two thousand dollars." He loosened a red-striped tie and opened his shirt collar.

"Shit, boy. He earns that in two days working offshore."

"Then Creed apologizes to Lejeune and chews me out in front of the staff," the young man whined.

Hammond set his lemonade on the table. "Good thing. We don't need Buddy Lejeune and his buddies running over to Biloxi on their seven days off."

"I run the casino, Avery."

"Don't take what's printed on your business card so damn seriously." Hammond held up a hand, then glanced at me. "Where are my manners? This is my nephew Eddie." Turning back to him, he said, "This is Detective Brenner."

"Who the fuck cares?" Eddie glared at me as if my mere presence offended him.

He stormed back to the big house. His insolence, no doubt bolstered by being born into wealth and privilege, reminded me of Jenna Meade's brother, Jason.

"Once again, I apologize for the actions of my family." Hammond picked up the flask from the table and drank directly. "My nurture, though not my nature."

"Children of your own?" I asked.

"My lawyer worries about one turning up someday, if you know what I mean." Hammond winked. "Finish your lemonade if you want, I have to go fix the mess my idiot nephew caused."

"Think I will," I said.

Hammond took a deeper swig from the flask, then leveled his eyes on me. "I'd ask you to let me know how your investigation goes, but my sources will keep me informed." His dark eyes flickered.

As he retreated across the lawn, I decided Hammond's remark about my digging things up was a figure of speech. Neither Graves nor Willow had reason to tip him off. Then, as I looked at the expensive slate tiles, presumably covering the buried murder weapon, I considered what I'd learned about Hammond. His last look had been a warning. He was a man used to being in control. A man who could order a murder if that control was challenged. So if the deaths of David and Deer had nothing to do with race or politics, maybe they'd stumbled onto something. Had lamb somehow threatened lion?

I was also intrigued at Hammond's discomfort when I mentioned his brother, the father of his hotheaded nephew and promiscuous niece, whose mother had disappeared. I wondered if her "running off" was related to the death of Hammond's brother.

I finished my lemonade. As I walked along the side of the house to the front drive, Hammond pulled out of the garage in a black Mercedes ML55 and tipped his tycoon hat. Once in the driver's seat of my car, I cranked the engine and turned the air-conditioning to max. The lemonade had left a prickly tartness in my mouth. Thinking perhaps the pie Faith had given me would extinguish it, I opened the Styrofoam box. All I found was a mass of pecans swimming in a thick brown puddle.

I headed back to town, wondering if Rhino Perrot already knew about my visit to Hammond. After stopping for gas and trashing the box holding my melted pie, I pulled up in front of Seven Angels Bail Bonds. One of those cardboard BE BACK AT signs with moveable clocks hands hung inside the door. Three o'clock. I didn't want him thinking I was holding out on him, but I didn't feel like waiting around for an hour, either. Having no way of leaving him a voice message, I decided to write him a note that I'd check with him later.

Faith Tilden's house was two blocks from the main highway. I parked on the street and strolled up the walk, observing that Faith's property was far from the least resplendent. Baskets of ferns and red-bloomed dwarf hibiscus hung the length of the porch. The garden lining the front of the house dazzled with daffodils, Mexican sunflowers, and nail-polish-pink impatiens.

I knocked on the door and was greeted by the bourbon-laced breath of Truman LaRoche.

"Come on in, Detective. I just dropped off some vegetables for Faith." His deep, jovial voice and unkempt beard reminded me of Santa Claus. Only the jagged violet line running down his face spoiled the image.

I followed Truman to the kitchen, where Faith stood at the sink washing eggplants. A round antique table and a matching china cabinet in the large country kitchen reminded me of Aunt Joyce's furniture.

"I guess you never get away from it," I said.

"Our chef does most of the cooking at the restaurant," she said. "I do most of it here. Did you enjoy your lunch?"

"The first course." I explained about the pie.

Faith dried her hands on a towel. "Wish I'd brought some home. But there's cheesecake in the fridge."

"Sounds good to me," Truman said. "I'll make coffee."

Faith folded the towel neatly on the counter, then grabbed my arm. "Let me formally introduce you to my parents while it's brewing."

"If it's not a good time—"

"Don't worry about Mother."

Faith led me back to the den, with picture windows stretching the entire width of the house and offering an even more magnificent view than the front landscaping. My aunt Joyce in her prime could never have competed with the color and variety of Faith's gardens.

"I was impressed with your front yard, but this backyard of yours is fabulous," I said.

"All Truman's doing," Faith said.

An alcoholic Martha Stewart. I noticed Constance Tilden sitting next to a small, withered man in a wheelchair with a tray fixed across the arms. He seemed to be watching the television eight feet in front of him. His right hand trembled as he turned a plastic straw to his lips. Constance grasped the base of the aluminum tumbler for him.

"I believe you've met Detective Brenner," Faith said to her mother.

"Nice to see you again," I said.

Mrs. Tilden removed the tumbler from the tray. "Faith, I need to change the bedclothes in your father's room."

She rose and left, her gaze never meeting her daughter's or mine.

Faith drew me closer to her father, whose eyes had a faraway but amused look, as though he was trying to recall a funny story he remembered parts of.

She touched his shoulder. "Papa, this is Jack Brenner. Jack, Jerroll Tilden."

"Good to meet you, Mr. Tilden." I started to praise his daughter's cooking, but stopped, worried his condition might not allow him to partake.

His eyes showed a little light at a playful yapping sound coming from the television.

"He loves the Animal Channel," Faith said.

I recognized the program, a show about working dogs called *K-9 to Five*. Our canine unit was featured on it once.

"He's not being impolite. Papa lost his speech when he had his stroke." Faith smiled, then elevated her voice and bent near his ear. "But he understands everything you say."

Mr. Tilden's gaze remained intent on a pair of dogs chasing geese from a golf course.

"Jack's with the New Orleans police, Papa. He's David Brenner's cousin and hopes to find out who killed him and Deer Jackson."

Mr. Tilden's eyes went dead and his whole body began to shake. On the television, the dogs snarled and barked loudly at a large Canadian goose who'd stood his ground.

Faith grasped his shoulders. "What is it, Papa?"

"Is there anything I can do?" I reached over and turned off the television.

Faith's voice was calm. "This happens every so often. Something agitates him and we have to calm him down." Then she called out, "Mother!"

Faith knelt and held her father's trembling body until Mrs. Tilden entered the room. The glare she directed at me showed little concern for her husband.

She looked down at her daughter. "What's going on?"

"Just the shakes," Faith said. "Some dogs barking on the television got him started."

"Or having strange people around," Mrs. Tilden said.

"Mother, stop it! Help me get Papa back to bed."

Mrs. Tilden huffed and lifted the tray attachment while Faith released the brake.

"I'll be back shortly." Faith looked at me and nodded toward the kitchen. "The coffee should be ready. And I'm sure Truman's already eating his cheesecake."

Then she pushed the wheelchair out of the room. Mrs. Tilden followed.

Returning to the kitchen, I saw Faith had it right. Bits of graham crust and cream cheese clung to the tines of a fork resting in the center of Truman's plate.

"You're going to love this." Truman pointed to another plate with a large wedge of cheesecake on it. "How do you take your coffee?"

"Black." I joined him at the table.

Truman poured coffee into a flower-design mug from a Pyrex pot, which he returned to a trivet next to a bottle of bourbon.

"I understand you're responsible for the impressive flora around here," I said.

"I'm far more successful nurturing plants and vegetables than I was at saving souls."

"You gave up the priesthood for horticulture?"

"Being the investigator you are, I'm sure you haven't failed to notice the road map on my face." He set down his coffee mug and leaned forward in case I hadn't.

I dropped my eyes to my plate and took a bite of cheesecake.

"Got into a tussle with a pimp in Baton Rouge and he bit my nose off. They had to graft skin from my cheek to replace the flesh he swallowed."

"Jesus," I said, then realized I'd taken his Lord's name in vain. "Sorry."

Truman grinned and waved it off. "The year after David and Deer were killed I volunteered for ghetto work thinking I could make a difference."

"But you gave it up after the pimp bit your nose off?"

"No. I wrestled the pimp away from a streetwalker because he was beating her. I was on top of him holding his hands down when he bit me. I quit the priesthood because the streetwalker stuck me with a four-inch blade when I got up. She was irritated that I'd interrupted their business discussion."

"You can only help people who help themselves," I said.

He stroked his beard the way a young child strokes a favorite blanket. "We helped some. But working in that environment finally got to me. You know what I'm talking about. Cops lead the pack when it comes to suicide, and since suicide's a sin, you guys don't get much competition from priests. But we have a narrow lead over cops when it comes to alcoholism."

I steered the conversation toward something more useful to me. "You knew my cousin?"

"David and I spent a fair bit of time discussing philosophy and religion that summer. He's the reason I left to save souls in city slums. You know what *tikkun olam* means?"

"It's Hebrew for 'healing the world.'"

"David said that's what his work here was about. It's why he was going to law school after college."

"And he encouraged you to go work with the urban poor?"

"Bon Terre's a cushy assignment for a priest. David encouraged me to find more challenging work because he thought it might help me quit drinking. *Tikkun olam* begins at home, you might say."

"Tradition teaches that saving a single life is like saving the whole world," I said. "Even if it's your own."

He reached for the bourbon. "The thing about the drinking is it helped me with the chastity vow by keeping my willie working full-time meeting the demands of my liver and bladder. It's one of two vows I still keep." He topped off his coffee.

"The other?" I asked, irritated that we were talking so much about him and so little about David.

"The sanctity of confession. No matter what the crime."

"I've run into that brick wall a few times."

Truman looked down into his mug as though it were a wishing well. "And will again, I'm sure." He took a deep gulp.

I'd just about finished my cheesecake when Faith returned to the kitchen.

"Your father okay?" I asked.

"He's asleep." Faith sat in a chair between Truman and me. "Truman, you'd better bring more plum tomatoes by the restaurant. The shrimp pasta did a brisk trade today."

"No problem. I love picking vegetables in the heat of the day." Truman pushed back his chair and rose, taking a last, long swallow of laced coffee.

I waited until I heard the back door close. "Tell me about your conversation with Willow Ashe, Faith."

"She's so nice. She asked about the work I did with Deer and David. What I knew about them. Things that happened that summer." She hiked her shoulders. "Pretty much what I told you, except she asked a lot of questions about Avery Hammond."

"Please don't talk to her again," I said.

Faith frowned. "I don't understand. She's only getting background information. Besides, I thought she was cooperating with you."

"She's acted entirely on her own. She's looking for a big story."

Faith screwed her lips as she might after tasting a sauce that had yielded an unpleasant result. "Why are you angry with her? She said you were best friends in high school, and she wanted to help you."

Or use me. But a fair assessment of Willow's actions was that her broadcast was the reason I'd been allowed to work this case. She was only doing her job, and what did it matter that she stood to gain from what benefited me? So then, why *was* I furious with her? Was my adolescent pride still so wounded? I'd accused her of using me to fulfill selfish needs, including even our lovemaking in high school. But I wondered if what truly angered me was my inability to believe I could be the subject, and not the object, of a woman's pleasure and emotions. Or her love. A love that, growing up feeling responsible for my mother's happiness, seemed always out of reach.

Maybe Willow was using me, but I owed her more than a one-sided, laser-sharp complaint. Just as I owed Alexis an honest inventory of my own needs, and an acceptance of the honest inventory of her own.

Faith's cracking voice broke the silence. "Did I do something wrong?"

A frequent question of mine. Then, hoping to break the tension with levity, I said, "Some of my best friends are reporters, but they still make me nervous." Wouldn't that make Odell Harris laugh.

"I thought I was helping," she said.

I placed my hand softly on hers. "You were. I really appreciate that. You're the kind of person I'm sure David was proud to know."

Suddenly her eyes misted over, like two mint leaves glossed with morning dew. "Would you like another piece of cheesecake?"

Rhino Perrot could wait a little longer. "How can I refuse?"

Faith recounted what she'd told Willow about Avery Hammond. Nothing I didn't already know, but it made me uneasy that Willow had followed his trail. If she knew something about Hammond I didn't, would she tell me? I wanted to believe she was the helpful friend she'd convinced Faith she was.

By the time I drove up in front of the sheriff's office, it was after five. I hopped onto the walk and entered the office. Rhino Perrot was at his desk fishing through a side drawer.

"Goddamn," he said. "Where'd I put those cigars?"

"One of those days, Sheriff?" I asked.

He continued rummaging in the drawer without looking up. "Where the hell have you been since this morning?"

"Didn't you find the note I left you? I stuck it in the door of your office."

"The hell you say." He slammed the drawer shut and pulled out the top tray.

"I've been trying to talk to you since this morning."

"Talk."

Before I could, his phone rang. He lifted the receiver with his left hand and kept rummaging through the drawer with the other. "Perrot. Can I hep ya?"

Two seconds later his face softened. "Honey. I was getting ready to lock up. Need me to pick up something?" As Rhino listened, his eyes narrowed and he slowly withdrew his hand from the desk drawer. Then he looked at me. "What channel?" He nodded. "I'll be home as soon as it's over."

He looked up at me. "My wife's got on the evening news, like always, and Don Samuelson says one of their top stories tonight comes from south Louisiana. Ain't no hurricane in the Gulf. What do you suppose the story is?"

13

Faith's cheesecake felt like a chunk of asphalt in my stomach. Had Willow done it again? I followed Rhino behind the justice of the peace bench and into Seven Angels, where a small television with rabbit ears sat on a table in the rear of the room. Rhino pushed the power button. Several seconds later, the face of Don Samuelson appeared on the snowy screen.

Samuelson pushed aside a sheet of news copy. "We now turn to a surprising update on a story we broke last week concerning a case where for thirty years, the deaths of two young civil rights workers have awaited justice. Live from Bon Terre, Louisiana, is Willow Ashe, of our Atlanta affiliate."

A head shot of Willow appeared on-screen. She wore the same ecru blouse she'd had on when I saw her at Meal Thyme.

Rhino whistled. "Even with that fuzzy damn picture, you can tell the woman is a knockout. She the reporter Constance Tilden complained to me about?"

I nodded.

Rhino squinted at the screen. "Lot nicer than any Biloxi whore."

I didn't ask how he knew.

Willow began. "Emmett Floyd Graves, an inmate at Angola penitentiary serving time for drug trafficking, is currently charged with killing a prison transport officer. Last week, I reported that he claimed to have information concerning the 1972 murders of two civil rights workers, David Brenner and Elton Jackson. He stated that he knew the location of the murder weapon and would reveal it if officials agreed not to seek the death penalty for murdering the guard. The Orleans Parish DA agreed to his demand.

"Yesterday I learned Emmett Graves confessed to Jack Brenner of the New Orleans Police Department, the cousin of victim David Brenner, that he took part in covering up these killings."

Willow's lush voice continued as the screen filled with footage taken from a moving vehicle. The emerald cane looked familiar.

"On the night of July twentieth, 1972, Emmett Graves gathered the bodies of the two victims and placed them into David Brenner's car. He then drove the vehicle into the swamps, where he submerged it with the bodies inside."

The television showed a black pond, cypress stumps piercing the surface, vines and moss dripping from an umbrella of trees.

"Emmett Graves claims to have no involvement in the murders, but says he was paid to dispose of the automobile and the bodies, as well as the murder weapon, a shotgun."

Willow returned to the screen. "But after dumping the car and bodies, Graves says he hid the shotgun as possible future leverage against the man who asked him to clean up after the killings. That man's name, according to Graves, is Avery Hammond."

As the camera zoomed out, revealing the entrance to Hammond's property behind Willow, Rhino exhaled heavily. "Goddamn."

Willow turned to glance briefly over her left shoulder, then reconnected with the camera. "Mr. Hammond's expensive home lies at the end of this Tara-like lane. He's a prominent businessman whose family has owned large parcels of property in this area for over a century. Today, Mr. Hammond operates several businesses in and around Bon Terre, including a casino. Yesterday, Graves told Detective Brenner that he buried the weapon Avery Hammond allegedly asked him to dispose of somewhere on the grounds of Hammond's home. Brenner plans to unearth the shotgun, hoping for evidence that will reveal the killer's identity."

Suddenly, above Willow's shoulder, a black SUV raced down the lane. She flinched, possibly at the sound of the engine. "Back to you, Don," she said hastily.

Rhino stepped forward and mashed the power switch with his heavy thumb, then turned and looked at me like a man whose livestock has found the one spot in the fence he'd failed to repair. "Was this what you wanted to tell me about?"

"I've been trying since this morning. But now's not the time. That SUV looked like it was on a collision course with the news team. We'd better get out to Hammond's place."

Rhino stared briefly into the blank television screen. "I'll radio Officer Thomas."

After dispatching her from a radio in his office, Rhino led me out the back door to his cruiser. He flicked on the flashing lights, but not the siren, then wheeled around the building and zoomed along Main Street. Fishing gear rattled in the backseat.

I watched the last of the Main Street shops whiz past my window. "What you heard is pretty much what Graves told me yesterday at Angola."

"I hope you weren't the one that told this reporter about it."

"Graves has been using the press all along," I said. "I don't know if he talked to her before or after he talked to me, but I'm going to find out."

"You expect me to let you dig up Hammond's property?" Rhino asked.

"I'm hoping you'll go along," I said, knowing I'd do without him if necessary.

Rhino drew in a deep breath. "This is a sight more than I'd planned on."

"What do you mean by that?" I asked, searching his narrowed eyes.

He glanced at me, then regripped the steering wheel.

Soon the lights of Jarla Thomas's cruiser flickered ahead of us. As we pulled in behind her vehicle, she knelt beside someone sitting on the ground near a green van. We jumped out of Rhino's car.

Jarla and a man with a ponytail and a worn-out T-shirt from a 1995 James Taylor tour helped Willow Ashe up from the asphalt.

"What's going on?" Rhino blustered.

"According to these two," Jarla said, "Ms. Ashe was assaulted by a young man who fled in a black M-class Mercedes. He sped down the driveway and almost hit the van, then got out and ripped the microphone away from Ms. Ashe, knocking her to the ground. He also took the television camera and tossed it in the weeds."

"That guy was juiced," the cameraman said. "The network had already cut our live feed, but we got tape rolling. I got him attacking Willow."

"Rather than put the camera down and try to protect her?" I asked.

Willow pressed a hand to the base of her spine. "I told him to, Jack. Derek and I were both doing our jobs."

"This morning we talked about the trouble that causes."

Rhino looked at us as if we'd been speaking in a foreign language. "Are you all right, ma'am? This isn't typical Bon Terre hospitality. 'Course, you ain't a typical Bon Terre guest."

"I landed on my tailbone and lost my breath," Willow said. "Nothing more."

"I'm pretty sure I know who knocked you over," Rhino said. "Eddie Hammond loves to drive his uncle's SUV. We'll bring him in, ma'am."

Derek grinned. "Got it all on tape if you need evidence."

"Did he say anything to you?" I asked Willow.

"He said he'd dig Jack Brenner's grave before they dug on Hammond property. And he called me names. Bitch was the kindest." Willow touched Rhino's arm. "Please, Sheriff. Let it go."

A cold, familiar feeling settled inside me like a dense fog on the morning of a trip you dreaded making. It came in the form of rage. I was slipping into the role of protector. Eddie Hammond had hurt Willow.

"If you don't wanna press charges, I'm going to the house," Rhino said. "Officer Thomas, see if these fine people need anything. Then take Detective Brenner back to his car."

"Sheriff," I said. "We still have a problem."

"I'm looking at it." He eyed me like I was a leaky faucet that had almost annoyed him enough to fix. "But it'll have to wait till tomorrow."

"I'm talking about the shotgun," I said. "Now that Ms. Ashe has let the proverbial feline out of the bag, what's to prevent Hammond from digging it up tonight?"

Rhino wiped his hand over his face. "This place is over a thousand acres. I don't recall this young lady specifying a location. You afraid he'll strip-mine the entire property?"

Willow had been vague on that point. I wondered if it was purposeful, or if Graves had given her less detail than he'd given me. There was nothing Hammond could do short of having his henchmen scour his land with metal detectors. And the last place he'd look would be under his slate patio.

"You've got a point, Sheriff," I finally said.

"Be in my office at eight in the morning. We're gonna have us a frank discussion. Your lieutenant gave me a choice of deputizing you or having your case turned over to the FBI's New Orleans field office. I'm thinking I picked the wrong poison." He tipped his hat to Willow. "Ma'am." Then he turned toward his car.

"You all okay?" Jarla asked Willow as Derek jogged around the van to retrieve his equipment.

"We're fine."

Jarla shrugged. "Okay. Ready, Detective Brenner?"

Willow smiled. "I'll take him back."

Jarla's crystal blue eyes searched mine for an objection. I suspect what she saw reminded her of a deer in her headlights.

"Tomorrow's my day off," she said before turning away. "Make sure you don't let Officer Trevino catch you coming around the bend in the highway. He's been known to hand-calibrate his radar gun."

Derek stowed his gear in the rear of the van, then drove Willow and me to Trahan's Bed and Breakfast. He got out and pulled some of the equipment from the back while Willow scooted over to the driver's side and I took the passenger seat.

He stopped in front of the window and waited for Willow to lower it. "I'm gonna look at the footage of that asshole. We'll call for a pizza later."

"Do it whenever you get hungry. I'm not sure how long I'll be."

Derek looked at me as though I were a poorly framed video clip, then hiked a nylon bag on his shoulder and left.

"My car's at the sheriff's office," I said. "It's five minutes away. I don't think you'll be missing dinner."

Willow smiled and turned the van around.

As we drove toward Bon Terre, I noticed a lone brown pelican flying south toward the peach-tinged clouds that hung over the Gulf. He'd probably strayed inland to raid a catfish farm. The bird could hold more in his beak than his belly. I knew the feeling.

"I'm sorry for what I said this morning," I said. "At least the way I said it."

"You made it clear you don't trust me. We're both used to that in our lines of work."

"I got personal. I have trouble thinking of you as just a reporter. As much as I wish you weren't, I know you're doing what you have to do."

Willow offered a bemused glance. "You wish I hadn't broken the story and given you a shot at solving your cousin's murder?"

I watched the pelican disappear beyond the treeline. "Guess I should thank you."

"At Molly's, you said it was a shitty thing to do."

"I was upset you didn't let me know ahead of time."

"And Jack Brenner doesn't like not being in control of a situation," she said.

"And I sure as hell didn't like Rhino Perrot finding out about the murder weapon buried on Avery Hammond's property from the evening news."

"Before you get indignant again, don't you want to ask me a question?"

"Yeah. Why don't you and your cameraman go back to Atlanta?"

She slowed the van as we approached town. "What if I'd broadcast the exact location where Emmett Graves buried the shotgun?"

I studied her face. Her eyes were golden in the early evening shadow. "Do you know?"

"That's the question I was expecting, Detective. Do I have to prompt you for everything?"

"Just tell me. Did Emmett Graves tell you where he buried the shotgun?"

She didn't speak until she spotted the sheriff's office and pulled into a parking space next to my car. She killed the engine, then swiveled toward me. "Under the oak tree in back of the house. Twelve feet from the trunk towards the bayou."

My body fell back against the van door. "When did he tell you?"

Her eyes, now facing the setting sun, lit up. "The day I met you at Angola."

"What did he tell you about the night of the murders?"

Willow repeated a sketchier version of the story Graves had told me. Graves had given me details because he was playing with my mind.

"He tell you anything else I might want to know?"

She shook her head.

I hoped she was telling me the truth. "Why did you try to talk to Hammond this morning?"

"Derek was ready to get his picture if he'd come outside and we could have shown it on the broadcast this evening. And I wanted to get a feel for the man."

Same reason I'd been to see him. "But Creed Beaumont turned you away."

"He thought I was buying his flirtations, but he gave me pretty good insight into what we're . . . you're dealing with. Kindly city fathers don't hire men like him."

"I warned you about him this morning."

"For which reason I had our research department check on him. Beaumont was an Army Ranger in the attempt to capture Noriega in Panama. His team took the airport."

"Beaumont told me Hammond hired him after he left the military."

"It's a little more personal than that," Willow said. "He saved Hammond's life in Panama. The army didn't count on the PDF defending the airport so vigorously and they also failed to recognize that two civilian flights had landed just before the assault. One was a private jet owned by a Louisiana oil man who'd taken some buddies sport fishing in Chile, including Hammond. He had the misfortune to walk into a men's room where two PDF were holed up. To make a long story short, Hammond shit in his pants, one Ranger took two bullets, and the PDF men ate a couple of grenades after Beaumont dragged Hammond out."

"Regards to your research department. Mine is an obese cop anxious to get back out on the street." I shook my head. "Tell me why you visited Faith Tilden."

"I was interested in seeing the site of the murders."

"What's the connection with Faith?" I asked. "Graves said he found the bodies at Beulah Baptist Church. I drove Escondido Road this morning and didn't see any church."

"The congregation outgrew their sanctuary and relocated five years after the murders. They sold the property to Faith Tilden. She built Meal Thyme on it."

I felt the chill you're supposed to feel when someone passes over the ground that will be your grave. I'd stood on the spot where David was killed.

Willow smiled. "I found that out by going to the library this morning. The director told me. Faith filled in the details. The building next to the restaurant is the old church. She said she couldn't stand to tear it down, so she removed the steeple out of respect and uses it for storage. I didn't know she worked with your cousin until she told me. She told me a lot about those boys. Faith was very close to them."

Willow turned her head, revealing the side of her face I hadn't been able to see as we drove.

My neck warmed as I noticed a bruise on her jaw. "Did Eddie Hammond hit you?"

She lightly touched her face. “The mike caught me here when he pulled it away from me.”

I reached across the console and used my forefinger to tilt her chin up. “Looks nasty.”

“I carry strong medicine in my makeup kit.”

“I’ll have a talk with the little weasel.” I started to remove my hand.

Willow grasped it. “There’s a saying I heard when I was covering some business guru’s seminar. He said if the only tool you have is a hammer, you see every problem as a nail.”

I didn’t resist her sure, but pliant, grip.

“Just because you ride a white horse, Jack, doesn’t make me a damsel in distress.”

“Make it all right, Daddy,” Sarah or Carrie would say, holding up a boo-boo. A daughter’s pleading, but also the voice of most adult women in my life. Women whose happiness, at least in my mind, depended on me. Willow was a woman who held no expectation of rescue, a woman confident in her own power. Which kind of woman did I fear most?

I slipped my hand from Willow’s. “I’m still uneasy about giving Hammond a heads-up.”

“You can always stake out his property,” Willow said.

“With you and your cameraman?”

“He’s off the clock, but I’ll volunteer.” She smiled.

No room in the beak, much less the belly. “I’m not worried about him digging up evidence. I’m worried about what else he might do. Be careful.”

I got out of the van and walked around it to my car.

She lowered her window. “There’s still one question you haven’t asked me, Jack.”

I moved up to her and placed my hand on the bottom frame of the open window. “Prompt me.”

“I didn’t give specifics about the location of the shotgun in my broadcast. I could have.”

“Alleged shotgun. Alleged location.”

“True. But if I’d done it, Hammond could have dug up the

evidence before you could have obtained a court order. Assuming it's there, of course."

The slate patio would have made that difficult but Willow didn't know about that. "Being helpful would have been not mentioning it at all so we could have surprised him with a court order."

She shook her head. "Hammond's lawyers would have you out of there in twenty minutes. It only takes one friendly judge to issue a temporary restraint. But now, he has no choice but to let you dig. A man like Hammond won't refuse with the kind of publicity I've created."

Her logic was sound. Willow had done me another favor. "Want me to thank you again?"

"There's an idea." She placed her hand on top of mine and leaned out the window.

"First tell me why you did it," I said, feeling the heat of her breath on my face.

"I did it for you." Willow placed soft but purposeful lips on mine. They parted—an invitation. Her tongue brushed my upper lip, but only once. She'd left an open door whose threshold could be crossed solely of my own volition.

I drew back, but only inches.

"How about that stakeout?" she whispered.

I kissed her on the cheek and whispered, "Your pizza's getting cold." Then I kissed her other cheek. "Thanks for the help."

Her hand lingered on mine as she slowly pulled her head inside the van. There was no disappointment in her eyes. Rather they beamed with the recognition that while this was not the time or place, we'd affirmed that those other times and places were real, and ours alone. Besides, her parting smile told me, tomorrow's another day.

I watched her drive down Main Street toward a sky streaked with orange and a nail-polish pink that reminded me of Faith Tilden's impatiens. I took the old route home, crossing the Huey Long Bridge to the West Bank. Then turning onto River Road, I lowered the windows and breathed in the sweet odor of wild grass along the levee as dry lightning flashed high in the darkening southern sky.

14

My cell phone beeped away my reverie and Lieutenant Forrest Utley's angry voice replaced the silent light show.

"Where the hell are you, Brenner?"

"Leaving Jefferson Parish on River Road."

"Keep heading east," Utley said. "I'll wait for you at the station."

When I arrived, Utley was outside pacing the pavement, still damp from late-afternoon showers. Ozone and bus exhaust mingled with the odors of wet brick.

"Guess you watched the evening news," I said.

He locked his hands behind him and stepped well into my personal space. "So did the DA and the superintendent. You've been responsible for too many surprises for too many people."

"I was as shocked as anyone by the broadcast," I said.

"You should have talked to someone immediately about what Graves told you."

I held up my palms. "I tried all day to talk to Rhino Perrot."

"Relentlessly, I'm sure. You try calling me?"

"Okay, Lieutenant. I hear you."

"Sheriff Perrot called me this evening to tell me he regrets agreeing to let you handle this investigation."

I laughed tentatively. "He'd rather have a gaggle of FBI agents in Bon Terre?"

The way Utley's eyes bore into me reminded me of my coach the year I played basketball in high school and missed two free throws near the end of a close game. "The FBI wouldn't touch this case. They didn't like the odds."

I furrowed my brow. "What are you talking about? Rhino said I got the investigation because he didn't want to be overrun by the Feds."

"You gotta love a good bluff," Utley said.

I shook my head. "I don't get it."

"I thought Sheriff Perrot would more likely accept having you investigate if he thought you were the lesser of two evils."

"*You* thought?" Then it hit me, causing me to feel like a kid learning Dad was the tooth fairy. "You set it all up?"

Utley's face turned from stone to flesh. "You're not on your own here, Brenner. I know you think I'm a hardass." He paused until I nodded sheepishly, then peered into the light filtering through the front doors of the station. "I was upset when I found out you'd been to Bon Terre on department time. But I understand why you did it. What I don't understand is why you run off on your own when there are people who want to help you."

Must be that white horse thing Willow had lectured me about.

"Be straight with me, Brenner," Utley said. "I'm on your side. What did you have to do with the broadcast this evening?"

"Nothing." I swallowed. "Directly."

Utley's eyes narrowed. I summarized my meeting with Emmett Graves, then told him about Willow and me.

"So you're right," I said after I'd finished. "People have been trying to help me. I guess I haven't shown much appreciation."

Utley chuckled as he unbuttoned his collar and loosened his tie, something I'd never seen him do. "You and Willow Ashe. That's rich."

"She started all this to get national exposure for herself," I said. "But she's worked everything to my advantage. Like you have. Thank you, Lieutenant."

He looked intently at me, but more like a cop than a commander.

"Sheriff Perrot considers you a tick buried in a tender place to scratch," Utley said. "But he's gonna be a big help, too."

"Like how?"

"He got Hammond to agree to let you dig on his property."

"Outstanding! Saves the hassle of getting a court order."

"Your friend Willow was right. The publicity leaves him no choice but to cooperate."

"Hammond's not the type to go down without a fight," I said. "That means he doesn't expect us to find anything that will hurt him."

Utley shrugged. "Maybe you won't. We'll know tomorrow. By the way, the DA wants Mary Evans to go with you to help make sure no evidence is compromised."

"There's something that's crossed my mind, Lieutenant. What if Rhino Perrot's working for Hammond? What if he's helping Hammond hide something?"

"Don't worry. Perrot's on our side."

"Hope you're right."

It was still dark when I left the house the next morning to pick up Mary Evans. Thirty minutes later we drove south along the highway. A saffron mist floated above the rice and soy fields like the breath of the rising sun. As I finished filling her in on events to date, I decelerated sharply at the bend in the road before the Bon Terre speed trap. No patrol car. But five minutes later, pulling in front of the sheriff's office, I knew why. A forlorn man wearing work clothes and a pipeline company cap stood on the walk. A pink receipt hung from his hand like a lifeless flag while an officer strode past him to the police cruiser. Probably Trevino. As I walked around the car to retrieve the wheelchair, he tipped the brim of his hat and eyed me like a man who'd netted his first speckled trout of the morning.

When Mary and I entered Rhino Perrot's office, I felt like a fish flipped on a frying pan. Rhino stepped from behind the justice of the peace bench at the back of the office and rambled toward us as though we were weeds he aimed to yank up from an otherwise immaculate lawn.

"Brenner, you're damned lucky you got Lieutenant Utley on your side. I was ready to trade you in for the whole goddamn FBI New Orleans field office." Then his eyes dropped to Mary. "Excuse me, ma'am."

"Sheriff, I'm Mary Evans with the district attorney's office." She held out her hand. "I understand you plan to remove evidence from a citizen's property this morning."

"Welcome to the party, ma'am." Rhino released Mary's firm grip and glared at me. "I've pulled in a couple of parish workers on overtime. I hope you get what you want out of this and then leave us alone."

"The workers bringing a jackhammer, Sheriff?"

"Goddamn, Brenner. I thought hemorrhoids was one senior frailty I'd escaped, but I feel a big one crawling up my butt right now. What the hell are you talking about?"

"Graves says the shotgun's buried twelve feet from the big oak in Hammond's backyard. His patio extends out at least thirty feet."

Rhino closed his eyes and exhaled. "Ow. Bet it's a bleeder." He glanced at Mary. "Excuse me, ma'am, but your friend's a pain— Hell. Let's get going."

"We'll follow," I said. "I've got evidence containers in my trunk."

Rhino walked around his desk to grab his keys and hat, then pointed his thumb to a doughnut-shaped cushion hanging from the wall. "A gag gift for my fifty-fifth. Looks like I'm really gonna need it."

When we reached the entrance to Avery Hammond's property, a stocky black man and a skinny redheaded kid with flesh the color of boiled shrimp were waiting in a utility truck on the side of the road. They fell in behind us as we followed the sheriff's cruiser past the circular drive in front of the big house and pulled around back. Willow Ashe and her cameraman, Derek, stood next to their green van.

"What the hell's she doing here?" I said.

"This should be interesting," Mary said.

I popped the trunk. Rhino beat me to the rear of my car, lifted out Mary's wheelchair, and helped her into it.

Mary smiled up at him. "You're so kind, Sheriff."

"I want you to understand my animosity is directed only toward your friend," he said.

"Can your wheelchair travel over the lawn?" I asked.

"As long as it's not muddy," Mary said.

"That won't be your problem, ma'am," Rhino said. "The Hammonds got a couple of big dogs."

"Morning, Jack, Sheriff," Willow purred as she approached us in a form-fitting black suit, hem well above the knee, the open jacket revealing a white silk blouse with the top three buttons undone.

Rhino's gaze lingered at the point of the V. "Any reason you're here?"

"Mr. Hammond will explain," she said.

Rhino scanned from Willow, to Mary, to me. "There was this reporter, a lawyer, and a dumb-ass cop. I think someone once told me a joke that starts out like that." He strode across the lawn toward Avery Hammond, who was sitting at the wrought iron table on his patio, sipping from a china cup.

"Your being here doesn't help our investigation," Mary said to Willow.

Willow looked down at her with a saccharine smile. "I promise not to get in the way."

"I can't believe Hammond allowed you on his property," I said.

"We came by early this morning and I had a nice little chat with Mr. Hammond. I told him if he'd let me tape the excavation, I wouldn't press charges against his nephew." Willow fastened button number three, then patted me on the chest. "We both have work to do, but I'd like to continue last night's conversation some time."

Mary put her wheelchair in motion. I followed her to the patio, where Rhino and Hammond were talking.

Hammond looked at Mary. "My, my. We are indeed blessed with beauty this morning. Who might you be?"

"I'm with the Orleans Parish DA's office. I want to have record of your permission to dig on your property." She pulled a document from her briefcase and handed it to him.

"This doesn't include the house or buildings, does it?"

"I can get it changed if you think it would help."

"Pretty *and* snappy." Hammond grinned. "I'd be happy to sign this. But we need to get something clear first." He turned to me. "The sheriff just told me you want to dig up my patio."

"The location Graves gave me was twelve feet on the opposite side of the oak."

He glanced toward the bayou. "I said I have nothing to hide. But those slate tiles are expensive."

"The parish will take care of restoring everything to your satisfaction, Mr. Hammond," Rhino said.

"Fortunately they're laid on a stone dust base, so the boys won't need to bust 'em out." Hammond tipped the flask into his coffee cup. "Let's get on with this subterranean Easter egg hunt, Sheriff."

Rhino whistled and waved at the workers who'd been waiting in their truck.

"Please, Mizz . . ." Hammond motioned to Mary.

"Evans," she said.

"Let's take care of this paperwork over coffee."

An hour later, the workers had lifted the slate from the bedding over an area six feet square and stacked the tiles neatly to the side. Then they dug in a three-foot radius from the center point, removing dirt in six-inch layers.

Avery Hammond passed the time sitting at the wrought iron table, taking nips from his flask and chatting with Willow. Rhino directed the work while Derek hovered over the site, periodically taking footage. I used the time to tell Mary about my conversation with Willow the previous night, sans the kiss.

"She's been pulling the strings all along," Mary said.

I shook my head. "This is Emmett Graves's doing. Willow fell into her big story by chance."

"What about your strings?"

My eyes followed the movement of the shovels. "I turned down a solid offer last night."

"Such self-discipline."

I looked down and caught the kind of sly grin I'd expect from Arceneaux.

"Got something, Sheriff!" the stocky man called as they reached a depth of two feet.

"Clear the dirt with your hands, Slim," Rhino commanded.

Derek, who'd taken a seat on a stack of tiles, jumped up. We all crept closer to the clearing, including Hammond, who suddenly showed an interest.

"You want in the shot?" Derek asked Willow.

She shook her head. "I'll do a voice-over if we use it."

Seconds later Slim held up a rusted horseshoe.

Rhino pulled a cigar from his mouth. "Put that aside. My son collects Civil War memorabilia. Union cavalry rode all over this area."

Another foot down and twenty minutes later, the redheaded kid's shovel failed to penetrate. He tapped Slim on the shoulder and they began to work with their hands.

"Have a look, Sheriff," the kid said.

Rhino peered into the hole. "I don't see nothing."

"It's something black and plastic," Slim said.

"Graves said he wrapped the shotgun in trash bags and wound it with duct tape," I said.

Slim nodded to me. "That's what it looks like. Whatever's inside is hard."

"Then shovel around it some more," Rhino commanded. "You oughta be able to lift it out of the dirt then."

Five minutes later the workers had cleared the dirt from around an object four feet long, bound in plastic. Avery Hammond stood near the giant oak, his dark gray eyes fixed on the crater as he tilted up his flask and swallowed. After fastening the cap and returning the flask to his back pocket, he crossed his arms and glared at me as though the scar in the ground were an offense that would not be repaired by the replacement of tiles.

Slim pulled out a pocketknife.

"Don't!" I shouted.

Rhino stepped next to me. "Ever learn in school about that Pandora woman?"

As I descended into the pit to recover the plastic-covered object, I suddenly realized Willow was talking to the camera.

". . . and Detective Jack Brenner has retrieved the evidence to be inspected later by forensics examiners. But if indeed it is a weapon, it remains to be seen if Detective Brenner can prove it to be the one used to kill David Brenner and Elton Jackson."

15

I pulled myself up from the large cavity in Avery Hammond's expensive patio holding what I hoped was the shotgun Graves claimed he'd buried. Willow had asked the right question. Even if it was the murder weapon and thoroughly wrapped in plastic, what could the forensics team find on it?

"Would you like to make a statement, Mr. Hammond?" Willow moved next to him and held the microphone to his face.

Hammond looked directly at me. "I don't care what you found. Emmett Graves is a lying son of a bitch."

Hammond swatted the mike away and turned for the house. Willow followed, peppering him with questions, while Derek backpedaled to keep him in his viewfinder.

Rhino motioned to the workers. "Fix this patio up good as new. You're on overtime, so I know you won't rush it." Then turning to me he said, "We may as well of pulled up a nest of water moccasins from that hole."

Despite Lieutenant Utley's intuition that Rhino was on our side, my gut told me he was hiding something. "You sound disappointed. If you didn't want me to find anything, why did you agree to let me investigate?"

He inspected his now extinguished cigar. "I told you. Didn't want the damn FBI crawling all over the parish like fire ants."

"Or maybe you were hoping a lone investigator wouldn't be successful."

Rhino threw the butt into the dirt. "That's a goddamn inflammatory thing to say to a another lawman, son."

The way his neck reddened and bulged, forming a white ring above his uniform collar, reminded me of Arceneaux. His reaction appeared sincere. If he was holding something back, perhaps it had nothing to do with the murders of David and Deer. But it might have everything to do with Avery Hammond.

"I'm sorry," I said. "I misinterpreted your remark. I know you'll have hell to pay with the lord of the manor. I appreciate your help."

"If you only—" Rhino stopped himself with a deep breath, then looked down and patted his shirt pocket. Finding it empty, he gazed down at the stogie lying in the dark, moist earth. "Aw, shit."

Mary and I returned to my car in silence. I popped the trunk and gently slid my discovery into a large yellow evidence bag, then helped Mary into the front seat and put her chair in the back. As we left Hammond's property, I called Lieutenant Utley and briefed him, promising a complete report later in the day.

"I overheard what you said to the sheriff," Mary said. "You doubting his honesty?"

"I believe he's a good cop and a good man. But I think there's something going on he's not telling me about. And it's all about Avery Hammond."

"If he's letting you do your job, why do you care if he keeps his business to himself?"

"Because I believe Emmett Graves was connected to Hammond then, and he's connected to him now. After Graves finished his story about the night of the murders, he made a remark that implied his drug conviction was Hammond's fault. And since Graves worked for him, Hammond's businesses likely include more than life insurance, appliances, and a casino. Maybe Rhino's onto something and my investigation is a complication for him."

"If you can prove Hammond killed your cousin, you might be doing the sheriff a favor," Mary said.

I shook my head. "I don't believe Hammond did it. At least not himself. And if he ordered the killings, who else would have done it for him other than Graves?"

Mary nodded. "In which case, why would Graves help you find the murder weapon and why would Hammond agree to let us dig?"

"This whole case is full of missing motives."

Passing through Bon Terre on our way back to the city, I spotted Officer Trevino's cruiser in the opposite lane following another speed trap victim. I waved to him and pressed the accelerator until I hit eighty. Thirty minutes later, we crossed the I-310 bridge over the Mississippi. I began to think about the River Road route I'd taken last night and the events that caused me to choose it, but my cell phone interrupted.

"Hey, Jack," Arceneaux sputtered. "Got some news for you."

"As long as it doesn't involve a reporter."

"Huh?"

"Willow Ashe is camped in Bon Terre."

Arceneaux whistled. "Saw her on the tube last night at Fuzzy's. She could do a report on hepatitis in the oyster beds and I'd still have a hard-on." He commenced a hearty chuckle, then aborted it. "Hey, Jack. Didn't mean no disrespect, her being your old girlfriend and all."

"She has that effect on guys," I said.

"Say. What's this about Graves leading you to a shotgun?"

"We dug it up this morning. I'll tell you about it in a little while. Mary Evans and I are on our way back. I've got to take the weapon to the crime lab first. What's your news?"

Arceneaux puffed a few breaths into the speaker. "Uh, it'll wait till you get here."

"Why so cryptic?" I asked.

Silence. Then, "Why can't you fucking speak English?"

Mary and I drove the shotgun to the forensics lab on Broad Street. When I asked the technician how long it would take for them to get to it, she told me Lieutenant Utley had pulled strings. Top priority, she said. I handed her my card with my cell phone number.

• • •

After dropping off Mary, I returned to the station and found Arceneaux sitting in my chair, a familiar collection of files, loose papers, Styrofoam cups, and food wrappings on *my* desktop.

Arceneaux looked up as I hung my coat on the cloak tree, then he glanced over the refuse covering my blotter. "I figured since you was part-time these days—"

My startled stare stopped him. I pointed to the handgun strapped to his side. "That have anything to do with what you wanted to tell me?"

Arceneaux's grin was as broad as his belly. "I'm back on the job, Jack. Utley caught me sneaking by his office this morning and said the doc cleared me."

"That's terrific, partner." But I wondered how much longer I'd be calling him that. Knowing Utley's plan to separate us dampened my joy. I clasped Arceneaux's shoulder. "Congratulations. Beer and oysters on me tonight."

"Anyone else I woulda hugged," he said. "But after the son of a bitch handed me my gun back, he orders me to run a background on some asshole named Creed Beaumont."

"I was the one who asked for that." I eyed two Styrofoam cups lined with sticky brown residue lying on their sides near the edge of my desk.

Arceneaux scowled. "He coulda told me. Who the hell is Creed Beaumont anyway?"

"You tell me when you find out," I said. "Start with military records."

Arceneaux shrugged it off, then said, "After Utley told me to run traps on this Beaumont character, he did something really spooky."

"What?"

"He smiled and shook my hand and said, 'Welcome back.' "

"Pretty strange for the Lieutenant, all right." I imagined Utley doing his best to strike a rapport with Arceneaux before dissolving our partnership. Suddenly I felt foolish and selfish. I'd been focused on my own feelings of impending loss and hadn't considered what a blow this would be to Arceneaux.

"Hey, Jack. Guess he's told you." Keisha swooped around us and began deftly lifting the scum-encrusted coffee cups, some empty wrappers, bits of potato chips, and loose peanuts from among the folders and papers on my desk.

"You can join us at Fuzzy's tonight to celebrate, if you'd like," I said.

She smiled like a blind person invited to a painting exhibit as she dumped the trash into the basket. Then she brushed off her hands and returned to her desk. Arceneaux's desk.

"Arceneaux may talk and look like a redneck, but he's one hell of a cop." Keisha pulled a sanitary wipe from her top drawer.

"Whaddaya mean, redneck?" A blush rose above his collar.

"Never give Arceneaux a compliment," I said. "He'll play it back on you for years."

Keisha dropped the wipe into her wastebasket. "No more bragging on you, Arceneaux."

"She talks more than you do, Brenner. But she don't use such big words." The chair creaked as Arceneaux leaned back and looked up at me. "Say. I been reading the Bowen file. So I'm going over your report where the store manager's telling you about the three shots he heard. I get an idea, so I call him up and ask him to tell me the story again, and he does. The manager says he heard a *blam*. Then he said there was a short pause, then *blam-blam*."

"He didn't mention that before," I said.

"Right. But I'd gotten to thinking about the missing slugs."

I plopped into the side chair by my desk and covered my face. "Return fire."

Arceneaux slapped the desktop triumphantly, causing a loose page to flutter to the floor. "Exactly. He told me maybe the next two shots sounded a little different than the first."

"We know Steven didn't have a gun," Keisha said. "Which means there was another person nearby. Lot of people pass by the store walking up Miro to Napoleon."

"Including those coming from the Blue Pelican," Arceneaux said. "You gotta believe most of their customers carry."

"And wouldn't be shocked at having someone shoot at them," Keisha said.

"For true," Arceneaux said.

"If someone returned fire, we've been looking for the other two slugs in the wrong location," I said.

Arceneaux retrieved the errant page from the linoleum and tossed it into the sea of paper in front of him. "Let's see if we can find them."

"They may be in the shooter's car," I said. "Or his body."

Arceneaux shook his head. "Already thought of the shooter taking a hit and checked local ER's. Didn't no one show up with an unexplained gun wound that night or the next day."

"Then send out a couple of crime scene analysts," I said.

"Let's do it ourselves." Arceneaux stood, my desk chair groaning in relief, the expression on his face like that of a bird dog bounding into the field from his master's truck on the first day of dove season. "It's my lucky day."

Twenty minutes later, the three of us stood next to the pay phone where Steven Bowen was shot. The heat was as ruthless as a police dog trained to bite and hold.

"It's dark at night along the sidewalk next to the store," Keisha said. "Someone could have been walking up the street from the Blue Pelican toward Napoleon and fired at the car from the other side of the phone booth."

"And assuming the car moving down Miro was the target of the second and third shot, and they missed, the slugs would have landed over there," I said.

Six eyes traveled up Miro across Napoleon.

"Did anyone canvass the places over there?" Arceneaux asked.

I looked toward a small strip center containing a patisserie, a barbershop, an insurance agent, and a psychic. "All those places were closed."

"Bullshit." Arceneaux pointed to Madame Charmaine's Fortune Boutique. "The Madame reels in her marks at night."

Keisha shook her head. "I'm telling you. The lights were out and there were no cars in the parking lot."

"Maybe the Madame was on a cruise to Haiti," Arceneaux said.

Keisha rolled her eyes as we followed him across the street. I wondered how much of her lighthearted welcoming of Arceneaux's return was an act. And I wondered how long it would be before Utley would make known his plan to pair me with Keisha.

Arceneaux stepped up to the raised walk in front of the Madame's and turned to scan the concrete between the storefronts and the crime scene. "Depending on where the car was when the second shooter fired, we could find a slug anywhere along here." He slapped the whitewashed cinder block.

We walked to the insurance agent's office at the end of the strip center. Then we slowly worked our way back toward Madame Charmaine's, inspecting the masonry and the grease-stained concrete parking lot.

It was obvious the return to street duty had reenergized Arceneaux with a quiet rapture. He scrutinized the facade of the patisserie with a concentration so intense his nose didn't even twitch at the sweet redolence wafting from the doorway.

"Maybe this isn't your lucky day," Keisha finally said, wiping the perspiration from her neck. "Unless you count losing ten pounds from poking around in this heat good fortune."

"We ain't checked the side of the building yet. If the shooter fired at the car straight on, the bullets could have landed back there." Arceneaux passed the patisserie entrance without a glance.

Keisha and I followed him to the end of the building where a narrow alley dead-ended at a wooden fence with razor wire mounted on top. The sweating cinder block and a half dozen overflowing trash cans crammed into the alley stirred an olfactory cocktail of mold and ripe refuse.

Undeterred by the stink, Arceneaux glanced back toward the phone booth across the street, then moved along the side of the building. He stopped at a doorway opening into the alley, inspected it, and moved deeper toward the collection of green plastic cans. Then he squatted in front of the one closest to us.

Keisha held her nose. "Nothing here. Can we go now?"

Arceneaux didn't look up. "We gotta check 'em all. Don't know what position they was in the night of the shooting."

Seconds later a large, dark form scuttled from beneath one of the cans Arceneaux was handling and vanished beneath the wooden fence.

Keisha gasped and backpedaled. "Shit! I don't do rats."

"What you saw was too big for a rat," Arceneaux said. "It's a roach."

"Don't do roaches, either," she said.

"We all do roaches in New Orleans," I said, holding my breath as I twisted one of the cans to check for bullet holes.

We reached the last can. Arceneaux pulled it away from the back fence, toppling a plastic bag that broke open, spilling chicken parts and greasy take-out boxes onto the asphalt. But as Keisha and I jumped back, the unmistakable *clack-clack* of a pump-action shotgun chambering a round echoed in the concrete canyon.

16

We turned slowly toward a woman whose delicate café-au-lait hands confidently leveled the barrel of a shotgun at us. Allowing for the red turban piled atop her head, the lady training her weapon on us wasn't more than five feet tall.

"What business you got with Madame Charmaine's trash?" she asked.

The voice was stern, with a clipped West Indian accent. She had lustrous chestnut skin and wore a rainbow-colored dress.

"We're police officers," I said.

"Never seen you before," Madame Charmaine said.

"That's 'cause we ain't Vice," Arceneaux sputtered. "Wanna aim that somewheres else?"

"Show me your badge." Charmaine gestured with her shotgun.

"Thanks for sharing your lucky day," Keisha grumbled to Arceneaux as I pulled my shield from inside my coat and held it out to the Madame.

She kept her finger on the trigger guard. "What you doing in my rubbish?

Arceneaux grunted. "We ain't interested in your headless chickens and goat guts."

"Entrails," Keisha whispered.

"Don't *you* start with them big words, goddamn it," he said.

I pointed to Charmaine's weapon. "Do you mind?"

Madame Charmaine lifted the muzzle upward. Her eyes took the shape of giant almonds.

"A young man was shot to death at the phone booth across the street last week," I said. "We believe someone returned fire in this direction. A bullet may have hit one of your trash cans."

She carefully leaned her shotgun against the wall. "The boy in the green jacket."

Keisha's eyes narrowed. "How do you know that? Your place was dark that night."

Arceneaux sniffed. "She got a full report from the good folks in the neighborhood who got so much disposable income they can afford the Madame's tea leaves."

"His spirit cries out." The fortune-teller's eyes glimmered intently, as if observing some action only she could see. "The boy was not meant to die."

"You have something you wanna tell us, Madame?" Arceneaux asked. "Or is your babbling coming from some lagniappe in your incense?"

"There is another man who wears a green jacket." she said. "He use the pay phone across the street. That boy die in his place."

"How often do you see this man in the green jacket?" I asked.

"Two, three times a week," Charmaine said.

"Mistaken identity," Keisha said.

Arceneaux's eyebrows rose. "Can you describe this guy?"

"The distance is great," she said. "Madame Charmaine sees better the spirits."

Arceneaux smirked. "Well, put on your voodoo contact lenses and tell us what you can."

She quickly scanned Arceneaux's body. "*Much* thinner than you." Then she nodded to me. "And shorter than you."

"Like Steven," Keisha said.

"Does the man park at the convenience store before using the phone?" I asked, hoping for a make on an automobile.

"He walk from the bar."

Arceneaux snickered. "Spend a lot of time looking out your peephole?"

"After sundown, my door wide open for all who seek help," she said. "Perhaps the bones of the saints will reveal this man's name. The moon will be right in two days time. Come back then."

Arceneaux narrowed his eyes. "Them bones is you going over to the Blue Pelican to question the bartender and patrons about a customer that wears a green jacket, hoping you'll get a name or a better description, which you'll then give us, expecting some payoff. We can work that mojo ourselves."

Madame Charmaine smiled. "You do not believe."

"I believe your magic causes fools' money to disappear. Mind if we get back to our business?" Arceneaux kicked away the chicken wings and food containers he'd spilled, then sat on his haunches to peer at the front side of the refuse can.

I turned to Madame Charmaine. "Looks like this garbage has been rotting back here for some time. How often is it collected?"

"This garbage stay here a month sometime. Why you think I got so many cans?"

"These are all yours?" I asked. "What about the other businesses?"

"Man who owns the building charge too much for service. Madame Charmaine waits for her lazy brother-in-law to move this trash."

"That's gotta be some kind of health violation," Keisha said.

Charmaine smiled. Someone in the city was getting his palm read and greased at the same time.

"Nothing here," Arceneaux said, whisking his palms together. "So much for my lucky day."

"At least the Madame's given us strong support for our theory. Thanks to you, we've got a lead on who may have been the intended target."

"Thanks for sharing your visions, Madame," Arceneaux said, heading from the alley, his spirits high over his return to his old routine.

"You come back to see Madame Charmaine," the fortune-teller called out. "I offer a public-safety discount."

Keisha and I smiled and thanked her, then followed Arceneaux back across Napoleon to the convenience store.

"No sense going to the Blue Pelican now," I said. "Let's come back tonight and see if the bartender knows a regular customer who wears a green jacket."

Arceneaux nodded. "That'll give me time to talk to my buddies in Narcotics. If the shooting was a case of mistaken identity, it was most probably a whack gone wrong. I'll find out if there are any dealer turf battles going on."

"Good idea. But don't forget I need research on Creed Beaumont, starting with his days in Special Forces. Keisha can talk to Narcotics."

Keisha glanced at Arceneaux, saw him start to protest, then said, "I'll do the research, Jack. Arceneaux will get a lot more out of the nar-cowboys than I can. You two do the Blue Pelican"

I tilted my head toward her. "Team player, Arceneaux. Look, listen, learn."

I needed to let my aunt Joyce know we'd dug up the shotgun before she heard it on the news. After dropping Keisha and Arceneaux at the station, I drove toward her home as leaden clouds rumbled in from the Gulf and doubloon-sized raindrops splattered sporadically on my windshield. By the time I pulled up to the house, splotches of wetness dotted the dry concrete on the sidewalk. I hopped from my car and walked quickly to the porch. Aunt Joyce's cat pounced up and flopped onto the dry planks beneath the living room window. She watched me, black-and-gray-striped tail swishing like a metronome driving the rain's lazy rhythm.

Aunt Joyce opened the door before I could knock. "I thought I heard a car door."

"Expecting a ride from someone?" I asked.

"From you, I'm expecting an explanation."

I followed her into the kitchen and sat at her table.

She walked directly to the coffeemaker at the end of the counter. "Would you like a cup?"

Because it was afternoon, I knew it would be decaf, but I didn't refuse. "Thanks."

She set a china cup and saucer in front of me, but remained standing. She steadied herself against the table, her eyes as brown and hot as burned roux. "I saw that woman on television last night. Did you know she's Fannie Ashkenazi's daughter?"

No crisis too great for her to point out family connections. "I knew her in high school, Aunt Joyce."

"I told you I didn't want all this."

"Justice belongs to the whole community, not one person," I said.

I'd taken a hard shot at her—an elderly cancer survivor, a woman who'd been more of a mother to me than my own. Aunt Joyce's hands pressed into the table as she sat, wavering slowly as if pushing up against a weight too great for her.

"You're right," she finally said. "Justice for David doesn't belong to me. But how do we know there'll be justice now? Thirty-one years ago we waited for the FBI to catch the horrible people who killed David. But they didn't find them. Is there hope now? Will I live through the memories for nothing?"

"I'll do my best to make sure you don't. But ours wasn't the only family affected. Another boy was killed, too."

Raindrops clicked on the windowpane.

"It's awful, but I've forgotten his name," Aunt Joyce said, glancing out the kitchen window at the sweet peas clinging to the lattice.

"Elton Jackson. But everyone called him Deer. He was a runner, like David."

"You know we never met his parents. If you talk to them, tell them how sorry I am for their loss."

When she turned her head from the window, her eyes had lost their forlorn flatness. They told me that, once again, she would endure. As she had when David died. As she did when she discovered she had cancer and when her husband died. She had the kind of strength I'd always wanted from my mother.

"It's a mitzvah for you to send your thoughts," I said.

Aunt Joyce ran her finger beneath the loose hair on her cheek and tucked it back into her wig. Then she looked down at the table and breathed deeply, as if shelving her emotions like a cookbook she frequently used. "Would you help an old woman whose memory is slipping?"

"What do you mean?"

"Bring your coffee." She tapped my hand and stood.

I grabbed the cup and saucer and followed her into the living room. Aunt Joyce sat on the couch and patted the space next to her. Several old scrapbooks were strewn across the coffee table.

"You know what a shutterbug your uncle was," she said. "And organized. Our anniversaries. Grandchildren's birthdays. Sam's Little League games. David's track meets."

I set my coffee on the end of the table and picked up one of the albums.

Aunt Joyce folded her hands in her lap. "I pulled them out this morning. Your uncle wrote the date and event on the back of every picture, but they're so old I'm afraid I'll tear them if I try to pull them loose."

I moved my hand over the frayed plastic cover thinking how much of David's life was held inside. And how much of my aunt's. "You want me to tell you about each of these pictures."

Her brown eyes flooded. "Help me remember."

My turn for a mitzvah. "Of course."

As we thumbed through albums over the next hour, I identified the year and event for each picture. She managed to laugh when she remembered things that had happened to David around those times. We had one more album left when I excused myself to relieve my bladder of the decaf. Aunt Joyce had already opened it when I returned to the couch.

"That's you, Jack!" She pointed to a picture of David, hands on knees to catch his breath, smiling at me. I was holding up a stopwatch to show him he'd broken the Tulane record in the three-mile run. A few of his teammates patted him on the back. In the background was a beaming young woman, her long auburn hair lifting in the breeze. Faith Ann Tilden.

I drove back to the station. As I sat at my desk, still cluttered with Arceneaux's half-finished paperwork, I was surprised with a call from Ennio Cribari.

"I was reluctant to offer my help last week because of Karl," the retired FBI agent said.

"The guy who let me in the other day," I said, remembering the younger man's edginess.

"He's worried about my health, Detective Brenner. Bet you couldn't tell I was wearing a hairpiece. Looks pretty close to the way it was before I started chemo."

"I understand." I was also beginning to comprehend his relationship to Karl. It wasn't by blood.

"I'd be happy to discuss the case with you," Cribari said.

I wanted more than a talk in his rose garden. "Take me over the ground you covered. Maybe you'll recall something important that didn't have meaning back then."

"Come by the house anytime. I'm sure Karl can overcome his irritation and whip us up some—"

"No. I mean literally cover the ground. Take a ride with me to Bon Terre tomorrow."

"I don't know," he murmured. Then after a pause: "Screw Karl. Let's do it."

I was walking toward Lieutenant Utley's office to fill him in on my unearthing the shotgun when my cell phone rang.

"Brenner," I answered, expecting Keisha or Arceneaux.

"This is Sally Ellis from the crime lab."

I stopped in the middle of the aisle. "That was quick."

"We found something you might want to know about," she said.

"Don't tell me it wasn't a shotgun inside that wrapping," I said.

"SKB, side-by-side double barrel."

"Fingerprints?"

"Working on that now," Sally said. "Everything's been well preserved, and the lacquer on the gun stock is pretty worn. That's good for picking up prints. But I didn't call to tell you that."

"What then?"

"Inside the outer wrapping, there was a separate plastic bag. It contained a gold necklace wrapped in a bloody swatch of denim."

A detail Graves had left out. Unless someone else had buried the shotgun and he didn't know about it. "What kind of necklace?"

"I'm not Jewish," Sally said, "but one of the girls in the lab called it a *high.*"

"*Chai,*" I said with a guttural inflection, as something hot and bitter rose in my throat. "The Hebrew word for life."

"Could it have been your cousin's?" she asked.

My mind riffled through images of David and me running barechested on late afternoons, steam rising from the asphalt while large drops of moisture fell lazily from the leaves of live oaks and magnolias lining the streets. "I never knew him to wear jewelry."

"Well," she said. "We'll find out if we have something to compare the blood on the *chai* and the denim against."

17

I stood frozen in the aisle. The ghoulish image of Emmett Graves taking the *chai* from David enraged me. Surely he hadn't forgotten such a calculated act when telling me his story. Had he failed to mention it to intensify my shock when I discovered it?

But the anger iced over as I contemplated the other possibility—Graves had lied. Did he somehow know another person had buried the shotgun, but didn't know the necklace had been hidden with it? Or maybe the *chai* wasn't David's and was planted by whoever entombed the weapon in Avery Hammond's backyard. But then whose blood was on it?

A large hand on my shoulder ended my speculation.

"Brenner," said Lieutenant Utley. "Follow me and fill me in."

I trailed him to his office, where he settled in behind his desk.

"Close the door," he said.

I mechanically shut it, then slowly lowered myself into a guest chair.

"Looks like I caught you in the middle of deep thought," Utley said.

"You might say." I wiped my face. "Let me start at the end and work backwards."

Beginning with the phone call from the lab, I told him everything that had happened in Bon Terre that morning. "Thanks for running interference with forensics," I finally said.

He waved it off. "I want to get this whole thing over with. Hopefully with answers to your cousin's death. What do you make of this necklace?"

"David never owned one as far as I know. I could ask my aunt Joyce or Faith Tilden."

He nodded. "How'd Arceneaux do his first day back?"

"He's back with a vengeance."

I told Utley about Arceneaux's theory of a second shooter in the Bowen case, our encounter with Madame Charmaine, and our plan to question the help at the Blue Pelican that night.

"Arceneaux belongs on the street, that's for sure," Utley said. "Guidry was about to resign in frustration. Arceneaux's as clumsy with computers as he is with people."

"Speaking of which, and with all due respect . . ." I swallowed, uncertain if I had energy right now to risk raising Utley's ire. "Arceneaux won't work well with anyone but me. Please don't split us up when this is over."

"Arceneaux's working with Lundy just fine. I've been watching."

"Let us work as a threesome, then. Other departments are trying it."

"Brenner, you have enough to do without trying to restructure my command."

Now *wasn't* the time. "I'm going to Angola this afternoon, Lieutenant. See if Graves can tell me about the necklace. Or if he'll admit he's been lying."

"Brief me again Monday morning," Utley said. "Say. You have time to drive to Angola and still hit the Blue Pelican with Arceneaux tonight?"

"Sure." *If I miss Friday night dinner and Shabbat services with my wife.*

The clammy gray walls of the interrogation room at Angola mirrored the mood that had followed me all the way from New Orleans. Justice for David drove me here, I'd told myself, just as justice led David to Bon Terre over thirty years ago. But when I finally listened to David's voice instead of my own, it told me nothing is as important as family. I could almost feel his strong fingers digging into my shoulders, sternly admonishing me that keeping myself from Alexis this evening, even to pursue his killer, was no honor to his memory.

I admitted to myself that my presence here was for neither justice nor truth. Though I was driven to avenge David's murder, I was compelled by the narcotic of the contest as surely as an alcoholic is driven to booze. Emmett Graves was another competitor running at my shoulder.

Across from me, Graves's flat black eyes trained on me like lasers.

"Get your evidence?" he asked.

"We dug up a shotgun right where you said we'd find it."

"I bet Hammond pissed his pants."

"He says you're a liar. I'm not in a position to disagree."

Graves sneered. "That shotgun was exactly where I told you. I'll testify to how I come to put it there."

"A con who cut a deal to save himself from the needle? Does me no good unless I can tie the weapon to the murders."

"You know I'm telling the truth." He cocked his chin, his eyes glowing brighter. "That shotgun ain't all you found."

"Tell me what else." A cold hollow formed in my chest. "Then tell me how it got there."

"Just remember, you asked."

Raindrops clicked on the car's windshield as the rays of Emmett Graves's flashlight found keys hanging from the ignition. He'd have to move the white boy's body to get them. The boy had fallen facedown, halfway into the front seat. Graves grasped the boy's green jacket with gloved hands and jerked the body toward him, then stepped aside as it thudded onto the gravel. The body landed face-up, skin as white as the oyster shells in the parking lot. Then something golden flickered in a flash of remnant lightning. Graves shined his flashlight onto the boy's body. Another shimmer. Graves knelt down and saw a necklace around the boy's neck.

He'd seen one like it before. A Jew-lawyer in Baton Rouge who got mob guys off on pinball-racket charges. He'd sat next to the fat kike at a bar. Graves had asked about the gold object dangling from his neck, but he couldn't recall the Hebrew word the Jew-lawyer used, only that it was two Hebrew letters. And he'd felt an old rage thinking they appeared to him as incomprehensible as English letters.

The chain and Hebrew letters around the white boy's neck were more delicate than those the Jew-lawyer sported. A thought flickered in Graves's mind, at first as far away as the retreating storm, but then it settled inside like a warm, steady rain.

He'd already decided about the shotgun. He'd get rid of it like Avery Hammond had commanded. But Graves would put it in a place that might do him good at some later time. Now, he thought, he'd bury something else with the evidence. Something that would prevent any confusion about what the shotgun was connected to. The gold object was hard to grasp with his gloves, but once he had it, he ripped the gleaming necklace from the dead white boy's throat.

Graves shrugged matter-of-factly. "Didn't mean no disrespect by what I done. Just protecting my interests."

My knotted jaw rendered me mute.

He sneered. "Telling a story's all in the timing."

"You've been salivating to tell me this part," I finally said. "But I think it's a lie. As far as I know, David never wore jewelry. You could have planted that necklace."

Graves leaned forward as far as his manacles would allow. "There's blood on them Hebrew letters."

The veins in my temples pulsed. "That's what the lab tech told me. But how do we know it's David's?"

"He didn't tell you what the necklace was wrapped up in?" The chains scraped across the metal table as Graves righted himself in his chair. "After I took the necklace, I cut a swatch from your cousin's jeans where his leg was nearly blowed off and wrapped it up in that. The denim was as red as a whore's lipstick."

I'd gotten what I came for. Emmett Graves's description of the *chai* was further validation of his account, causing me to believe I'd unearthed the weapon used to kill David. But Graves had also planted in my mind a hideous moving picture on a continuous loop. I drove back to the city feeling as whipped as a runner overtaken on the final curve, a hollow pain in my tightening chest, arms and legs as rigid as the trusses supporting the causeway over the swamp.

Arceneaux and I had agreed to meet at nine o'clock in the strip center across from the Blue Pelican. Three cars sat outside Madame Charmaine's Fortune Boutique. Arceneaux had parked his in front of the insurance office at the opposite end. I pulled up next to him. We both got out.

"Do any good with Graves?" he asked.

I told him.

"I know you don't like Graves fucking with you like that, but maybe the son of a bitch is actually telling the truth."

"I'm tired of thinking about Emmett Graves right now," I said. "Let's cross the street and see if we can stir up something about our mystery man in the green jacket."

"Back in action. Hot damn!"

Arceneaux and I entered the Blue Pelican. The room was long, narrow, and dimly lit. It was one of those places where eyes never meet, but everyone is looking. Clusters of men sat in circular booths lining the wall to the left, and at several tables scattered in the middle. But no one's back faced the entrance. No green jacket in sight.

The row of empty stools fronting the long bar on the right told me this wasn't a drinking man's place. The classic rock pumping from the speakers in each corner of the room was neither for dancing nor mourning lost love. It was for masking conversations. The Blue Pelican served as headquarters, sales office, and boardroom for criminals.

"Sol, get us another round over here," a man called from one of the booths as we approached the bartender. He was a dark-haired man, with a large body as mushy as grits.

"Sol," I said. "That short for Solomon?"

He glared at me. Then at Arceneaux. Then he glowered back at me as though I were a counter stain that hadn't disappeared with the first application of Comet. "No. Sol as in aero-*sol.*"

"You mean like hair spray?" Arceneaux asked.

Sol cackled. "Naw. Like bug spray. Cockroaches like you run from me."

"Pesticide's a good thing to have in this place," Arceneaux said.

Sol steeled his face as much as he could, but his jowls were as limp as the rest of his body. Even his stubble looked like bits of pencil lead floating in a bowl of oatmeal. "Cops come in here all the time pretending they ain't. You two don't even try to hide it."

"We're new on the job," I said.

Arceneaux gave me a what-a-weak-line look, then turned to Sol. "We want to know about one of your regulars. Wears a green jacket."

"I look like some fag notices what guys wear?"

Arceneaux grinned. "And if you ain't cooperative, *Sol,* everyone's gonna think you're a blabbermouth."

"What do you mean?"

"All these lowlifes in here." Arceneaux scanned the room. "You can bet they're all looking to see if you hand out some information."

"Which I ain't gonna do."

"But not out of any sense of honor. Your palms get greased by doing favors, the biggest of which is keeping quiet."

Sol nodded. "Heard nothing. Seen nothing."

"But you telling us something and them not knowing about it is a whole lot better than you claming up and them thinking you're a stoolie."

Sol gripped the bar as though the sudden vacancy in his mind had affected his balance. It was a classic squeeze. Get someone to cooperate by threatening to make everyone believe he's given something up if he *doesn't* talk. I admired how cleverly Arceneaux had presented this simple paradox to Sol. I wanted to say so, but Arceneaux wouldn't have recognized the word and it would have spoiled his rhythm.

Sol's eyes burned. "You can't con me, motherfuckers."

"Not a con, Sol. Just us doing business."

Arceneaux reached over the bar, grabbed Sol's collar, and pulled until their noses were only inches apart. The upper half of Sol's belly spread on top of the bar top like cookie dough.

"Now look real mean and defiant-like," Arceneaux said. "Grit your teeth at me like I was the biggest goddamn roach you ever saw and you're ready to knock me dead."

Sol had trouble looking vicious, especially in Arceneaux's grasp, but he did an okay job.

"There's a guy comes in here a lot," Arceneaux said. "Wears a green jacket. You give me his name, tell me where we can find him. Mumble it soft like you're cursing me."

"Fuck you."

"Now that's not a name," Arceneaux said. "That's a bad attitude. You got five seconds to give me a name and where we can find this person. You do that, and you can shove me and yell at us to leave. I'll let go and you won't see us no more. Unless of course you're lying. If I don't hear a name and location by the time I count to five, I'm going to let go anyway. And then in loud voices, we're going to lay money on the bar and thank you for being so cooperative. One."

"Go fuck yourself." The words leaked from Sol's throat like air from a faulty tire nozzle.

"Two, three." Arceneaux slid his eyes in my direction. "What this guy's got to say is worth at least a hundred. You got five twenties, partner?"

"A couple of fifties do?"

"Four." Arceneaux's fingers started to slip from Sol's collar.

Sol's puffy cheeks quivered and his crude scowl started to fade. He glanced toward the patrons, then at me. "Don't, man," he whispered.

"Don't what, asshole?" Arceneaux retightened his grip.

Sol's eyes darted around the room again. Then he drew a long breath and refocused his furious glower on Arceneaux. "Fuck your goddamn money!"

Arceneaux jerked him closer and glared back.

"Please." Sol exhaled quietly.

Arceneaux squeezed harder. Then Sol mumbled something I couldn't hear. As Arceneaux loosened his grip, Sol pressed his mushy palms into Arceneaux's chest and shoved hard.

"Hey," Arceneaux barked, as he pretended to stumble backward.

"Get the fuck outta here," Sol bellowed. "I ain't telling you nothing, you fucking cockroaches."

Arceneaux grabbed my arm and stifled his guffaw until we were out the door.

"Partner, I love this job." Arceneaux clapped my shoulder as the rumbling bass sounds from inside the bar faded into the hiss of traffic up the way on Napoleon. "For true, that Keisha's all right. But you and me is an unbeatable team."

I took a breath. The outside air smelled as stale as the barroom haze. "Never thought I'd hear you give passing marks to a woman."

"Partner her full-time with someone experienced, one who don't spend the shift trying to get in her pants, and she's gonna make a good one."

Utley's plan, exactly.

We walked past the convenience store, slowing as we eyed a young man at the telephone booth where Steven Bowen had been shot, then crossed Napoleon. We stood in front of our cars at the end of the strip center, darkened because of a defective security light.

"So what did you get from Sol?" I asked.

"The guy with the green jacket is named Mousey Trivette," Arceneaux said. "Main man for Maurice Silva. The Blue Pelican's their hangout."

"I've heard of Silva."

"Big Easy native. Went to Brother Martin High School. He has the coke and ecstasy trade in the ritzy neighborhoods along the lakefront, City Park west to Kenner. Sloughs off crack and heroin to homeboy dealers. Marijuana, he sells everywhere."

"If we hold to our theory that Steven Bowen was killed by mistake, that means someone wanted to take out this Trivette. Why?"

"The narcs think someone's trying to muscle into Silva's territory. An interesting name came up in the conversation. Someone you know." Arceneaux smiled like a cat who'd left a garden snake as a gift on the front porch.

"Who?" I asked.

"Creed Beaumont."

His image blazed in my mind—muscled arms crossed over his chest, sunglasses dangling from the earpiece stuck in his mouth, as he leaned against his fiery red Camaro.

"How'd they run across him?" I asked.

"The plates they ran on a car spotted a couple of times outside the Blue Pelican came up with Beaumont's name. Might be he's a customer. Or he could be a middle-man supplier maybe wants to move into retail. Markup's double between Banana Land and the States, but it don't take a big stash of coke to score six figures on the street. And if you've got the volume of a supplier . . ." Arceneaux held up his palms. "Then again, it could be nothing."

"Somehow I doubt that." Creed Beaumont's cool greeting that first morning in Bon Terre was starting to make sense. "Wonder if Keisha dug up anything on Beaumont."

Arceneaux raised a finger. "Glad you mentioned it. She found out he stayed in Panama till the end of his stint, a year after they bagged Noriega. Didn't re-up either. Keisha says he fell off the radar screen until he shows up in Louisiana a few years ago. He might've stayed in Central America after helping the gov cool Noriega's action."

"Maybe he took a piece of it," I said, thinking everything Keisha had found on Beaumont tracked with what Willow had told me.

Arceneaux leveled his forefinger, cocked his thumb, and made a clicking sound. "You think your Avery Hammond could be in the drug business?"

My eyebrows rose. "The casino operations Beaumont supposedly runs would be a great money-laundering machine."

"This tie in to what you told me about Emmett Graves blaming Hammond for his drug bust?" Arceneaux asked.

"Maybe Graves was freelancing. It's the only time he's ever gotten into trouble in the city. I can't see Hammond trusting anything other than intimidation or enforcement to a freewheeling psycho like Graves."

Arceneaux shrugged. "Guess Maurice Silva's next on our dance card."

"Not tonight," I said.

"Hell no, not tonight. I was thinking of them oysters and beer at Fuzzy's you promised, celebrating my return."

"Gotta give you a rain check."

"Come on. Just a beer to celebrate my first day back."

I sighed. "I need to get home to Alexis."

"All right, Jack. I know you got stuff going on." Standing by his car, he reached into his pocket, then jangled the keys in his palm. "Say. About next moves here. I heard what you said this morning. Being a team player and all. I came into the middle of this case. If you wanna take Keisha to interview Silva, I got no problem. Maybe she'll get a collar out of this."

"Thanks, Arceneaux."

The reflection of headlights off the storefront windows illuminated his face, making it look almost cherubic. "You and me'll catch the next case together."

Then the words slipped from my mouth like foam gushing over the rim of a beer mug. "It may not happen."

A carload of teens moved slowly by. I felt the *thump-thump* of their subwoofer in my chest.

Arceneaux's eyes narrowed. "Come again?"

"Utley told me he's seriously thinking of partnering me with Keisha full-time."

The humid air buzzed like a faulty fluorescent bulb. Arceneaux stared at me like a little boy who'd left his tooth in a glass the night before and had woken to discover the fairy hadn't replaced it with coins.

"I've been trying to talk him out of it," I said. "He doesn't take advice from his staff."

"So that's why the cocksucker tried acting so nice." He slammed the roof of his car. "Son of a bitch."

"I haven't told you because I've been hoping he'd change his mind."

Arceneaux looked up toward the stars, only there weren't any. The cloud cover looked like dark gray bubble wrap. "Well, thanks for telling me on my first fucking day back."

"I'm sorry, partner." The word went down like dry cornmeal. "Hey, I've got time for one beer."

"You got someone at home needs you." Arceneaux drummed his fingers on the hood and looked off toward the street as though each passing car were a memory.

"It never lasts for me, Jack. What's it been, me and you? Five years?"

I nodded, then stopped myself from saying something stupid like *we'll still be friends.*

"Least you ain't running off to Florida and taking the kid like my wife done." Without looking back at me, he lumbered into the driver's seat and slammed the door. Headlights flared like angry eyes, the steaming night air roiling across them like smoke. Arceneaux's tires whirred on the pavement as he backed out of the parking lot. Then his car jerked into drive and roared off. I heard the tires squeal around the next corner.

I tried to tell myself Arceneaux would have eventually found out about Utley's intentions. But like he said, I could have waited, and I cursed myself for unburdening myself at his expense.

I drove home and entered the kitchen around eleven o'clock.

Checking upstairs, I saw the light was out in our bedroom. I slipped quietly back downstairs, then slunk onto the couch and clicked on the television. As the channels flicked past my eyes, I thought about the Angel of Death, who on the night of Passover cut living branches from Egyptian families. Though more ancient than the patriarchs, the angel was alive and well in twenty-first-century New Orleans. She was a mercurial destroyer who took many forms. The loss of a partner. An evil miscreant defiling the memory of my cousin. A bullet meant for someone else destroying the life of a promising young man. A disintegrating marriage.

But the last in this string of misfortune didn't fit. There was no outside agent threatening my marriage, the turmoil no more beyond my control than the images flashing before me at the beck of my hand on the remote. The fabric of my marriage was rent not by the capricious angel but by neglect. And perhaps my fear was not in losing control, but in seizing it. Maybe what I dreaded was having it all within reach, the responsibility mine. And failing.

Another press of the remote filled the screen with a car dealer on Chef Menteur Highway promising zero interest and the lowest prices in the state. Though I wasn't in the market, the low-slung red sports coupe next to him caught my eye. Happy Larry Larrieu slapped the shiny surface just behind the left front headlight.

The driver's side. I jerked myself upright on the couch. That would have been the side of the car facing the phone booth where Steven Bowen stood. The side targeted by the man who returned the shooter's fire. And as Happy Larry Larrieu slid his thick palm along the waxed crimson body of the deal of the century, I recalled the replacement panel above the left wheel of Creed Beaumont's Camaro the day I met him.

18

I worried about bringing an ill and aging man anywhere near Creed Beaumont and considered reneging on my promise to take Ennio Cribari with me to Bon Terre. But the purpose of my trip was to see if I could unlock any useful memories from Cribari's mind. There was no reason to expect we'd cross paths with Beaumont.

I pulled in front of Cribari's house in the French Quarter and ran my right-side wheels over the curb to allow other cars to pass on the narrow street. I walked around the car and pressed the call button next to Cribari's door.

"Detective Brenner?" Cribari's voice crackled through the speaker.

"Yes, sir," I replied.

Within seconds, I heard a door open on the other side of the wall, then footsteps on the courtyard tile, followed by yet other footsteps.

The entry lock clicked and Cribari opened the thick oak door, revealing a sliver of his rose garden. He wore gray slacks, a navy blazer, and a white button-down shirt. A hand grabbed the edge of the door from behind him as he slipped out onto the sidewalk next to me.

"Good morning!" Cribari shook my hand with a firmness I guessed came from the expectation of adventure, or possibly the opportunity of gaining a respite from his mate. He nodded to Karl, who now stood in the opening to the courtyard. "See you when I see you." Cribari betrayed the attempted singsong tone with a catch in his throat.

"May I have a word with you, Detective?" Karl said as Cribari walked toward the car. He clenched his arms across a Tabasco T-shirt tucked into his jeans.

"Sure." I decided offering my hand would only make a tense scene worse.

"Ennio is not well," Karl said.

"He told me. I understand your worry, but this is something he wants to do."

"He can't let anything go."

"Maybe you should let some things go and try to enjoy your day," I said.

He shook his head. "You cops are all alike."

I glanced toward the car. Cribari looked twenty years younger than he had the day I met him. "Maybe he feels he has unfinished business."

"I have unfinished business too, Detective." Karl waited until my gaze returned to him. "And I'm running out of time."

"Why are you slowing down?" Cribari asked as we reached the stand of cypress trees along the highway near Bon Terre.

"There's a speed trap just around the bend," I said.

He pressed me with a quizzical grin.

I nodded. "Yeah. I got caught."

We made the turn. Jarla Thomas sat in her cruiser studying the radar readout. She raised a coffee mug to acknowledge our passing.

"That trap must keep the town's property taxes near zero," Cribari said as we passed by. "Got nailed myself thirty-one years ago. The sheriff let me out of it, though I'd have gladly paid it to get a little cooperation from him."

"Jurisdictional jealousy?" I asked.

"FBI always gets that. Often with good reason, sad to say. But Sheriff Vern Hammond went beyond the usual passive resistance. He got to most everyone in town before I could talk to them. Guess he figured the less people talked, the sooner we'd leave. He was certain the boys' murders were done by outsiders, probably Klan, and we were wasting our time."

"A sensible theory," I said.

"But only one theory."

"Consider him a suspect?"

"Wife claimed they were together in a roadhouse waiting for the storm to clear out before going back home," Cribari said. "Have you spoken with either of them?"

"Vern Hammond was killed six months later. The wife took off and left her kids with brother Avery."

"Who has it all now, I see." Cribari flung a hand toward the series of billboards flying past us advertising Hammond's businesses. "Used to be Burma Shave signs where those are."

A glint of sunlight off the windshield of an oncoming vehicle seared my eyes as I slowed before making the turn onto Escondido Road toward Faith Tilden's restaurant. The red Camaro slowed as it approached. Creed Beaumont touched a forefinger to the rim of his sunglasses then pointed it at me in a sort of arrogant salute as he punched the accelerator. The Camaro roared off. Through my rearview mirror, I watched the crimson coupe fade away up the highway. Business in the city with Maurice Silva? I wondered.

Cribari and I stopped in front of the old storage building next to Meal Thyme that was once Beulah Baptist Church. As I gave him a full account of what Graves had told me, we watched Faith Tilden gathering herbs from the garden that stood where rain and blood had drenched the oyster-shell parking lot over thirty years before.

"Graves's story sounds plausible," Cribari said when I finished. "Like I told you before, we suspected the boys were abducted from the church."

"Graves says they were each shot once. Deer in the stomach,

David in the leg. That doesn't fit the Klan assassination theory you said Vern Hammond was pushing."

Cribari nodded. "We figured it was a single perp with a double-barrel shotgun. The Klan didn't do solo jobs and never lacked for ammunition."

"And you'd expect a Klan killing to be preceded by threats and other violent acts," I said.

"And we found none of that. Bon Terre was no hotbed of racism. People seemed to get along." Cribari reached inside his blazer and pulled out his pipe. "You mind?"

"Go ahead."

He held a match over the bowl and sucked the flame downward. After several puffs, he pulled the stem from his mouth. "I hope bouncing your theories off me helps, but that's not the main reason you brought me to Bon Terre."

I looked toward the bayou. Cloud shadows passed over, turning the water dark and thick, like congealed blood. "Show me where you found the bodies."

"Let's go."

We drove until we reached the fork in the road I'd encountered before. The cane quivering in the wind looked olive drab in the penumbra of a large thunderhead.

"That way leads to Avery Hammond's estate," I said, pointing to our left.

Cribari scanned the asphalt lying straight ahead. "The pavement ended here back then, but I remember this right-of-way road follows the bayou. Your cousin's car was found about three miles up."

We snaked our way through wetlands strewn with ash and black willow. The only evidence of human beings was the occasional beer can and pipeline markers. The road turned sharply, swinging within ten feet of the water's edge. The matted grass and dirt clods on the shoulder told me the curve had been missed more than once. A few minutes after entering a stand of cypress trees, Cribari spoke.

"Stop here," he said.

I pressed the brake. An egret took flight from a limb overhead.

"See the rise in the land?" Cribari pointed to our left. There was a break in the canopy of leaves and moss. Ferns and wild grass covered a gentle grade. "Let's get out."

We stood in the middle of the road. To our right, there was a gentle tremor on the surface of the bayou from either a rising wind or feeding alligators.

"I wonder how far downstream Avery Hammond's house is," I said.

Cribari slapped the pipe against his palm. The spent tobacco fluttered away in the breeze. "If I remember correctly, about a mile as the crow flies." He returned the pipe to the inside of his blazer and started toward the swale.

As Cribari and I left the road, we pushed through thick groundcover. Surprised at the firmness underfoot, I remembered David's car had been driven over this ground. But moisture from the vegetation quickly soaked the cuffs of our trousers.

"This is it," Cribari said when we reached the top of the rise.

Twenty feet beyond us lay an ebony pool, maybe fifty yards across and a hundred yards wide. The surface was as still as the space between the breaths of a sleeping child. The musk of decay drenched the air.

"How did you find the bodies?" I asked.

"The state police searched the area, wherever they could go on foot. The bureau gave me two divers for one week. They got lucky on their last day."

"Maybe Graves left his boat at that spot about a quarter mile back where the bayou comes close to the road."

Cribari nodded. "Pretty clever for a guy who can't read."

There was a sheen on the water from the oils left by centuries of decomposed plants and animals. I squatted, my eyes trying to penetrate it and see the past. "The bodies in the trunk like Graves said?"

He drew a breath before answering. "Yeah."

I thought of Emmett Graves heaving them into the back of the car like blown-out tires. "The divers open it?"

"I'd ordered any agency finding a vehicle or container to leave it alone until I could get there. The state police dragged the car out. I was the first one to see the bodies."

I transferred my gaze to him.

Cribari's jaw flexed. "Don't ask me to describe it."

I shook my head. "At least they were dead when they went under."

"My God." Cribari's expression was as somber as the murky pond. "There's no way you would know."

"Know what?"

"It wasn't something we publicized. Didn't even tell his parents. But the autopsy showed David had water in his lungs. He was alive when the car sank."

I stared at the water, devoid of oxygen, dark as India ink.

"He didn't suffer," Cribari said. "The ME said he was unconscious. He'd lost a lot of blood."

A report crackled like thunder, but a sudden spray of dirt and grass told me the sound was man-made. Cribari dropped down onto the wet carpet. Then another explosion of damp turf rose six feet in front of me. I was the target. As I dove for the earth, I saw the smoke from the opposite side of the pond. A hundred yards.

"Cribari," I hollered, figuring I'd draw the next round. "Run for cover behind the car."

Another shot ripped into the earth near me. As Cribari neared the rear of the car, I rose and scrambled across the asphalt toward the front end. A shot roared overhead, whapping into the bark of a cypress tree on the bank of the bayou. I slid face-first into the ground behind the car next to Cribari. He raised his head and smiled at me. "This is more excitement than I bargained for, son. If we get out alive, don't you dare tell Karl about this."

19

"What now?" Cribari looked at the thirty-eight I held in my hand as if it were a wilted rose.

"Judging from the last shot, the rise shields us from the shooter's view. We're okay if we stay where we are."

"And the shooter stays on the other side of the pond," he said.

I looked back down the road. We could drive off safely enough, but was the assailant already on the move, positioning himself to cut us off?

"Moving now's our best chance." I reached up and pulled open the rear passenger door. "Stay on the floorboard."

Then I heard the throaty resonance of a large engine and the squeal of rubber around a sharp turn. Maybe there's more than one of them, I thought. The car sounded seconds away. I had six rounds, some extra ammo, and one civilian.

"What's plan B?" Cribari asked.

I could hear road debris pinging the underbody of the approaching car, its motor growling louder and louder. Suddenly, blue and red sparkles dazzled my eyes.

A police cruiser glided toward us. Jarla Thomas passed us, then spun her car, peppering the cypress trees and the surface of the bayou with chips of asphalt. She slung open her door and burst out low, the body of her cruiser protecting her from gunfire.

"Lucky you were in the area," I called out, wondering what had brought her here. "Any way someone could get here from the other side of the pond?"

"Not without hip boots, a machete, and breath bad enough to keep the alligators away."

"When I heard you squeal around the bend back there, I was afraid you were part of the problem."

Jarla cautiously peered over the cruiser's hood. "Let's get you guys out of here."

"One way in, one way out," I said. "What if the shooter's able to get back to Hammond Lane and is waiting for us at the fork?"

"I'll radio Sheriff Perrot and tell him to meet us at the fork. You follow me."

"The shooter's after me. Let me lead. Cribari, you ride with Officer Thomas."

Jarla hustled Cribari to the cruiser, keeping her body between him and the pond. She opened her rear door and soon Cribari was safely out of sight. I slipped into my car and cranked the engine. I flipped a U-turn, then looked back and saw Jarla slide behind the wheel of her unit. When she nodded, we hit our accelerators simultaneously, the engines whining in harmony like a fiddle and a slide guitar at an icehouse concert.

I followed the road, anticipating trouble around each bend. But I couldn't resist constantly flicking my eyes at the rearview mirror to make sure Jarla Thomas was there, even though I knew she'd have no trouble staying close on a serpentine road she knew much better than I.

As we neared the spot where Hammond Lane intersected the road, I spotted a cruiser parked on the left. Rhino Perrot leaned against the trunk, an unlit cigar in his mouth, fanning his face with his hat and staring ahead as though counting the stalks of cane on each side of the lane. He didn't acknowledge our presence until I drew to a stop and lowered my window.

He pulled the stogie from his lips, his eyes still focused on the cane. "I've finally figured out why there's so much crime in the city. It's city cops. You attract it. Hadn't had more'n a domestic disturbance or two this whole year till you showed up."

"I appreciate your help, Sheriff. If you don't mind, I'd like Officer Thomas to follow me to Meal Thyme. I'll pick up my friend there."

"He can ride back with me. Thomas has an incident to investigate. Probably just some coonass poacher trying to scare you off or some kid showing off for his girlfriend after you disturbed their fornicating."

"I have a good idea who shot at me."

He finally turned his eyes from the emerald-lined asphalt and fixed a glare on me. "You never lack for ideas, do you, son?"

Rhino walked back to Jarla's cruiser and said something, then opened the back door and helped Cribari out. As Rhino approached his car, I could hear him speaking to Cribari.

"Sorry all this happened, sir. We hardly ever have trouble like this. 'Cept when Detective Brenner's around."

Minutes later, we pulled into the Meal Thyme parking lot, where a lone pickup told me lunch was nearly over.

"Well, that was a trip," Cribari said as he got out of Perrot's cruiser. "The sheriff said some rednecks were having some fun with us."

I looked at Rhino fanning his face with his hat as he walked toward the shade of the gallery fronting the restaurant. "Ennio, go on inside. I need to speak to the sheriff."

I followed Rhino up the steps past the bees fertilizing the snapdragons in the planters lining the gallery.

He nodded to an exiting patron, waited for him to descend the stairs, then flicked away a drop of sweat from his cheek. "Once again you've disturbed our peaceful town. Don't you ever stop to wipe the shit off your shoes when you come into someone else's house?"

"My conduct's not at issue here. Someone shot at us. I'm guessing Officer Thomas showed up because she knew something might happen."

The sheriff settled his hat on his head. He cut his eyes toward the man pulling out of the parking lot and watched the wheels of the old Ford 150 kick up dust.

"What the hell's going on?" I demanded.

He shot his hands into his pants pockets, then drew them out and patted his chest pocket.

"I think I've stumbled into your business," I said. "And it involves Creed Beaumont."

He slowly withdrew a fresh cigar. "Oh, you do, now?"

"One of our Narcotics officers told my partner Creed Beaumont may be involved in drug trafficking. In addition to shooting at me, he may have killed an innocent teenager while trying to muscle into the New Orleans action."

"What makes you think that?" Rhino asked.

"Creed Beaumont's car had bodywork that could have been done to repair bullet holes."

Rhino stared at the cigar and sighed as though lighting it might be one of those irrevocable decisions that haunt a person later in life when he least expects it. He returned it to his shirt pocket. The resigned expression on his face reminded me of the way my father looked when he'd realized he couldn't put off the birds-and-bees talk any longer. "Creed Beaumont ain't your shooter, son. Not that poor kid in New Orleans. Not you and your friend."

"Your protecting a thug like Beaumont forces me to draw a conclusion I don't like very much," I said.

"And what goddamn conclusion is that, genius?"

"Beaumont works for Avery Hammond. And Hammond doesn't control a whole town without some help—people doing business with him, or at least looking the other way. So when you tell me Beaumont's a choirboy and you write off an assault on my friend and me as some drunk poacher—"

"Goddamn it, Brenner! It don't take much to get your bowels in an uproar. Your mother should have breast-fed you." Rhino held up his large hands as I started to respond. "If I got the story right from what you told Officer Thomas, shots were fired from across the pond. I know how wide it is. You think a former Army Ranger like Beaumont would miss from that distance?"

My face burned not so much from the foolishness I immediately felt for not having asked myself that question, but from a new, more intriguing string of questions. What did the sheriff know about Creed Beaumont's background? How did he know it? And why?

"Maybe he was trying to scare me off, worried I might uncover his activities," I said.

Rhino chuckled. "You're as big a pig knuckle in his boudain as you are in mine. But I promise, he won't hurt you and jeopardize his deal."

"Deal?"

"The DEA flipped Beaumont several months ago."

I think the buzzing I heard was the bees in the snapdragons, but it might have been between my ears. "He's an informant?"

Rhino grinned. "Don't start distrusting your instincts, son. You were starting to figure some of this out. You're as smart as your lieutenant says you are."

I recalled the night I'd spoken with Utley outside the station. "He promised me you were one of the good guys when I told him I wasn't sure of you."

"I like that lieutenant of yours," Rhino said. "Reads people pretty well."

"But how can you be sure Beaumont wasn't involved in a shooting in New Orleans or wasn't the one who shot at us today? His cooperation doesn't make him any less a criminal."

"The night that boy was shot, Beaumont was unloading three kilos of Colombian coke in Lafayette. After that, he delivered a load of rock to Baton Rouge. Right now he's in the Crescent Cesspool looking to make a big sale to catch some whopper daddy rats."

"You said not to doubt my instincts," I said. "Avery Hammond is one of the rats."

Rhino nodded. "The DEA's hoping to draw him out from behind his legitimate businesses to find a new market."

"These businesses being money-laundering operations," I said.

"Good'ns, too. Never been delinquent on any tax payment, local or federal."

It now made sense what Graves had implied. "Did Hammond set up Emmett Graves to get caught on that drug deal?"

"The DEA stung him with Beaumont's help. They wanted his reckless ass out of the way."

The knob on the front door clicked. Rhino and I turned to see Grace Tilden step onto the porch. "Hello, gentlemen."

Rhino tipped his hat.

Grace smiled at me. "Mr. Cribari finished off the crab. But I have some excellent snapper left." She cast her eyes to Rhino. "Can I interest you in a bite to eat, Sheriff?"

"Thank you," Rhino said. "My wife's got me some potato salad and a couple of sandwiches back at Seven Angels." He started down the steps to the parking lot, then turned back. "Take your friend home, Brenner."

As I watched him leave, I suddenly remembered that one of my tasks for the day was to ask Faith if she'd seen David wearing a *chai*, particularly on the day he died. "Is your mother here, Grace?"

"She's in the kitchen with Mr. Cribari." Grace motioned me inside.

I walked through the restaurant to the kitchen, where my nostrils flared with the smells of rosemary and hot butter. Cribari sat at a table, intent on large portions of bread pudding in whiskey sauce. Faith stood next to Cribari pouring coffee.

"I'm glad no one was hurt, Jack," she said when she noticed me. "Please sit down and eat."

"May I talk to you for a minute?" I nodded toward the back door.

Faith set the coffeepot on the table, and I followed her onto the back porch. I gazed over the rows of plants and herbs descending toward the bayou, the tranquil scene vastly divergent from the earlier chaos.

"So what did you want to speak to me about?" Faith asked.

"You know we dug up a shotgun on Avery Hammond's property. I believe it's the weapon that killed David and Deer." The image of Emmett Graves removing the bloodstained necklace from David's body stirred in my mind. "But there was something else wrapped up with it. Do you know what a *chai* is?"

Faith's face paled. Her neck hardened like frozen pipe. She folded her arms and stared toward the bayou as a gust kicked up smells of moss and oak. Fine strands of hair waved before her eyes like silver and auburn filaments of a scattered memory.

"Faith?"

Her eyes moistened and grayed. "Life. *Chai* means life."

"Yes. Did you ever see David wearing the Hebrew letters for life?"

The wind rippled the bayou. Limbs creaked and the low-slung clouds were as hard and splotched as tarnished sheetmetal.

"The day he died," she said.

That confirmed Graves's story, but it brought me no elation or satisfaction. This was the price of personal involvement. Homicide investigations fuel my competitive nature the way whiskey feeds an alcoholic. But this case was not a contest, it was an ordeal. The closer I came to the truth, the more my anger flamed as the loss became more visceral and intimate. I felt more victim than cop.

Faith wiped away a tear and turned to me. "How did the *chai* get buried with the shotgun?"

I recounted what Emmett Graves had told me. But I indulged myself in my own emotions and spoke in too much detail. As I described Graves ripping the *chai* from David's throat and dumping the bodies in the trunk like bags of compost, Faith's face grew as leaden as the clouds and her eyes milked over like drawn shades.

"David never wore rings, watches, and such," I said after concluding the story. "They distracted him when he ran and he didn't want to keep putting them on and taking them off. I'm surprised to learn he was wearing a necklace."

"I gave it to him," Faith said. Then she pushed the unruly

strands away from her face and pressed them into her hair, like thoughts best buried beneath her consciousness. “Excuse me. I need to help Grace clean up.”

She turned away. As she opened the screen door, the rusty spring keened like a nutria caught in the blades of an outboard.

I cast my eyes beyond the gardens and settled them on the waves of grass below the wisteria clinging to the old church building. Suddenly the lush green turned as white as bleached bone. Staring at the spot where Deer and David were shot, I saw the profane light of a savage midsummer storm flicker across the face of Emmett Graves. He stood above the bodies of two young men, their lives washed away like the rose-colored rivulets of blood gushing through the oyster shells toward the bayou. I saw him rend the red-stained symbol of life from David’s neck as easily and lustfully as he would gut a ten-point buck.

Emmett Graves had warned me: you sometimes get things you don’t want along with things you crave. Things so loathsome you regret the wish you made. I’d taken an important step toward my goal of unraveling David’s murder, but my only palpable possessions were vile and humiliating images—as though Emmett Graves had hurled me back thirty-one years and had defiled David’s body before my eyes.

20

When I finished wolfing down the lunch Grace had prepared, she made me promise the whole family would come for dinner one night after Sarah and Carrie returned from camp. Then Cribari and I headed toward the city, a straight-down rain drumming the car roof.

"Pretty handy for us that Officer Thomas happened by," Cribari said.

I watched hundreds of tiny silver crowns erupt from the blacktop.

"Bet it wasn't a coincidence," he said.

I glanced right. "Haven't lost the knack, have you?"

He grinned like a man who'd just beaten his teenage son at one-on-one hoops. "Thanks for inviting me along so I could find that out."

I told him about the DEA flipping Creed Beaumont, hoping to squeeze Avery Hammond.

Cribari narrowed his eyes and nodded slowly. "So that's how Hammond paid off their tax bill."

"What do you mean?" I asked.

"You see what he owns now, but in 1972 the family was land poor. The sharecroppers had gradually succumbed to big agriculture, and Vern and Avery Hammond held to their father's tradition of refusing oil and gas exploration on their property."

"Naturally you Feds rummaged though their finances during your investigation."

Cribari grinned. "Our stock and trade. But their problems were common knowledge. Almost everyone we interviewed was concerned about it. The Hammonds were good for the town and people were afraid the Hammond's selling off their land to pay taxes would change things."

"Looks like Avery solved those problems by joining the Dixie Mafia," I said. "Wonder if his brother the sheriff would have had a problem with that?"

Cribari reached into his coat pocket and pulled out his pipe. Then he glanced at me. "Not gonna light it. Helps me think." A few minutes later he pulled the bit from his mouth. "Didn't you tell me Vern was killed six months after the boys' murders?"

I nodded.

"Well, since we're thinking out loud here, what if your cousin and Elton Jackson stumbled across something that had nothing to do with adding a few black voters to the parish rolls? Maybe Vern somehow connected the killings to brother Avery's intention to save the family holdings through drug trafficking."

I'd contemplated the possibility that David's death wasn't related to his work, but had uncovered nothing to suggest it. The theory was intriguing. "And Avery could have killed Vern to silence him."

"A possibility." Cribari tapped his cheek with the pipe. "Unless the good sheriff was in on it, meaning he had certain knowledge the boys weren't killed by some outsider Klansmen. The theory he tried hard to push on me."

Was Vern Hammond an insider or outsider? "Didn't you tell me Vern had an alibi?"

"His wife, Genevieve."

"Who ran off without her children," I said.

"What would make a parent do that?"

To answer that question, I'd need to find Genevieve Hammond.

The rain followed us into the city, but it was a silent sprinkle when we pulled in front of Ennio Cribari's home in the Quarter.

He clasped my shoulder. "Thanks for letting me help you."

"Sorry for getting you into a dangerous situation," I said.

He brushed at the grass stains on his slacks and looked at the red wooden door to his property. "I'll have some explaining to do."

I drove away pondering the image of the sinkhole where the bodies of David and Deer Jackson had been immersed. But before I could study on it too much, my cell phone rang.

"Gotta hot date tonight," Keisha Lundy said. "Wanna be my chaperone?"

Anything to get out of the house. "Been out of action so long you figure the guy'll need protection, huh?"

She huffed. "Jack, when *I* say I haven't had a man since Emeril Lagasse was at Commander's Palace, it's funny."

"Okay. I hear you."

"Arceneaux arranged a meeting with Maurice Silva, Prince of Blow. He said he was busy and asked me to go with you."

Either Arceneaux was making good on giving Keisha a chance to make a collar on the Steven Bowen case, or he was still pissed at me. "Silva going to tell us who shot Steven?"

"If he knew, he probably would've taken care of it already. Arceneaux says Silva believes Steven was mistaken for his lieutenant, Mousey Trivette."

"The green jacket," I said. "Looks like Sol the bartender told us the truth. We'll take help from wherever we get it."

"I hate getting it from dope pushers. Far as I'm concerned, these guys are just as guilty as the man who shot Steven."

"Wouldn't be the first time we've used bad guys to nail bad guys."

We parked directly in front of the bar behind a stretch Lincoln Town Car. No other vehicles were parked within thirty yards in either direction. Keisha and I approached the entrance, drawing disciplined attention from two massive men in black flanking the door, both wearing wraparound sunglasses.

As we entered the bar, the jukebox died in the middle of Bruce Springsteen's "Dancing in the Dark." Sol's beefy fingers punched at the buttons with all the certainty of someone trying to negotiate the automated checkout in a grocery store. A man sat alone at a table, a Riedel single-malt crystal filled to proper proportion in front of him.

He rolled his eyes wearily toward the ceiling. "Is there a problem, Sol?"

"Just a sec, Mr. Silva." Sol bent closer to the keypad, his polyester pants stretched over the quavering layers of flesh on his buttocks. A rear view of the Pillsbury Doughboy.

Two men, clones of the sentries, were perched on stools at the bar to our right. Pects, lats, and sidearms bulged beneath their sport coats. Two more raven-clad goons, one a Van Damme knockoff, sat in one of the booths running down the left side of the room. A slightly built fifth man with dark, kinky hair and swarthy skin sat next to Jean-Claude and would have gone unnoticed were it not for the contrast of his white linen shirt.

Silva closed his eyes and spoke through clenched jaws. "Sol, I'm—"

Frank Sinatra's "Strangers in the Night" cut him off in midsentence. The irritation melting from Silva's face suggested Sol had managed to finally make good on his request. Silva then turned his gaze on us and nodded, apparently all the invitation to join him we were going to get.

Keisha and I sat at his table. He wore gray flannel slacks and a short-sleeve black silk T-shirt. Silva was trim, his upper body solid but smooth, like a gymnast's.

"I know you're here 'cause of the boy," he said. "Shame."

"Maybe in your grief you can tell us who shot him," Keisha said. "We know he was mistaken for one of your men. We hear someone's muscling in on your territory and you'd be real thrilled if we'd take care of that for you."

She'd made the statement with conviction. But it was only conjecture. We waited while Silva sniffed his scotch and took a sip.

"I hear stuff," he said, placing the Riedel glass silently on the table. "You know? Anyway, the way it happens, so I'm told, this guy's coming up the street minding his own business and hears this car coming round the corner. Tires squealing and all. Then *pop!* This guy happens to own a gun, figures he's being shot at, fires a couple rounds at the car. He don't see this poor kid. He hits the dirt while the car zooms by then gets the hell outta there."

Theory confirmed, if he was telling the truth. "You hear anything about this guy who happened to be packing getting a make and model on the car?"

Silva frowned as though he were considering philosophical subtleties. "Maybe."

My sciatic nerve burned. I shifted in my chair. "You mean maybe you want something in return."

"Not exactly." Silva's aquamarine eyes became as hard as blue zircon. "We have a common interest here. Maybe I can help you. But maybe you learn a thing or two goes beyond our shared interest. Maybe causes you to interfere with other interests of mine."

Keisha matched Silva's hard look with obsidian. "We don't give a shit about your other interests. We want to find the man who killed Steven Bowen."

"You know they got undergarments besides sports bras, honey," he said. "Like me to send something over? Bet you'd look spectacular in purple."

The cartilage in her jaw rippled. "Make. Model. License plate."

Silva sneered. "Couldn't go wrong with hot pink."

My cool-it look was too late.

"Don't jive us, asshole." Keisha hammered her fist down on the table.

Silva's crystal glass toppled and rolled toward the edge of the table near Keisha. I heard two bar stools creak behind me, relieved of the weight of their occupants. The glass dropped from my sight. In a motion too fast to see, Silva snatched up the crystal with his right hand and held it up in front of Keisha's face. The man in the linen shirt snickered. Sol rushed up with a towel and mopped up the rivulet of scotch from the table, then bent over to wipe the floor.

"Get your fat ass out of here." Silva returned the empty stemware to the table.

"Yes, sir." Sol retreated, despoiling the myth that fat men are light on their feet.

I knew Keisha wasn't being thin-skinned about the sexual innuendoes, but she'd let her association between her brother and Steven Bowen compromise her poise.

"Guess some broads belong in flannel." Silva softened his look then turned to me.

The man in linen snickered again. Keisha glared at him. The man's crow-colored friends grinned at her.

"We came for one thing," I said.

"Good." He looked down at his empty glass and nodded as though answering his own question. "They say everything happened so fast and it was too dark for a plate. But that car come racing around the corner was a new-model Camaro. Red."

Creed Beaumont. "This citizen put a round into the Camaro?"

"Popped the headlight out with his second shot." Silva lifted his glass. "Looks like I've had my limit. Gotta run."

The goons rose in unison as he stood. The man in the white linen shirt slid toward the end of the booth.

"Let's go, partner," I said, pushing back my chair.

Keisha looked at me as though I'd drawn her attention away from a thought she'd been trying to lock on to.

"After you." Silva motioned toward the door.

Keisha and I walked ahead, she to my right. The sound of heavy footsteps told me Silva's bodyguards were right behind us. Reaching for the door handle, I saw Keisha glance backward. Her cheekbones suddenly became chiseled black marble and fire shot from the slits of her eyes. I turned to see what had caused this transformation.

The man in the white linen shirt had drawn up next to her. He was wearing a green nylon jacket, a football with NY centered above it, stitched on the left breast.

"You're Trivette," Keisha snarled, inching toward him.

He grinned. "What's the matter? You don't like the Jets?"

She was well inside his personal space. "An innocent boy dies 'cause someone thought they were shooting your sorry ass. And you sit over there giggling."

"Sorry about the kid, lady." Trivette smirked. "Just glad it wasn't me."

Keisha whipped her forty-five from her holster and thrust it beneath his jaw. "Next time it will be, dickhead."

Silva's henchmen moved quickly forward with the sound of metal scraping leather. I resisted reacting, not for fear of my life, but to avoid acknowledging to these men that my partner had done something incredibly stupid.

"Brenner, your partner here's a little edgy," Silva said. "Maybe a hot oil massage would do her good."

I carefully placed my hand on Keisha's shoulder.

She took her eyes off Trivette and looked at the bodyguards as if noticing their presence for the first time. She slowly lowered her firearm, then grasped Trivette's jacket and slung him into the wall next to the door. The impact of his reeling body rattled the wood paneling. A framed beer poster featuring a lingerie-clad woman fell from the wall, glass spattering over the floor.

Silva laughed. "Finally managed to break something, honey. You all right, Mouse?"

"Bitch." Trivette held his gaze on Keisha as he slowly zipped up his green jacket. He passed through the door held open by one of the men in black. The other three clustered around Silva.

"Good luck taking care of this common interest of ours," he said to me as Silva and his entourage left the bar. "It Was a Very Good Year" began to play.

I looked back at Sol, who stood up from behind the far end of the bar. The sweat running down his forehead and cheeks made his face look like a scoop of melting ice cream.

"Let's get out of here," I said.

Outside the bar, the Town Car was gone.

“What the hell you think you’re doing?” I asked Keisha, my voice low but forceful.

Keisha rammed her weapon back into its holster. “Back off, Jack.”

“No. I’m gonna chew on your ass, which is intact only because none of those thugs lost his cool the way you did.”

“That asshole was the one supposed to die. Not Steven Bowen.”

“I know you reacted the way you did because of what happened to your brother,” I said. “But you can’t let those thoughts put both our lives at risk.”

Keisha leaned back against the wall. “ ‘Glad it wasn’t me.’ ” Then louder: “He said, *‘Glad it wasn’t me.’* Goddamn him!”

“I heard him, Keisha.”

She shook her head. “I’m not talking about Trivette, Jack.” Something shifted behind her eyes. “My brother thought the noise he heard was our father coming in drunk, and I followed him from the kitchen into that dark living room, him swearing he’d never let my father beat us again, and the door burst open and, Jack, I’ve never seen such bright lights and I know I screamed but the blast was so loud.”

While that sound reverberated in her mind, we stood in near silence, the hiss of traffic on Napoleon like white noise in a library.

Keisha took several coarse breaths. “ ‘I’m glad it wasn’t me,’ is what my father said when he came home while they were taking away my brother’s body. He’d double-crossed a drug dealer. The shooters thought my brother was my father.”

21

Keisha's revelation shocked me as much as the first shot fired at me by the pond that morning. I said nothing while she drew a few deep breaths as though struggling to shake off a hideous vision gaining purchase in her mind.

She finally looked up. "I was wrong to let the personal shit get to me. It won't happen again."

I squeezed her upper arm. "Want to get a beer?"

"Take me home. Ben & Jerry's in the freezer. Those two guys don't ever disappoint."

We drove in silence until we reached her apartment.

"Listen, there's something I need to tell you," I said, and filled her in about my suspicion of Beaumont as Bowen's possible assailant.

"What time you picking me up in the morning, Jack?" Keisha asked.

"We had an appointment?"

"The man who killed Steven may be in Bon Terre. That's *my* case."

"Only maybe," I said. "According to Sheriff Perrot, Creed Beaumont has an alibi. Assuming Silva's telling the truth, someone else could have been driving Beaumont's car."

"And that someone could have shot at you when you were at the pond with Cribari."

She had a point. Her case was now linked to the world of Bon

Terre. And having her along might help dilute my own precariously personal involvement in my cousin's murder. "Maybe we oughta let Utley know what's going on first."

"Tomorrow's Sunday," she said. "Brief him Monday morning. When should I be ready?"

I sighed and thought a moment. "Noon. We both need to sleep off tonight's excitement."

Keisha stepped out of the car, then, before closing the door, stuck her head back inside. "Thank you for the verbal slap up side the head this evening. But I didn't deserve your lame joke about the absence of men in my life. We cool?"

"Cool."

As I pulled out of the parking lot admiring Keisha's resilience, my cell phone rang.

"Hi, Jack. It's me. Willow."

"Hello, me Willow," I said, immediately grimacing at my adolescent rejoinder.

"Cute," she said. "We need to talk. In person."

"Now?"

"Creed Beaumont told me some things you'll want to know about."

"What the hell you doing talking to Creed Beaumont?" I practically shouted.

"Keep your white horse in the stable. Let's meet somewhere."

"My cell phone battery's fully charged. Talk."

"See you at Molly's in half an hour." She said it with the quiet certainty that I'd obey.

Willow was waiting in front of the plate-glass window wearing black jeans and a white tank top that reached an inch above her navel. The light from the restaurant created a golden glow about her hair. She looked like the subject of a Renaissance painting, the backdrop of diners inside Molly's like the myriad of religious and mythological characters whose sole purpose is to adorn and accentuate the revered personage. More Mary Magdalene than Madonna, I thought.

"You move fast," I said, approaching her.

"It's what keeps me employed."

I nodded and started toward the door.

She grabbed my elbow. "Let's not go in."

The scented blooms on the magnolia trees lining the street more than held their own against the odors of auto exhaust. A cool breeze hummed through the leaves.

I pointed at the street lamp above. "Let's get out of the glare."

We walked to the corner. I glanced across the street at her green van, then directed her down a side street and under an awning of a used bookstore that was closed for the night. The recessed entry protected us from traffic headlights, and the magnolia perfume was stronger on the dark side of the building.

"Not quite the levee, is it, Jack?" Willow said, leaning against the brick.

"Nothing will ever be the levee," I said, hoping I hadn't sounded overly wistful. "Now tell me what you were doing talking to Creed Beaumont."

"He's working for the DEA. They have Avery Hammond in their crosshairs."

I should have long before given up being astonished at the things Willow knew and how fast she found out about them. But I was sure Willow interpreted the surprise on my face as a reaction to new and unexpected information, and I decided for the time being not to let her know Sheriff Perrot had already informed me.

"Creed Beaumont's dangerous and not someone to consider a reliable source," I said.

"But everything he's told me fits with my research. He left the military shortly after that operation in Panama and worked as a private contractor in South America."

"Mercenary," I said.

Willow nodded. "Then he found the drug trade paid better. Anyway, when he was a hired gun, he got a bit reckless with civilian lives. The Peruvian government finally got around to indicting him. Our government gave him the choice of extradition or taking a bust here and helping to bring down Hammond. Beaumont will do about as much time as Sammy the Bull."

"Why would Beaumont tell you all this?"

"Because he's broke. He figures if he can hook up with a decent writer and some connections, he's got a book deal. He doesn't want to come out of Leavenworth penniless."

"The print world's not as glamorous as television, Willow."

She puffed, "I don't want to write the damn book. I want to produce a prime-time newsmagazine feature. He's hoping the publicity from that will interest a book publisher."

"You sure know how to use other people's problems to your own advantage."

A wave of light passed over us as an SUV turned onto the side street. By the time my eyes had readjusted, Willow was within inches of me. Magnolia blossoms gave way to her fragrance.

"You saying you aren't interested in using me for your own purposes? That you really want me to stay away from that big bad wolf Creed Beaumont because you're so-o-o worried about my safety that you'd give up access to information you couldn't get any other way?" She laid her hands on my chest. "Jack. You have such a cute way of exempting yourself from scrutiny when *you* make one of life's little compromises."

I gulped on that one. "Guess I had that coming."

"Well then, if it's morally acceptable to you, I'll tell you a few other things Creed Beaumont told me." Her hands slid inside my coat. "Like maybe who shot at you today."

This surprise was accompanied by anger. I stepped back so that her hands fell to her sides. "What does Beaumont know?"

"We were having a drink late this afternoon on the deck behind the B-and-B—"

"You and Beaumont were having cocktails?"

Willow cocked her head. "Ever had a Pisco sour? It's the national drink of Peru." Her lashes flickered above her amber eyes. "We were sitting at a table near the bayou. Eddie Hammond and some young skinny guy come trolling past in Hammond's boat. Beaumont says, 'That asshole took a potshot at your boyfriend this morning.'"

"Eddie?" I asked, trying to let the boyfriend comment pass.

Willow caught my twitch and grinned. "Yeah. I'd heard nothing about it, so Beaumont filled me in."

Beaumont could have found out about the incident in dozens of ways. "How does he know it was Eddie?"

"Beaumont was having a late lunch with Hammond on the patio under the oak when Eddie and this kid pull up at the dock, then get out of the boat and walk up to the house. Eddie's carrying his rifle. Seems Eddie likes to take the boat out on the bayou with a cooler of beer, some weed, and a rifle in case he runs into a bull gator. He's fond of stuffing them and hanging them around the casino. Beaumont didn't know what had happened at the time, but later, he put two and two together. He says Eddie was just trying to scare you. He's shot over the heads of hunters who've wandered onto Hammond property before."

"What makes him so sure Eddie wasn't trying to kill me?"

"He said Eddie wouldn't have missed. Creed taught the kid to shoot himself. The only thing Eddie's not a screwup with is firearms."

So now it was *Creed.* "While we're on the subject of Eddie, maybe you can do a little more research for me."

She smiled. "Quid pro quo."

I told her I wanted to find Genevieve Hammond so I could ask her why she'd abandoned Eddie and Annie after Vern Hammond had been killed.

"Could be a story in there somewhere," she said. "I'll see what I can do."

"It'll give you something better to do than spend time with Creed Beaumont."

"I'll manage my own time, thank you. Beaumont says something big involving cocaine is going down soon and he's giving me an insider's view of a sting. I'm his one chance to salvage something from it before he does time."

"You'll let me know if you get specifics."

"Of course. Life's little compromises." She moved close to me again. Her breath was hot in my ear. "Care to make another?"

Sharing vital information portends even greater intimacy than sharing feelings. It's why cops of both genders sometimes find themselves in bed with confidential informants. And for Willow, revealing things she knew, off-the-air and in person, without the surety of either fame or recompense, was intercourse of the most personal kind. I closed my eyes as though opening them again would hurtle me into another life. But my lids lifted onto the workaday world of job and family and consequences. "That would be more than a little compromise," I finally said.

She kissed my cheek and patted me on the chest. "I thought so."

I felt a little guilty for not having told her that I already knew about the DEA flipping Creed Beaumont. And I wanted to tell her about Maurice Silva claiming the car driven by the man who shot Steven Bowen might belong to Beaumont. But I was tired of talking and more attuned to the bouquet of the magnolias and the subtle musk emanating from Willow's skin.

"Maybe a small compromise." I pulled her to me without the ferocity of our youth, but with a tender resolve to let her know that what I was about to do was not the abandonment of self-control but an act of closure. Her mouth parted even before my tongue could breach her lips, which melded with mine as though guided by the kind of ancient memory that returns spawning fish to their place of birth. We held each other for a while before gradually letting go.

"What you've told me really helps," I said. "Thanks for the heads-up."

Willow grasped my hands and stepped back, her topaz eyes sparkling. "Jack, didn't anyone ever tell you the pun is the lowest form of humor?"

Our hands didn't part until we'd reached the corner, where Willow darted across the street toward the green van. The warmth from her palm dissipated slowly, the way details from a pleasant dream languish in the dawn.

Driving home, I felt Willow settle into a place in my heart where the blood flows warm and gentle. Where the past is remembered but not longed after. Where lightning flickers softly over the levee, and a storm passes with a contented sigh.

22

Alexis and I made small talk the next morning over coffee and bagels. When I told her I was going to run by the station for a while before spending the afternoon in Bon Terre with Keisha, the talk stopped.

I was about to enter the Second District when I recognized a woman crossing Napoleon. As she made her way toward me, I had the feeling that her presence would somehow shift the landscape into a different perspective. The way lightning causes rebirth in ancient forests. With fire.

"Grace. This is an unexpected pleasure," I said, my instinct telling me there was more to it.

"I was in the area and called your house. You'd just left. Your wife told me I might find you here."

"What can I do for you?"

Her face held a quiet intensity. "Detective Brenner, my mother told me something last night that you need to know about."

"What?"

"It's not a coincidence that your daughter Sarah and I are allergic to shellfish," Grace paused and smiled. "And I'd really like to know what ancestor is responsible for passing that along to us."

A glint of sunlight pierced my inner eye—a flashing white radiance. I saw David's *chai,* cleansed of blood, pure and shining, the hands of Emmett Floyd Graves powerless to profane it.

Quavering, I felt the conjoining of bonds, long denied. "Grace, are you telling me you're David Brenner's daughter?"

A tear slipped over her cheek. "Your daughters are my second cousins. You and I are first cousins once removed. Google search."

"Welcome to the family, Grace." But the implications of the discovery quickly transcended my astonishment. "As you can imagine, I have some questions."

Grace's jaw hardened. "Like how my mother could have kept this from me?" She glanced at a bus moving along Magazine. "We were cleaning up after the restaurant closed last night. When I mentioned that you told me Sarah and I had the same allergy and skin color, Mother started crying and dropped a plate. I asked her what was wrong. But she kept sobbing. I figured she was just tired because Grandpa had a bad day.

"Mom finally stopped crying and that's when she told me. Imagine how I felt growing up believing I was the product of a one-night stand. She'd always told me she'd met a soldier in San Francisco who went off and got killed in Vietnam."

"She give you a reason for not telling you the truth about your father?" I asked.

"My father . . . Gosh. It feels strange to talk about him like he was a real person." Grace rubbed her left cheek with the back of her hand. "She was afraid of how my father's family would react. I got angry and said she had no right to keep me separated from them. She cried some more. I left and spent the night with Truman." She wiped the other cheek. "I am *really* mad at Mother."

"Parents make mistakes," I said.

"This isn't quite the same thing as the time she cut my bangs too short."

I chuckled, then considered how much of a shock this discovery would be to Grace's grandmother, my aunt Joyce. Before I could contemplate the implications of that, my cell phone rang.

"You're not planning on standing me up, are you?" Keisha Lundy asked.

I looked at my watch. I was late. But I needed to talk with Faith

Tilden, and Keisha couldn't be part of that conversation. "Some things have come up."

"So, you'll be a little tardy."

I took a breath. "We'll go to Bon Terre in the morning."

She picked up on my hesitation. "Don't bullshit me. What's going on?"

"I have to talk to someone. Alone. It's a long story."

"Tell it on the way. Ten minutes?"

After the previous night, I couldn't refuse her. "Make it fifteen."

As I closed the phone, Grace grasped my hand. David's flesh pressing mine. "I want to meet my family. You tell me when the time's right."

"I promise." For the first time I noticed the faint crease down the tip of her nose. Like David's.

I picked up Keisha and by the time we reached the speed trap outside Bon Terre, manned by Officer Trevino, I'd finished filling her in on Grace's announcement. I said nothing about seeing Willow the night before.

"That's some heavy shit," Keisha said. "I can't believe a mother would tell her daughter she'd been knocked up by a stranger to hide her real daddy's identity."

"That's the private conversation I need to have."

"No problem, long as we get to Creed Beaumont today."

As we neared the turnoff for Meal Thyme, red and blue sparks erupted in my rearview mirror followed by a high-pitched wail.

Keisha glanced through the rear window. "Your heavy foot's gonna cost you again."

As I peered over my left shoulder, Jarla Thomas sailed past and pointed ahead. We followed her into a dirt clearing next to a daiquiri shack. GEAUX CUP was painted crookedly across a weathered eight-by-four pine panel leaning against an even more weathered structure.

Keisha and I stepped out of the car. The morning coolness was gone and the air smelled of dry chalk and scorched metal. Jarla exited her cruiser, hat and sunglasses in place, and motioned toward a nearby picnic table. The surface was encrusted with beverage spills, while Styrofoam cups, straws, and plastic tops lay scattered underneath. Jarla went to the service window and quickly retrieved three thirty-two-ounce containers and set them on the table.

"On-duty specials." She lifted a drink, put the straw to her lips, and tilted her head toward Keisha as though sizing her up.

"My partner, Detective Lundy," I said. "You have some reason for stopping us?"

Jarla's shaded eyes left Keisha. She picked up a cup and handed it to me while Keisha scooped up the remaining beverage, lifted the lid, and sniffed.

Jarla watched her carefully replace the plastic top and jab the straw into the icy concoction. "I want to finish off a conversation you had with the sheriff yesterday, Detective Brenner."

"Damn!" Keisha said. "This tastes like gunpowder and bull nettle stirred into a flat Pepsi."

Jarla made a toast with her frozen blend. "Tea, lemonade, mango syrup, Red Bull, and Tabasco."

Keisha tossed the cup into an open trash can next to the table. Most others had missed.

"Nice shot," Jarla said, watching the slush-filled Styrofoam land with a hollow thunk. Then she fixed her gaze on mine. "I know the sheriff told you about our little problem with Mr. Hammond."

"Detective Lundy is here with me because your problem and our problem seem to involve the same people."

"You think Creed Beaumont is involved with a shooting in New Orleans. He's not."

I'd always had trouble seeing Jarla Thomas as a big-city cop looking for a more pastoral setting. "You speaking for the sheriff or by some other authority?"

Jarla let the straw slip from her lips and set her drink on the hot, viscous tabletop.

"You don't fit the profile of a small-town deputy," I said. "And I'm not talking about gender."

"I was with Lubbock PD. Now I'm in Bon Terre. That hard to understand?"

"You left Texas for this job?" Keisha cast derisive eyes toward Jarla's cruiser.

Jarla slowly peeled away her sunglasses. Her crystalline blue eyes were as frozen as her jaw.

"Let me guess," I said. "You're federal. Probably DEA, because my partner found out they're after Maurice Silva and his suppliers. Creed Beaumont connects Silva to Avery Hammond. I think you're working the sell side of a big deal."

Keisha raised her eyebrows at Jarla. "That *Special Agent* Thomas, or what?"

Jarla folded her sunglasses and slid them into her shirt pocket. "All out of business cards."

"We have a dead teenager in New Orleans," I said. "The boy had a helluva future."

"I'm not unsympathetic. If I thought Beaumont was the shooter, I'd drag his ass into the Second Precinct myself. Believe me. But he was in Lafayette the night your vic went down."

"You know for sure?" Keisha asked.

"One of our undercovers was involved in the Lafayette deal."

"DEA," I said.

"Yeah. DEA. So I know for sure."

"Yesterday we talked to Maurice Silva and his punk sidekick Mousey Trivette," I said. "They made a big effort to let us know the shots that killed Steven Bowen came from a red Camaro and were meant for Trivette. The day you caught me in your speed trap, the left front end of Beaumont's car had bodywork done to it, but it hadn't been painted yet. What do you know about that?"

Jarla looked down, eyes in motion, like she was counting the empty cups strewn about. "He'd left the car in the parking lot at the casino that night. Found it damaged when he came back early the next morning. Probably plugged by some drunk roughneck who'd lost a whole week's pay."

"How'd he get to Lafayette?" I asked.

"Hammond's ML55. The gas tank's been modified to hold product. Even the dope dogs can't sniff it out."

"Someone else could've borrowed his wheels," Keisha said.

"We don't assign agents to watch parked cars."

"But you've been watching me." I set my untouched drink on the picnic table. "How did you happen to be so close by yesterday?"

"Eddie Hammond likes to hunt over by the sinkhole. Except for the pipeline easement, it's their property. He's been known to send a salvo over the heads of trespassing sportsmen."

Exactly what Beaumont told Willow. "The shots came from across the pond. We were in the open. There was no mistaking us for poachers."

"He's a reckless kid. Thought I'd come by and tell you to be careful."

"Or is there something near that pond you don't want us knowing about?" Keisha asked.

Jarla watched an old Dodge truck wheel into the Geaux Cup lot, sending up a light brown billow that looked like steam rising from a sulfurous pool. Suddenly the two young boys in the cab spotted her cruiser. The driver gunned the engine.

"Not even legal to drive but they'd have been served if I wasn't standing here," Jarla said.

Her concern seemed genuine, if not on point. "My partner's question wasn't rhetorical, Special Agent. We'll go back to the sinkhole if you don't answer it."

Jarla rattled the ice in her quart cup as her narrowed eyes followed the fleeing adolescents. "Rather you didn't. Eddie set up a small meth lab back in there a couple of months ago. I was worried Eddie and his buddy might decide to fire a warning shot."

"His buddy?" Another matching detail from the story Beaumont gave Willow.

"Some rich kid from New Orleans who likes to gamble. Beaumont's seen him with Eddie at Hammond's casino. Sometimes the guy's with a well-dressed forty-something ex-cheerleader, not always the same one. From Beaumont's description, he's the same character we've seen traveling with Eddie on his boat to the meth lab."

Drugs. Rich, well-preserved matrons. I slowly turned to Keisha, who looked like she was waiting for me to figure out a *Wheel of Fortune* puzzle she already knew the answer to.

Jarla glanced between us. "Sound like someone you know?"

"Jason Meade," Keisha and I replied in duet.

"Who's Jason Meade?" Jarla asked.

"Brother of Steven Bowen's girlfriend," I said. "It's not surprising he and Eddie Hammond are hooked up. They both have the personality of a feral hog with roundworms."

"Assuming Eddie's friend is who you think it is," Jarla said.

"Eddie part of the family business?" I asked.

She shook her head. "He's on his own with his meth lab. We haven't done anything about it because it might queer our operation, but Avery Hammond would shit if he knew. He's pretty protective of his niece and nephew."

"I'm protective of my friends. A retired FBI agent fighting cancer got close to a couple of live rounds. What have you done about that?"

"Sheriff Perrot went out to the Hammond place last night, but no one seems to know where Eddie is. It's not unusual for him to just take off. He likes playing Texas Hold 'Em in Vegas."

"Coulda taken off last week in Beaumont's Camaro and shot Steven Bowen," Keisha said.

"If this were my case, I'd have to ask myself why," Jarla said.

An obvious but unexplored question. But I recalled Eddie's rage at being overruled by Beaumont, then reprimanded by Avery Hammond. "Maybe he wants to force his way into the family business."

"And killing Mousey Trivette would help how?" Jarla asked.

"Maybe he wanted to set up Beaumont," I said. "Doesn't matter whether Silva or the cops take him down."

"Not sure Eddie's brain can handle that many moving parts." Jarla slurped the remainder of her drink, then dumped it into the trash can. "I don't want to interfere with your case, and I expect the same courtesy from you two. If Eddie's your guy, let me know before you take him down. It's taken the DEA two years to get this far with Hammond and we've about got him. We square on this, detectives?"

Keisha rolled her eyes.

"If not, we can work it out with your lieutenant." Jarla removed her sunglasses from her pocket and flipped out the earpieces. "We square?"

I nodded, then noticed Jarla eyeing the sweating cup I'd left on the table. "All yours, Special Agent Thomas. I didn't touch it."

Keisha grabbed me by the arm. "Lord, you best be thankful for that."

Returning to our car, I switched on the ignition. Before I could shift into gear, my cell phone rang.

"Make any compromises today, Jack?"

"Willow. Where are you?"

Keisha laid her arm on the backrest and swiveled in my direction.

"Baton Rouge."

"On your way to Angola?"

"My hair loses its bounce in that place. Remember that research project you gave me?"

"Don't tell me you found Genevieve Hammond."

"*Formerly* Hammond. She married Alton Baron, a judge turned state legislator who died last year."

That was quick even for Willow, but at the moment I was more eager to question Faith Tilden about my newfound family connection. "Can it wait till tomorrow? I need to see someone else this afternoon."

"Jack," she snapped. "You asked me to find this woman. It took some doing to get her to talk and she's in the mood now. Meet me at the Coffee Connection across from the Hotel LaFonte at four-thirty. At five o'clock, she's no longer your witness. She's my source."

"Willow—" I heard her beep off.

"Ah, the bottled blond flame." Keisha cackled. "And you got the nerve to ask her to wait?"

I explained the situation, including why talking to Genevieve Hammond could be important. "There's time to take you back to New Orleans," I said.

Keisha waggled her index finger. "Uh-uh, sugar. I'll be damned if I'll miss the chance to personally inspect that girl's dark roots."

23

We made good time to Baton Rouge and arrived at the coffee shop a little after four. Willow was seated near the window with an espresso.

"There she is," I whispered to Keisha as we entered the door.

"Golly, Jack. I could never have picked her out on my own."

"This is my partner, Keisha Lundy," I said as we approached Willow's table.

"Pleasure, Ms. Ashe," Keisha said. "You and Jack have sorta been partners, too,"

The women traded tentative smiles.

Keisha tapped my arm. "I'm gonna get me one of those fancy chocolate drinks."

"How'd you find this woman?" I asked Willow as Keisha wandered toward the counter.

"A guilty conscience marinating in alcohol. Genevieve's carried a heavy load for thirty-one years. She called for me at the station after watching my last broadcast. Our news producer gave me the message this morning. She's got a hell of a story."

The skin on my face tightened. "You've already talked to her? You told me she was your source if I didn't rush up here."

"You assumed that meant I hadn't interviewed her. I wanted to make sure it was worth your time."

I took a deep breath and reminded myself that my purpose was to shed new light on my cousin's death, not engage in verbal judo with Willow Ashe. "She involved in David's murder?"

"Not exactly. See the hotel concierge. She'll take you to Genevieve's suite." Willow lifted her demitasse. "I'll be taking off as soon as I finish this. Call me tomorrow, Jack."

I crossed the street hoping she'd led me to something useful. Inside Hotel LaFonte, I gave my name to the concierge, who nodded and reached for the phone on her desk.

"Finished with her?" I heard her ask. She chuckled softly. A few seconds later, the concierge covered her mouth to stifle a giggle, then replaced the receiver and flipped up a placard that said, WILL RETURN MOMENTARILY.

"Mrs. Baron's expecting you," the lanky, coffee-skinned woman said. "I'll take you up."

We stepped off the elevator on what the hotel called the Grande Level and I followed the woman down a corridor. A muscular young man exited the double mahogany door at the end of the hallway pushing a cart that appeared to be a portable massage table. He wore Nike sandals and an unbuttoned Hawaiian shirt. The concierge smiled furtively at the man, who responded with a double pump of his eyebrows.

"He come with the suite?" I asked.

"I'd be happy to discuss our Grande Level amenities with you on your way out, Mr. Brenner."

A moment later she knocked on the mahogany door.

"You forget something, sugar?" a voice called from inside.

"It's Clara," the concierge responded. "I've brought Mr. Brenner."

"Oh. Come in."

The concierge seemed amused as she swiped a card through the door's magnetic reader, turned the brass doorknob, and stood aside while I entered the marbled foyer of the suite.

Genevieve Hammond, rather Genevieve Baron, stepped away from a well-stocked bar dividing the entry from the living room. One hand clutched her black silk robe just below her breasts, the other gripped a pint glass a third full of liquid that I was pretty sure wasn't tea.

"Can I get you anything?" the concierge asked her.

Genevieve looked me over. "You've done real well so far this afternoon, Clara. I'll let you know."

I heard the lock click behind me.

"Can I get anything for *you,* Detective?" She placed the glass on the bar and quickly tied the sash of her robe.

"No thanks," I said, noticing the hem clinging to her thighs just above the knees.

She shrugged, picked up her glass, and motioned me toward the living room. The entire back wall was glass and overlooked the Mississippi. The sky from western to northern horizons was a pallid blue, and the July afternoon sun burned formlessly through it like a flame inside a rice-paper lantern. In the south, swollen purple rain clouds assembled for their late-afternoon commute into New Orleans.

Genevieve slipped onto a couch and patted the space next to her. "Please sit."

"Quite a view." I parked myself in an easy chair across the coffee table from her.

"Funny how someone can charge so much to look at something that doesn't belong to them." She took a sip from the pint glass.

I could see the resemblance between Genevieve and her children, particularly Annie, though the physical trait revealed by the deep V in her robe could hardly be shared with a son. Like daughter, the mother's complexion was smooth and richly tanned, and her eyes were such a delicate composite of emerald and sienna that calling them hazel was inadequate. Wealth provides advantages when it comes to physical appearance, but Genevieve Baron's figure and facial features were well beyond those associated with handsome and well-preserved women in their fifties. She could have easily passed for Annie's older sister.

"Sure I can't interest you in a drink? Every batch of this bourbon has a different proof. They handwrite it on each bottle." She leaned forward to set her glass on the table, presenting me with another stunning view.

"You wanted to talk to me," I said.

She gave me the kind of smile that refused to acknowledge business and pleasure as separate enterprises. "I want to tell you about the night your cousin was killed."

"Thirty-one years ago you told the FBI you were riding out the storm with your husband. You going to tell me something different now?"

"Very."

"And I should believe you?"

She placed her hands on her bare knees and looked down into the pint glass as though merely looking at the high-octane whiskey would fortify her. "I know I lied about being with my husband that night. But I had no choice."

I cocked my head. "But now you do?"

She shrugged. "I'm independent now."

"Have to wait out a prenupt to get there?" I asked.

The lines around her mouth revealed themselves for the first time and her eyes were as sharp as broken glass. "I've paid my dues, Detective."

I raised my palms in apology. "I'm listening."

Genevieve reached for her glass of small-batch bourbon and acknowledged my gesture with a mock toast. After taking a deep swallow, she drew up her legs, settled back into the couch, and looked off toward the windows.

Bam, bam, bam. The wind battered the one-room trailer, the thunder so loud Genevieve Hammond could barely hear her own moaning. Nearing exhaustion, she thrust her hips furiously upward, cursing herself for sharing a second bottle of bourbon with Emmett Floyd Graves. The torrent of alcohol that had removed any restraint from her also held her short of passion's meridian for what seemed an hour.

There. Finally. "God," she whimpered. "That's it."

"'Bout goddamn time." Graves rose on his elbows and jackhammered her until her pubic bone ached. "Ahh."

"Oh, baby." She shuddered as the lightning seemed to crackle through her loins.

Bam, bam, bam. But it was neither the thunder nor her climax. It was a fist against the trailer door.

"Goddamn!" Graves rolled off her and grabbed his jeans from the floor.

"Please don't." But she was sure her breathless voice was lost in the rain, which clanged like marbles against the trailer walls.

"Hold on!" he hollered toward the door.

Genevieve gulped, her words finding greater timbre. "Don't, Emmett. What if it's—?"

"If it was your husband, honey, he'd a-blowed off the locks by now, and whatever slugs he had left over would be in my butt and your brains."

Bam, bam, bam. Graves pulled a pistol from the nightstand.

She hopped out of bed, snatched her clothes from a chair, and rushed into the bathroom.

"Hang on, goddamn it," she heard Graves shout. "I'm coming."

Could someone have followed them from the juke joint and called her husband? Her car was hidden from view behind the trailer. But what if Graves allowed him inside and what if he needed to use the head? She ducked into the shower stall, pulled the curtain shut, and sat clutching her clothes to her breasts, her buttocks cold against the fiberglass.

She heard Graves open the door. The wind fumed and pellets of rain rattled the hardpan outside the trailer, making it impossible to discern the muffled voices. Seconds later, she heard something clunk on the trailer floor, then the whistles of wind became slightly muted. Eventually she stood, put on her clothes, and ventured cautiously from the bathroom. With an eye to the door, she crept to the window above the bed and carefully parted the curtains.

Twenty yards away, a mud-splattered police cruiser was parked nearly parallel to the trailer in a crushed-shell turnabout. Lightning flashes revealed two men inside the car. Emmett Graves and her husband, Sheriff Vern Hammond.

She trembled at what might have happened if Graves hadn't moved her car behind the trailer, despite her lustful cooing that she couldn't wait for him. But she'd waited inside, loosening all but two buttons of her rain-soaked blouse. Then she pulled down her panties from beneath her skirt as whiskey burned the upper regions of her chest, and she'd told herself that her absence from home could be explained by her discretion in waiting out the storm.

Had Graves boastfully told her husband that they must talk in the car because he'd offered shelter to some needful woman, had his way with her, and would again once the two men had finished their business? And had Genevieve's husband laughed, affirming his shared regard for floozies whose self-abasement was totally unconnected to the esteem of the men they pleased?

Shame burned Genevieve more than fear because she knew Emmett Graves had protected her by telling her husband the truth. Save for her name.

The two men got out and walked to the back of the cruiser. Vern lifted the lid of the trunk. Graves looked into the well and exchanged words with her husband.

Suddenly Vern pulled his fist from his pocket, grabbed Graves's hand and slapped something into it. Money?

Graves peered back into the trunk and nodded, then shoved his hand into his jeans pocket. He leaned into the trunk and lifted out something wrapped in a blanket.

Vern shut the trunk and nodded toward the trailer. Genevieve drew back. Could he have seen her? Then Vern turned and said something else to Graves, who nodded again, and a grim smile flickered beneath the brim of Vern's tycoon straw hat.

The cruiser's engine fired up in the rain. Graves carried the rolled-up rug toward a destination she could not see.

Minutes later, Graves stepped inside the trailer and shook like a retriever who'd just fetched a duck from the water. He picked up his handgun from the floor—the clunk heard while hiding in the bathroom—and laid it on the nightstand. Genevieve sat on the footstool in front of an easy chair, the burning tip of her freshly lit cigarette the only light in the trailer. Then a glimmer of lightning flashed through a part she'd left in the curtain.

Graves glanced toward it. "Been watching out the window, have you?"

Genevieve hoped the darkness masked the trembling of her hand. "What brings my husband out in this godawful storm?"

"None of your concern."

"Did he question why you didn't invite him in?" She knew the answer.

"Told him I'd offered refuge to some woman whose husband was riding out the hurricane on a rig in the Gulf."

"And you got lucky." The words were as raw as her whiskey-coated throat.

"What you did to me first was lucky. What I did to you next was work, honey." Graves pulled out a rain slicker and a hunting cap. "I got business to attend to. Don't be here when I get back."

She may have no self-respect, Genevieve thought, but she was the goddamned sheriff's wife and Emmett Graves was an ex-con. "I wonder who'd get the worst of it if my husband knew he'd driven up to your trailer just as you spent yourself inside his wife?"

Emmett Graves opened the top drawer of the nightstand. She didn't see what he removed, but a second later a hand gripped her hair and she felt cold steel against her cheek, the tip pressed into the tender skin beneath her eye, the blade flashing like mercury with each lightning bolt.

"Understand there's no end to what I can do. And ain't nowhere to hide that I can't find you."

She nodded, slowly, as Graves drew back the knife. "Can I use the bathroom?"

The cold left her cheek. Graves let go of her hair and let his hand fall to her neck. He bent down and kissed her lips gently, his breath smelling of smoke and stale bourbon. "Now that we have an understanding, you're welcome back anytime, honey." Then he stood and said, "Go on and pee before you leave."

The whiskey curdled in her stomach. "No. I'll go."

Seconds later, Genevieve Hammond felt her car fishtail in the mud behind the trailer as she tried to speed away. She eased back on the accelerator, then lurched onto the drive. She hit the gas again and found traction this time. The engine whined and the oyster shells clattered beneath the undercarriage. The veins in her temples pulsed with every burst of thunder.

The windowpanes in the hotel suite rattled as the thunderheads moved over Baton Rouge. The living room was dark. Genevieve Baron's body was merely an outline, while lightning flashes etched her face in high relief, like a white marble bust with vacant eyes. The details of her story matched all that Emmett Graves had told me. Except the visitor she saw was not Avery Hammond, but his brother, Vern, the sheriff. Why did Graves change the most important detail? Perhaps Graves did it to cause trouble for Avery, whom he blamed for landing him in prison. Graves never expected me to hear the story from another point of view.

"Excuse me." Genevieve rose and took her glass to the bar.

I went to the window and looked out toward the Mississippi. Shadowy vessels studded with watch lights moved slowly in both directions. The I-10 bridge shimmered in the smoky atmosphere.

"Guess I'm not as free and independent as I pretend," Genevieve said when she returned.

"Memories can bind a person as much as the present," I said, almost as a reminder to myself. "You lied to the FBI. But you had to lie to Vern, too."

Genevieve moved closer to the window, crossed arms squeezed against her breasts, whiskey glass in one hand. "My husband was working that evening. I called dispatch from the bar after Emmett Graves and I polished off our first bottle of bourbon. Told him if my husband inquired that I was all right, I was on my way back from visiting a friend in Houma, and I'd pulled into a bar to wait out the storm. Said I wasn't sure of the location, but I'd stay put all night if I had to. The dispatcher told me that was a smart thing to do. Later, after leaving Graves's trailer, I went back to the same bar. I called dispatch again and said I'd had too much to drink and wasn't sure when I could drive again. It was a different dispatcher, so I had to tell him the whole story I'd told the other. But this time I stupidly told him where I was." She laughed scornfully. "Didn't think he'd actually come get me."

"The dispatcher?"

"This dispatcher radioed my husband, who showed up twenty minutes later." She shook her head. "Vern asked me where I'd been and I told him I'd been visiting a friend in Houma and was on my way home, but pulled into the bar sometime around eight."

"You weren't afraid Vern would check out your story with the bartender?"

"The bartenders in this place never know anything, if you know what I mean." She took a pull of bourbon. "Then Vern told me that if anyone asked, he came for me around nine."

"So he covered his tracks by hitching on to your fabrication," I said. "Do you believe Vern killed David Brenner and Elton Jackson?"

"He had no reason. Avery and Vern were paying Elton's way through college, along with some other kids. They couldn't come right out and say it to the white public, but they had no problem with blacks voting."

There it was again. Missing motive. "He at least helped someone else cover it up. Why?"

"The Hammonds are big into favors," she said. "Need money? Need someone out of the way? A Hammond takes care of it. But they're into you for life."

"That why Avery Hammond paid college tuition for kids like Deer Jackson?"

"Put the parents on his payroll."

"Vern died six months later," I said. "That got someone off the hook."

She scoffed. "Thanks to a passing motorist so intent on not getting a ticket that he shot my husband in the face."

"Sounds like you don't believe it was a random event," I said.

"There are no coincidences in Bon Terre."

"Like you didn't just one day up and leave your kids for no reason. What makes a mother abandon her children?" I asked.

"I had a choice. Leave without them or leave them without a mother."

"Someone threatened to kill you if you didn't leave without your children?"

She wiped her eyes. "Emmett Graves came by six weeks after Angélique and Edmond were born and told me I had two days to get the hell out of Bon Terre."

Annie and Eddie. "What would Emmett Graves gain by that?" I asked.

"Graves did the bidding of both brothers. Avery considered me unstable. Can't deny that." She cast me a humorless smile. "Vern was gone, and I wasn't really a Hammond. But Avery figured the children were. And his goal in life is to preserve the Hammond name and property. He wanted to raise his legacies without interference from me."

"That was then. What's kept you away all this time?"

"Oh. Did I forget to tell you how much money I paid Emmett Graves over the years?" She turned away and headed toward the bar.

I followed.

She grabbed a fresh pint glass from an open shelf. "Two years later, and three weeks after my honeymoon with my second husband, Graves was back. The night I told you about was the last but not the only time I slept with him. Graves threatened to tell the press about our affair. Judge Baron was running for his first term in the state legislature and did not need a wife with a tawdry past." She pulled the cork from a bourbon bottle.

"Emmett Graves is locked away for life," I said. "Even if you couldn't go back to your children before, you can now."

She poured four fingers into the pint glass, then raised a toast to me. "Not only memories bind."

"But they're your children," I said.

The heavy glass clunked on the granite counter. She covered it with her other hand to steady it. "And mothers protect their children. Even from their father if they have to."

"You're not making any sense," I said. "Your kids' father has been dead for over thirty years."

"Then let's leave it at that. Please go."

"I think a nest of vipers is crawling out of hibernation in your head about now. I think you're trying to tell me something."

She picked up her bourbon and looked scornfully at me. "For God's sake, Detective. Just do the math."

Genevieve turned and walked uncertainly toward the windows overlooking the river. I followed her into the living room then stopped, suddenly realizing what she had told me. Through the glass I saw lightning pulsing weakly along the northern horizon as the spent thunderclouds moved out of the city. Barges floated around the bend beyond the I-10 bridge. But other vessels moved up river, their forms growing larger, their cargo revealed by new light.

24

Genevieve Baron took a long pull on the whiskey and gazed at the majestic view that had cost her so dearly. Without speaking, I made my way to the elevator and descended from the penthouse.

I'd learned that two men who'd violated my family and me in different ways were bound by blood. Eddie Hammond had terrorized me at the same sinkhole where his biological father, Emmett Graves, had dumped my cousin's body thirty-one years earlier. Then Graves may have killed the man who'd either murdered or covered up the murders of David and Deer Jackson. I had yet to discover a purpose for their killings, but there was another motive to contemplate.

What reason did Graves have for killing Vern Hammond? Did Graves learn he'd fathered Eddie and Annie, then murder Vern and terrify Genevieve into leaving her children behind to protect the secret? Or did Vern learn the truth and confront Graves, with fatal consequences?

I passed through the hotel lobby, the brilliancy of polished brass fixtures, white ash walls, and gilded mirrors displacing the dark scene I'd left behind.

"Come back soon, Mr. Brenner," the concierge cooed as I walked past.

When I returned to the coffee shop, Keisha's hands were

clasped around a tall cup covered with a clear plastic dome, a straw protruding from the center. "This mocha something cost me as much as a quart of Ben & Jerry's."

She pushed back her chair and followed me outside, where we stopped at the curb and waited for traffic to pass.

"Willow Ashe leave right after I did?" I asked.

"You mean, did we talk about you?"

"Well?"

"She said you were a great athlete back in high school."

"And?"

"And she's glad she got a chance to see you after all these years. You turned out to be the man she always thought you'd be. Her only disappointment is you don't trust her."

I wasn't sure what I believed. "You pump all this out of her?"

"I may have encouraged her a little. But she doesn't say things she doesn't want other people to hear."

As we cruised the interstate toward New Orleans, I told Keisha everything Genevieve Baron had revealed.

"Sounds like Eddie Hammond's got killer genes. Suppose Uncle Avery knows where he is?" Keisha asked.

"Let's find out," I said.

By the time we reached Avery Hammond's home, burnt-orange streaks arched over the water oaks and cypress trees lining the bayou.

We parked in the circular drive, climbed the steps to the front door, and rang the bell. Annie Hammond opened the door. She rested her cheek against the mahogany as though it were the shoulder of a sleeping lover and hooked a thumb into the pocket of her tight denim shorts.

"Hey, Detective."

"Your uncle home?" I asked, gazing into eyes that could have belonged to Genevieve Baron at a time when her desperation was still germinating.

"Who's she?" Annie said, looking at Keisha.

"Miss Annie. You no answer door." Cho grabbed her arm and pulled her back. "Please enter," he said to me, as he ushered Annie into a room off the foyer and closed the door. "Mr. Hammond outside. Please follow."

Cho stopped when we reached the back porch and motioned toward the patio, where a dozen citronella lamps lined the perimeter. Avery Hammond sat at the same table from which he'd viewed the extraction of the shotgun. We descended the steps and crossed the lawn, the damp grass swishing beneath our feet. As we approached, Hammond lifted a stainless shaker from the table and poured a clear liquid into a cut-glass tumbler.

"You have this unique ability to attract gorgeous women," Hammond said. "Bet your wife's a looker."

"This is Detective Lundy," I said, noticing even in the waning light that his slate tiles had been perfectly restored.

"Y'all sit down." He clicked a fingernail against the metal shaker. "I'd offer, but of course no New Orleans cop would drink on duty." Grinning, he turned to study Keisha. "I'm surprised you'd bring another officer into your case, Detective Brenner."

"Someone shot at my partner yesterday," Keisha said. "He doesn't need to be spending time alone around here."

"The sheriff came by last night asking about Eddie." Hammond took a sip from the tumbler. "I got the idea he thinks Eddie popped those shots at you. I can't think of a single reason why he'd do that."

"Where's Eddie now?" I asked.

"He's irresponsible. And—I admit I'm to blame—he has enough pocket change to come and go as he pleases."

I nodded. "He have friends in New Orleans?"

"He has friends all over the Gulf Coast."

"I'm talking about the friend he brought here yesterday," I said.

"You must mean the little twerp who made advances on Annie."

"I'm sure she offered resistance."

"Well, as you can see, she has a problem in that regard."

"What's his name?" Keisha asked.

"Ran him off before I could catch it. You'll have to ask Eddie."

A sudden glare from the bayou drew my attention. A lamp now glowed over the dock.

"Automatic timer," Hammond said.

The bass boat I'd seen previously was still there. The jet boat was gone.

"Look," he said. "When Eddie shows up, I'll tell him to call. I have your card."

I had the feeling Hammond really didn't know Eddie's whereabouts and was content with his absence. He may have even ordered him away. If something was going down soon, as Willow had suggested, having a screwup like Eddie temporarily off the board was a plus.

"Eddie's sister know where he is?" Keisha asked. "Or maybe he has a girlfriend we could talk to?"

"Anything Annie hears gets processed through her liver. And Eddie doesn't have a steady girl. I'm afraid he cuts into casino profits by erasing young ladies' debts off the books."

"Seems you've had your hands full raising your brother's children," Keisha said.

"We're a family. I'm sure Detective Brenner's told you their daddy's dead and their mama ran off."

"I spoke with their mother today," I said.

The corners of Hammond's mouth twitched. His tumbler clinked hard as he set his drink on the glass table. It was the first time I'd witnessed a chink in his composure. Even though genuinely surprised when the shotgun was unearthed from beneath his patio, he'd expressed nothing but controlled indignation over the intrusion into his private life. I was sure he was truly shocked by what I'd just told him.

"You seem to have a way of unearthing useless relics of the past," he said, recovering his complacent smile.

"She thinks Emmett Graves killed your brother."

"That woman has swamp gas for brains. Vern wasn't the first lawman gunned down 'cause he was unlucky enough to pull over an outlaw on the run."

"Vern insisted to the FBI that my cousin and Deer Jackson were killed by outsiders. Six months later your brother's shot by a stranger." I thought about Genevieve telling me there are no coincidences in Bon Terre. "That's a lot of random murder for a small town."

"Why the hell would Graves want to kill Vern?"

I wasn't ready to float the idea of Graves being father to Eddie and Annie, one reason being that Hammond's assessment of Genevieve wasn't far off and she could have been unloading a hallucination on me, though I didn't think so.

"Graves says Vern directed him to dump the boys' bodies. He also told him to dispose of the shotgun."

"Look. I know you're looking for—what does Dr. Phil call it? Closure? But you can't believe my brother killed those boys."

"Either that or he covered up for someone else."

Hammond slapped his arm to kill a mosquito the citronella hadn't deterred. "Goddamn it! You've brought nothing but speculation with you, all based on the fabrications of that miscreant Graves and a deranged whore."

"The miscreant worked for you."

"Graves delivered new cars and trucks to customers' homes and took their trade-ins. Worked security at the casino. He may have had what you call a checkered past, but who knew he was into illegal drugs?"

"I think your brother used him for general dirty work. After Vern died, you continued using him for off-balance sheet projects."

Hammond narrowed his eyes as though wondering how much we knew about his real business.

"You called Genevieve a whore," I said. "Did you know her to be unfaithful to Vernon?"

"This is the sort of trash I was afraid you and that pinup girl reporter would kick up." Hammond rose suddenly, his chair grating across the slate. "You came to talk to Eddie. He's not here."

I glanced back toward the dock. Moths and june bugs flitted about the lamp. Then something clicked in my mind as I saw

Hammond lift his drink to his lips. "Mind if we check with Annie on the way out?"

He finished a deep swallow, then turned and walked away.

"Doubt if talking to Annie's gonna do us any good," said Keisha as we made our way back to the house. "Apparently things don't stay long in that girl's head."

"Maybe she'll give us something," I said.

Annie was on the veranda overlooking the stables, sitting on a cushioned chair, drink in hand. Her feet were propped on the railing, one slender ankle crossing the other.

"Hey, Annie," I said. "We'd like to talk to your brother. Know where he might be?"

"He doesn't tell me anything." Her feet dropped to the deck. She rose and turned, then sat straddling the chair, her arms draped over the back. "No one does."

"He have any special friends?" Keisha asked. "Certain places he likes to hang out?"

Annie shrugged and took a swig of spirits.

"How about the fellow who was with him yesterday?" I asked. "You know him?"

"I just met Jason yesterday. He's young, but I think he knows his way around, if you get my drift. Uncle Avery made him go away." She said it like a six-year-old who's been dragged off the playground at suppertime.

Annie had confirmed that Eddie's friend was who Keisha and I suspected. Jason Meade.

Her pout became a smile. "Jason told me to look him up whenever I'm in New Orleans."

"Maybe that's where Eddie went," Keisha said.

"If you see Jason, tell him I'm still here." She tilted her glass upward, swallowed the contents, then waited to catch my eye before letting a solitary ice cube slowly emerge from her lips and slide down her tongue until it clinked into the bottom of the glass.

"All gone," she said.

"Let me take care of that." I grasped the bottom of the glass with one hand and covered her wrist with the other until the glass slipped from her fingers and I'd secured it.

Annie caressed my fingers. "Be right back?"

"We have to go, Annie. I'll have Cho refresh your drink."

We walked back into the kitchen, where Cho was chopping onions next to the sink. Keisha followed me toward the front door.

"You gonna bring that empty glass with you?" she asked when we reached the foyer and opened the door.

"Got an evidence bag?"

"Got gloves," she said as we descended the porch steps.

When we reached the car, Keisha pulled a glove from the inside pocket of her blazer while I held up Annie's glass, my fingers firmly around the base.

Keisha smiled as she slipped the glove over the rim. "Cool move, Jack. Gotta be some of Graves's DNA stored somewhere."

"Why settle for Genevieve Baron's word that Emmett Graves is Annie's father?"

25

My day had started with a jolt: Grace Tilden was David's daughter. Then a detour on my way to question her mother, Faith, led me to the discovery of another family's hidden bonds. If only I could connect these secrets to my cousin's murder.

Keisha and I drove back to the city to drop off Annie's glass at the crime lab on Broad. It was Sunday evening, so I left Sally Ellis, the lab tech who processed the shotgun, a note telling her the comparison I needed wasn't for case evidence. I only needed to know if the DNA she took off the glass came from someone related to Emmett Graves.

As we returned to the car, my mind refocused on a case starting to show signs of progress.

"Why would Eddie Hammond borrow Beaumont's Camaro to attempt a hit on Mousey Trivette?" I asked as I swerved around a bus, only to catch a light.

"Eddie's trying to break into the narcotics business," Keisha said. "He uses Beaumont's car hoping to pin the shooting on him, then moves in to strike his own deals with Silva."

I shook my head. "Gunning down Maurice Silva's top lieutenant is a dangerous play for a punk like Eddie and it doesn't guarantee him a piece of the action afterward. Another thing. Eddie was clowning around with Jason Meade at the Hammond estate Saturday. Then he vanishes. Why so suddenly?"

"He knows someone's looking for him. If not us, then Silva."

"I don't see word of our meeting with Silva getting out that quickly."

Keisha flicked her eyes toward the traffic signal, which had turned green. "Beaumont probably told him. Even if he thinks Eddie tried to set him up, he isn't going to take out Hammond's nephew. He tells Eddie that Silva's figured him for going after Trivette and he should lay low for a while. Gets Eddie out of the way for whatever's going down."

Beaumont's best seller. "Works as a theory. Let's pay Beaumont a visit tomorrow and see if he knows where Eddie is. But Faith Tilden's first on my dance card in the morning."

"Don't forget about the lieutenant."

Utley had been emphatic about seeing me in person and I didn't want to ruin the good turn in my relationship with him. "Let him know I'll be in before noon to brief him."

"Sure," Keisha said, her attention suddenly drawn to a Winn-Dixie looming on our right. She rapidly patted my shoulder the way my girls did when they wanted something from me. "Jack. Could you pull in for a sec? I ran out of Ben & Jerry's last night."

I drove south to Bon Terre the next morning under a cloudless sky that blazed like the blue flame of a gas broiler. I pulled in front of Meal Thyme and stepped out of the car, hoping to catch Faith Tilden alone. Finding the restaurant's front door locked, I walked around back. If she'd hidden the identity of her daughter's father, what else had she kept secret?

Faith was kneeling on the lawn near the old storage building that was once Beulah Baptist Church. Bees flitted frenetically about the wisteria that clung to the clapboard. An overturned basket lay next to her. Cuttings of basil and rosemary were strewn on the grass.

As I approached, Faith's freckled shoulders shivered. Her right hand cradled her left.

"What's wrong?" I asked.

She turned pale, wet cheeks upward. Her eyes were as gray as the wood on the storage building where the whitewash had worn off.

"Thirty years and I've never been stung." She brushed the swollen heel of her upturned palm with her fingertips. "Guess I've even upset the honeybees."

"It's hard to let loose of a secret you've kept for so long," I said.

She continued stroking her hand. "You didn't come here to tell me that. You want to know why I never told Grace about her father."

I sure as hell did, but I needed to stay focused on finding David's killer. "That's between you and your daughter. I need you to tell me anything else you've left out about you and David or the night he and Deer Jackson were murdered."

"David and I were lovers." A wounded smile crossed her face. "Guess that's obvious now."

"Did he know you were pregnant?"

"I didn't realize it myself until a couple of weeks after he died. I went off to California so my parents wouldn't know. I'd planned on giving the baby away, but after I felt Grace's first kick, there was no way."

"So you made up the story about the dead soldier rather than tell your parents David was the father?"

"I better take care of this." Faith rose, holding her smitten hand close to her body.

I followed her to the back of the garden. She stooped down and reached for a plant with narrow leaves as glossy and deep green as a magnolia's. She broke off a branch and cracked a twig, then rubbed the juice into the heel of her hand.

"Daddy had his first stroke soon after Grace was born," Faith said. "Mother asked me to come home. I didn't see any good in telling them about David. And no harm in not. Until now."

"When did you give David the *chai*?" I asked.

"A few weeks before he died."

"I ran with him a couple times, always bare-chested. I don't remember him wearing it."

She glanced up. "What if he had worn it?"

"I'd have asked him where he got it."

"So maybe he wasn't ready to tell his family he had a gentile girlfriend," she said, like a schoolteacher feeding an answer to a dull student.

"Were you and David going to get married?" I asked.

Faith split another herb sprig and drizzled the juice onto her palm. "We broke it off the night he died."

"Was it mutual?"

"David was a passionate *and* practical man," she said, massaging the heel of her hand. "When you're young and in love, you think anything's possible. But he helped me see our lives were headed down different paths."

"Your differences in religion part of that?"

"That may not be such a big deal now, but back then it was. Neither of us told our parents we were seeing each other. I knew breaking up was the right thing for both of us. Though I don't for a second regret having his child."

Faith stood silently drawing circles with her fingertips, working the balm into her swollen hand. Then she gazed at the old church building as though it were a creditor come to settle old accounts. She began to weep again, but I could tell it wasn't from the bee sting.

"Is there something else?" I asked.

"David might be alive if I'd gone with him to the church that night."

"Or you'd be dead. Don't hold yourself responsible." My words were scant tonic for her guilt.

"Even though a hurricane was blowing through, we had to assemble a bunch of flyers for the next day. I told David I was too upset to go." Her jaw tightened as the tears dribbled down her cheeks. "I cried in my room until after midnight, when my father stumbled home drunk."

"He was out in the storm?"

"He was the evening-shift dispatcher. Being alone most of the time allowed him to drink on the job."

"You may have broken up," I said. "But David didn't return the *chai* you gave him."

"He was wearing it that night and he started to remove it. But I stopped him. Life is something you don't give back. You pass it on."

"Guess you both did. Her name is Grace."

A parched breeze rattled the herbs as Faith reached for another branch. She smiled at me through a moist veil. "Savory works wonders."

Once back at the Second Precinct, I intended to brief Utley, then grab Keisha and get back to Bon Terre to question Creed Beaumont about the whereabouts of Eddie Hammond. But my plans got a quick adjustment.

"The lieutenant ran out about an hour ago," Keisha said, looking up from her desk. "He wants to see you soon as he gets back."

I plopped into my chair. "He say when that'll be?"

"He's part of the mayor's dog-and-pony show for a bunch of Homeland Security officials doling out grant money. They got a luncheon afterwards."

"Shit." The mayor was famous for impressing important visitors with the finest New Orleans cuisine. At a leisurely pace. I glanced around the squad room for signs of Arceneaux. "Where's our teammate?"

"Back at the computer with Guidry."

"Let me see what he's up to," I said, thinking this was an opportunity to see him away from Keisha. I wanted to apologize for spoiling his first day back and assure him I'd do my best to talk Utley out of splitting us up.

But my cell phone beeped before I could stand.

"Hey, Jack." Willow Ashe's voice lingered like the fragrance of the magnolia blossoms outside Molly's. "Get anything useful from Mrs. Barron?"

"She spins a good yarn. Will I hear it again on national television?"

"Until you make a breakthrough in your cousin's case, I've got bigger fish to fry, Jack."

"Meaning Creed Beaumont," I said. "You're the one who's going to get dunked in hot Crisco."

"Thanks for that fresh rejoinder to my cliché, but I called to tell you he's stopping by the B-and-B this evening. Come by tomorrow and I'll fill you in on everything I pry out of him. I'm pretty sure the climactic chapter of his book is being written soon."

"You're playing with fire."

"I've tamed lightning," she said.

"Then try thinking of Beaumont as a plunge into the deep end."

At a high school party at the Jewish Community Center, I'd shoved her into the pool beneath the high dive and learned not only that Willow couldn't swim, but deep water trumped snakes and spiders in her fear department. It was two weeks before she went back to the levee with me.

"You jerk. Anyway, Beaumont's a land shark. Did I tell you I've perfected his Pisco sour recipe?"

"Damn it, Willow."

The line went dead. I flung the cell phone onto my desk.

Keisha looked at it as though it were the discarded toy of a spoiled toddler. "I don't think Miss Willow's gonna take orders from a high school sweetheart with a paternalistic attitude."

"She's in over her head."

"So says the knight atop his white stallion." Keisha grinned.

An unwelcome flush warmed my cheeks. "She tell you about that yesterday?"

"Girl talk's exempt from the partners-share-everything rule."

"I hope you got a headache from eating that ice cream last night." My chair clacked across the linoleum as I pushed it back.

I went looking for Arceneaux, but a clerk next to Guidry's cubicle told me the two of them had gone to lunch. I figured Arceneaux knew I was in the squad room and they went out the back way, meaning he was still sore at me. Keisha and I left to grab poor boys at a nearby deli.

When Lieutenant Utley still hadn't returned by late afternoon, I went to check with his administrative assistant, who told me the superintendent had dragged Utley into doing some last-minute analysis for the Homeland Security grant proposal.

"We've wasted half a day," I said as I dragged Keisha from her desk to head for Bon Terre.

"Hope we find Beaumont before his date with Willow," Keisha said as we crossed the Huey Long Bridge.

"Me, too," I said. "But what I really wish for is a way to make the son of bitch back away from her without blowing Jarla Thomas's operation. What if we just hung out near Willow's B-and-B and happen by while he's there?"

"Steady your steed, Sir Jack."

Before I could snicker, Sally Ellis rang me on my cell phone.

"Got the note you left last night," the forensic tech said. "We have Emmett Graves's DNA. Whose is on the glass?"

"Can't say," I said. "Just find out if the person's related to Graves. You got something on the shotgun?"

"The prints on it were good enough for comparison, but no hits in AFIS."

I knew that was a long shot. The only real hope for a match was someone who'd done prison time in the last twenty years. "So they didn't belong to Graves."

"No. We were also able to make comparisons with those of every sworn peace officer working in Bon Terre during the seventies. And we took a look at Avery Hammond's prints. They're required for a casino operations license."

If Graves had guessed that one of the Hammonds was David's killer, he was wrong. And I had nothing. "Thanks, Sally."

We continued south toward Bon Terre and once again found the speed trap unmanned. As we passed signs touting Avery

Hammond's businesses, I kept wondering why a man like Creed Beaumont would roll over so easily for the DEA. He was trusted by Hammond and close to much of his wealth. I would've expected Beaumont to find a way to rip off Hammond and steal away to some exotic locale that didn't extradite.

The whoop of a siren and the sight of a cruiser in my rearview mirror ended further speculation. "Looks like the sheriff's out from behind his desk this evening."

He tucked in behind us as we pulled onto the shoulder. I lowered my window and awaited his approach.

"Been a hot sonovabitch today, even for July." Rhino stooped to gain full view of our front seat and tipped his hat to Keisha. "Don't believe I've had the pleasure, Detective. Officer Thomas tells me you're as unsure of her favorite frozen beverage as we are of your partner here."

"*Special Agent* Thomas isn't unsure of anything," Keisha said.

Rhino chuckled. "She ain't too bad for a federal type."

"You didn't stop us to vouch for Jarla Thomas's character," I said.

"Detective Brenner." Rhino placed his hands on his knees and fixed his eyes on mine. "I done you a courtesy the other day, telling you about this DEA operation involving Avery Hammond and Creed Beaumont. Now I need you to honor a request I hope I don't have to repeat to your lieutenant. Stay out of Bon Terre for a couple of days."

Willow was right. Something was going down. "We think Creed Beaumont's car was used in the murder of Steven Bowen, and Eddie Hammond may have driven it. We want to find him."

"I'm curious about his absence myself, but Eddie's not a player in our game here. Wait two days and I'll help you all I can. In the meantime, there's something else I can do for you." Rhino stood erect and stretched upward, his hands pressed into the small of his back. "You'd think fifteen hunnert dollars would buy a decent mattress. Y'all follow me."

Keisha and I left our car and trailed Rhino to the rear of his cruiser.

"Thomas told me y'all's thoughts about the damage to the front end of Beaumont's Camaro. I paid a visit to Marv Brister this morning. He does most of the bodywork around here." Rhino opened the trunk, then stood back to let us look inside.

Lying atop a couple of fishing poles and a tackle box was a bright red auto-body panel. The round hole in the crumpled fiberglass hadn't been caused by a fender bender. Even if it did no more than confirm our theory, it was a big find.

"It's been two weeks," Keisha said. "This Brister fellow didn't see what's obviously a bullet hole and call you?"

"The car was parked outside the casino," Rhino said. "Not uncommon for an innocent vehicle to get plugged by a sore loser. That panel's all yours."

Keisha grabbed the misshapen fiberglass and carried it to our car. As she slid the panel onto the backseat, the radio in the sheriff's cruiser squawked.

"Goddamn dispatch better not be patching my wife through to me again," Rhino grumbled as he waddled to the front of his cruiser and reached through the window for the mike.

Dispatch. Suddenly in my mind, two threads joined, like the first stitch in the repair of a torn garment. The dispatcher was the tie between the recollections of Genevieve Baron and Faith Tilden.

"There's something else you can help me with, Sheriff," I said, after his last "yes, honey."

"Make it quick. I gotta be getting home."

"I understand Jerroll Tilden was a dispatcher back in seventy-two."

"And for a year after that till I caught him with a mostly consumed pint of whiskey on day shift after I became sheriff. My predecessor overlooked things like that."

Vern Hammond also overlooked murder. "Can you remember if he worked the evening shift the night my cousin was killed?"

Rhino closed his eyes and massaged his forehead before answering. "Yeah. The night dispatcher, Mike, was there when I came in the next morning. His shift began at midnight."

"Could he have come on earlier?" I asked.

"Maybe. Those guys swapped time with each other and kept track of it themselves. We didn't have a time clock."

Without other information making either Jerroll or Mike persons of interest, Cribari would have had no reason to pin down their activities that night.

Rhino opened the door of his cruiser. "What's this got to do with your cousin's murder?"

"Probably nothing. Just one of those details I like to nail down."

Rhino flopped behind the wheel. As he pulled onto the highway and headed toward town, I thought about the night David was killed. If Jerroll Tilden was the first dispatcher Genevieve Baron talked to, when had the second dispatcher replaced him? And what was Jerroll doing between then and midnight, when he came home drunk?

"Where are you going?" Keisha asked as I put the car into gear and continued heading west.

"I still owe you for covering my ass last week. Meal Thyme beats Clancy's any day." Making sure we didn't catch up to the sheriff, I turned onto Escondido Road a few minutes later.

"Isn't that it?" Keisha asked as we drove past the restaurant.

"Let's go somewhere for cocktails first."

"I wasn't happy about it, but you promised the sheriff we'd stay away."

"We're not going after Eddie Hammond or Creed Beaumont."

Keisha's eyes narrowed. Then as the car dashed past the water oaks lining the road leading toward Hammond Lane, her eyes popped open as though an image in her mind had materialized on the windshield. "You're going to that B-and-B Willow Ashe is staying at, aren't you?"

"And you're going to help me talk some sense into her."

"Uh-uh, child. White stallions don't take double riders."

26

The evening sky was the blue-gray of gunmetal as Keisha and I drove past the main house of Trahan's B-and-B, where june bugs and gnats had begun congregating around the porch light. We rumbled over the wooden bridge crossing a creek and approached the cottage Willow had rented. The green van was parked directly in front of the door. We stopped on the grass to the right of the cottage and got out.

"Let's walk around back," I said, noticing that one of the rear cargo doors on the van was ajar. We made our way along a crushed-brick path until we reached the deck at the rear of the house, where the bayou flowed silently in the dimness and crickets rasped like out-of-tune fiddles. A kitchen light was on, but I didn't see any activity through the windows. The sliding glass door was open.

"No screen," Keisha said. "They're gonna be slapping at mosquitoes all night." Then she pointed to a redwood table on the deck where a pitcher filled with ice, limes, and a clear liquid rested next to a tumbler. "Looks like Willow decided not to wait for Beaumont."

I moved closer. The glass was nearly full and remnants of ice cubes floated on the surface. "This has been sitting here awhile."

Keisha shrugged. "Let's check inside."

As I took a step toward the cottage, my foot bumped something and sent it rolling on the deck. I reached down and picked up an empty tumbler. It was wet inside and smelled of citrus and alcohol. I held it up next to a garden light near the edge of the deck. Lipstick stuck to the rim of the glass.

"Something isn't right here. This tumbler's heavy. The wind didn't knock it off the table." I pulled out my revolver.

Keisha followed my lead and drew her forty-five. Perhaps we were overreacting. But embarrassed is better than dead. The incident at the sinkhole was evidence of the violent side of Bon Terre.

Keisha moved at an angle that allowed me to approach the door. Through the raised window blinds and open slider we could see the entire first floor, a combination living room, dining room, and kitchen. I slipped through the door and moved right. Keisha followed me in and moved left. We inched toward the stairway at the front of the cottage. I peered up the steps. There was a landing halfway up, the stairs turning to the right.

I hugged the wall going up, careful to allow Keisha a line of fire if the worst occurred. Reaching the landing, I peered around the corner and saw nothing but empty hallway. I nodded for Keisha to join me. From that point, we searched the bedrooms.

"Clear," called Keisha, after popping open the door to the bathroom in the room that must have been Willow's. A Gucci purse rested atop a knotted pine bureau by a four-poster bed.

I checked the open handbag. "Her cell phone. This is her baby. She left here in a hurry."

"Possibly not of her own free will," Keisha said. "And what about her cameraman?"

"Maybe that open door on the van means he left just as suddenly."

"C'mon."

We kept our weapons drawn and carefully descended the stairs, then opened the cottage's unlocked front door. The van was parked directly in front of the porch. We moved to our left and stepped down from the porch at the far end of the cottage and crossed the lot to our car. A full moon had crested the treeline, giving the gravel the appearance of crushed bone.

We popped the trunk and grabbed Mag-lights, then slowly approached the van from the rear. Though one cargo door was wide open, the inside was obscured by darkness. But as we drew close, the beams from our flashlights penetrated the van's dark cavity, revealing a pair of work boots, legs attached.

Keisha covered me as I slung open the van's other door. Derek's body was draped awkwardly over a video camera. His bulging eyes were cast upward as though some horror were descending upon him. Droplets of blood clung to the corners of his eyes from burst veins in the sclera.

I placed my fingertips on his bruised neck. "Still warm." I pulled out my cell phone. "Sheriff. We have a DOA at Trahan's B-and-B. Willow Ashe's video guy."

"Accident?"

"Professional. I think maybe your CI Beaumont is running a play that's not in the DEA's game plan. And another thing. Willow Ashe is missing."

"How do you know?"

"She's not here, but her cell phone is. She's either been abducted . . ." I had to swallow hard before delivering the next thought "Or her body could be in the bayou."

Rhino puffed into the speaker. "Goddamn." Then he hung up.

"You think Beaumont did this?" Keisha asked.

"Look at the bruises." I pointed to Derek's neck. "This was done with bare hands. Not many men capable of that."

"We wait for the sheriff?"

Two shots echoed from a distance, followed by a burst of several rounds.

"Guess not," Keisha said.

The shots had come from the north. Maybe a mile away. Avery Hammond's property. We jumped into the car and peeled up the drive toward the highway.

"What do you think?" Keisha asked.

"Beaumont's got better ideas than spending time in federal prison and making money off a book deal. He's taking care of business the way he did in South America."

"And Willow?"

I might have suspected she didn't know about Derek's murder and had gone with Beaumont willingly, but the overturned tumbler and abandoned cell phone suggested otherwise. "I'm hoping Beaumont took her and has some reason to keep her alive."

Within two minutes we were racing up the lane toward Hammond's home. The shots sounded like they'd been fired outside, so I drove the car to the rear of the mansion. Keisha and I drew our weapons and exited, taking cover next to the carriage house where Hammond's black Mercedes SUV was parked. Scant light filtered through back-room windows, and the citronella lamps lining the patio beneath the oak tree offered no more illumination than a swarm of fireflies. But the full moon hung like a pewter watch lantern, exposing two figures crouched on the dock next to the bayou. The bass boat was moored close to the pier, the slow-moving current causing the fiberglass hull to scrape gently against the pilings.

As we crossed the lawn, I noticed large pockmarks in the ancient oak tree, which I presumed were consequences of the shots we'd heard. We soon reached the dock. A man sporting a tycoon hat knelt next to Annie Hammond, her legs curled beneath her buttocks, her eyes brimming with refracted moonlight. The torso of Hammond's servant Cho lay face-up across Annie's thighs, legs dangling into the gently rocking bass boat, his knees rising and falling as though attached to puppet wire.

Avery Hammond rose and turned toward us, a gun pressed against his right thigh.

"Whatever you're thinking, drop it," I commanded.

Hammond looked down at his side, then released his grip. A small pistol bounced onto the weathered deck with no more malevolence than a potting shovel.

"Sorry," he said. "Forgot I had it."

Keisha moved to retrieve the discarded gun, then knelt next to Annie, who cradled Cho's head in her hands. Annie's shoulders quivered as her muted whimpers barely registered above the croaking bullfrogs. Keisha reached down and placed a hand on Cho's neck, then looked up at me and shook her head.

"What the hell's going on?" I asked.

"Beaumont," Hammond said.

"Why would Beaumont kill Cho?"

Hammond considered his response for a long time while the bayou lapped against the boat, and a breeze blew down from the stables carrying the odors of hay and horse manure. "Cho was the only person I ever really trusted."

"He was part of your business," I said.

"Ever since you showed up around here, you've made a number of gratuitous claims about both my business and my family." Hammond's eyes fell to Cho's body. His knotted jaw was that of a man forcing himself to acknowledge an irreparable loss.

Did he consider the injury business or personal? I wondered. "That's the second corpse we've discovered tonight. The other is Willow Ashe's cameraman. And she's missing. Now tell us what happened, Hammond."

He rubbed the center of his forehead with his fingertips. "Cho was in the bass boat when Creed Beaumont drove up in the Yamaha inboard and tied it at the end of the dock."

"You were expecting him?"

"I was on the patio waiting."

"The three of you were planning a business transaction?" I asked.

"Call it what you want, but I didn't tell Beaumont I was taking Cho along. I saw him climb up onto the dock and start talking to Cho, but I took a moment before walking down there. If I hadn't taken those last swallows of vodka, I'd be lying next to Cho right now."

Hammond took a breath. "Just as I set my glass on the table, Cho got this excited look on his face and pointed to the Yamaha. Beaumont glanced back and shrugged. Then he said something else to Cho. Beaumont shook his head while Cho kept yapping at him. Cho finally started to get out of the bass boat. Then Beaumont took a long look toward me standing on the patio, like he was making up his mind about something. Cho must have seen it coming because he reached inside his jacket. But Beaumont whipped his pistol from under his shirttails so fast Cho barely got his gun out of his holster. He took two slugs and fell where you see him now. Cho's gun splashed into the bayou."

"The shots we heard after the first two sounded different," I said.

"Those shots came after Beaumont reached into his boat and brought up a semiautomatic rifle. I dove for cover behind the oak. He tore the hell outta my patio."

"What kept him from coming after you?"

"I fired my pistol once from behind the tree. Guess he figured there was too much open ground and he didn't have time to wait me out. I stayed hunkered down till I heard him zoom off full throttle."

"Which way?"

He pointed in the opposite direction of Willow's cottage, toward the sinkhole.

"Was Willow Ashe with him?" I asked.

"Far as I could tell, he was alone."

My eyes drifted in the direction of Trahan's. I wondered if Beaumont had docked behind Willow's cottage, quietly killed Derek, and then gagged her and forced her aboard his boat? Was she the cause of the noise or motion that had attracted Cho's attention?

I looked at the bass boat, then at Keisha. "Ever handled an outboard, partner?"

Her eyes narrowed. "You're not thinking what I think you're thinking."

"Beaumont could have Willow."

"I don't know what the hell you think you're gonna do," Hammond said. "Beaumont's carrying a hell of a lot more firepower than I suspect you have, and I dare say he has more professional experience using it."

I didn't need this statement of the obvious. Acknowledgment of the danger I was contemplating for my partner and myself brought images of Sarah and Carrie to my mind. "Where's he headed, Hammond?"

"How would I know?"

"Your appointment. Where is it?"

Hammond pushed up the brim of his hat. "I thought you knew everything about my business."

I holstered my revolver and moved toward him. I grabbed his hat and flung it into the water. My face was within a foot of his. "Tell me where to find Beaumont."

Hammond took a slow step back. "I don't know the exact spot, but it's on the water. Not too far away.

I pointed to the bass boat. "I presume this has plenty of fuel."

"Yes," Hammond said. "But if you fire up that engine, Beaumont'll hear you coming. You don't need to be giving him more advantage than he's already got."

"We'll have to take the chance."

"Not if you use the electric trolling motor mounted on the bow," Hammond said. "It'll only get five miles an hour, but there's no sound. Twist the rudder handle to control the speed."

"That's charitable of you," I said.

"No generosity involved. I want you to kill Beaumont before he kills you. Hopefully I've upped your odds to something greater than zero."

"You figure out how to run that thing," Keisha said. "I'll grab our Kevlar from the trunk,"

"If Beaumont's shooting at us with a military weapon, it may not do us any good," I said.

"Humor me." Keisha started past me. "The vest matches my blazer."

The tremor in her voice told me her fear matched mine.

27

Keisha jogged across Hammond's lawn to our car. I called the sheriff and told him about the situation at Hammond's.

"Brenner, you're having a stellar day," Rhino said. "Two bodies in thirty minutes."

"Jarla Thomas with you?" I asked.

"She's in Lafayette tonight."

"Can you give me her cell number?"

"Why?"

"We may have business to discuss."

He recited the number. "What business?"

"Check you later, Sheriff."

"Goddamn it. Don't you cut me off—"

There was no use listening to him try to dissuade me from pursuing Beaumont. After saving Jarla's number on my cell phone, I clipped the phone to my belt. I saw Hammond surveying the moonlit grounds as though burning into his mind images he'd never see again—the stables, the mansion, the ancient oak, and finally the carriage house and the impenetrable wilderness beyond. He reached down and patted Annie on the shoulder. "Come on, honey. There's nothing we can do for him."

She carefully lowered Cho's head onto the dock.

Hammond helped her up and put his arm around her. Then he

turned to me and lifted a hand as if to touch the brim of his hat. Realizing it was floating in the bayou, he offered a salute instead. "Good luck with Beaumont."

"Willow's in the boat with Creed," Annie said to me, her sorrow-ripened face now fully her mother's. "Don't let him hurt her."

"Did you see her?" Annie had overheard my speculations and I worried she'd twisted them into memory.

"Cho told me before he died."

Willow's alive. Or was. "You're sure?"

She nodded.

"I told you something spooked Cho," Hammond said.

"Annie, did Cho say anything else?" I asked.

Moisture percolated through the dry coals in Annie's eyes. "He said he loved me."

I wondered how often she'd heard those words. But there was no time to appreciate their bittersweetness. I hopped from the dock onto the deck of the bass boat near the bow as Annie and Hammond started toward the house.

Keisha approached wearing a Kevlar vest and holding up mine. "You want this or not?"

"Toss it. Loosen the rope from the cleat and let's get moving."

She stepped onto the boat. "Don't get in such a hurry. This thing sinks and the gators dine on two of NOPD's finest."

"Beaumont has Willow," I said, finding the motor and lowering it into the water. I repeated what Annie had told me while Keisha unwound the rope and dropped it on the deck.

I pointed to the dual consoles near the rear of the bass boat. "Take your pick."

She settled into the seat on the port side. "Can you drive this thing?"

"We'll see." I knelt by the column of the trolling motor, found the switch, and flipped it on. As I grabbed the handle, the boat moved forward and scraped the dock. After a few seconds, I got the feel of it, and soon we were floating along the bayou in the right direction.

"We're not moving very fast," Keisha whispered.

"Hopefully fast enough." I grabbed my cell phone to call Jarla Thomas.

She answered on the first ring. "Where are you, Brenner?"

"In a bass boat on Bayou L'enfant chasing Creed Beaumont."

"After you tell me why you're doing that, maybe you'll explain why you're talking so soft I can barely hear you."

I summarized everything, starting with my first call to the sheriff.

"What the hell's Beaumont doing with Willow Ashe?" Jarla asked.

"Probably took her as a hostage in case he can't make a clean getaway. Beaumont's got a ten- or fifteen-minute head start. I think he's planning to trade the coke for the cash and pass on the all-inclusive package at Leavenworth."

"You happen to know where?"

"Somewhere on the bayou north of Hammond's house. Real soon. What can you put together?"

"Maybe a chopper from Lafayette with however many agents can meet me at the hangar in ten minutes."

"My phone's on vibrate. Keep in touch."

I let my sport coat fall from my shoulders, picked up my Kevlar vest, and secured it. I clipped the phone to my belt, then tossed the coat to Keisha. "Fold it with the lining out and lay it in the other seat, please."

"Uh-huh. Terrific time to be worrying about your threads."

As the trolling motor pulled us through the water with calm efficiency, I stayed a course in the penumbra of the treeline, hoping to avoid submerged cypress knees and other vegetation along the right bank. Muted moonlight exposed the opposite shore. Keisha, only six feet from me, was a motionless silhouette.

My cell phone vibrated.

"Yeah," I whispered.

"The fuck you doing, Jack?" Ferrell Arceneaux's Cajun diction sputtered like an engine with a bad spark plug. "Some Special Agent Thomas called Utley, who commandeered a chopper and caught me in the middle of my first beer at Fuzzy's. He asked me if I wanted to take a ride with him."

"Glad you guys are on your way, but I have no idea where this is going down."

"The DEA bird's gonna fly north along the bayou from Hammond's place. We'll start where the main highway crosses the bayou and move in the opposite direction."

"DEA cooperating with NOPD. Amazing."

"Hope to see you soon, partner. And tell Keisha to keep her fine-looking ass outta the crosshairs. Clear."

I clipped the phone back onto my belt.

"Who was that?" Keisha's hushed voice floated from the stern.

"Arceneaux. He and Utley will be in a chopper approaching from the north. Says to tell you to be careful."

"Sweet man."

We agreed the plan sounded like a desperation backcourt shot. Bon Terre was an hour's drive from New Orleans and a little more than that from Lafayette. A chopper could get here in thirty or forty minutes from either city. But would they spot us?

We clung to the shadowy side of the bayou, so I couldn't read my watch. But I guessed we'd been traveling for fifteen minutes. Beaumont would be well ahead of us and increasing his lead. Our only hope was that he'd have to wait on Silva. And even if we caught up, how would we approach him without being killed or causing Willow to be killed?

Our boat glided on black water. The stillness belied the turbulence below, like the bouillabaisse of emotions simmering beneath my professional composure. Fear was the prime ingredient. Fear for Willow, for Keisha and myself, for my daughters. Even for Alexis. But the acid taste in my mouth was anger. Willow had danced near the flame and I had failed to stop her. No white knights, she'd told me, but I'd used it as an excuse to allow her dealings with Creed Beaumont to go on too long. I was the romantic teenage boy who watched her, excited by her full-tilt abandon, her craving to draw the lightning to herself when others sought cover, with no second-guessing or remorse. Despite the claim she'd made that afternoon at Molly's, Willow was not like me. Her intoxicant left her each morning with eyes lucid and unswollen, her gut free of bile, her mind uninfested by doubts. Maybe I didn't stop Willow right away because I wanted the life I thought she had—uninhibited by introspection, constant vigilance, and feelings of responsibility. Maybe I was angry at that.

"Jack," Keisha said. "Up there."

A hundred yards ahead, the bayou doglegged left, then turned hard right behind the feathered silhouettes of water oaks and black willows. Letting up on the foot pedal, I heard nothing but trilling crickets, croaking bullfrogs, and thrashing surface feeders.

I closed my eyes as though the crystalline reflection of moonlight on the bayou was a distracting noise. To my right, something slipped into the water through the reeds lining the bank, perhaps a snapping turtle or nutria. A distant thunderhead rumbled over the Gulf. Blood pulsed in my eardrums. Then another sound emerged. A high-pitched whine that in other situations could have been an off-road motorcycle. Out here it had to be watercraft.

I opened my eyes and nodded to Keisha, who pulled herself from the console and knelt beside me, her gaze fixed on the point ahead.

"Think Beaumont's heading back this way?" she asked.

I shook my head. "Another guest has joined the party. Either Silva or whoever he's sent to do the deal."

"So we just sail around the bend and say, 'Stick 'em up'?"

"Whatever we do, we'd better do it quick."

"Let's call Thomas and Arceneaux," she said. "Let 'em know what's going down."

"They won't make it in time. Beaumont'll be in and out in a heartbeat. He doesn't know you and I are tailing him, but he's gotta figure Hammond dropped the dime on him after he killed Cho."

Keisha inhaled deeply through her nostrils. "So what about Willow?"

I drew on my earlier anger. "I told her not to get mixed up with Beaumont."

The motorboat sound was louder.

"Well, she is," Keisha said. "Step on it."

We reached the bend in less than a minute.

Keisha touched my arm. "Let's get off on the bank and check out what's round the bend."

"We're more mobile in the boat."

"More exposed, too."

"Okay," I said. "You go ashore and try working your way to the other side of the point. I'll be the one with fiberglass between me and the alligators."

"Well," she said. "Those gators could take exception to my belt being made from their kinfolk's hide. Let's move up a little further."

I gently pressed the pedal and steered closer to shore.

Seconds later Keisha grabbed my shoulder.

As I cut the motor beneath a drapery of water oak branches, the boat nosed into a clump of rushes. Beyond, the bayou widened and made a horseshoe. A tight stand of bald cypress stood fifty yards from us in the middle of the hairpin. The limbs, barren of leaves, bent out from the trunks like fractured bones. Tied to a cypress knee was a watercraft, no doubt the jet boat Creed Beaumont had taken. A woman sat upright near the stern. Willow Ashe.

28

In the moonlight, Willow's face was as hard and bloodless as alabaster. Though dressed in the same attire she'd worn at Molly's two nights earlier, a white tank top with black jeans, she was not the lustrous figure who'd stood before the picture window.

"What's Beaumont doing?" I whispered, wondering if he lurked within the gloomy mantle of foliage on the far shore. Or close to us on the near bank.

Keisha nudged me. "Well, we sure don't know what we're doing."

"We gotta get Willow outta there before something bad happens."

"Maybe we can somehow let her know we're here," Keisha said. "If she stayed underwater most of the way, she could swim to us."

"I happen to know Willow can't swim."

I studied the jet boat gently bobbing in the slow current. If Beaumont's plan was a drugs-for-money exchange, I doubted he'd leave himself exposed in the middle of the bayou, but there was a chance that he was positioned out of sight next to Willow.

"If Beaumont's hiding in the brush, we can't reach her without him spotting us," Keisha said. "For all we know, he already has."

I shook my head. "We'd be dead by now. These branches and shadows are good cover. You're fine right here."

"*I'm* fine?"

I unfastened my Kevlar vest.

"You're not gonna—"

I handed my revolver and cell phone to her. She stuffed the gun under her blazer between the small of her back and her alligator belt. Then she cast her eyes toward Willow. "What'll you do when you reach her?"

"Teach her to swim." I pulled off my shoes and socks.

Keisha placed them, along with my phone, into the starboard console. "Those motorboats are getting closer. Sounds like more than one."

Keisha was right—three distinct pitches, each growing louder.

"You may not get there in time," she said.

I could now hear the hulls of the boats slapping the water's surface. They were moving fast. I was convinced I had no other option.

I dangled my feet into the water. "I want you to create a diversion. When you see me pull Willow overboard, fire off a couple of shots into the water on the other side of our boat so they can't pinpoint your location from the muzzle flash."

"Be careful, Jack." She squeezed my hand quickly then let it go, like a person offering a final touch to a loved one being wheeled into surgery.

I slipped into the bayou as the boats moved nearer. Though the surface retained the heat of the day, I shivered as my feet sank into mud and detritus. I quickly forced my body into a horizontal position and took tentative strokes. I hoped I wasn't in the company of the alligators I'd joked about with Keisha. The water was neither putrid nor viscous, but knowing bayous provide filtration for the land the way blood flows through the liver of a drunk reminded me I wasn't in a lap pool. I propelled myself forward, inhaling the odor of sodden bark and a faint ammonia essence from effluent fertilizer and dead fish.

Suddenly, the engines sputtered as if they'd reached their destination. As I neared the shimmering current beyond the shadows, I took a breath and pulled myself beneath the water. Knowing I couldn't see anyway, I squeezed my eyes tightly. Soon I broke the surface, to breathe and reckon my position.

I repeated this cycle until reaching a point ten yards downstream from Willow. Unfortunately, another craft with two men on it idled next to her boat.

"What the fuck's going on, Beaumont?"

Voices carry well over water. This one belonged to Mousey Trivette.

"Simple exchange. Leave the money with her." Beaumont's voice boomed like that of a drill sergeant from the far side of the bayou. I no longer had to worry about him being in the boat or onshore near Keisha.

"What about our product?" Trivette said.

"It's in the bow. All fifty pounds of it. Take it and put the money in its place. Then stay put until I'm sure it's all there." Beaumont raised his voice. "That goes for you clowns upstream, too."

He was speaking to the occupants of the other boats Keisha and I had heard.

"I don't care if you are knocking half off the price," Trivette said. "I ain't gonna put the money in that boat till Hector here tells me you've given us a good load. Where the fuck you at anyway?"

"On the business side of a sniper's rifle with a night-vision scope. Now take the coke. I'll give you three minutes to put the money in its place. After my associate brings it to me, I'll tell you when you can leave."

Trivette cackled. "Associate, my ass. What happens to the bitch?"

"Not your problem."

"She goes to the cops, it is."

"Unless you morons get caught holding, there's no evidence of this meeting. You've got less than three minutes."

"All right, Beaumont," Trivette said. "We appreciate you stiffing the Feds and Hammond and giving us this steep discount, but don't forget Silva and the boys are back there if you try something funny."

"And you keep telling yourself that little red dot in the middle of your chest is a lightning bug."

Beaumont telling Silva about his association with the DEA surprised me, but I guessed he'd cut the price in half to lure him into the deal. And he didn't have to split it with anyone. His plan was starting to make sense. Beaumont had protected himself by staying out of sight and insured compliance from both Willow and Trivette by making it clear he'd take out anyone who made a false move. Then, in his words, he'd evaporate. Hard to do with Willow in tow. I was certain now he wasn't planning on taking her hostage. He had the skills, and no doubt the plan, to spirit himself though the swamps and out of the country. I didn't really care if he did. That was Jarla Thomas's problem. Willow was mine.

I couldn't let her take the money to him. The choppers were too far away to keep Trivette and Silva's goons from letting loose a hail of lead after Beaumont had his money. My only chance to save Willow was to take her while the deal was in progress. Criminals are like hungry dogs after table scraps. They tend to have focused objectives. If Willow went overboard, Trivette would be far more concerned with protecting his drugs than analyzing her actions. Even if it meant exchanging fire with Beaumont.

Willow's boat shielded me from Trivette. As I approached, I considered whispering to Willow, preparing her for what I was about to do. But I worried she'd have the same hysterical reaction she had in high school. I wouldn't give her time to think.

My left hand found the stern. My right foot found purchase on a submerged cypress knee. I gripped the edge of the boat for leverage and flexed my knee, preparing to push off hard. My calf and thigh muscles tensed. I was right in back of her. I'd use both arms to elevate myself and I'd grab her from behind.

"Here's the money, Beaumont," Trivette shouted.

I heard a thud.

"Willow," Beaumont called out. "Start the engine like I showed you."

I hadn't counted on her doing that before untying the rope. I heard the engine turn over. Then a jet stream of water blasted me, the backwash burning my nostrils and propelling me away from the boat.

Willow reached to loosen the rope. She'd be gone before I could get to her.

"Willow!" I shouted, stroking toward the boat.

She turned her head toward me. "Jack!"

I grasped her wrist.

"No! No!"

As I yanked her into the water, Keisha's shots cracked like dry timber rent by lightning.

I tried to take Willow deep, but she fought me, wriggling loose and thrashing to the surface like a leaping bass. There was more gunfire, now muted by the water in my eardrums. I remained submerged, holding my breath, as I pulled her down again.

Willow was reacting like she had that summer at the pool in high school. She kicked loose from my grasp. I resurfaced, wrapped my arm around her neck, and dragged her down, keeping her beneath the water for several seconds. More shots reverberated above us.

I wasn't making the progress with Willow I'd hoped for, but Keisha's shots had created the right effect, a gunfight among bad guys. On our next trip to the surface, I looked back and saw Hector blown backward, fragments of his flesh and jacket catching moonlight as they spewed from his back. He crashed into the bayou. Trivette was nowhere in sight, certainly the victim of Beaumont's sniper's rifle.

I pulled Willow down again as the shooting continued from a greater distance. Silva's men were in a gun battle with Beaumont. If they kept each other occupied long enough, I could get Willow to our boat and we could motor down the bayou and get picked up by the DEA chopper moving up from Hammond's place.

The next trip to the top, Willow shrieked and slipped beneath the surface as though she'd fallen through a trapdoor. I reached back and felt for her, the murky water resisting my leaden arms.

"Jack!" Willow popped up, tangles of wet hair matted across her face.

Then another voice: "Move ahead to the bank, Brenner. I have a knife. I'll gut her."

Mousey Trivette appeared from behind Willow. He shook his head, clearing his eyes of water, and grabbed her by the collar. A silvery object trailed him. I quickly made it out to be a suitcase, one too small to carry fifty pounds of coke. It was the money.

"Let her go, Trivette," I said, my feet touching bottom. "I have no interest in you."

Willow screamed and flailed at him.

"Shut up or I'll cut you, bitch." Trivette locked his arm around her throat, the knife in his hand catching a spark of moonlight. Then he pulled her up, the water chest high, and pushed her from behind. His eyes focused over my shoulder. "Move it. We're going for a ride on that bass boat."

I kept backing up. Once Willow was safely ashore, Keisha could surprise him with a round from her forty-five. I stepped onto the bank next to the boat and into a small clearing lined with dense foliage, protecting us from Beaumont's view as long as he remained on the opposite side of the bayou.

Trivette shoved Willow forward. She fell to the ground about six feet from me.

"Beaumont was planning on using this money for a long vacation," Trivette said. "Guess it's me who's off to the tropics."

Where is Keisha? "You don't have much time, Trivette," I said. "Beaumont's not going to let you take his money. He was Special Forces and he can span the bayou underwater in one breath. Leave her here."

Trivette glanced around, then looked down at Willow. "Aw, fuck her." He started to sling the suitcase onto the deck of the bass boat. But instead, the money dropped next to his feet as the first shot tore into his shoulder. The next shot punched into his stomach, and as he started to double over, the third sent him back with one side of his face missing. I knew the shots had not come from Keisha.

"Understand you've been looking for me, Brenner." Eddie Hammond moved into the clearing wearing camouflage fatigues. Black camo cream covered his face. He held his scoped rifle waist high, muzzle directed at my midsection. "Well, here I am."

29

Mousey Trivette's body lolled facedown in the bayou, the trapped air causing his jacket to billow about him like a green hot air balloon. Eddie Hammond eased closer to Willow and me.

He cocked his head toward the aluminum travel case bobbing in the water next to the corpse. "Bring me the money, Brenner."

My first impulse was to ask him what he'd done to Keisha, but I held off in hopes she'd evaded him and was waiting to make a play. "It doesn't belong to you."

"Don't fuck with me. That cash floats away, your girlfriend gets what Trivette got."

I glanced down at Willow, her knees in the dirt, head down, bare shoulders spreading and contracting like the bellows of an accordion. Having no choice at the moment but to follow Eddie's instructions, I fielded the suitcase from the shallows and carried it ashore, my gaze probing the darkness beyond the clearing for signs of Keisha. I set the luggage on the spongy turf at his feet and surveyed the shadows again.

He sneered. "Forget it, Brenner. I coldcocked your partner and tossed her gun. She's facedown in the weeds beyond the bass boat. Now move over next to Blondie."

I retreated and helped Willow struggle to her feet, my mind

flipping through empty options. If Eddie Hammond was fresh from the slaughter of several men, he had nothing to gain by keeping us alive.

He eyed the money, his rifle still directed at my gut. "How'd you and your dyke partner come to crash the party?"

I told him.

It's hard to read the expression of someone whose face is smeared with grease paint, especially in dim light, but I thought I saw the muscles around one eye quiver.

"Annie loved Cho," Eddie said.

"Beaumont didn't care about that."

"He's an asshole."

"Then why are you working with him?" I asked.

"Because Uncle Avery's a bigger asshole." Eddie shifted his feet. "And because me and my partner get two million dollars worth of cocaine."

"Let me guess. Your partner's Jason Meade. He was the third point in the crossfire Beaumont set up for Silva and his goons."

"Taught him everything about guns Beaumont taught me."

"Which one of you took the potshots at my friend and me at the pond?"

"We were just playing." He glanced between Willow and me and tilted the rifle barrel toward my heart. "Now we're not."

"I'm not the only one who's been looking for you. Maurice Silva claims you mistook Steven Bowen for Mousey Trivette and killed him."

"So Jason and Beaumont tell me. That's why I've been laying low. But I didn't try a hit on anyone in Silva's crew. And I didn't kill that kid."

"Then someone's gone to a lot of trouble to make it look like you did."

"What the hell for?"

I was in the realm of speculation, but Eddie didn't know it. "How about to grab your share of the cocaine and make you the fall guy for someone else's crime? If I hadn't interrupted, Beaumont would be on his way out of the country with Silva's cash, leaving the authorities to find the bodies of a bunch of gangsters. And a dead man who killed a high school honor student."

"What are you talking about?"

"Jason Meade kills you and takes the drugs. He wouldn't be tied to any of it. You might want to reconsider your plans."

"Bullshit. You're having near-death delusions." Eddie's jaw tightened as he glanced down at the suitcase next to his feet.

"Take the money and get out of here," I said. "Beaumont's not going to sit on the other side of the bayou waiting for a delivery."

"Goddamn right he's not." Creed Beaumont slipped into the clearing from behind Eddie, a semiautomatic sidearm directed at Eddie's spine. Eddie's arms froze, the evil end of his weapon still pointed at me.

I'd had a decent chance to overpower Eddie. Beaumont presented far worse odds.

"Weren't thinking of leaving, were you?" Beaumont asked, water dripping from his amphibious wet suit. He pressed his pistol into the back of Eddie's neck.

"Hey, Creed." Eddie's voice cracked. "Trivette almost got away with your money."

"Easy, sport." Beaumont reached around and grasped the barrel of Eddie's rifle and pressed it downward. Then he jerked the gun from Eddie's hands and slung it into the bayou.

"Hey, man," Eddie whined. "I wasn't gonna stiff you."

"Well, now we're sure of that," Beaumont said, pushing him next to me. Willow stood on my right, her arms wrapped around her midriff, nipples hardened against the thin, soggy material of her white tank top.

Beaumont grinned at her. "Chilled, are we?"

Willow glared back.

There was a rustling to Beaumont's right. He crouched and directed his semiautomatic toward the sound.

"What the hell happened, Creed?" Jason Meade stumbled into the clearing.

"What almost happened is I nearly blew your brains out."

"Sorry. I'm kinda stoked."

Judging by the jerky movements of his eyes and the way he kept loosening and tightening his hands on his assault rifle, it was more from speed or coke—maybe both—than from the action. I wondered if Beaumont recognized Jason's condition. Either way, Beaumont hadn't planned on crossing to Jason's side of the bayou for his money.

"Figured you'd be halfway to Mexico by now," Jason said.

Beaumont gestured to the suitcase on the ground. "Trivette dove into the water before I could kill him and managed to make it to shore with my money. Who started the shooting anyway? I didn't see a muzzle flash from either your position or Eddie's."

"I took those shots as a diversion to save Willow," I said quickly. As far as Beaumont and Jason knew, I was alone.

"And you're here why?" Jason squinted at me as though blinded by the moonlight.

I explained before Eddie got a chance to mention Keisha.

"Why aren't you out collecting your goods, Jason?" Beaumont asked.

"Wanted to neutralize Eddie before going out on the water."

Beaumont smirked. "Neutralize? You've been watching too much TV. How about the others?"

"Dead in the water." Jason snickered and turned to Eddie. "Sorry. This is the end of a beautiful friendship."

"Fucker." Eddie spat his words.

"Ouch." Jason grinned.

The two reminded me of kids on a playground, their camouflage fatigues more like Scout uniforms on their slight frames. But while Eddie had a boy's look of fear and confusion, Jason's eyes held a seasoned malevolence.

Beaumont moved behind us. He patted down Eddie first, then started on me. "This would have been a lot easier if you'd let the thing play out, Brenner. And safer for you and Willow."

"I dropped my revolver in the water when I grabbed her."

"Like I'll take your word for it." He quickly finished his search, then slipped behind Willow, his lips near her ear. "I've already secured you."

Her shoulders stiffened. "You son of a bitch."

"Hey, Beaumont." Jason giggled. "She as wild in bed as she looks?"

"Keep your focus, amigo. This isn't a frat party." Beaumont walked over to the suitcase and knelt beside it.

Jason held his gun on Eddie, Willow, and me. His fingers kneaded the stock as if it were a string of worry beads.

"Beaumont," I said. "Tell me why you set Eddie up for being the shooter who killed Steven Bowen."

Beaumont tried the latches to the suitcase. "What makes you think I did that?"

"Finding a hole in the panel you had replaced on your Camaro was way too easy." I waited for confirmation, but Beaumont was intent on the lock. Then I noticed Jason grinning. I took their silence to mean I had it right. And that they didn't expect my conclusions to ever find voice beyond this moonlit clearing overlooking the bayou.

"I needed my car to be positively identified as the one used by the shooter," Beaumont finally said. "My alibi and a little false rumor made Eddie the driver. Silva assumed Avery Hammond ordered Eddie to hit Trivette in a play to move into the retail side of the business. That made it real easy for me to sell Silva on a plan to let me rip off Hammond. Offering Silva a fifty percent discount on the coke clinched it." Beaumont slapped his fist on the suitcase. "Goddamn!"

"When did he bring you in on this scheme, Eddie?" I asked.

He stared at Beaumont like a man who'd just dropped the largest wager of his life to a casino dealer's blackjack. "He asked me and Jason to help him take out Silva the day after that kid got shot."

"But it wasn't the first time you'd heard about his plan, was it, Jason?"

Eddie slowly returned his gaze to Jason. "You've both been using me."

"Which wasn't very hard, stupid," Jason said.

Beaumont tugged on something near the ankle of his wet suit. A knife emerged, the blade like a splinter of blue ice in the moonlight.

Hoping he'd drawn it as a tool and not a weapon, I decided to test one last notion. "The store manager heard two rounds after the one that killed Steven Bowen. Silva claimed someone returned fire and one of the shots punched a hole in the car. Either that's true, or Steven's killer fired twice into the air after shooting him and put the hole Sheriff Perrot found in the panel you replaced on your Camaro sometime later."

Jason's chuckle was laced with amphetamine.

"You're good, Brenner," Beaumont said, twisting the point of the knife into one of the locks, snapping the latch like a dry twig. "But not quick enough."

"Jason, you asshole," Eddie blurted. "You told me you had a date that night."

I connected my own final dot. "Jason was near the convenience store when he called Steven's pager from his cell phone. He left his sister's cell as the callback number, knowing it wouldn't take long for Steven to show up to return her call. Jason knew Steven always wore that green jacket, like Mousy Trivette. Silva and the police would think it was you, Eddie, who tried to hit Trivette."

"The nigger boy never left home without that stupid green jacket," Jason said.

"So another crackhead's off the streets," Beaumont said as the second lock gave way.

"He was an honor student and a friend of Jason's sister," I said.

Beaumont slipped the knife back into its sheath. "Well, Jason. Maybe you aren't so smart after all. If the kid had been a lowlife junkie like you told me, Brenner wouldn't be here to complicate things."

I thought of the rabbinic maxim David had taught me—saving a single life saves the entire world. "You're wrong. Every life matters."

"Only one life counts as far as I'm concerned." Beaumont

shrugged an empty backpack from his shoulders and dropped it to the ground next to the money.

"Steven Bowen died so you could manipulate Eddie," I said.

"Collateral damage," Beaumont said.

"Learn that on TV?" I asked.

"I learned it in places that would make your worst nightmares seem like wet dreams." Beaumont zipped open the backpack and began stuffing money into it.

"How long have you been working on this scheme?" I asked.

"Since dropping the dime on Emmett Graves after the DEA jammed me up."

Graves had given up the location of the shotgun that killed David because he believed that Avery Hammond was the cause of his incarceration. Yesterday I'd learned the DEA had set Graves up. Now it looked like Beaumont would be the beneficiary.

"Whadda we do with these three?" Jason's eyes flitted randomly, like neon lights on the broken marquee of a low-rent bar.

"They're your problem, bubba." Beaumont slapped another stack of bills into his backpack. "Sorry, Willow. I wouldn't have let you get hurt. Your boyfriend here's taken things out of my hands."

I realized he was right. His goal all along was to take out Silva and his men and leave the country with the money. By trying to rescue Willow, I may have cost us both our lives.

Jason's finger moved inside the trigger guard.

I'd written Keisha off, but the choppers couldn't be far away. Maybe if I could stall a few more minutes, they'd locate us.

"Jason," I said. "At least give me time to tell Eddie about his mother."

"My mother?" Eddie looked at me as though I'd delivered a grievous insult. "The bitch ran off when Annie and I were babies."

"Then there's nothing to tell," Jason said. "You all step toward the water."

I wasn't going to beg Jason. My best hope was to continue as if he'd given permission. "I talked to your mother yesterday, Eddie."

"Then you must have been in a whorehouse. Look. If Jason's going to do us, I don't want to die thinking about my mother." He looked out at the water, as though thoughts of abandonment were worse than death. Maybe they were.

"Emmett Graves threatened to kill her and harm you and Annie if she didn't leave and stay gone. I believe Graves killed your father."

"That was thirty years ago. So where's my mother been?"

"She hasn't made contact because she's still afraid of Emmett Graves."

"He's been in jail for six months."

"She had some things to take care of." It was the best I could do.

"Whoa! Too bad there's no time for Dr. Phil to fix this boy's head." Jason pointed toward the bayou. "You first, old buddy. Brenner and Blondie follow."

The pitch was rough and mechanical, but under the circumstance, the reverberation of an approaching helicopter sounded like the flutter of angel wings.

Beaumont glanced up at me as he slammed down the lid of the empty silver suitcase. "I'm guessing that chopper isn't here by coincidence. DEA or your guys?"

I said nothing.

Beaumont zipped up his backpack and stood. "Well. I've enjoyed listening to these little stories, but my money's stowed and my exit's overdue."

"Hey," Jason whined. "What about my drugs?"

"All yours," Beaumont said. "Just like we planned."

"I'll be a sitting duck if I go out on the water."

"Send Ms. Ashe after them. She's already wet."

"Funny. Help me get my coke."

"You may not be as dumb as Eddie, but you've never worked for a damn thing in your life. Figure it out for yourself, amigo."

Jason looked toward the bayou as though watching a bus roll through a stop before he could catch it. For a second, he appeared totally calm, a look I'd seen many times on the streets of New Orleans. Jason was harnessing the meth-injected energy that zapped across the synapses in his brain like wild horses spooked by lightning. He was conjuring up the will and control for one violent and decisive act.

Creed Beaumont sensed it, too, and he was ready when the barrel of Jason's gun swung toward him. I pulled Willow to the ground while Beaumont dove for the dirt in front of Eddie. Jason sent a round high of his target. Eddie took it square in the chest, his arms flailing upward as he jerked backward, a muffled grunt erupting from his throat. Beaumont fired his semiautomatic several times as he rolled over the damp ground, evading Jason's second shot. At least one of Beaumont's bullets found its mark.

I leapt for Beaumont as Jason spun toward the water, his third shot piercing nothing but the foliage behind him as his rifle flew upward.

Beaumont, who must have felt me coming, flipped onto his side, but I reached him before he could swing the gun around to fire on me. I was on my knees, pushing his weapon hand into the ground and tightening my grip. He clawed at my fingers with his left hand, but I hung on and managed to get a finger inside the trigger guard to prevent him from switching the gun from one hand to the other. Suddenly Beaumont released his left hand. Could he reach the knife he'd used to pry open the suitcase? Or did his suit conceal another?

"Run, Willow!" I shouted, knowing I was no match for Beaumont's strength or skill.

But the implement of combat he came at me with was not a knife. It was the one Beaumont had used to break the neck of Willow's cameraman—his bare hands. He slung his arm around my throat and jerked my head back, causing me to roll on top of his now supine body, my face to the sky. I maintained a firm grip on the gun with my right hand, but my left clawed uselessly at his rigid forearm.

Then he slid the bend of his elbow beneath my chin and wrenched it back violently. I heard the grind of bone against bone from the intense compression of my upper vertebrae, as though a hot rail spike were being driven between my shoulder blades. I rocked from side to side, but each futile motion gave him greater purchase of my throat. I dug my heels into the ground in an effort to counter his leverage, but the soft soil gave way, rendering my legs as useless as those of a box turtle, shell side down. Trying to counter some of the pressure, I threw back my shoulder blades and tried lifting and relaxing my chest. But my breaths grew ragged and I knew I couldn't last. Beaumont would break my neck or he'd choke off the air to my lungs.

His infernal breath was the only sound I heard. Where were the beating wings? Had the chopper passed over without seeing? Was it because the moon had suddenly fallen and they'd lost their way in the darkness exploding in my eyes?

A burst of air shrieked down my windpipe like a category-four hurricane. But the banshee cry was not from life-redeeming oxygen, it came from Creed Beaumont. I felt his arm uncoil from my throat like a retreating python. I saw the moon above me again. Had Keisha or a sniper from the chopper shot him? I hadn't heard the blast. And he held on to his gun as tenaciously as ever. He howled again, like a hunting dog who's wandered into a coon trap. I managed to turn from my back to my knees and grip his pistol with both hands to keep it aimed away from me.

Then I saw the source of his outcry. Willow Ashe knelt above his head. She'd lacerated one side of his face and was tearing the skin from the other side with her nails. Blood mixed with grease paint, covering his face like raspberry glaze on a scored pork loin.

Beaumont grabbed Willow's wrist. She cried out and slashed him again, this time along the neck. It did little damage. The nails that had dug deep into his flesh were torn and, like a bee's stinger, couldn't be replaced. Then I heard bone snap, and a piteous moan. Willow had dispensed all the havoc she could. And Beaumont still had the semiautomatic in his grasp.

I had to risk letting go with one of my hands. Using my knees for traction, I forced his arm above his head, then released my right hand and drove my fist into his face below his left eye. I felt his cheekbone crack. My knuckles connected again, this time an uppercut to his chin. Electricity arced from my hand to my spine, but it was Beaumont who lost teeth. And his grip on the pistol. He tried to recover as I pounded his wrist into the soft ground. With one last pull, I dislodged the gun, causing it to sail into the underbrush bordering the clearing.

"Willow! Find that gun!"

Her face was dappled with dirt and blood. She cradled her wrist in the palm of her other hand. The whine of the helicopter grew louder. I flipped Beaumont onto his stomach and placed his hands together in the small of his back. I had nothing to tie him with other than my belt and I worried about the knife still strapped to his ankle.

"I can't find it, Jack," Willow cried.

"More to your left, closer to the bayou."

But Willow stood motionless, like a doe catching the scent of a predator. Jason Meade labored up from the soggy carpet, his right hand grasping the assault rifle, muzzle pointing to the ground. His fatigues were soaked with blood and his left arm dangled limply at his side. He took two faltering steps toward Beaumont and me, struggling to lift the barrel, as my heart pulsed like the beating wings of angels beyond our reach.

30

Jason Meade labored toward us, his right index finger curled around the trigger of his assault rifle. He'd take out Beaumont first to avenge his betrayal, but he wouldn't stop there.

"Get out, Willow!" I shouted.

As she crashed into the underbrush, I released Beaumont and moved out of the line of fire. I eased to my left toward the shadows, hoping Jason's maimed condition and his single-minded purpose would provide me with an opportunity to circle behind him. Beaumont looked up at Jason, his face streaked with dirt and blood and etched with resignation that this flirtation with death was his last. The muscles in Jason's neck and right arm tensed as he struggled to maintain command of his weapon. He shuffled toward Beaumont.

"You won't need that money where you're going." Unlike the even drone of the approaching helicopter, Jason rasped and coughed like a dying engine.

"Drop that rifle now!" Keisha Lundy's voice rang from the darkness.

Ignoring the command, Jason raised the muzzle.

Then a blast rocked the clearing. Jason took a wavering step forward, still holding his weapon, trying to draw a bead on Beaumont. Two more flashes erupted. With his mouth open as though posing a silent question, Jason's legs buckled, then his body collapsed. His rifle bounced into the dirt.

Beaumont rose to his knees, ready to lunge for the gun.

"Freeze." Keisha Lundy used a two-handed grip to train my gun on Beaumont. "Hands behind your head." She moved closer, the muzzle pointed at his midsection.

"Good to see you, partner." A shiver coursed through my body as the adrenaline that had kept my terror in check during the past several minutes began to ebb.

"Just happy my lights came back on. Who was it went upside my head anyway?"

"Eddie Hammond." I pointed to him, lying motionless, as I snatched Jason's rifle.

"Where's Willow?" Keisha asked.

"Over here," she called, her words almost drowned by the roar of the helicopter soaring over the clearing and bathing us in an intense radiance that drowned out the moonlight.

Keisha looked up and shielded her eyes from the chopper's searchlight. "This isn't doing my headache any good."

I suddenly remembered she'd been knocked unconscious and could be a bit woozy. "Hand me my gun. I'll cover you while you cuff Beaumont."

The moon reappeared as I slung Jason's gun over my shoulder. Keisha handed me the revolver, her hand shaking.

"Hope they spotted us," she said, moving behind Beaumont and pulling his wrists one at a time into the small of his back, then securing them with her stainless cuffs.

"They see everything the searchlight picks up," I said. "They'll circle back."

Willow stepped in front of Beaumont, cradling her wounded hand in her right palm. "You wanted to know if this talking head with tits has something below the belt?" She dropped her eyes toward his lower extremities. "How about you, asshole?"

Willow delivered a solid kick to Beaumont's groin. He howled, then toppled facedown into the soggy turf and continued to whimper.

"You go, girl," Keisha said. "Thanks for putting him into position."

"He's got a knife in an ankle sheath," I said.

Keisha quickly flex-cuffed his ankles and removed the weapon as Willow moved next to me, sucking air through her teeth, obviously in pain.

"I ruined a hundred-dollar manicure on that bastard," she said.

Keisha knelt over Jason's body. "Nobody home here."

"When he thought he was going to take us all out, Jason admitted to killing Steven Bowen," I said.

Keisha stood and looked down at Jason's body as if it were roadkill. "Then cancel the wish-I-hadn't-had-to-shoot-him feeling I was getting." She went over to Eddie. "He's barely breathing. Got a hole in his chest."

"Jason put it there." I knelt next to him.

Keisha carefully rolled Eddie to one side, then shook her head and laid his body back to rest.

Then we heard a voice that seemed far away, like a conversation carried over water. "Tell me about my mama."

I saw Eddie Hammond's eyelids quiver as though inner visions were flashing across a screen visible only to him. I wondered if the child had captured a mother's image for the man to reclaim. "She misses you and Annie," I said.

"Is she coming for us?"

"Soon," I said. "She'll be back soon."

Eddie's eyelids grew still. The helicopter circled back and hovered above, illuminating the clearing like home plate at a night game. I rose and gave a thumbs-up to let them know things were under control. Figuring the space was too tight for a landing, I wasn't surprised when a few seconds later someone secured to a tether slowly descended from the chopper.

DEA Special Agent Jarla Thomas touched down and extracted herself from the harness. "You never returned my calls, Brenner."

"My cell's been unattended." I gave her a sixty-second summary of events and showed her the empty suitcase and Beaumont's backpack full of money.

"Anyone need medical attention?" she asked.

"Beaumont's missing half the skin on his face and his big brass balls are cracked. All compliments of Ms. Ashe. She has a broken wrist, and Officer Lundy has a serious headache."

Jarla spoke into the mike clipped to her shoulder. Then she grasped Keisha gently by the arm. "No telling how long it'll take to get a boat in here. Let's not take any chances."

Keisha lifted her eyes to the hovering aircraft as Jarla fastened the harness. "Going for a ride in that thing's taking chances."

Willow touched Keisha's hand. "Thanks for being my white knight."

"Broke the color barrier again," Keisha said. "Whoa!"

Keisha rose like a marionette pulled offstage.

Willow put her hand on my shoulder. "I'm sorry I got myself into this. More sorry for bringing you and Keisha into it."

"You got a hell of a story," I said.

She glanced toward the bayou, where earlier she'd been the flash point of a fatal conflagration. "I'm too much a part of it. Someone else can have this one."

Frightful situations can cause people to make all sorts of promises they later break, I thought. But whether or not she kept this one wasn't my concern. Willow rested her head against my chest while another DEA agent descended from the chopper. His boots thudded on the dirt and he unfastened the harness, then helped Jarla secure Willow into it. I squeezed Willow's good hand and didn't release it until she was airborne.

"Whadda we got here?" asked the other agent as the glare from the helicopter retreated.

Jarla pulled a Mag-Lite from her belt and switched it on. "Let's see. We've extracted the wounded, which leaves the dead and this renegade asshole snitch." She drilled her toe into Beaumont's side, producing a muffled grunt. Then she trained the beam on me. "But let's not forget the meddling city cop who's left behind a mile-high pile of shit. And I fear there's more than meets the eye."

I looked down at Eddie, his life brutally concluded, and wondered if his fate had been fixed the day Genevieve Hammond fled from her home, believing the abandonment of her infant twins was their only hope of survival. Or was Eddie's cruel providence preordained on a violent night in South Louisiana, when swollen purple clouds crackling with fire spewed out torrents of rain that rushed over the land and washed away the blood of David Brenner and Deer Jackson? Was it on that night in a small trailer where his mother sought comfort in whiskey and sex that Eddie Hammond was irrevocably bound to evil through the wicked seed of Emmett Floyd Graves?

"Yeah," I said. "There's more."

31

I was thinking the night's mayhem had done nothing to further my mission to find David's killer when a raucous clatter erupted over the bayou. The water dazzled like quicksilver as I shielded my eyes from the searchlight flooding the clearing. "That chopper would be my lieutenant and my partner."

"You get hit on the head, too?" Jarla asked. "Your partner lifted out of here five minutes ago."

"My other partner."

Jarla narrowed her eyes and started to say something, then shook her head and flipped open her cell phone. "Got your boy down here, Lieutenant Utley."

The other agent checked the cuffs on Beaumont as she explained that Willow and Keisha were on the way to the hospital. Then Jarla listened to Utley for a few seconds.

"No, I don't want his help," she responded. "Get him out of here. Brenner's left us with a frigging mess. He's a two-legged disaster."

Whatever Utley said next caused her to shoot a look up toward the helicopter with a knot in her jaw. She slapped her cell phone against my chest. "Here. Talk to him yourself."

I grabbed the phone and put it to my ear. "Lieutenant?"

"Apparently you're persona non grata," Utley said. "We'll send down a harness."

"My coat, badge, and cell are in Hammond's bass boat. Let me take it back to his place and meet you all there."

"We'll be waiting," he said.

I took a few steps away from Jarla. "Lieutenant. What did you say to piss off Thomas?"

"I suggested her gratuitous remark about the mess you made was inappropriate."

"That's it?"

"I also called her a bitch."

I was starting to like my boss.

After tossing Jarla her cell phone, I made my way back to the boat and was soon navigating down the bayou, where moonlight glistened on the surface like sequins on a silver gown. Sounds that on my journey upstream had seemed cold and ominous now echoed with life. Every chirping cricket, croaking bullfrog, and splashing nutria cheered me as though I were the last runner in a marathon I'd been lucky to finish.

Arceneaux and Utley were waiting for me at the dock.

"DEA agents arrested Hammond," Arceneaux said, helping me off the boat. "They were taking him away when we touched down out front."

"What about Annie?" I asked.

"Found her passed out drunk," he said. "A female agent's staying the night with her."

"This isn't what you came to Bon Terre for, is it, Brenner?" Utley said.

I knew he was talking about my search for David's killer, but I answered him by explaining Jason Meade was involved in Beaumont's plot to rip off Hammond and had admitted to killing Steven Bowen.

Staring at the bayou, Utley slowly nodded. "Things sometimes fit together in ways you never expect. Wished you'd found the answers to your cousin's murder, but I'm gonna have to shut you down."

It was a long shot, but I had one thing left to do. "Give me a couple of days with my family, Lieutenant. Then Arceneaux and I are first up."

Utley immediately caught my oblique plea to let us remain partners and regarded me the way I'd eye one of my girls trying to con me. "Well. Lundy's out of commission for a while. We'll see after that."

He insisted I ride in the chopper while Arceneaux took my car back. And after ordering me to wait until the next day to visit Keisha in the hospital, Utley drove me home himself.

I didn't return to a dark house. Alexis sat at the kitchen table, her fingers wrapped around a coffee mug.

"Long night?" she said, studying my disheveled attire.

"Yes." The arctic white appliances and bare ivory countertops made the room seem as bleak as Eddie Hammond's eyes. Noticing a half-full pot at the end of the counter, I pulled a mug from the cabinet, poured a cup, then slid into a chair across the table from Alexis.

"You were in danger?" she asked.

"A little."

"A little." Her eyes were sharp and dark. "Tell me how someone gets in a *little* danger."

I looked down at my coffee, the steam rising and dissipating as swiftly and irrevocably as the lives of the men who'd died that night. I took a sip, then laid the mug back on the table and did something I'd never done before. I gave her every detail.

I finished thirty minutes later knowing I'd taken her on a journey to a place well beyond the reach of her imagination. If she ever believed that not knowing was worse than the truth, I'd brutally demolished the notion. Tears clung to her eyes like ice crystals. The skin on her face was taut and pallid.

"Well." Her voice came from another room in her mind. "Guess that answered my question."

"While Keisha and I were floating up the bayou, I thought about how much you hate me being in dangerous situations. I know you can't live like this."

"I'm used to you not taking my feelings into account. But I was hoping you'd think about your daughters."

I left the guilt card she'd dealt on the table. "They need a father who lives true to his nature."

"The people you send to prison live true to their nature."

"The difference is, I accomplish something good. I'll admit the risk is part of what I love about it, but I *need* my work."

"You needed running track and playing basketball. But damn it, Jack, you don't die from those things." She let out a long breath. "I'm sorry, but I won't play second fiddle to your need for danger and competition."

"I can't expect you to change. You need a man who's certain to come home at night and stay there. You need someone less consumed by his job. You need—"

Alexis held up her hands as though pushing back some invisible force. "Please, Jack. Don't tell me what *I* need. Be man enough to say it. You don't want to be with me."

It was true, but hearing it like that chilled my heart. "I'm saying I can't be the person you want me to be."

She threw me an acerbic smile. "If it helps you to put it that way."

"We're both who we are."

Alexis's gaze grew distant and she slowly nodded. "Yes. And I'm a good mother. And you're a good father, Jack. Whatever we decide, that doesn't change."

"No," I said. "That doesn't change."

She slid her mug toward me. "My coffee's cold."

I pushed back my chair, grabbed our mugs, and returned to the coffeepot. In a single night, I'd nearly died and my marriage was over. Now we were celebrating it all by drinking weak coffee in the wee hours of the morning. I poured the cold brown liquid from our mugs and watched it sluice down the sink, wishing I could drain my churning gut.

Needing to fortify my next serving, I filled my mug halfway with coffee. "I'm having a shot of Grand Marnier in mine. How about you?"

Alexis stared at me as though watching some sojourner retreat down a trail, perhaps an apparition of who she thought I was or might have been. Then she leveled a smile at me that distilled everything that had drawn me to her in college—her sense of duty, her ability to seize control when others were afraid, and yes, her unpretentious sensuality.

"Thanks, Jack," she finally said. "I'd like that."

32

I slept in and woke up to an empty house. I grabbed lunch and reached Bon Terre in the late afternoon. Lieutenant Utley had made it clear my time was up for investigating the murder of my cousin, and the only lead I had was the discovery that Faith's father, Jerroll Tilden, had left his dispatcher post and was unaccounted for during the time frame in which David and Deer were likely slain.

Though I wanted closure, I almost hoped I was wrong. I'd imagined avenging David by unveiling the evil acts of a monster like Emmett Graves or the treachery of a moral degenerate like Avery Hammond. Jerroll, the invalid grandfather of David's daughter, did not fit that picture.

I ran from the car to the veranda of Faith Tilden's home as a late-afternoon shower splattered the walkway and rippled her daffodils and Mexican sunflowers. The front door opened before I could knock.

"Detective Brenner," Truman LaRoche said, the floral perfume not quite masking the alcohol fumes on his breath. "I was coming out to water the hanging baskets."

"Don't let me interrupt."

"Nonsense. Come on in." He stood aside, the scent of bourbon taking command as I slipped past. "Faith's mother never misses bingo night at St. Lucy's. I'm baby-sitting her father. Something I can do for you?"

Finding an object with Jerroll Tilden's fingerprints would be easy, particularly without Mrs. Tilden around. But Truman was a problem. I needed to lift the prints without him knowing what I was doing because if I was wrong about Jerroll, I didn't want Truman telling Faith and needlessly alarming her. And if I was right, I wanted to tell Faith first.

So I lied. "Faith said you might know how to contact Elton Jackson's parents."

Truman shut the door behind us and studied me with muddled eyes. "Haven't had contact with them since they left town almost thirty years ago . . . when I was in Mississippi. You could have called and saved a trip."

"I was on my way home."

"If you were talking to Faith, you were at the restaurant. Coming here is backtracking."

Pretty lucid for a drunk. I heard the sound of canned television laughter coming from the back room. "Mr. Tilden watching TV?"

"*Planet's Funniest Animals.* But I have to change it before *Animal Precinct.* He can't stand seeing those abused creatures."

Truman followed me toward the den as I tried to think of something to say that would make him forget his skepticism. Jerroll Tilden sat in his wheelchair in front of the television. Four kittens were attempting to nurse from a border collie who seemed oblivious to it all. Jerroll's hand shook as he maneuvered a plastic straw to his lips and drew a cranberry-colored liquid from an aluminum tumbler on his tray. Juice dribbled down his chin. He put the straw aside, his head bobbing as if suffering a small convulsion.

"He okay?" The man's decrepit condition tempered any rage I might have felt.

"He's laughing." Truman nodded toward the screen, where a white mouse rode on the back of a black cat riding on the back of a golden retriever. He crossed over to the other side of the wheelchair, grabbed a kitchen towel from an end table, and started to dab away saliva and juice from Jerroll's chin.

I lifted the tumbler and straw from the tray. "I'll freshen this up for him."

Returning to the kitchen, I set the tumbler on the counter next to the sink and fished a plastic evidence bag from inside my coat. As I lowered the open end over the straw, the floorboards creaked.

I sealed the plastic straw and tumbler in the bag, then turned to face Truman, whose gaze was fixed on the evidence bag.

"Get what you came for?" he asked.

"I'm not sure," I said.

"Maybe if you knew what really happened that night . . ." Truman cut his eyes to the kitchen table, where a half-empty fifth of Jack Daniel's sat next to a more-than-half-empty old-fashioned glass. "Let's sit awhile. Can I get you a glass?"

I shook my head, but took a seat across the table from him. Truman's statement implied knowledge of David's murder. There was nothing to lose by hearing him out. I was curious to learn what he knew. And how.

Truman topped off the lone tumbler, then took two sips. "Remember I told you I still honored my vow of confidentiality?"

"Yes."

"I'm going to violate it," he said. "For *tikkun olam.*"

Healing the world. "How will telling me what you know about the night David and Deer were murdered contribute to that?"

"Hopefully, you'll see." Truman took another draw of bourbon. "One night after the FBI had packed up and left Bon Terre, Jerroll came into my confessional booth at St. Lucy's. He was drunk. But the way he trembled had nothing to do with alcohol."

Jerroll Tilden's shift ended at midnight. The wall clock showed three hours remaining. He opened the desk drawer and pulled out a pint of Wild Turkey. Two fingers left. His chair creaked as he raised his bulk and slipped the whiskey bottle into his back pocket just before the graveyard shift dispatcher walked through the door.

"Thanks for coming in early, Mike," Jerroll said.

Mike shivered out of his yellow slicker. "Nasty out."

"'Lectricity's out all over the east side of the parish. People mostly staying in." Jerroll patted the hard object in his back pocket as Mike turned to hang the slicker on one of the wall pegs.

Mike thunked a thermos on the desktop. "Leg acting up again?"

Jerroll nodded. "Diabetes is a helluva thing to have when your wife's the kinda cook mine is." But not so tough as being fond of bourbon, he thought. "Listen. I got a call from Genevieve Hammond an hour ago. She's stuck out west somewhere. Been visiting a friend."

"Friend?" Mike raised his eyebrows.

Jerroll didn't want to get into another discussion of the social activities of the sheriff's wife.

"You radio Sheriff Hammond?" Mike asked.

"She asked me not to bother him unless he asked about her." Jerroll grabbed his nylon jacket from the row of pegs. "That's fifty hours I owe you. Don't tell the sheriff or Deputy Perrot you spelled me. They've been onto me about my sick time."

"It's between us," Mike said. "Be careful going home."

As Jerroll tapped the brake to take the last turn toward his house, his right foot felt like a watermelon. He stopped after rounding the corner, pulled the whiskey from his hip pocket, and drained the bottle. Usually he threw the empties into the weeds along the road, but the rain was rattling the window like buckshot. Jerroll screwed the cap on the bottle and slid it under his seat.

As he approached his house, he saw two red flashes that reminded him of the eyes of a dragon in one of the stories he used to read to his daughter, Faith. He was almost upon the sixty-four Ford as it pulled away. He knew that car.

"Goddamn," Jerroll muttered. He didn't mind the work they were doing. The Negroes deserved to vote like anyone else. And the Jacksons were fine folks. He'd shared breakfast in town with the elder Jackson more than once. But he didn't see how Faith and the boy they called Deer needed help from a city boy. Especially a Jew.

Jerroll hadn't wanted Faith to go to Tulane. He worried about her marrying some rich Catholic kid from somewhere else, but he never dreamed she'd get involved with a Jewish boy. Faith hadn't told him about it, but Jerroll had seen them exchanging quick kisses in his car, and once he saw them holding hands in town. He had no more ill feeling toward Jews than Negroes, but what if she ended up marrying a Jew? Jerroll passed by the house. The lights were out, just like his wife had said when she called him at work to ask where he'd put the spare batteries. He pressed on the gas with his swollen foot as the red eyes of David Brenner's taillights grew dim in the silver threads of rain, and he thought again about the dragon in the mist and about the fire in his leg.

Jerroll followed the Ford for a couple miles until it pulled into the empty oyster-shell parking lot of the old Negro church on Escondido Road. He stopped the truck and killed the engine as he watched David sprint from his car. He could never run like that, even when his legs were young and his nerves not ruined by diabetes. Jerroll fished out a spare pint of Wild Turkey he'd hidden inside a tear in the padding beneath the bench seat and waited.

Fifteen minutes later his throat was as raw as the wind rocking his truck. Glancing to his right at the old Ford and figuring the boy must be alone, Jerroll grabbed his shotgun from the rack, stowed the half-empty bottle of Wild Turkey in his hip pocket, and pushed on the door. The rain stung his face like bull nettle. He traipsed through the sheet of water rushing over the asphalt until he heard the oyster shells crunching beneath his boots.

Soon he was standing, back to the wind, thirty feet from the entrance to a house of God, holding a shotgun. What the hell was he doing? He only wanted to talk sense into the kid. Civil rights was one thing. His daughter was another. Maybe the kid just wanted to sow his wild oats with her. Well, that wasn't right either. But Jerroll couldn't bring himself to come any closer. He'd wait for the boy to come out.

Five minutes later he was reaching back for the bottle. His right foot felt like a Brahma bull was standing on it. His left foot was numb from taking all his weight. He grasped the neck of the flask protruding from his pocket and pulled.

"Goddamn!" The whiskey slipped from his hands and fell onto the oyster shells. He bent over to find it intact, then stood with his back to the gale, cradling his shotgun in the bend of his elbow to free both hands. As he unscrewed the cap and raised the bottle to his lips, a loud pop startled him.

Jerroll looked up to see David Brenner fighting to close the church door, which the wind had slammed into the whitewashed clapboard. Jerroll took a snort, placed the bottle back in his pocket, then grasped the shotgun with both hands and moved toward the old Ford. The boy had pulled the hood of his green windbreaker over his head and he ran with long, smooth strides toward the car, unaware he wasn't alone until Jerroll grasped the boy's shoulder as he reached for the door handle.

The boy spun around and tore back the hood, his deep brown eyes as wide as a treed possum's, his dark curly hair plastered against his forehead. "Mr. Tilden!"

"Stay away from my girl," Jerroll said, stepping back to allow some space between his shotgun and the boy.

The kid eyed the shotgun. "Faith isn't a little girl, Mr. Tilden."

"I got nothing against Jews, but we're a Christian family." The combination of whiskey and bile working its way up his craw tasted like scorched iron. "There's plenty of your own kind back in the city."

Suddenly the boy looked toward the road, the rain pummeling his squinted eyes. "Deer! Stay back!"

"What the hell?" Jerroll looked over his shoulder to see the Jackson boy coming hard at him. Was that a knife in his hand? Jerroll started to raise his gun, hoping a warning shot would make him keep his distance. He felt a tug on the barrel. Jerroll planted his throbbing foot into the oyster shells and yanked the gun to dislodge David's grip. But as Jerroll jerked the shotgun away, he heard an explosion. And he knew the sound wasn't thunder, nor the flare of a lightning bolt.

The recoil sent Jerroll stumbling backward, his attempts to

stay upright no match for his drunkenness. As his buttocks crushed the wet gravel, all grew silent, as though he'd been cast into a deep pool. Had the shotgun blast deafened him? Or was he stunned by the sight of David Brenner on his back, legs splayed, a huge patch of red growing on the jeans around one knee?

Jerroll rose and spun around, the wind no longer roaring in his ears. The lightning flickered without thunder, the black boy screamed without voice, and the shotgun flared in silence. Deer Jackson's knees buckled, his eyes as white as the bleached oyster shells. A small silver flashlight dropped from his hand. Before the young man's face hit the gravel, Jerroll saw the black hole that obscured the lettering in the boy's gold jacket.

Truman averted his eyes from the amber liquid as though waking from a trance. "Jerroll panicked. He knew Vern Hammond was cruising the town and found him on Main Street checking on businesses. He told him what he'd done, but Sheriff Hammond told Jerroll to put the shotgun in the sheriff's trunk and go home. Said no one would ever believe it was an accident and that the federal government and the press would come in and crucify the whole town right along with Jerroll if he confessed. What Sheriff Hammond did was wrong, but he was right about that."

Truman's story confirmed my suspicion that Jerroll Tilden's fingerprints would match the latents lifted from the shotgun we dug up from Avery Hammond's backyard. But I felt no joy in it. I'd discovered that David died because of the fear and recklessness of a killer already buried in a coffin of flesh and bone.

"So you kept all this a secret because of your vows," I finally said.

Truman took a long swallow of bourbon. "It's a mortal sin for a priest to reveal a confidence. I've never done it until now. I didn't absolve Jerroll and I urged him to turn himself in to federal authorities. But he was afraid to act against the sheriff's wishes."

"You believe it happened the way you've told it?" I asked.

"My erstwhile profession is a lot like yours. You learn to know when people are lying."

I studied Truman's face. The alcoholic fog had lifted. His eyes were as blue as the sky on a cloudless fall day. "You're telling me this now, even if it's a sin, because I'm going to prove Jerroll Tilden killed my cousin and Deer Jackson. And you want me to let it go."

Truman returned the wise and compassionate expression of a priest. "Doesn't your faith allow you to sidestep the law for a higher purpose? Aren't observant Jews permitted to eat nonkosher food if the alternative is starvation?"

I nodded. "If there's truly no other choice."

"So you get to choose right now between some awful alternatives," he said. "You can do what I did and disregard your vows as a police officer. Or you can arrest a decrepit old man who unintentionally killed two fine young men thirty-one years ago when he was scared and drunk. You'll force Faith and her family—in part, your family—to endure the pain of knowing that Faith's father killed Grace's father. And it'll all play out on prime-time."

I thought about that, tossing my aunt Joyce, David's mother, into the simmering moral sauce piquant. Then, perhaps like a plant whose thirst has drawn the rain, I recalled a Jewish teaching I'd learned from David.

"Remember when Moses killed the Egyptian?" I asked.

Truman nodded. "Who'd been beating the Hebrew slave."

"The ancient rabbis used that story to establish the principle behind the example you gave of violating the laws of *kashruth* to preserve life," I said. "The Torah says before he acted, Moses looked this way and that. Seeing no one, Moses killed the Egyptian and buried him. But the rabbis worried that checking around before taking action made Moses look more like someone afraid of being caught than a rescuer."

Truman smiled. "Not the patriarch we've been taught to venerate."

"Exactly. So the rabbis came up with this. They said when Moses looked this way and that, he was really searching for a way to save the slave without taking the Egyptian's life. The rabbis concluded that drastic or normally forbidden actions are permitted to prevent serious harm to someone, but only if a person makes certain there are no other options. Like taking a life to save an innocent one." As Keisha had done the night before.

I pulled out the evidence bag. The straw and tumbler inside were like high-powered weapons aimed at the heart of the Tilden family, one of them David's daughter. But would sparing them from humiliation and heartbreak justify my failure to take action? My responsibility as a cop was to apprehend suspects and deliver evidence to the DA, to let the justice system determine innocence, guilt, and punishment. But what if that system threatened blameless people? What if my sworn duty imperiled innocents, Faith and Grace, as surely as the hostile Egyptian assailed the Hebrew slaves?

And what purpose was served by punishing Jerroll Tilden? He was not an Emmett Graves, whose depraved acts fueled and comforted him. And his crime was less the killing and more the weakness he showed by allowing Vern Hammond to conceal his actions. Rather, he was a man whose suffering, perhaps rendered by guilt, was far beyond what any jury could impose.

I went to the refrigerator, found a jug of cranberry juice, and set it on the counter next to the sink. I grabbed Jerroll's tumbler from the evidence bag, rinsed it, and filled it halfway. Finally I removed the straw, held it briefly under the faucet, then placed it in the glass.

When I entered the den, Jerroll Tilden's wide eyes brimmed with tears. The animal comedy show had ended. On the screen, a patrolman restrained an angry man while two animal control officers hurried past, one cradling a rotweiler, her hide dotted with abscesses and furless patches, while the other officer held a box of emaciated and whining pups. But it was Jerroll Tilden's whimpering that filled the room. His face was contorted and gray, like a gargoyle in a French Quarter courtyard, and his body trembled as though spiked with electricity.

I set his glass and straw on the tray, found the remote on the end table, and switched the television to the evening news. Then I walked back into the kitchen, where Truman sat at the table pouring whiskey into two fresh glasses.

"David and I spent many an hour talking of things great and small," he said. "I got to know him real well and something tells me he'd be proud of you right now. Not about what you chose to do, but because of what you put into the decision. I have a feeling you spend a lot of time looking this way and that, Detective Brenner."

Truman waved his hand over the glasses of bourbon.

I pulled out a chair. "Never been a whiskey drinker."

Truman lifted a glass. "To healing the world?"

I picked up the other glass and clinked mine against his. *"Tikkun olam."*

33

The rain had moved toward the Gulf, cooling the air by July standards, so I lowered the windows for my drive back to the city. The southern sky was veined with lightning, the thunder too far off to be heard above the hissing of my tires on the wet asphalt. The mucky odors of sodden rice and soy fields swept through the car as an uneasiness swelled in my gut, like a stain from a drop of wine spreading slowly through the fibers of a white tablecloth. Hiding the truth about Jerroll Tilden covered up my own inaction from those who would view it as a grievous violation of trust. And my childhood had taught me the emotional price of concealment. I knew a sliver of shame would be lodged forever in my heart, and even David's wisdom could not extract it.

Concealing the true cause of David's death also cheated me of the retribution I'd anticipated, and understanding the futility of throwing a man with little left of mind and body into the criminal system didn't fill the void. But perhaps tomorrow my hunger for justice would be sated when I tasted vengeance by proxy with as fine a surrogate as I could have.

I drove the River Road into town and to the hospital where Willow Ashe was spending her second night. When I asked for her room, the front desk attendant pointed out it was five minutes short of eight o'clock, the end of visiting hours. I flashed my badge and thanked him.

Willow reclined in her bed, head raised, arm in a sling, watching the credits of a movie I recognized.

"The book's better," I said.

Willow smiled and pressed the mute button on the remote. "Isn't it always?"

"You're looking great." I wasn't stretching the truth to cheer a patient. Without the distraction of makeup, Willow's iridescent eyes and ivory skin looked like topaz floating in cream.

She brushed aside a yellow strand of hair. "I got a chance to thank Keisha for saving my life when we were flying back on the helicopter. I need to thank you, too."

"If I hadn't shown up, you'd have been out of danger," I said. "Creed Beaumont would have left you with a cell phone in a swamp somewhere after he secured the money."

"You sure of that?"

"Not a hundred percent."

Her eyes locked on mine. "Like a lot of things, we'll never know."

"We can always wonder." Which is exactly what I did. What would have happened if I'd swallowed my pride and not left her waiting at Molly's that winter break?

"Odell Harris, from our New Orleans affiliate, came by this morning," she said.

"Not to bring you flowers, I bet."

"I gave him an interview. I meant what I said back on the bayou. I'm finished chasing stories."

"They put painkillers in these IV's. You may feel differently after they release you."

"Which they say is tomorrow, thank God. But I'm serious. No more investigative reporting. I talked with Trent for over two hours on the phone this afternoon. We agreed to quit going through the motions and really try to make it work."

"I'm glad for you," I said, thinking of my situation with Alexis. "I couldn't walk away from my job."

"After losing a colleague and nearly dying myself, I'll be quite satisfied doing the morning show. Or the weekend desk. Or anything they'll let me do, except the weather. Did I ever tell you what they wanted me to wear in Chattanooga?"

"Tell your boyfriend Trent," I said.

"I've shown Trent."

The detective in me changed the subject. "There's some things I want to tell you." I started with all that had happened at Faith Tilden's home.

"That was a tough call to make, Jack. You did the right thing. But why tell me?"

"You've been straight with me the whole time. You deserve to know."

"But you want me to keep quiet."

"If it makes the news, Truman LaRoche and I will deny everything."

Willow smiled. "I appreciate your confidence in me."

"There's something else only you and I know about, with the exception of the people involved. I informed Genevieve Baron this afternoon that her son was killed. She doesn't want people knowing Emmett Graves is Eddie's and Annie's father."

She nodded her assurances.

"But you won't have to sit on the story I'm going to give you next," I said. "ADA Mary Evans and I are going to Angola tomorrow morning."

"I told you. I'm out of investigative reporting. Tell Odell Harris about it."

"You want to deal him in, that's your call. And I hope that's what you choose."

"This some kind of test?"

My face warmed, realizing she was right. I'd unconsciously offered Willow a hard choice to prove she was serious about giving up something to salvage a relationship. Something I was unwilling to do. "Maybe I'm being unfair."

"Maybe you're being the obtuse Jack Brenner I'll always love. And thanks to the past two weeks, it's Jack Brenner the man, not just a teenage memory."

"You're a fine person, Willow Ashkenazi," I said. "I see no harm in remembering the lightning on the levee."

"Jack, *we* were the lightning."

She reached across with her right hand and I took it. Her skin was cool, her grip firm. We held our grasp, not with the regret of parting lovers, but with the quiet comfort of two old friends restoring a bond.

"So what's the scoop?" she asked, her hand slipping away.

"Emmett Graves is going down."

I gave her the details, then grasped her hand again before walking to the door. As I turned for one last look at her, Willow smiled and brushed back her unkempt flaxen strands. And I imagined the lightning flickering across her face as thunder rumbled over the Mississippi, and I breathed in the scents of summer rain and wild grass.

When we reached the interview room at Angola the next morning, Mary Evans stayed outside the door with a guard like we'd planned. Graves was waiting for me when I entered, his shackled hands folded in front of him on the metal table. His hair was undone, and it fell to his shoulders in twisted black and gray vines. His cheekbones were as sharp and hard as angle iron.

I'd underestimated Graves's intelligence the first time, so I knew I had to be careful in the ordering and phrasing of my questions and statements. I needed to keep from spooking him before putting him away.

"Brenner," he said. "Hear you and that blond reporter with the tight ass nearly got yourselves killed."

He didn't know how unlucky he was about that. "All in a night's work."

"You put down some bad hombres."

"And sent Avery Hammond up the river, which is what you were after all along. To pay him back for setting you up in the sting that put you where you are now. And to sidestep the needle. Turns out Creed Beaumont's the one who dropped the dime on you. He did it to get you out of the way so he could double-cross the DEA. Beaumont might be your next cell mate."

Graves sneered and eased back in his chair. "I got Hammond. Beaumont's a bonus."

"Take the credit if it makes you happy."

"I only offered information so's you could get justice for your kin. How's that coming?"

"Dead end."

"Really? No matches on them prints they took off the shotgun?"

I had no way of knowing if Graves knew that Jerroll Tilden had shot the boys, but I doubted Vern revealed anything that wasn't necessary to a man like Emmett Graves. "Were you expecting a match?" I asked. "Maybe Vern Hammond?"

The skin crinkled at the corners of Graves's narrowed eyes as he flexed his jaw. "Why would I expect Vern Hammond's prints on that shotgun?"

"Because he was the one who paid you to cover up the killings. Or did you think he hired you to cover for Avery?"

"I was paid not to ask questions. And what makes you think it was Vern who come to my trailer that night?"

"Genevieve Barron told me."

Graves straightened up in his chair. "Who the hell's that?"

"The woman you forced to abandon her children and who you've been blackmailing up until the death of her second husband. Yesterday, I had to tell Genevieve that her son was killed in a shootout."

"Eddie?" The name came with a slight catch in his throat, and I wondered if the purpose of the quick glance he flashed me was to see if I had caught it.

"Your son is dead."

He leaned forward, his manacles scraping on the steel table. "Bullshit. I ain't got any fucking kids."

"We compared your DNA sample to one of Annie's. You're the father. Genevieve Hammond was the woman in the trailer with you the night my cousin was killed and she saw you talking to her husband, Vern. That's when the twins were conceived. I believe you killed Vern because he found out."

"You're trying to trick me."

"You don't have to confess to killing Sheriff Hammond, but you could tell me if I'm right about him knowing."

"He knew they weren't his. But it coulda been others that knocked his wife up. Genevieve was a weak woman."

"You may not be able to read, but you can cipher. I think you guessed they were yours and Genevieve admitted it to you. Like you say, she was a weak woman. You couldn't take a chance she'd let it slip to her husband. So you killed Vern Hammond before he found out, because if he had, you'd be off the Hammond payroll. What's it been like seeing your children grow up without a father?"

The muscles around Graves's eyes quivered. It was a moment before he spoke. "You've dug up a lot of useless notions. None of it has a thing to do with your purpose."

He'd given me as much confirmation as I was going to get. I rose from my chair, Graves watching me with the wary eyes of a predator who suspects the chosen prey may possess the strength or cunning to swap roles. I pressed the button on the wall.

The door opened and Mary Evans wheeled into the room.

"Won't be much longer," I said to the guard.

The door fastened with a sucking sound.

Graves glared at Mary. "What's she doing here? You didn't need to bring the lady district attorney all the way from New Orleans to tell me about Eddie."

Mary settled next to the chair I'd been sitting in. I leaned toward Graves, my fingers gripping the chair back. "We're finished talking about Eddie. It's about David Brenner now."

"I done my best to help you. I got nothing else to say."

"Well, I do." This was my last visit, so I ignored protocol and moved closer, just beyond his reach. His arms stiffened, causing the restraining chains to creak. I felt like a kid staring down a viper on the other side of a glass cage in the zoo. "David Brenner was alive when you pushed his car into the sinkhole."

"You're lying. That what you brung this crip lawyer here for, to trap me?"

"The actual cause of my cousin's death was never in the papers, but you can't read anyway."

Graves's jaw muscles quivered. "Even if what you say is true, you'll never pin that murder on me in court."

"Our agreement exempts you from the death penalty in the murder of the prison guard," Mary said. "It specifies, however, that if you in any way contributed to the death of David Brenner or Elton Jackson, the agreement is null and void. In your statement to us, you indicate that you immersed David Brenner's vehicle with his body and the body of Elton Jackson inside the trunk. David Brenner was no doubt unconscious the entire time; however, the autopsy found drowning to be the cause of death. So, if what you told us is true—"

"Maybe it ain't," Graves said. "You can't prove it is."

Mary's glare had the exquisitely lethal look of a jeweled scimitar. "Are you saying you provided us with false information, Mr. Graves? If so, that will also nullify the agreement. Shall I read you that clause?"

Graves jerked up from his chair and raised his fists until the chains clanked. He lurched forward, his restraints allowing him within four inches of me. His eyes were black maelstroms and his skin clung to his cheekbones like weathered parchment. There was an evil gurgle in his throat.

"Graves, you're going down for the guard," I said. "And I'm going to be here with his family. But while I watch them pump the potassium chloride into you, I'll be thinking about my cousin and his friend and how much better this world would be if they'd lived. And how much better it will be when you're gone."

"No way they'll ever get that needle into my arm. I got ways to reach out to you."

I didn't totally dismiss his threat as bravado, but he'd never know it. "Graves, what you got is a little time to earn a GED."

Mary moved to the wall and pressed the button while I took one last look at him. The earth would soon be rid of his dark presence, but I wondered if his execution would truly rid us of his evil. Did the deaths of men like Emmett Floyd Graves diminish the vileness in the world, or is their wickedness reincarnated in other forms? I knew David would say that evil is the denial of spirit and only spirit survives. But David wasn't there to convince me.

Epilogue

Predicting November weather in New Orleans is rolling craps. The waning hurricane season can bring monsoon winds, stalled fronts with sunless drizzle, or dog days straying into autumn, when walking outside is like donning a wet wool overcoat. But sometimes the cold air from Canada punches across Lake Pontchartrain with enough force to briefly rebuff the warm breath of the Gulf. On those days, the sky is a fire-baked blue, the air laced with cayenne, and the magnolia leaves are as opulent and polished as if they'd been carved from wax by Old World craftsmen.

It was that kind of Sunday afternoon that caused me to take Sarah and Carrie rollerblading on the asphalt road looping Audubon Park. We passed dogs leaping for Frisbees, couples lolling on blankets next to coolers of wine, and the same senior tai chi practitioners that Keisha and I had encountered on our search for Jenna Meade.

That July morning after leaving Graves's evil presence at Angola, I'd paid a visit to my aunt Joyce and told her that David had fathered a daughter named Grace Tilden. When she'd finished soaking her handkerchief with tears, she ordered me to take her right away to see her granddaughter. On the way to Bon Terre I told her I'd failed to find David's killer. She cared nothing about that, she said. What was important was knowing David had a family. She wanted to make sure they were welcomed.

Sarah and Carrie returned from summer camp. In mid-September, Sarah had her first period. In early October I went to City Park and stood next to Coach Goldberg as Jenna Meade passed a runner from St. Mary's in the last ten meters to win the first cross-country race of the season. The next evening, Erev Rosh Hashanah, Grace Tilden wore the golden *chai* her mother had given her father and stood with her grandmother Joyce reciting Kaddish in David's memory.

After morning services the next day, I'd taken Carrie and Sarah to Meal Thyme. As I stood on the back porch watching them help Faith and Grace pick herbs from the garden, Truman LaRoche approached holding two large tumblers of iced tea with sprigs of mint. I thanked him and took one, and he let me know his tomatoes were struggling and Faith was having to get them from some guy in Thibodaux. He also mentioned he'd run into Genevieve Baron and Annie Hammond at a twelve-step program in Bon Terre and that Sheriff Perrot had agreed to fix his next three tickets if he could stay sober.

Skating now along the asphalt, I sucked in the bracing fall air thinking the only thing left broken was my marriage. And my sorry physical conditioning, which forced me to drop out as Sarah and Carrie glided off together, taunting each other with the kind of cruelty only sisters understand as love. I sat on a bench, pulled off my skates, and put on my Nikes. Having silenced my cell phone earlier, I decided to check my messages. There was one call from Arceneaux, no code attached, so it wasn't a call-out. He was probably at Fuzzy's watching football and wanted me to join him for beer and oysters.

But it was too fine a day to spend indoors. I rose from the bench and walked briskly up the road. The sun was below the treeline and the shadows of the oak trees spread across the grass and asphalt like spilled paint. Runners passed me, each breathing with a timbre and cadence as unique as a fingerprint. Most were gasping or panting, but less than a quarter mile into my walk, I heard the measured inhalations and hearty expulsions of a trained runner. When I glanced to my left, Jenna Meade floated by. She slowed as I called her name and caught her eye, then she smiled and soared on with a wave of her hand, her ponytail swinging back and forth like a golden metronome.

I responded with an ancient instinct, and suddenly my legs were no longer my adversaries. I fell into rhythm, my lungs drawing in oxygen as if I were breathing for the whole world. As Jenna faded into the distance, a fine film of sweat anointed my body, and my skin prickled in the cool autumn air. Suddenly a ray of sunlight burst through the branches. I saw David Brenner to my right, sweat glistening like diamonds on his chest, his feet touching the road as softly as a kitten's paws, his face as serene as the space between thoughts. Deer Jackson and Steven Bowen joined him, and together they moved ahead like perfectly moving parts of a single organ. They glanced back and beamed kindly as a twelve-year-old boy, straining to hold form, fell off the pace. And as the road twisted beneath a canopy of oak and pecan trees and the shadows vanished, the boy knew that one day he would catch up and join them.

But voices from behind reminded me that this was not the day.

"Look," Carrie cried above the rumble of in-line skates. "Daddy's running!"

"He's gonna hurt himself," Sarah said.

"No, he's not!"

Sarah cackled. "Just you wait."